"*I'm asking you to do me the honour of becoming my wife, Miss Melville.*"

"*Why?*"

"*I believe we should suit admirably—I admire and respect you—*"

"*Admire! Respect!*" she echoed mockingly. "*Admiration and respect will not do. There must be stronger feelings.*"

"*You are speaking of a romantic attachment?*" he asked. "*A headlong, neck or nothing passion? Such transports are only for the very young.*"

Henrietta shook her head. "*I like you very much, sir, and I think you like me, but that is not enough.*"

He took her hand, hesitated, then carried it to his lips. It was trembling slightly. "*Good day to you, Miss Melville.*"

After he had gone, Henrietta stood for some time at the window. And all the while, the tears were falling unbidden and unheeded down her cheeks . . .

A
Conformable
Wife

Alice Chetwynd Ley

BALLANTINE BOOKS • NEW YORK

Library of Congress Catalog Card Number: 81-66862

ISBN 0-345-28390-2

Manufactured in the United States of America

First Edition: August 1981

A
CONFORMABLE
WIFE

❧ *Chapter I*

LORD ALDWYN was lying in bed, propped up by a bank of pillows, when his son, on his way down to the dining room, looked in to see him. A strong odor of medicaments hung about the sick room. His lordship's face was still drained of all colour, but there was more alertness about the deep-sunken eyes this evening.

"He'll do," whispered Franton, Lord Aldwyn's devoted valet. He was a short, spare man with deft movements. "But don't be staying too long, Mr. Julian, or setting him in a bustle—not that *you're* likely to do that."

The Honourable Julian Aldwyn nodded, accepting without umbrage the dictatorial manner of this old and valued servant, who had known him all his life.

"What're you whisperin' about, Franton?" demanded the invalid peevishly. "Damme, no need to go creepin' around talkin' in church voices! I'm in prime twig now, and fit for anything—anything bar talkin' to my daughter Jane, that is, and I'll never feel up to the mark enough for that. Be off with you. I want a word with my son." He broke off, panting a little.

Franton obeyed, with a final warning grimace at Julian.

Julian Aldwyn advanced to the bedside, taking his father's hand for a moment in a firm clasp.

"Capital to see you so much improved, Father, but don't set too hot a pace for a while. I'll sit with you for ten minutes, no more. And don't start to argue, mind, for I'm under orders," he added, as he saw the bloodless lips open to protest. "Devil of an autocrat, Dr. Gillingham. Beats Old Hookey into fits, and that's a bold word!"

Recognising His Grace the Duke of Wellington under this irreverent appellation, Lord Aldwyn grinned and subsided for a moment, surveying his son.

The Honourable Julian Aldwyn was a young man of

1

eight and twenty, a little above medium height, slim but
with broad shoulders. His crisply curling dark hair was
brushed forward onto his forehead over a lean, tanned
face. His calm expression showed sensitivity as well as
intelligence. Although his well-cut evening dress obviously owed its inspiration to one of London's modish tail-
ors, there was nothing of the dandy in his appearance.
He looked what he was: a gentleman of birth and
means. But his quiet air of assurance carried with it a
hint of the self-reliance and decision acquired during
his years spent campaigning in the Peninsula under the
redoubtable Wellington.

"You'll do, m'boy," pronounced Lord Aldwyn, having
recovered his breath. "You look just as you should.
Never fear, I'll not overtire myself. But there's something
I must say to you."

"No need to say it now, sir. I'm fixed here for some
time, so why not save your breath until you're stronger?"

Lord Aldwyn shook his head. "No time like the present. I damn near had my notice to quit, know that?"

Julian nodded, his brown eyes compassionate.

"Might happen again, any day," went on his father.
"This matter's on my mind; has been for some time. May
be too late if I don't speak now." He paused, panting
slightly.

Julian cast him a swift, appraising glance, trying to as-
sess whether he would do more harm by quitting his father's side at once, or staying to hear whatever Lord Aldwyn wished to communicate. The latter would be less
likely to upset the invalid.

"Very well, Father, if you must. Fire away. But I beg
you to spare yourself as much as possible. No long
speeches, mind."

"No need for that. It's a simple enough matter. Don't
know that you'll like it, though."

"We'll chance that. In any case"—he smiled affectionately at the older man—"I'm scarce likely to fly up in
the boughs with you at present."

Lord Aldwyn attempted a chuckle. "No. Got you
there, ain't I? Well, it's this. You're my heir: when I
quit, you take the reins. That's all right and tight."

Julian nodded. His quick mind had already seen what
was to come.

"Thing is, there's no one to follow you. Must have a

successor. Aldwyns been here for close on two hundred years. Time you married, m'boy."

He leaned back wearily against the pillows, having shot his bolt. It had taken more effort than he could well spare, but he felt a strong sense of relief that it was done, even though he had some qualms about its reception.

His son said nothing for a moment, then nodded calmly.

"Yes, of course. I, too, have come to realise that necessity, of late."

"You have?" The invalid leaned forward again, almost eagerly. "Someone in mind, eh?"

"Not yet. But I assure you that I shall, as the politicians say, give the matter my most earnest and immediate attention."

Lord Aldwyn grunted. "It's to be hoped you mean more by that than they do!"

Julian rose to his feet and bent to kiss his father's forehead.

"You may safely trust me, Father. Think no more of it. And now, good night. I'll send Franton in to you."

Closing the door softly, Julian sent in the hovering valet, then continued on his way downstairs.

His mother and two sisters were already in the dining room about to take their places at the table. Lady Aldwyn, a faded blond-haired woman, who still showed traces of her former youthful beauty, looked up anxiously as her son entered.

"How did you find Papa? He would insist on seeing you tonight, after Dr. Gillingham said he was to have no visitors today but myself. It always excites him to be crossed, you know, even when he's in health. That's why Franton thought it might be best to let him have his way, provided you did not stay long. I myself may stay only ten minutes at a time. But I'm sure you did not stay too long."

"Be easy, Mama."

His smile was gentle, for he knew his mother could not meet trouble with resolution. She had always relied on her husband's support; now that he needed hers, she scarcely knew how to meet the challenge, and had thankfully passed it on to her family. They had all been hastily summoned from their various domiciles at the onset of Lord Aldwyn's illness. Julian had come reluctantly.

knowing that the alarm might well be a false one; but he soon saw that the matter was serious. Lord Aldwyn had suffered a seizure from which, the physician said, recovery would be slow.

"He seemed tolerably comfortable when I left him," Julian went on, "and I understand Gillingham is to look in later."

"And you know, Mama, Dr. Gillingham may be relied on completely," put in Jane Hyde, Julian's elder sister. "I have never forgotten how he pulled my dear little Timmy through the chicken pox. The worst case he had ever seen, so he said, and not a pin to be placed between any of the spots, and Nurse quite at her wits end how to comfort the poor lamb, for you know how active he always is, and certainly not a child to take kindly to being kept in bed! Of course, I did feel at the time that perhaps Dr. Gillingham was too severe with my darling, but his papa made me see that at least Timmy would stay quiet for the doctor. And I am sure, dearest Mama, that if we all think hopeful thoughts about poor dear Papa's recovery, it will make all the difference, for such things have a stronger influence than perhaps we are aware of, you know."

She paused for breath, a respite for which Julian and his other sister, Almeria, were thankful. Jane Hyde was a pretty woman with soft blond hair, pink cheeks, and blue eyes, but somehow she always contrived to look insipid. Instead of the alert intelligence that animated the faces of her younger brother and sister, she had a certain vacuity of expression. She was thirty years of age and had been married for the past ten years to Fabian Hyde, a squire in another part of the county. So far, she had presented her husband with three children. Julian had once found darling Timmy, the eldest, playing with his razors, and, exasperated, had remarked to his sister Almeria that he trusted Jane would foist no more of her brats upon her long-suffering relatives, as the youngest of her progeny was now six years old.

Lady Aldwyn, however, seemed much comforted by her daughter's remarks. She was the only member of the family not to find Jane a bore. Indeed, they were very much alike: kind-hearted, clinging females occupied with the trivia of domestic life, which they were prone to make the sole subject of their conversation. Predictably, Jane began to speak of her children again as soon as the soup had been served.

"I'm so very thankful that dear Papa is on the mend at last, for my darlings will be missing me, and I do not altogether trust Nurse to keep them out of mischief. They are so high spirited! But of course healthy children should be so, shouldn't they, Mama?"

"Very true, my dear," replied her mother.

"If only I could have brought them here!" said Jane, not for the first time. "They would have cheered up their grandpapa prodigiously! But dear Fabian thought it better to wait awhile, until Papa was truly on the mend, which I do think he is, at last."

Julian and Almeria, an attractive, lively young woman with black curls, exchanged surreptitious glances of comical dismay.

"I think perhaps I may safely promise to return to Nemphett in a day or two," Jane continued. "Do you not agree? I may see dear Papa tomorrow, so Dr. Gillingham said, and after that he will go on splendidly, just you wait and see. Of course, it was only natural that he should wish to see Julian first," she added with a touch of pique.

Almeria intercepted another of Julian's cynical glances and almost choked over her soup.

"Oh, take care, my dear!" said Lady Aldwyn solicitously. "Is it too hot? Smithers, a glass of water, please, for Lady Barrington."

The footman brought the water, and after some pressure from her mother, Almeria reluctantly took a few sips.

"That was your fault!" she whispered to her brother after the meal, when they were able to snatch a few moments of private conversation.

"Well, if it isn't enough to turn anyone's stomach!" he retorted. "Jane's become worse, if anything. I realise I've seen little of her since I joined the Army, and she never was the brightest of females, but I don't recollect her ever being quite such a dead bore."

"It's the petrifying effect of domesticity," replied Lady Barrington, her green eyes dancing. "No doubt you observe the same ravages in myself, only you're too civil to remark on it."

"When have you ever known me trouble myself to be civil to you?" he asked with a grin.

"Whenever you wished something from me," she answered in the same spirit. "But tell me, why did Papa insist on seeing you tonight? Jane didn't like it above half, for it had been settled we were none of us to visit him until tomorrow, except of course Mama."

"He had some maggot in his head that what he had to say wouldn't wait for tomorrow."

"Well? Don't be so provoking! What was it?"

"He wished to urge me to lose no time in marrying and providing an heir for the estate."

"And how did you feel about that?" she asked, eyeing him warily.

He drew a snuffbox from his pocket and inhaled a pinch before replying.

"I dare say you were tempted to tell him to mind his own business," she prompted, "but I know you would not, just at present."

"I don't believe I was even tempted," he said slowly. "After all, the succession *is* his business. Moreover, I've been thinking along much the same lines myself lately."

"Have you? And I thought—everyone else, too, for that matter—that you were a confirmed bachelor! Who is the lady? Do I know her?"

"How like a female to jump to conclusions! Because I've been considering that perhaps it is time I settled down, does not necessarily mean that I've already selected a suitable partner."

"Well, it usually does," replied Almeria defensively. "And since you've been in London ever since you sold out of the army, it seemed quite likely that you could have met some eligible female there. I can't help but know, of course, that there have been countless *in*eligible females in your life."

"Can't you, indeed? I should wonder you will be so barefaced as to admit it, but you always were a shameless baggage!"

"Oh, come, Julian, I'm an old married woman! Besides, such things get noised abroad."

"I suppose they do. Much I care for that. And I'd scarcely describe you as an old married woman at five and twenty."

"All the same, I've been married to Giles for five years, and I can thoroughly recommend the state. I think it excellent that you should be considering wedlock at last. Perhaps I may be able to introduce you to someone of my acquaintance; there are scores of pretty girls in Bath."

"There are scores of pretty girls in London too. I've had a whole season in which to observe them, and I saw none to my taste," replied her brother. "They're empty-headed creatures, who wish to be constantly flattered and courted, and think of nothing but balls and parties."

"Well, what do you expect? They go to town to come out into polite society and to find themselves suitable husbands. Of course they appear empty-headed and given over to gaiety. But once they are married, be sure they will settle down to make excellent wives," retorted Almeria with spirit. "Why, I myself was no end of a flirt during my London season, but it didn't stop Giles from falling in love with me! I tell you what it is—you haven't yet met the right girl, my dear brother. When you do, you won't speak in that patronising fashion!"

"I have no expectation of meeting the right girl, if by that you mean falling in love," he replied soberly. "Once was more than enough."

"Oh, Julian!" She drew in her breath sharply, her eyes troubled. "Dearest, you can't mean that you still wear the willow for Celia Haldane? Why, that happened all of eight years ago; you were barely twenty at the time. By now you must realise how worthless a creature she was!"

"My disillusionment is complete." His expression was grim. "I most certainly do not cherish any tender feelings toward her, make yourself easy on that score. But the memory of making a most thorough-going fool of myself over a worthless female preserves me from any inclination to make a further trial of falling head over ears in love. No, Almeria, what I intend now is to find a sensible woman, perhaps not in her first youth. A young romantic female would expect ardent courtship, and that would be tedious."

"Well, I declare! What a cold fish you are become!"

"Quiz me if you wish, my dear, but all I require in a wife is that she shall be presentable and of amiable disposition. And, too, she must be fitted to take her place one day as mistress of Aldwyn Court. Of course, once the succession is assured, we may each agree to go our own ways. I think such a match would answer very well."

Almeria made a wry face. "Oh, prodigiously! I believe

you must look for a candidate at one of the Employment
Registry Offices. She sounds more like a good housekeeper than a wife!"

He tried not to laugh, only half succeeding.

"You must admit, Almeria, that scores of marriages
are made simply for convenience. And it occasionally
happens that a quite pleasing female has been left by
some accident on the shelf. Such a one might be very
ready to settle for what I can offer."

"Julian!" Almeria's eyes lit up with sudden inspiration.
"Do you know, you are quite right about that? Indeed, I
can tell you the very person who fits your description!"

"Can you indeed? And who may she be?"

"Why, Henrietta Melville! She is everything that you
could wish—and far more than you deserve, you odious
wretch!"

"Henrietta Melville." He repeated the name, frowning
in an effort to remember the woman. "I recall that she was
always an intimate friend of yours. In fact, did you not
both attend the same seminary in Bath? I must admit
that I can't remember her in the slightest. Never had
much to do with that family, myself, even though Nick
Melville and I were at Winchester at the same time. Isn't
he come into the title and settled at Westhyde Manor? I
believe Mother mentioned in one of her letters that old
Melville died last year."

"Yes, that is so. Sir Nicholas brought his wife and family to live at the manor about eight months since, I be-
live. That's what makes Henrietta's situation so odiously
disagreeable! She had been mistress there ever since her
mother died seven years ago, and now she's obliged to
give place to her sister-in-law, who by all accounts is a
most difficult woman. Even Henrietta admits to me that
she's no longer quite comfortable at home."

"How is it that Miss Melville remains single, since she's
well past an age for marriage? Is she an antidote?"

"No such thing!" retorted his sister indignantly. "She's
a charming creature, as you'll readily see when I make
you known to her. She's simply been somewhat unfortunate in her circumstances."

"As long as that hasn't turned her into one of these
plaintive, whining females—"

"How dare you say so! Really, I'm out of all patience
with you, Julian. If only you will be quiet and listen!

Henrietta left school at seventeen, as I did, and we were both to have a come-out in London in the following spring. But Lady Melville died that winter—you were overseas then—so not only did Henrietta have to forgo her season in London, but she found herself taking charge of the household of Westhyde Manor. I believe Sir Walter was a selfish sort of father, totally absorbed in his own grief, and took some odd notions of economy into his head after his wife's death. Henrietta had two younger sisters in her charge, Cecilia and Pamela, and she devoted her life to them. When they were old enough, they both made their come-out in London and made good matches, but Henrietta never stirred from the manor. Now she stays on in a house where she was once sole mistress."

"But if she has so much to recommend her why has no one come forward to offer for the lady?"

"You must see that it's not quite as simple as that," replied Almeria defensively. "Henrietta is my own age, approaching six and twenty. Most men hereabout are already married or betrothed, and she has rarely been away from home. So you see, Julian, the poor darling might be very ready to receive your addresses. I promise you, she's the most delightful creature, with a quirky sense of humour very like your own. As for the other qualities you mention—birth, breeding, experience of managing a household of consequence—she has them all, with amiability and common sense besides!"

She broke off with a little gesture of distaste.

"I don't care to be speaking of my friend in this way, Julian! It all sounds rather like some odious business transaction, like—like buying a horse! Yet I would give almost anything to see dear Henrietta creditably established, and I'm sure there's no female I'd rather have as a sister. And you are not so bad a catch, you know—besides being quite a dear, when one comes to know you."

He bowed ironically. "Thank you, ma'am. You relieve my mind, for so far you've successfully managed to depress my pretensions."

"Pooh! That is very likely!"

"I am far more sensitive than you describe."

"I do hope so, else all is lost."

"I only hope Giles has the good sense to beat you oc-

casionally, vixen! It's no more than you deserve. Well,
I think I shall meet your female paragon and judge for
myself, if that can be arranged before you return to
Bath."

"There's only one matter," said Almeria hesitantly.
"You musn't be expecting a female decked out in the first
stare of fashion. Henrietta has never paid much heed to
dress. She's led a restricted life, as I've explained. But
that could soon be changed if she became your wife, for
she has ample means—her father left all the girls handsomely provided for—and it would give me the greatest
pleasure in the world to assist her in choosing a trous-
seau!"

"So she's a dowd, is she?" asked her brother ruefully.

"Now you are being odious again! You don't deserve
that I should introduce you to her. But I will, if only for
her sake. There is no reason why we should not spare
a few hours to make a call at the manor. Mama has
Jane's company."

"And then they can talk uninterruptedly of Jane's dear
little ones. How delightful it will be, don't you agree? I
can hardly bear to miss it."

"You are a wretched cynic," remarked Almeria severely. "Only wait until you set up your own nursery. I
dare swear you'll be the most besotted parent of us all!"

🐾 Chapter II

WESTHYDE MANOR WAS a pleasant, warm, red brick house with diamond-paned windows and tall chimneys. Henrietta was at work in the garden when a smart curricle swept into view along the drive and would have passed by on its way to the house, had not the female passenger suddenly espied Henrietta and urgently commanded the driver to rein in his horses.

The passenger quickly scrambled down from the vehicle and ran across the short expanse of lawn to Miss Melville.

"Oh, my dear Henrietta!" Almeria exclaimed breathlessly as she flung her arms around her friend. "What a fortunate chance to find you at home!"

"Almeria! You, of all people! I haven't seen you this age! How do you do? And how is Lord Aldwyn? We heard that he had been unwell. Nothing very serious, I trust?"

"Well, I fear he did give us grave cause for concern," replied Almeria, detaching herself and taking Henrietta's arm to draw her across in the direction of the waiting curricle. "But I'm thankful to say he's on the mend. I expect I shall be able to return home in a few days, but I could not leave without seeing you, my dear! My brother Julian drove me over—you must allow me to present him. I'm sure you won't at all recollect him from those early days when we were still at school."

Henrietta glanced across at the curricle's driver. He was elegantly attired in a close-fitting coat of Bath superfine, fawn pantaloons, and an intricately tied cravat. Her gaze took in Lady Barrington's modish blue carriage dress and high-crowned bonnet ruched with blue ribbon. Henrietta reddened, suddenly conscious of her own undistinguished appearance.

11

"Oh, dear, I'm in no case for company," she said rue-fully. "I hadn't the least expectation of seeing anyone this morning, so here I am, dressed in my old gardening things!"

"Goose, as if it matters! We are come to see you, not your attire! I've been telling my brother so much about you—he'll be delighted to meet you."

Any delight the Honourable Julian Aldwyn felt on seeing Miss Melville was easily contained. Her gown, if such it might be called, was made of a serviceable brown holland, which had evidently seen several seasons, though the figure beneath it seemed trim enough. It was impos-sible to tell what colour her hair was, since it was con-cealed under an unbecoming, shapeless sunbonnet, which shaded most of her face. Only her smile made a pleasing impression. But he reflected ruefully that his sister had warned him not to expect a fashionable beauty. What-ever Miss Melville's other virtues might be, her appear-ance would scarcely inspire a man instantly to thoughts of matrimony.

He began to regret having come, but there was no way now to make his excuses gracefully. So he bowed and followed Miss Melville's directions to the stables, where he left his equipage in the hands of a capable head groom. He then strolled back to join the ladies, who were still standing where he had left them, chattering away like magpies.

Miss Melville conducted her visitors to the drawing room, introducing them to her sister-in-law. Sir Nicholas was summoned. He was a well-built man, whose good-humoured smile welcomed his former schoolfellow with a cordiality that compensated for his wife's stiff civility. Refreshment was offered and, as it was a warm day, ac-cepted, the ladies taking tea while the gentlemen pre-ferred a tankard of ale.

Lady Melville busied herself with the tea tray. She was a good-looking woman in a frigid, aristocratic way, with high cheekbones, a classical nose, down which she often looked when she wanted to intimidate someone, and cold green eyes.

Almeria seized the opportunity to exchange some local news.

"You'll remember Louisa Randall that was, Henrietta? Well, she is come to live in Bath; she's been there three months or more. I chanced on her one day in Milsom Street, and since then we've been together frequently."

"Why, of course I recall Louisa! I've had little news of her, though, since she and Mrs. Randall moved away from this neighbourhood after Mr. Randall's death. The last I heard was that she had married an Irish gentleman and gone to live in Dublin—that must have been full three years ago. Is not her husband's name Fordyce? Well, it's good news that she is not so far off as formerly."

"Louisa is alone now. Unfortunately, she is widowed."

"Oh, poor Louisa, how very sad! And not so very long married! What was the cause of poor Mr. Fordyce's death?"

Almeria shook her head. "She seems reluctant to speak of it, and naturally I do not press her. But I must say she does not appear to be overcome by grief, for she's amusing herself tolerably well in Bath, going to balls and parties. It may be that the marriage was not altogether happy."

"Does Mrs. Randall live with her?"

"No, I collect Louisa's mama died in January of this year. She lives quite alone in a pleasant house in Pulteney Street, close to the Sydney Gardens."

"Alone? Does she indeed?" asked Henrietta, much struck by this.

Lady Melville, cutting into the conversation, requested Sir Nicholas to hand Almeria her tea, an interruption which was not especially welcome to her spouse, who had been hearing a lively account of Aldwyn's experiences in the Peninsular War. Her quelling accents had the effect of putting an end to any but general conversation, so Henrietta was unable to learn anything more at present of the young woman who had once been a schoolfellow and close friend of both Almeria and herself.

After twenty minutes or so of the desultory chat that inevitably followed Lady Melville's inclusion in a conversation, the visitors rose to take their leave.

"Are you to be staying long at Aldwyn Court?" asked Sir Nicholas. "If so, you must do us the honour of dinng with us one evening, must they not, my love?"

Thus appealed to, Lady Melville condescended to second the invitation.

Julian bowed. "You are very good, ma'am. As for myself, I shall be fixed at my parents' house for some little while yet, as I must attend to some duties of the estate. But my sister tells me she intends to return to her own family in Bath in a few days' time."

He glanced at Almeria, and she nodded.

"You're to go so soon?" echoed Henrietta in dismay. "There is still so much I wish to tell you, and to hear from you! Would it be very selfish in me to beg for a few more hours of your company tomorrow afternoon?"

"I would remind you, Henrietta, that I have an engagement elsewhere tomorrow," put in Lady Melville before Almeria could answer.

"Then you'll not be obliged to sit through our endless prattle, Selina," replied Henrietta, who had certainly not overlooked this fact when she issued her invitation. "Now pray say you'll come, Almeria! We see each other so seldom nowadays."

Almeria readily consented, relieved of the constraint of including Lady Melville, hitherto unknown to her, in their conversation. It was arranged that her brother should drive her to the manor tomorrow.

"Why not stay to dine with us later?" Sir Nicholas suggested hospitably. "No need to stand on points, Lady Barrington, just a family meal, y'know. Now pray say you will."

"You are very good, sir," Almeria replied, hesitating a little, "but I think perhaps Mama would not quite like it if I were to dine out, when I am obliged to leave her altogether in a very few days. I beg you'll excuse me and understand how I am placed."

"You are quite right, Lady Barrington," said Lady Melville sententiously. "A mother's feeling must always be considered."

"Oh, to be sure, very true," echoed her husband. "But there'd be no such objection in your case, I take it, Aldwyn? Since you're to make a lengthy stay with your parents, I mean to say. Now do say you'll take your pot luck with us, there's a good fellow."

Lady Melville graciously endorsed this invitation. It was an object with her to form an eligible circle of acquaintance in the neighbourhood and the Aldwyns, being the most important landowners thereabouts, came first on her list. Julian had little alternative but to accept.

"I think it a splendid arrangement," commented his sister on their way home, "for you'll have a better opportunity of becoming acquainted with Henrietta if I'm not there to monopolise her conversation. That's to say, if that odious sister-in-law of hers permits you to exchange anything but small talk! Did ever you meet a more frosty female? I wonder an amiable man like Sir Nicholas should have chosen such a wife!"

"No accounting for tastes, when it comes to matrimoney, m'dear. But tell me, did you make your excuses in order to throw Miss Melville and me together?"

She laughed. "Well, it did just cross my mind, you know!"

"Hm. You're an artful baggage," he retorted with a grin. "I may as well tell you at once, though, that your Miss Melville did not vastly impress me. For one thing, not to put too fine a point upon it, she *is* a dowd."

"I must admit I've seen her appear to more advantage," said Almeria. "That dreadful sunbonnet! But recollect that she apologised for that in the first minute. Not," she addd reluctantly, "that dear Henrietta is ever precisely a fashion plate. I did warn you of that. But I *know* that once you and she are better acquainted, you'll like her extremely, for she's a perfect dear. Moreover, she's the very female to suit your exacting requirements, you unfeeling wretch! That is, if you haven't changed your mind and decided that, after all, you'll wait until you meet some dazzling female who will at once inspire you to a wild passion, in the manner of a romance!"

His face took on a grim look. "No fear of that, make your mind easy on that score. I shall undertake to reserve my judgment on Miss Melville until our meeting tomorrow. After all, I had very little opportunity of pursuing my acquaintance with her today."

"I suppose you will say that is my fault, but I am doing my best for you! I declare, you are the most ungrateful man."

"Not so much your fault as Lady Melville's. I can see I shall have to contrive some way of getting the fair Henrietta to myself, if I am ever to discover these sterling qualities that you tell me exist beneath what might fairly be described as an unpromising exterior."

"There are times," declared Almeria indignantly, "when I could *hit* you! And smartly, too."

He laughed. "My dear sister, you are most welcome to try."

✨ *Chapter III*

ALTHOUGH STILL FAR from striking, Henrietta's apparance was certainly more creditable on the following day. She wore a plain grey gown, and her hair was so primly braided under a cap that no curls were permitted to stray onto her face.

Almeria rightly guessed why her friend should choose such a dull colour: Henrietta had not yet troubled to discard the half mourning into which she had gone six months after her father's death.

When they had been chatting together for some time with the old, familiar ease of bygone days, Almeria ventured to mention this matter. They were quite alone, for Sir Nicholas had taken Aldwyn off to the stables to inspect his horses.

"Why am I still wearing grey?" repeated Henrietta with a shrug. "I really don't know, for I don't think it becomes me above half! I suppose I'm simply too lazy to set about providing myself with a new wardrobe. I wear whatever first comes to hand. Now that the girls are gone, there's no one to keep me up to the mark, I fear. The thing was, you see," she admitted awkwardly, "Papa took some odd notions into his head after my mother's death—such as a positive passion for economy. It meant that our dress allowance was pitifully slender."

"Economy?" echoed Almeria, with a creditable apparance of never before having heard of this matter. "But surely there was no need!"

"Not the least in the world. He left all three of us girls so well provided for that I can be considered quite an heiress!" She laughed, then sobered again. "I think, perhaps, Mama's death perverted his sense. Such penny-pinching ways were quite alien to his former habits. The result was that I had the utmost difficulty in extorting money from him for anything other than the most

17

necessary household expenditure. Why, he even withdrew from social intercourse with our neighbours, as you well may know, and became, more or less, a recluse. Altogether, the house became rather a dull place for two young girls."

"*Three* young girls," corrected Almeria.

"I never thought of myself in that category," said Henrietta reflectively. "I suppose that having two younger sisters in one's charge tends to make a female feel older than her actual years. Besides, *I* was never dull, I assure you. What with the management of the household and the lively companionship of my sisters and intimate friends, such as yourself, the time simply whizzed by! But I was most thankful for my sisters' sake when Aunt Frayne offered to bring them out in London as soon as each of them reached a suitable age. Of course, Bath is only fifteen miles off, and they could have attended the Assemblies there, but a London season is vastly more exciting. And only see how well it answered, for they are both very happily married. My only regret—a selfish one —is that they live too far off for me to see them as frequently as I would wish. We do manage to keep up a lively correspondence, however," she finished cheerfully.

"Have you considered making your home with one of them?" asked Almeria.

Henrietta wrinkled her nose. "Oh, no! What young married couple could wish to have a spinster relative foisted on them? I wouldn't for a moment entertain such a notion!"

"And yet," said Almeria hesitantly, "I dare say you must find your situation here a trifle difficult, now that Lady Melville is mistress of the house."

Henrietta did not answer for a few moments, so that Almeria began to wonder uneasily if she had given offence. It was true that Henrietta's letters had hinted at some difficulties since her sister-in-law's taking up residence at the manor, but nothing had been openly stated. Perhaps it was a subject on which her friend preferred to maintain a reserve.

But Henrietta's next words showed that she was, after all, prepared to confide in her girlhood friend.

"Yes," she admitted presently. "It *is* difficult. I do my best not to upset Selina, but it's the servants, you see. They've been so used to consulting me over everything.

They are gradually accustoming themselves to the change, but there are still times—"

She broke off and sighed.

"I think, Almeria, I will soon be obliged to make a change. But what, I can't think. I positively will *not* foist myself off on either of my sisters! Yet what else is there to do?"

"You might marry, my dear."

"Marry?" Henrietta laughed shakily. "Why, I'm already at my last prayers—I'm almost six and twenty, as you well know."

"What nonsense! You are as delightful as ever, and there must be many men only too eager to make you an offer. Do you mean to tell me there has been no one in all these years?"

"No one whom I would consider acceptable," replied Henrietta. "But there is a dearth of eligible gentlemen in this neighbourhood."

"Then you must look elsewhere. I wonder your aunt did not invite you to London again after you were out of mourning for your mother."

"Oh, but she did. At the time, however, I could not be spared," replied Henrietta. "She pressed me again when Cecily went there for her come-out, but I didn't see how I could possibly leave poor Pam at home alone. She was only sixteen, and it would have been too cruel to deprive her of the companionship of both her sisters, would it not?"

"I tell you, Henrietta," declared Almeria warmly, "you need to consider yourself a little more! You are altogether too heedful of the claims of others."

"Fustian!" Henrietta reddened a little. "In my place you would have done exactly the same."

"Fortunately I was never put to that test. I would do a good deal for Julian, though," she added with some intent. "I'd like to see him comfortably settled in life with the kind of woman who could make him happy. For that end, possibly, I wouldn't object to a little self-sacrifice."

"But I've always understood you to say that your brother had not the slightest inclination for matrimony?"

"No more he had, but this latest illness of Papa's has changed his mind. He sees now that it's time he took a wife and produced an heir for Aldwyn Court."

Henrietta nodded, a twinkle in her eye. "And I collect

he has someone in mind who will call for a sacrifice on
your part?"

Almeria laughed. "No such thing! Apart from associa-
tions with ladies of a certain sort, he has never shown any
interest in females since that unfortunate affair with Lady
Haldane."

"I know little of that, for it happened when I was
quite young. There was some kind of scandal, I collect?"

"She played him a monstrous cruel trick!" exclaimed
Almeria vehemently. "Of course, he was very young and
a trifle foolish. Poor Julian!"

She saw that her friend was interested.

"There is no reason I shouldn't tell you the whole,"
she continued. "It's all so long ago, and you are unlikely
ever to meet the Haldanes, since they now live in Italy."

"But possibly Mr. Aldwyn would prefer that you
shouldn't?"

"I don't think it makes any odds to him now. It has all
become ancient history. He was only nineteen when he
met Celia Haldane, a mere boy, with a boy's trust and
credulity. She was ten years older than he, and married to
a nobleman almost twice her age. She really was the
most prodigiously beautiful woman; there were scores
of men at her feet. But what must she do but make a determined onslaught on Julian particularly! Of course, it was
all a hoax on her part, but he took it in earnest. She told
him the wildest stories of her husband's neglect and phys-
ical cruelty toward her, and poor Julian believed every
word! He believed, too, that he was the only true love of
her life, which just goes to show how thoroughly she
went to work on him! In the end, she persuaded him
that she must escape from her husband for fear of her
life, and so he arranged to carry her off."

"Oh, dear. And did he succeed?"

Almeria laughed, but totally without humour. "He had
a chaise and four waiting for her in a quiet lane near the
Haldane residence one night, for that very purpose. And
the lady came—but accompanied by her husband and
an attendant group of merrymakers to mock at Julian!
She informed him it had all been a jest done only for a
wager. You may imagine his feelings."

"She must have been unbalanced," Henrietta at last
replied, shaken. "How could any female so treat a young

man in the throes of calf-love? Cruel—cruel to excess!
What could she possibly gain?"

"The wager. And a sense of power, I suppose. Females of her stamp," said Almeria bitterly, "do not care
who is hurt by their petty self-indulgence."

"I am thankful to say I don't number any such among
my acquaintance. But what of your brother? Do you
imply that he has never completely recovered from that
unfortunate experience."

"No more he has, in a way. Of course, he had a
wretched time of it at first, for that kind of story soon
spreads abroad, and he became a laughing stock. In the
end, he quitted England to join Wellington's forces in the
Peninsula, and for years did not return home."

"One cannot wonder that he has avoided females ever
since," said Henrietta sympathetically.

"I suppose not, though eight years is a long time. But
while he still feels so much bitterness towards our sex, I
fear that any marriage he makes will be no more than a
matter of convenience. And he deserves so much more!"

"And so," remarked Henrietta quietly, "would his wife."

After Almeria had been driven back to Aldwyn Court
by her brother, Henrietta went up to her bedchamber. It
was too early yet to change for dinner—never a lengthy
process for her—but Selina would be returning in a few
minutes, and Henrietta had no wish to talk to her sister-
in-law at present.

It had been a relief to speak freely to Almeria. They
had exchanged frequent letters, of course, but it was
much more difficult to commit one's most private
thoughts to paper than to give vent to them in conversation. She sadly realised how greatly she had missed
having a confidante since Pamela's marriage. As for
other female friends, those in whom she had been most
ready to confide had married, like Almeria and Louisa
Randall, and moved away. It had never before struck
her how solitary, in fact, she was. The thought made her
melancholy.

She had realised for some months now that she could
not continue to make her home at the manor. Do what
she would to make matters smooth, her sister-in-law obviously resented her presence. Nicholas, too, must always
be in an uncomfortable situation while she remained, un-

easily attempting to smooth down his wife's ruffled feathers while trying at the same time to avoid making his
sister feel unwelcome.

Yet what alternative was there? She was determined
not to make a home with either of her sisters. Though
she had paid visits to each of them after Papa's death
and been made very welcome, there had never been mention of a permanent arrangement. In her view, it was
just as well, for such a situation would certainly give rise
to tensions that might in time fracture their affectionate
relationship with each other.

Almeria had spoken of marriage as a way of escape.
There had already been the offer of marriage from the
Reverend Thomas Claydon, vicar of the parish, a widower
with two young children. He was an agreeable gentleman
of five and thirty, who lived with comfortable means in a
snug house surrounded by a pleasant garden. Henrietta
had known him for several years, and she both liked and
respected him. But she believed that his proposals had
been made chiefly in the hope of providing a suitable
mother for his children. She was sure her refusal had
given him no pain. Of course, it would have been more
sensible to accept, as Selina had not scrupled to point out
afterwards. But at the moment of his declaration, it had
come suddenly upon her that she wanted more than this
from marriage.

She had never yet been in love—absurd that it should
be so at her age, she reflected wryly. Though there must
be many females like herself who were on the shelf simply because no opportunity had been granted them to
meet suitable partners. Doubtless they were every bit as
attractive and amiable as others of their sex who had entered the married state. Unclaimed blessings, she told
herself, and laughed a little at the phrase.

But perhaps, in her case, it was not entirely a matter
of failing to meet many gentlemen. She knew that she
was not as pretty as her sisters.

She moved over to her mirror to again confirm this
long-accepted notion. There was a certain family like-
ness; all three had oval-shaped faces with small features
and fine, smooth skin. They differed in colouring and expression. Cecilia's hair was dark, and her hazel eyes
frequently held a mocking look that matched her cool
elegance. Pamela's chestnut curls and soft brown eyes

had a melting effect on any man, old or young, who came within her range. The eyes reflected in Henrietta's mirror were between blue and grey; they neither mocked nor melted, but turned a direct, frank gaze upon the world, seeking both to discover and understand its foibles. There was little here, she thought with a rueful smile, of feminine mystery, though she had to acknowledge that her smile did do something to redeem what must otherwise appear rather an austere countenance. As for her hair, no one could deny that it was mouse coloured; but since she had long ago taken to wearing a cap, very little of it appeared in view.

She wondered what such a gentleman as the handsome, dashing Mr. Aldwyn, used to the fashionable belles of London society, might think of her. She laughed aloud. What a quiz she must have appeared to him yesterday morning, in her old gardening dress and sunbonnet! But Mr. Aldwyn, by his own sister's report, took no account of any female, fashionable or otherwise. She thought of the story she had been told of his youthful folly, and her eyes softened with compassion. Although she was a stranger herself to love, her imagination told her how deeply he must have suffered. Although he certainly showed no slightest trace of it now, assured and elegant and so very much in command of himself and the world about him.

Her thoughts moved on to Almeria's news of Louisa Randall, now Mrs. Fordyce. Louisa had always been a close friend until four years ago, when she and her mother had removed to Harrogate in Yorkshire. Louisa had not proved a satisfactory correspondent; her last letter had come almost three years since, announcing the news of her marriage and saying that she was to live with her Irish husband in Dublin. After that, Henrietta had heard nothing more of her until Almeria's visit yesterday. Poor Louisa! How sad that she should have been so soon widowed. And now she was living alone in Bath.

This information had at once caught Henrietta's interest. If Louisa could set up an establishment on her own, why should not Henrietta do so? True, she was not a widow; but was she not a spinster of sufficiently advanced years for such an arrangement to be considered proper? If she were obliged to leave the manor, a home of her own would be far more agreeable to her than any other solution. Not until now had the idea fully taken form in her mind. She would think it over for a little longer, and then perhaps write to Almeria to ask her opinion.

She realized it was time to be changing her dress for dinner. Accordingly, she rang for her maid Ruth, a middle-aged, comfortable-looking country woman who had been with the family when Henrietta's mother was alive.

"Will you wear the purple or the grey, Miss?" asked Ruth briskly, when her mistress had finished her ablutions.

"Oh, either," replied Henrietta indifferently, then added suddenly, "No. That is to say, have I anything else suitable, Ruth, do you suppose? We are to have company to dinner this evening."

Ruth opened the wardrobe, inspecting its contents doubtfully. "Well, there's naught but what's old, Miss. Now that you can be out of mourning altogether, 'twouldn't hurt to have one or two new gowns made up in prettier colours, if you'll pardon the liberty."

"Yes, I dare say you're right."

❧ Chapter IV

WHEN HENRIETTA DESCENDED to the drawing room, Mr. Aldwyn was already taking a glass of sherry with his host. She could not help thinking how well he looked in evening dress and she wished that she had worn the blue gown, after all. She dismissed the thought as stupid and vain, and went over to sit beside her sister-in-law on the striped satin sofa.

The conversation at first followed much the same insipid course as that of the previous day. But Henrietta noticed with amusement that Mr. Aldwyn was using considerable address in an attempt to thaw out the frigid Lady Melville. He succeeded so well that by the time they were all seated at table in the dining room, Selina had unbent sufficiently to ask after all the latest London news, and Sir Nicholas felt able to issue an invitation to look in at the Manor any time.

"Dare say you'll welcome a change now and then, my dear chap. We could take out a gun together, or have a day's fishing. My wife and I are only just settling in here ourselves and getting to know the neighbours. These things take time, what? Especially as my father more or less cut himself off from local society. Henrietta's acquainted with most of 'em, of course, having lived here all her life. And I'm sure she'll be very happy to take you sightseeing. Couldn't have a better guide, too, in many ways; she knows all the history of those dashed places! Never could understand what she and my father saw in it, but no accounting for tastes, what?"

"Fortunately, Miss Melville's taste and mine are at one on that subject," replied Aldwyn easily. "If I recollect aright, there's a ruined castle not far from Westhyde. Now, what was the name of it?"

"Do you mean Farleigh Hungerford, sir?" asked Henrietta. "It's only three miles distant. I often go there; it's one of my favourite rides."

"Ah, yes, that is it. So you enjoy riding, too, do you, ma'am?"

"Oh, of all things!" she exclaimed eagerly.

He gave her a swift but penetrating glance. Perhaps she was not, after all, quite so plain as he had at first thought. It was a pity that she should scrape her light brown hair so relentlessly back instead of allowing it to form a soft frame for her face, and even more regrettable that she should crown it with a cap that added years to her age. After all, her face was not unpleasing, with fine delicate bone structure and a pair of expressive grey blue eyes that reflected her changing moods.

Lady Melville struck in at this juncture. "It is an exercise to which my sister-in-law is particularly addicted, though I could wish that I might persuade her to take a groom out with her. It is not at all the thing for a lady to go jauntering about unaccompanied. I was never allowed to do so."

"You weren't brought up in the country, Selina," protested Henrietta gently. "Besides, you were much younger than I, in the days when you went riding."

"It is true that I never venture out on horseback nowadays, but if I did so, I should most certainly take a groom with me," replied Lady Melville stiffly. "Quite apart from the conventions, one never knows when an accident may occur."

"I have an incurably optimistic disposition, you know, and never think of such things as accidents. But perhaps yours is the wiser course," added Henrietta diplomatically, in response to her brother's warning frown.

"May I suggest that I should take the place of a groom when next you decide to ride to the castle?" asked Aldwyn. "That is, if you will indulge me with the pleasure of your company, and if Lady Melville considers me a suitable escort?"

Selina, mollified at being consulted, graciously assured him that she did. He went on to press the matter until a definite arrangement had been made for three days hence.

"Is it possible that your friend has developed an interest in Henrietta?" Lady Melville demanded incredulously of her husband later, when they were alone together. "I can scarcely credit it."

He stared for a moment, then laughed. "No such thing! Aldwyn's not in the petticoat line. Leastways, not with females of his own quality. There have been ladybirds, so rumour has it . . ."

Selina stopped him with a gesture. "I don't wish to hear gossip of *that* nature," she said coldly.

"No, no, of course not, m' dear! But I believe the truth of the matter is that he's at a loose end in this dull neighbourhood and glad to snatch at any chance of a little social diversion. I must say I welcome his company. I trust you haven't taken him in dislike?" he added anxiously.

"Not at all, though I am not best pleased to learn of his rakish disposition—he appears so very much the gentleman," replied his wife. "But as my dear mama warned me, men are notoriously unreliable in such matters, so I suppose one must not refine too much upon that. And there is no gainsaying that he will be a prestigious addition to the social circle we are endeavouring to form about us, as he comes from one of the first families in the county."

"Just so, my love." Sir Nicholas was relieved. "Though I don't expect he'll remain here for more than a few months, y' know—just long enough to see the old fellow fit to take up the reins again."

The day of their expedition turned out to be dry and sunny, though with a cool breeze that presaged autumn. Shortly after eleven o'clock, Aldwyn presented himself at the manor in buckskins and a well-cut cinnamon riding coat. His immaculate appearance gave Henrietta some doubt for the first time about her own riding habit, a garment that had served her well for the past three or four years but had long since faded from its original olive green to a drab, indeterminate colour. Almeria's gentle hints now presented themselves to her more forcefully. She really must soon take a trip to Bath, she thought, and see what could be found in the Milsom Street shops to refurbish her wardrobe.

Their ride took them through undulating countryside with a fine view of the river winding among open fields, where sheep grazed or reapers gathered the corn. Here and there were stone farmhouses sheltered in the lee of tree-covered hills, but there were few cottages to be seen along the lanes.

"I had forgotten how splendid my native countryside is," remarked Aldwyn, gazing about him appreciatively as they topped a rise and saw the sunlit landscape spread out before them. "There's something quite mellow about Somerset, do you not agree, ma'am?"

"Oh, yes, I delight in it! Lush meadows, fine woodlands, the river: what more might anyone wish for?"

He glanced at her face, which was alight with enthusiasm, and he thought once again that she was not really plain. How could he have supposed her so at first? Her figure was pleasing, too, and she sat a horse expertly enough, even if her riding habit was more than a trifle shabby.

"You must allow me to say, Miss Melville, that you look at home to a peg in the saddle," he remarked.

"Oh, I'll allow you to say anything of a complimentary nature!" she retorted, laughing. "You need only ask my permission if you intend to make derogatory remarks. But I am sure you have too much address for that, sir."

He gave an answering chuckle. "Perhaps so. But don't depend upon it when I come to know you better. My sister tells me I have a caustic tongue at times."

So he means to know me better, thought Henrietta. Aloud she said, "How fortunate that you warned me! Else my sensibilities must have been completely overset."

"I wonder?" He smiled down at her. "I have a feeling that you'd stand up to more Turkish treatment than I'm ever likely to mete out, ma'am."

"So you fancy you can read my character, do you, in spite of our short acquaintance?"

"Well, perhaps I'm cheating a little," he admitted, with another sidelong glance. "You see, Almeria has told me a great deal about you already."

"Oh, dear! That quite casts me down."

"It need not. She has a very high opinion of you."

"And so have I of her loyalty, for she must have suppressed some of the truth to have given you a favourable impression," said Henrietta, laughing once more. "But see, here is the castle."

They had begun to descend the hill leading to the hamlet of Farleigh. The castle stood on their left. Lying among the rolling Somerset hills, the ivy-covered walls of the ruin stood picturesquely on an area of level ground overhanging a gulley through which a busy stream ran to a mill a short distance down the valley. Although little remained of the great hall and most of the main buildings, the gatehouse, close to the steep hill, stood whole and impressive. Behind it rose a great tower, still as high as when it had been built more than four hundred years before. The curtain wall that surrounded the ruins was broken only by the priest's house, still complete, which hid the fourteenth-century chapel from those outside. They drew rein before the fine gatehouse emblazoned with a coat of arms.

"That's the Hungerford crest, I suppose," he said.

"Yes, but the castle passed from their hands many years ago. I believe it's now in the possession of a family named Houlton."

They rode through the gateway and dismounted, leaving their horses to crop at the grass growing in the outer court.

"It's certainly a magnificent pile, but in a sadly ruinous state," remarked Aldwyn, looking interestedly about him. "Shall we walk round a little, or are you too tired, Miss Melville?"

"Goodness, I hope I am not such a poor creature as to be overset by a gentle ride of three miles!" exclaimed Henrietta. "Where would you like to start, Mr. Aldwyn? Perhaps you would care to look into the chapel first, as it's near at hand. There are some very fine tombs there where generations of the Hungerfords, dating from the fourteenth century are buried."

"This was once the parish church," Henrietta explained, as they descended the short flight of steps that took them into the chapel. "But when Sir Walter Hungerford constructed the outer court in the fifteenth century, he decided to include the church and convert it for his own use as the family chapel."

They lingered for a time looking round the interior before moving to an arch that led into a small chantry with a low-pitched roof where the Hungerford tombs stood.

"This is the tomb of Sir Thomas, builder of the castle," said Henrietta, pausing by a crypt. "I can't help but feel that his lady has more comfort from that cushion under her head than he does from the helm on which he's rest-

ing, even though both are carved in stone. But pray don't
regard my nonsense! Do you not think it very fine?"

He agreed, and they were about to pass on to inspect
another, when a piercing scream from outside suddenly
shattered the surrounding peace.

"Heavens, whatever was that?" cried Henrietta.

He made no answer, but ran back into the courtyard.
She followed close at his heels.

They stood for a moment, uncertain. One of the horses
threw up its head and whickered; otherwise they heard
no sound.

"I think the scream came from this direction," said
Aldwyn, walking rapidly toward a ruined section of the
wall on their left. "It was high pitched—a child's or a
female's, I would think. Oh!"

He broke into a run, and Henrietta followed as fast
as she could over the piles of broken masonry.

When she reached his side, he was bending over the
recumbent figure of a fair-haired boy, about ten years
old. She recognised the child at once.

"Oh, dear God! It's Ben Florey! Is he—surely he can't
be—"

"No, no," said Aldwyn reassuringly. "Stunned, merely.
I dare say he'll be round in a few moments. Yes, here
he comes."

The boy opened his eyes, blinked, shook his head, and
sat up, staring at them dazedly. Then he attempted to
struggle to his feet.

"Steady on," advised Aldwyn, putting an arm about
the child to assist him. Then, seeing the boy wince as he
started to put his left foot to the ground, "Hm, hurt
your foot, have you? Sit down again, and I'll take a look
at it."

Aldwyn gently removed the shoe and stocking to ex-
amine the extent of the injury. He smiled approvingly as
he noticed the child bravely suppress a second wince.

"Nothing serious; a sprain, I'd say. You know the lad,
do you, Miss Melville?"

"Yes, he's the youngest son of our neighbour, Mr.
William Florey. Poor Ben, you must be feeling all on
end! How did you come to such a grief?"

"I took a tumble, Miss Melville, when I was climbing
that curst wall," answered Ben, who, though pale, was
now recovering rapidly from his swoon. "Regular mutton-

headed thing to do, seeing that I'm forever climbing trees! I remember falling, then knocking my head on the ground, then nothing else until I saw you and this gentleman bending over me. Must've swooned, I s'pose —just like a silly girl!" he added, in disgust.

"No need to be ashamed on that account," Aldwyn reassured him. "I've seen plenty of soldiers knocked out cold in similar circumstances."

"I say, sir, are you a military man?" demanded Ben eagerly, forgetting his troubles in the excitement of this discovery.

"I should perhaps introduce you to Mr. Aldwyn," put in Henrietta at this juncture. "He was until lately a major in the Duke of Wellington's forces."

"That's famous! Should I call you Major Aldwyn, sir?"

Aldwyn shook his head. "I renounced the military title when I quitted the army. But I think we'd best be getting you home, young fellow. How did you come here; did you ride?"

"My pony's cast a shoe and the blacksmith's too busy to see to it until this afternoon," explained Ben. "Well, it seemed a pity to waste a capital sort of morning like this, sir, so I thought I'd hoof it to the castle—that is to say, walk it, Mr. Aldwyn," he amended, with the wary glance of one who is frequently being reprimanded for his use of slang.

"Well, it's plain that you won't be returning on foot," replied Aldwyn, with a grin. "I fear, Miss Melville, that we must postpone our tour of the castle until some future occasion. I'll take our young friend up on my horse, and we'll accompany him home."

"Yes, indeed we must," Henrietta agreed. "Do you feel more the thing now, Ben?"

"Right as a trivet, ma'am! But I'm sorry to be giving you and Mr. Aldwyn so much trouble," said Ben politely. "If you wouldn't object to lending me your arm, sir, so's I can get up, I dare say I can hop over to the horses."

"Possibly, but I don't propose to put it to the test," said Aldwyn with a laugh. "There's any amount of loose masonry hereabouts, and we don't want you spraining the other ankle, do we?"

Without waiting for an answer, he took the boy up easily into his arms, carried him over to the waiting horses, and lifted him to the back of his own animal.

Then he turned to assist Henrietta to mount, before swinging himself into the saddle.

"I say, sir, this is a sweet goer!" exclaimed Ben, when they had covered a few hundred yards. "What do you call him?"

"Pericles. Yes, he gets over ground readily enough."

"Pericles?" echoed Ben in tones of disgust. "Why, wasn't he one of those Greek chaps?"

"I am gratified to see that your classical education has not been wholly neglected," said Aldwyn.

"No fear of that, sir, with old Master Finnemore, regular Tartar that he is! But I must say, Mr. Aldwyn, it seems an odd sort of name to give a horse. Though I don't mean to be impertinent," he added, glancing warily at his companion.

"Well, perhaps it is an odd name, but I'm possessed of a somewhat odd sense of humour."

He glanced at Henrietta as he answered, and they shared a smile. She reflected that he seemed to have an easy way with the boy, considering his bachelor state. Then she remembered that he had several young nephews, and must be quite used to children.

They rode on in silence for a time, until Ben suddenly asked Henrietta how long it would take for his ankle to recover.

"It depends on how severe the sprain may be," she replied. "But I dare say you'll be able to use it by the end of the week."

To one of Ben's restless temperament, this seemed like a life sentence. His expression grew glum.

"Not till then? Oh, Lud, and Father was to take me over to the Limpley stables tomorrow! He's to buy a new hunter, and I wouldn't miss it for anything! This is the most curst thing!"

"I shouldn't let yourself get cast into a flat despair yet," consoled Aldwyn. "If your father's to drive there, you know, I expect you can still accompany him."

"Yes, that's true," agreed Ben, his face brightening. "I could hobble around with a stick or something, I dare say. But it'll be pretty flat at home for the rest of the time."

"You must persuade your sister Anna to play some indoor games with you," suggested Henrietta. "That will soon pass the time away."

"Anna—not she! She spends all her time reading

trashy novels. At least Mama *says* they are trashy, though I saw her reading one of them herself the other morning, when Anna had gone out. Mama said it was to make sure such matter was fit for Anna to read, but I'm not so sure about that."

Henrietta had hard work not to laugh at this, and from a quick glance at Julian Aldwyn, she saw that he was experiencing a similar difficulty. He turned the subject with some adroitness, however, and the rest of the journey was accomplished without the emergence of any further insights into the foibles of the Florey family.

❦ Chapter V

ANNA FLOREY WAS curled up on the window seat of the front parlour in Maxtead House, her fair head bowed earnestly over a copy of Miss Frances Burney's novel *Evelina*. At first she had not been anxious to read the book, which had been handed to her by her mama with the recommendation that, if she must waste her time in reading novels, she might as well choose one with a high moral tone. But a lack of other reading matter had forced her to make the attempt, and now she was deep into the story, her blue eyes devouring every word of the affecting scene set out before her.

If only she could have been Evelina, she thought wistfully, and had the good fortune to meet such a handsome, elegant, charming gentleman as Lord Orville—and one with such striking nobility of character! Of course, one would need to go to far-off London and enter polite society to meet such a gentleman, for Anna was sure there were none in Somerset. She lowered the book a few inches and let her gaze wander as she passed in rapid review all the single young gentlemen of the immediate neighbourhood.

They were mostly schoolboys like Jack Bovill, she reflected scornfully, either that, or boring older gentlemen of the sporting fraternity who hunted or went shooting with Papa. They always greeted her heartily, if they deigned to notice her at all, with no trace of the romantic approach due a heroine. For fifteen-year-old Anna saw herself as the heroine of a romance, in spite of the determined efforts of the rest of the world to treat her as a very ordinary schoolgirl. She knew that she was a trifle too plump for a truly romantic heroine, but she had strong hopes that this was only puppy fat, as Nurse said, and that time would remove it. Had not her sister Catherine become slim and willowy in her seventeenth year, just before Mama had taken her to London for her come-out? And was Katie not now married to a dashing baronet, and quite one of the toasts of the town—or so Mama said. For the rest, Anna was aware that she was tolerably pleasing to look at, with her golden curls, deep blue eyes, and, looking earnestly in her mirror, a mouth that she would sometimes—but this was a great secret—consider kissable.

She sighed deeply. It was a melancholy fact that life was not nearly so exciting as one hoped it might be, so that there was really nothing else to be done but to seek vicarious thrills between the covers of a novel. The summer holidays were almost over, and she had never once fallen into the smallest adventure or met anyone in the least way interesting; it was enough to sink her in mortification. In little more than a week, she would return to Bath, immured in the stultifying, correct atmosphere of Miss Mynford's Select Seminary for Young Ladies, in Queen Square. Although, as a senior student, she had many privileges, and she and her chosen friends often had good times there, she indulged herself for the moment in imagining the seminary as nothing better than a prison. How absurd that she should remain there for another whole year! She would speak to Mama about it.

Having made this momentous decision, she was about to return to her book when she heard the sound of horses on the drive. She looked out of the window and saw two riders approaching. She immediately recognized the familiar riding habit of Miss Melville. But the other . . . She looked again, this time with a quickly caught breath and a leaping heartbeat. The other was the hero of her dreams!

Tall, elegant, sitting his horse with masterly ease in spite of the encumbrance of—Ben, of all people! What in the world was *he* doing in such an enviable situation? If only it could have been herself!

Casting Miss Burney's masterpiece aside, Anna made her way into the hall just in time to see the newcomers admitted by a footman and greeted by her mother, who had chanced to be passing through the hall at that moment.

Inured to her young son's mishaps by years of experience, Mrs. Florey made no fuss, but summoned the family nurse to bear Ben off and deal with his injury. She then invited his rescuers into the parlour and sent for Mr. Florey to join them.

It was some time before Anna found herself being presented, and then the business was accomplished in what, she thought indignantly, was the shabbiest fashion.

"Oh, this is my daughter Anna, Mr. Aldwyn," Mrs. Florey said, carelessly. She invited the visitors to be seated. Then, in a sharper tone to Anna, "Come, girl, don't they teach you how to make a curtsey at that school of yours? Pray, don't just stand there with your mouth open, but mind your manners!"

Glancing at the now fiery face of the schoolgirl, Aldwyn felt a pang of compassion. Why were mothers so often maladroit in their dealings with their adolescent offspring? To make up for the girl's obvious discomfort, he executed his most graceful bow as he pleasantly made her acquaintance. Anna bestowed a grateful look upon him before seating herself in a chair opposite his so that she might look her fill at him.

She could not be sure that he was precisely like Lord Orville in looks, of course, for the author of *Evelina* had left her readers with no very clear impression of her hero's appearance. Mr. Aldwyn had crisply curling dark hair, an interestingly tanned face, which somehow had a look of strength, and deep brown eyes. A thrill ran through her as she encountered a glance from them. From that moment, Lord Orville relinquished his previous hold upon her imagination, stepping back into the shadowy pages of fiction from which she had summoned him. If she were to meet the counterpart of Evelina's suitor tomorrow, she told herself scornfully, she would pay no heed to him at all.

But how to interest this demi-god in someone as young and inexperienced as herself? As she listened to the account of Ben's accident, she railed against fate. If only *she* had been climbing among the castle ruins and come to grief instead of Ben, then *she* would have been lifted in his arms and carried home on his horse. But, of course, she would never have been permitted in the first place to wander off alone on foot farther than the quarter of a mile to the village. It really was too bad that boys were allowed so much more freedom than their sisters.

Her thoughts were interrupted at this point by a further

remark from her mama, which again cast her into confusion.

"Anna, I wish you will not stare so! Upon my word, our visitors will be setting you down as half-witted."

It was Miss Melville who came to her rescue this time, as Mr. Aldwyn was deep in conversation with Papa.

"On the contrary, I know Anna to be very quick witted," said Henrietta with a laugh. "Do you recall how we used to play at charades when your sister Catherine and my own sister Pamela were still at home? You were nearly always the first to guess."

"She can be sharp enough when she chooses," conceded Mrs. Florey, bestowing a relenting smile on her offspring before turning to join in the gentlemen's conversation.

"Oh, that all seems so long ago," Anna replied with an adult air. "More than a year. I was quite a little girl then."

"I suppose so. You are fast becoming a young lady. When do you return to school? But how stupid of me!" Henrietta added contritely. "I know I should never ask that question; it seems to make the holidays shorter, somehow."

"That is what I like about you," declared Anna, with the candour permissible among lifelong acquaintants. "You always know how a girl feels about such things."

"It would be strange if I did not, as I've once been a girl myself."

"Yes, but most grown-up ladies seem to forget that," said Anna, a shade bitterly. "They are forever expecting one to behave as if—oh, as if one were thirty!"

"Thirty being the end of the road?" asked Henrietta quizzically. "At half that age, I dare say it may seem so."

"I shall be sixteen in February, and that's almost grown up, at any rate. But Mama says I must stay at Miss Mynford's until the end of the summer term. Only in the *following* spring may Catherine bring me out in London. Oh, Miss Melville, it's all so far off. I simply can't wait that long!"

"It will soon pass," Henrietta consoled her. "And you couldn't make your come-out before you are at least seventeen, you know. So you may as well be among your schoolfellows in Bath as kicking your heels at home with nothing to occupy you and very few companions of your own age."

"I suppose you are right, but I do so wish that . . ."

She broke off, looking across at Aldwyn with so much open admiration in her eyes that Henrietta at once guessed how matters stood. She smiled; girls of Anna's age were very prone to sudden attacks of fancy, and as far as she could see, it could do the girl no harm. No doubt it would be forgotten when the doors of Miss Mynford's Seminary once more closed behind her, and she found other distractions.

As Henrietta turned her attention to the others, she heard Mrs. Florey inviting Mr. Aldwyn to join a small evening party, which she was planning to hold in a few days.

"Nothing formal, you know, Mr. Aldwyn, just a few of our neighbours. We have been meaning to introduce Sir Nicholas and Lady Melville to some of our friends. They have as yet made few acquaintances in the neighbourhood, having lived until lately in London. If we can prevail upon them to join us, that is. In country districts, neighbours should keep together, do you not agree, sir?"

Aldwyn bowed. "Indeed I do, ma'am, and I shall be happy to make one of your party, if circumstances at Aldwyn Court permit."

Anna's face glowed as she heard his reply, and she wondered if she could possibly prevail upon her mama to allow her to be present for at least part of the evening. It now being Monday, a tentative date for Friday was fixed upon. Henrietta would bear the invitation to her brother and sister-in-law. Mrs. Florey accordingly absented herself from the room for a few moments to pen a suitable note.

While she was gone, Anna, greatly daring, moved into the chair left vacant beside Aldwyn. She was almost overcome with delight when he good-naturedly turned to address a few remarks to her. They were the merest commonplaces, but in her ears they sounded like heavenly music, and every word was treasured. Henrietta hoped sincerely that the father might fail to read the message that came over so clearly to herself, and that poor Anna would be spared the inevitable teasing that would result if her half-fledged admiration became known to her family.

Youth was so very vulnerable, Henrietta reflected, and her thoughts went once more to the story she had heard of the youthful Julian Aldwyn's sufferings. She had to acknowledge that this shadow of his past had somewhat influenced her opinion of him, presenting him to her in a more sympathetic light than her slight acquaintance with him could possibly have justified.

But later it occurred to her that he seemed intent on cultivating that acquaintance; for when he escorted her back to the manor, he urged her to visit the castle again with him on the following day so that they could resume their interrupted exploration. It was a natural enough request, she supposed, and yet he seemed unduly insistent. She could scarcely flatter herself that he had conceived a sudden, wild passion for her, she reflected wryly; there was too much calmness, and even calculation, in his manner. No, it was most likely, as her brother thought, that Mr. Aldwyn was bored, being away from his London friends and pursuits, and had no congenial company at Aldwyn Court now that Almeria had returned to her home in Bath. That might account, too, for his willingness to accept an invitation to Mrs. Florey's evening party, for Baron Aldwyn's family and the Floreys had never been on any other than formal terms.

She agreed to his suggestion, dismissing from her thoughts a small, uneasy feeling that it might not be wise for her to see too much of this new arrival to the neighbourhood. She was not altogether sorry, however, when the following day brought heavy rain, making the outing impossible. A note delivered at the manor from Mr. Aldwyn early in the day suggested a postponement until Wednesday or Thursday, whichever should prove most convenient to her. She returned an agreement, saying she would look to see him tomorrow, weather permitting.

She then settled herself down to a day of reading, writing letters, and the dubious delights of Selina's company. She was granted a respite from this, however, for the afternoon brought better weather, and before long, the Floreys' coach drew up at the door of the manor, bringing Mr. and Mrs. Florey and Anna on a social call. They were received cordially by Sir Nicholas and his sister, but only condescendingly by Selina, as the Floreys came rather low on her list of desirable acquaintances. Still, she had no insuperable objection to accepting their invitation for Friday evening. It might even prove the very way to extend her circle in more rewarding ways.

"And how is Ben today?" asked Henrietta, after the preliminary civilities.

"Oh, he's in the rudest of health, except that his ankle is not quite recovered, of course," answered Mrs. Florey. "It takes more than a little tumble to affect Ben, I can tell you!"

Lady Melville thereupon interrupted and engaged Mrs. Florey in a conversation from which neither seemed to derive much pleasure, leaving Anna the opportunity to discuss with Henrietta the subject that at present occupied the young girl's mind to the exclusion of everything else.

"Do you know, Miss Melville, how long Mr. Aldwyn is to stay in the neighbourhood?" she asked diffidently.

"Certainly until Lord Aldwyn is sufficiently improved in health to attend to estate matters. I cannot say how long that may be—weeks or even months, possibly."

Anna's face lit up at once. "Oh, capital! But then I shall be returning to school in a fortnight," she added glumly.

Henrietta suppressed a smile at the girl's unthinking admission of interest. "Well, I know the thought of going back to school is rather apt to cast one into a fit of the dismals," Henrietta said, sympathetically. "But I always found that no sooner was I actually there, than something interesting or amusing turned up. After all, it's more fun being among a group of girls of your own age, don't you agree? I'm sure you have many good friends."

"Yes, indeed I have, but that isn't quite . . ."

Anna's voice trailed off, but after a moment she began again. "Do you not think, Miss Melville, that Mr. Aldwyn is very like Lord Orville?"

"Like Lord Who?" repeated Henrietta, puzzled. "Is he someone with whom I'm acquainted?"

Anna giggled. "No. That's to say, he's not someone you've met. He's—"

"Absurd girl, how can I possibly compare Mr. Aldwyn to someone I've never met! I ask you, Anna!"

This only served to increase Anna's giggles until her mother noticed. Mrs. Florey sent her daughter a reproachful glance.

"Hush!" said Henrietta in a low warning tone. "Your mama has her eye upon you."

Anna tried in vain to stifle her mirth. "I can't help it, Miss Melville. Oh, you're so droll!"

It was obvious that having started to giggle, Anna would find it difficult to overcome the attack, so Henrietta remarked loudly that she was sure Anna would like to see some of her sketches, and hurriedly shepherded the girl out of the room and into the library across the hall.

"There, now you can laugh as much as you like!"

She watched, smiling, while Anna took full advantage of this permission.

"And now, my dear," Henrietta said, when the worst of the fit was over, "perhaps you'll explain: who *is* this mysterious nobleman?"

"Oh, when you understand, you will laugh too, I promise you. I mean Lord Orville from *Evelina*, Miss Burney's novel, you know! And when you said that you couldn't t-trace a re-resemblance to—to—!"

She dissolved into laughter again, and this time Henrietta joined her, though with less abandon.

"No wonder you had me in a puzzle!"

"I thought I should die laughing!" Anna showed signs of attempting this feat afresh. "And, and Lady Melville and Mama and the others being there, only m-made it worse!"

"Yes, it always does," said Henrietta, chuckling. "It's most irritating. The more sober the occasion, the more ready one is to succumb to inconvenient mirth. Well, I was very obtuse, wasn't I? I should have recognised your literary allusion."

"Oh, as to that, there's no reason why you should." Anna was calmer now, having had her laugh out. "I happen to be reading the novel at present, so naturally it was in my mind. But what do you think, ma'am? Is Mr. Aldwyn not very like Miss Burney's hero?"

Henrietta shook her head decisively. "I would not say so."

"You wouldn't?" Anna sounded surprised, almost shocked. "Oh, but he is everything that the author describes: handsome, elegant, and charming."

"Yes, he is all these things, but I think him too—" Henrietta paused to consider, then went on—"too virile, perhaps, to compare with the hero of Fanny Burney's romance. Truth to tell, Anna, I've always thought Lord Orville an unrealistic character, unlike many of the others in that excellent book. He is such a prodigious paragon of all the virtues that no living, breathing man could ever

match him! I dare say Mr. Aldwyn has his fair share of
faults, like the rest of us. Though, of course, my acquaintance with him is of the slightest," she added quickly.

Anna thought this over in silence for a moment.

"I dare say you may be right," she admitted reluctantly. "But it does seem to me that Mr. Aldwyn is—oh,
never mind! Do you really wish to show me your
sketches?" she concluded, with a polite show of interest.

"Heavens, no! I'm the poorest hand at sketching, and
wouldn't inflict my efforts on my worst enemy."

"I declare you're like no one I know, Miss Melville!
You are never in the least stuffy!"

"I've had two younger sisters at home, you know. But
come, I think we'd best return to the company now, do
not you?"

"Oh, must we? I would much rather stay here awhile
and talk in private to you," Anna pleaded.

Henrietta wondered if this meant that she was about to
be forced into enduring a further session of raptures over
Mr. Aldwyn, but nevertheless she gave way.

"If you wish. But possibly we'd better make some show
of looking at my drawings, in case we are interrupted. We
don't wish to appear uncivil to the others."

Henrietta took down a bulky portfolio from a shelf and
placed it on the table.

"Now you may laugh as much as you choose," she
said, opening the volume at random. "I offer no prizes for
your guesses as to what the subjects are meant to be."

"But these are not nearly so bad," said Anna, slowly
turning the pages. "Oh, look a ruined castle. How pretty!"

"I'm amazed and flattered that you should recognise it,
for it's odiously poor! I suppose it's too much to hope that
you will be able to identify it? No matter, really. I've in-
scribed the name underneath."

Anna studied the inscription. "Why, Farleigh Hungerford castle! That's where you and Mr. Aldwyn found Ben
yesterday. Do you go there often, then, Miss Melville?
This drawing is dated last year."

"It's always been a favourite haunt of mine."

"I've never been there at all, but I've no interest in
such places. That's to say," Anna hastily amended, recollecting that her hero had been interested enough to visit
the castle, "I never did have, when I was younger, though
I think I might like to see it now."

"Greater maturity does, of course, expand one's interests," replied Henrietta quizzically.

"Oh, you are roasting me. It's too bad of you. But I really do mean it."

"Well, possibly it can be arranged then," said Henrietta on a sudden impulse. "Mr. Aldwyn and I are to go there again, either tomorrow or Thursday, whichever day the weather will be fine. Do you suppose your mama would permit you to accompany us?"

Anna clasped her hands together in ecstasy.

"Oh, would you really and truly take me? I should like it of all things! Oh, Miss Melville, you're the greatest dear in the word!"

"You may find it odiously boring, I must warn you," laughed Henrietta.

"Never! As if I could ever be bored in Mr.—that's to say, in your company, Miss Melville! Oh, I do hope Mama will let me go. It would be so shabby if she did not. Besides quite ruining my holiday. Indeed, I shall tell her so!"

"I beg you'll do no such thing. You may set her against the scheme at once. Why not leave it to me to ask her permission?"

Anna considered this then, realising Henrietta's wisdom, agreed. Almost at the same moment, the door opened to reveal Mr. and Mrs. Florey, come to collect their daughter. They were about to take their leave. When Henrietta asked, they readily agreed to allow Anna to join in the excursion to Farleigh Hungerford.

"You are very good to take her, Miss Melville, but pray, don't permit her to make a nuisance of herself," said Mrs. Florey. "We shall look forward to seeing you with us on Friday evening, as Lady Melville has graciously accepted my invitation to our small party."

After they had departed, Henrietta began to wonder why she had been so ready to include Anna in the outing. It was certainly not to encourage the girl in her sudden fit of worship for Mr. Aldwyn, although Henrietta took no serious view of this. She came to the reluctant conclusion that perhaps she had designed to protect herself from passing several hours in the sole company of Mr. Aldwyn. And it annoyed her to think so.

✒ Chapter VI

ANY DISAPPOINTMENT Aldwyn felt at the inclusion of Anna in their outing was concealed with his usual polite address, and the girl was even more charmed by him. He was no more fortunate in getting Henrietta to himself at the Floreys' party on Friday. Among the guests present were the Lavertons, a local family whom he had occasionally met in London where they had recently taken their pretty, dark-haired daughter of nineteen, Isabella. Henrietta noticed that Aldwyn spent some time by Isabella's side. Not at all his type, she thought, but several times during the following weekend, she found herself wondering exactly what his type might be.

Tuesday's post brought a letter for Henrietta in a handwriting she could not at first recognise. When she opened it, glancing in curiosity at the signature, she saw that it was from Louisa Fordyce. With a pleased exclamation, she quickly scanned the contents.

Louisa wrote to say that she had seen Almeria since her return home to Bath from Aldwyn Court, and that they had been speaking of Henrietta.

"Our conversation gave me a great wish to see you again, my dear, and Almeria seemed to think that you would not be averse to a change of scene. So why do you not pay me a visit at my new home in Bath? I am on my own here and have no one to please but myself. Pray, say you will come—as soon as you like, for as long as you like. It cannot be too long a stay for me."

The rest of the letter accounted all the pleasant diversions they might share in Bath. Henrietta noticed that Louisa said little of her personal concerns; perhaps she was saving all her news for when they could indulge in a cosy tête-à-tête.

"Who's your letter from, Hetty?" asked her brother carelessly. "One of the girls?"

"No, it's from Louisa Fordyce—Louisa Randall, as she used to be. I dare say you won't recall her, Nick, but she and I were very friendly at one time, before her family moved away from the neighbourhood. She's been married and is now widowed and living in Bath. She writes inviting me to go and stay with her in Pulteney Street."

"Capital notion, I should think," replied Sir Nicholas, turning to his newspaper again. "Dare say you'd like a change."

"Yes, indeed," put in Selina promptly, with unwonted enthusiasm. "A change would do you good, Henrietta, and there is nothing to keep you here."

Henrietta knew quite well that her sister-in-law was always wishing her away, and she could not altogether blame Selina for this. Her mind reverted to the idea that had first come to her after Almeria's visit: she, too, might possibly set up an establishment for herself in Bath, just as Louisa had done. If she went to stay with Louisa, she would have an ideal opportunity for inspecting suitable properties and informing herself on other matters necessary to the scheme. Added to that, of course, would be the pleasure of having a congenial companion of her own age. There seemed nothing against her going—well, only a matter that she refused to acknowledge, even to herself.

Her brother and his wife left shortly after breakfast on an errand, so Henrietta decided to walk into the village and pay some calls on the cottagers there. She had been doing this welfare visiting for many years, but nowadays she always tried not to obtrude it on Lady Melville's notice, for fear of arousing resentment. She never went on these visits empty-handed, and on this occasion, so heavy was her basket with delicacies that the gardener's boy, a stout lad of fourteen, had to be pressed into service to carry it.

Her last call was on Mrs. Gurney, wife of one of the labourers on the home farm. The woman had been in poor health for some months from overwork and undernourishment. Beside her husband and a family of five young children, Mrs. Gurney had to care for an elderly father, and her husband's wage of eight shillings a week allowed only a meagre diet of bread and potatoes. Although Henrietta feared she was wasting her breath, she laid strict injunctions on Mrs. Gurney to eat her share of the joint of beef that had just been taken from the basket.

"For what is to become of them all if you don't keep up your strength?" she demanded. "You'll not wish Matty to leave her employment in Bath to take charge at home, I'm sure."

"Oh, no, ma'am, indeed I'd not serve poor Matty such a turn, and her so pleased with her place, which you was good enough to get for her, writin' a letter to the school-ma'am, and all! She likes working at the school, Miss Melville. I'll try to do as you say, ma'am, and thank you kindly for all them good victuals, and your trouble, too."

Henrietta took her leave, sending the gardener's boy ahead with the empty basket while she walked back to the manor at a more leisurely pace. She was deep in thought as she reached the gates to the house, so she started a little when she heard herself addressed. She looked up to see Mr. Aldwyn coming toward her.

"Good day, Miss Melville. They told me at the house that you might be expected back from the village at any moment, so I thought I would stroll along to meet you. I rode over to see your brother, but it appears he's driven out this morning."

"Oh, yes, what a pity! Did you wish to see him particularly?"

"No, not at all, I simply came on the off chance of finding him at home. So you've been walking this morning instead of riding?"

"Yes, I've been taking comforts for some of our needy and ailing cottagers. It's a melancholy business, though. There's so little one can do for them."

He nodded. "The wars have brought about a depression in agriculture as in all else, I fear. Even on my father's estate I find a deal that needs doing, from buildings in disrepair to deeper problems not so easy to remedy. But I must not weary you with such matters."

They had now reached the house and he paused, as though about to take his leave of her.

"They don't weary me," replied Henrietta. "When my father was alive, he often consulted me on the management of our land—though, of course, our holdings are small compared with those of your family. But will you not come in and take refreshment? I dare say my brother will be back from Trowbridge shortly, and he would not like to miss you."

He accepted the offer, and soon they were comfortably seated together before a bright log fire in the morning room, a small parlour on the ground floor. A servant brought in coffee for Henrietta and some wine for her guest.

"I've been giving some consideration, for instance, to the management of the farms on our land," said Aldwyn. "Our tenants, even those with the greatest acreage, seem still to be working their holdings by the old methods. Can you credit that the majority do not make use of the seed drill for sowing? Why, it was invented close on a hundred years since. Culture in rows, as it is with this device, means that they can use horses for hoeing, at vast savings of time and labour. I name only one example; there are many more."

"I see you're bent on emulating His Majesty King George," replied Henrietta, smiling. "They call him Farmer George, do they not?"

He laughed. "You do well to quiz me for prosing on with such stuff, ma'am! You must be wishing me at the devil."

She bent toward him earnestly. "No such thing. My father used to speak to me of like matters, and I miss hearing of them. Pray continue, sir."

He took her at her word, for he believed her to be a sincere woman. "The thing is, Miss Melville, for so long I've been used to an active life, campaigning in the Peninsula, that I cannot settle to idleness. Oh, the social diversions and sporting pursuits in London are well enough in their way, but they cannot altogether satisfy me. And since it's plain that my father can no longer hold the reins at Aldwyn Court, the time has come for me to take over from him. I have much still to learn, but I believe that the life of a country landowner would suit me beyond anything."

He paused for a moment, and she nodded in understanding.

"Have you every heard of Coke of Norfolk?" he asked suddenly.

Henrietta considered for a moment.

"Why, yes, I've heard Papa mention the name," she said at last. "He's the owner of a great estate at Holkham,

is he not? And—I *think* I am right—hasn't he carried out
so many improvements there that others go every year to
study his methods?"

He gave her a look of warm approval. "Excellent
female! No, do not blush. Who else of your sex would
have known that? But so it is: Thomas Coke has so transformed farming methods on the Holkham estate that his
tenants have become the most prosperous in England.
That is what I would like to achieve, ma'am, a prosperity
shared by all who live on my land. The first thing I
mean to do is to go to Holkham, to one of Coke's sheep
shearings, as they call his annual gatherings. I'm told he
does it handsomely, with five hundred guests to dinner
each day!"

Henrietta gasped.

"I dare say," he laughed, "it takes one's breath away.
But dinners are the least of benefits to be found there!
The meetings, lasting four days, are for discussions, demonstrations, tours of different areas of the estate, exam-
amples of various farming methods, and so on. Agricul-
turists and men of science come from all over the country,
even from as far away as America."

During this speech his dark eyes kindled with enthusiasm, completely banishing the cynical look that he most
often wore. Henrietta was moved, answered with the
glow in her own eyes.

"It's plain to see that this scheme has fired your imagination, Mr. Aldwyn. You are fortunate, for few people
ever find their true vocation in life, I think. I wish you
every success, most sincerely."

He leaned over in his chair toward her, a piercing,
serious expression replacing the former, more buoyant
one.

"And will you not help me to achieve it, Miss Melville?
I cannot do all this alone. A man needs to have a worthy
helpmate at his side, to rejoice in his successes and con-
sole him in failure. You could be such a helpmate, I
know. Will you be one to me?"

Her limbs suddenly felt weak.

"I—I am not—quite sure what you mean, sir," she
stammered awkwardly.

He took one of her hands. "Why, I'd have thought it
was plain enough," he said with a smile, which caused her

to lower her gaze. "I'm asking you to do me the honour of becoming my wife, Miss Melville."

There was a deep silence in the room. Henrietta felt as if she had suddenly taken a headlong plunge over dangerous rapids in a paper boat.

She struggled resolutely for the mastery of her feelings. Astounding as his declaration was, it had not escaped her notice how calmly and unemotionally it had been made. Pride required that she should govern herself sufficiently to answer him in the same manner. And, dear God, she must not make the wrong answer! A mistake now would lead to a lifetime of regret; she must be quite, quite sure.

She drew her hand gently away and forced herself to meet his eyes with a challenging look.

"Why?"

He gave a slight start, then, raising his quizzing glass in a defensive gesture, surveyed her for a second with a puzzled air before letting the glass drop.

"I beg your pardon, Miss Melville?"

"Why do you wish to marry me?"

"I hoped that I had made the matter plain just now when I referred to you as a worthy helpmate. I believe we should suit admirably. I admire and respect you—"

"Admire and respect." she echoed mockingly. "Meaningless words, Mr. Aldwyn. You cannot pretend that you —are in love with me."

He studied her again for a moment without speaking. Damn the female. Was she then expecting an impassioned declaration? This was more than he had bargained for; she must realise that this was a business arrangement, to be of mutual benefit.

"Can I not?" he temporized.

She darted him a scornful look. "I know quite well I am not in your style!"

Well, that was true enough in a way, he acknowledged, looking at her dowdy grey walking gown and prim cap. He would certainly prefer a bride who took more pains with her appearance.

"Indeed? And how, may I ask, do you know my style? We have not been acquainted for so very long."

She coloured under his critical survey.

"Oh, there have been rumours. And even if my acquaintance with you is recent, I have known your family since childhood, after all. Why, Almeria has spoken of you often, and given me to understand that—that—"

She faltered and broke off.

He nodded. "That might account for it. I scarcely supposed that a well-bred female such as yourself would be likely to give attention to idle gossip."

"Well, I'm not so sure." She laughed uneasily. "Even well-bred females must have a little entertainment now and then."

"Yes, my sister told me you were possessed of a quirky sense of humour. So, I must confess, am I. That is surely one way in which we may be considered to suit?"

"Oh, yes, but—" She broke off, for a moment losing the words in which to express her feelings. Then, after a pause, she went on with more assurance. "You know very well that there is more to marriage than laughter, sir. Even admiration and respect will not do. There must be stronger feelings, a more emotional involvement."

"You are speaking of a romantic attachment?" he asked, with a slight sneer in his tone. "A headlong, neck or nothing passion? I should have supposed, ma'am, that by now you might have realised, as I do, that such transports are only for the very young. At a more mature time of life, one comes to value an attachment based on more solid qualities, such as those you have just scornfully repudiated."

"Oh, dear," she said, with lips quivering on the brink of a smile, "you sound just like Mr. Claydon."

"Mr. Claydon?" For a moment, the name did not mean anything to him.

"The vicar. I think you two may have a vast deal in common, though you do not realise it. He, too, professes that admiration and respect alone will make for a happy marriage."

"You are doubtless quoting from one of the reverend gentleman's sermons?"

"Well, no. As a matter of fact, he said so to me in a private conversation of—of an intimate nature."

He started. "Do I understand you to mean that he has made you an offer of marriage?"

She nodded. "Yes, indeed. It was some months since. He is a widower with two young children, and I'm good with children, you see. So he decided I would make a suitable wife and that marriage would not be unwelcome to me because"—she broke off, slightly embarrassed for a moment, but then continued stalwartly—"because now that I am no longer mistress of the house I have managed for more than seven years, my situation at home has become a trifle awkward."

He nodded sympathetically, although he could not help feeling guilty that his reasons for making an offer to Miss Melville were so like those of Mr. Claydon.

"I'm afraid my brother's wife was not best pleased when I refused the vicar. Not so much Nicholas; he's easy-going enough on his own account. But Selina has been very short with me since. She hoped to be rid of me. I can scarce blame her, I suppose. It cannot be agreeable to be burdened with a relative whom the servants still look upon as mistress of the establishment."

"You are more tolerant than many would be in your situation, ma'am. It's perhaps fortunate, then, that I did not first apprise your brother of my intentions."

"Oh, that would have been carrying propriety too far!" He laughed mirthlessly. "Well, I never expected to be reproached with that, at all events! But seriously, Miss Melville, will you not think over this matter awhile before rejecting my proposal? I hope I am no coxcomb, but I can offer you more than the vicar—in worldly goods, at least. Though doubtless he is a worthier man than I."

"Oh, much!" she replied irrepressibly. "As one might expect, his reputation is spotless."

He raised his brows ironically. "And mine is not? Well, I don't intend to offer you false coin, ma'am, so I won't deny the imputation. Nevertheless, I can assure you that you would have nothing to complain of in that way after our marriage. And it does seem to me that marriage would be the best solution of your present difficulties. An establishment of your own—"

She flung up her hands. "Don't suppose I haven't already told myself the selfsame thing! But it's no good, don't you see? I can't accept the price."

"Really, ma'am, you have the most effective way of depressing one's pretensions. I was used to consider myself a tolerably acceptable fellow."

"Oh, but you are, you are!" she said earnestly.

He bowed. "Thank you. But I am somewhat uneasily reassured, ma'am, for I have a presentiment that you're

soon to add a rider that will completely detract from the
pleasant impression of your remark."

"You see how it is," she said, a twinkle in her eye. "Already you begin to discover the less endearing side of my
disposition."

"On the contrary, I've discovered nothing yet which
does not lead me to suppose that we shall deal extremely
well together. I find you amiable, unselfish, tolerant, capable, . . ."

"Pray stop, sir! Such a catalogue of virtues makes me
sound the dreariest, prosiest creature alive."

"I wish you will ever let me finish what I'm saying," he
complained. "Since you will not allow that admiration and
respect are suitable enough for you, I must do my poor
best to find others in your praise. Tell me, what terms
would *you* suggest?"

"You might say that my beauty maddens you," she replied in a mocking tone that held a hint of underlying
wistfulness.

The laughter went out of his eyes. "If you desire me to
talk in such an extravagant style, I fear you're doomed to
disappointment, Miss Melville."

She sighed. "Yes, I suppose."

"Pray be serious for a moment, ma'am. Will you not
agree to wait a while longer before giving me my answer?
Our acquaintance is little more than a fortnight old. Give
it another few weeks, a month or so, whatever you wish.
Perhaps I've rushed my fences in speaking to you now."

She shook her head sadly. "It will not do. I like you
very much, sir, and I think you like me, but as I said before, that is not enough. Long ago I decided on what
terms I would marry; and just because I am at my last
prayers, as the saying goes, I see no good reason to change
my mind."

"In other words," he said abruptly, "you are awaiting
the onset of a romantic passion?"

She nodded, colouring a little. He gave her a serious
look.

"Tell me, Miss Melville, have you ever been in love?"

"No. Though I had few opportunities . . ."

She broke off, obviously embarrassed. He said nothing
for a moment, staring into space almost as if he had forgotten her.

"You have never known what it is to be in love, ma'am,

but I have." His mouth took on a grim line. "Let me assure you that it is a most unenviable state, a form of torture beside which the rack and the thumbscrew are mere child's play."

"Oh, but that is only when one loves in vain. What of the many instances of love affairs ending in happy marriage?"

He smiled bleakly. "I see you are an optimist. For my own part, I believe a marriage in which there is mutual esteem and respect has more chance of bringing true felicity to the partners than any impassioned transports, which, plunging one from Heaven to Hell, usually end in total disillusionment."

Her eyes softened. "You have been unfortunate, sir. I have heard something of that from your sister. Pardon me if I tread on delicate ground. but that was all a long time ago. Surely you do not still—?"

"Of course not," he replied brusquely. "As you say, a long time ago, and almost forgotten. It has, however, successfully deterred me from further expeditions of foolishness. I seek now to settle down with an amiable, sensible woman, who will be content with what I can offer, and not expect a courtship in the first flight of romance."

"And you naturally thought I was such a woman," she mused. "I am nearly six and twenty, still a spinster, neither beautiful nor even especially talented."

"You do yourself less than justice, ma'am. And, incidentally, you make my offer sound an unpardonable insult."

His tone was stiff, so impulsively, she leaned forward and let her hand rest lightly on his arm for a moment.

"No such thing. Pray don't suppose that I intended any reproach. I was merely reflecting that this is the way in which others must see me, and the notion came as something of a shock. Because, you know, one never realises how much one has changed with the years. We carry an inward image of ourselves, I think, which remains forever the same."

"That's true enough," he agreed. "It's said that inside every old man there's still a young lad. But all this is nonsense as far as you're concerned, ma'am. Why, you are pretty well three years my junior, and I hope I am not yet come to the sere and yellow!"

"Ah, but gentlemen are different," she insisted. "At my

age, a female who is still unmarried is considered to be on the shelf. But I do wonder," she continued, half to herself, "what kind of person I really am? For so many years I've tried to be what others expected and needed me to be: my father, my sisters and brother, the household. There was never time nor opportunity to discover what I wanted for myself—even whether I am truly the sensible female everyone considers me."

"Only accept my offer of marriage, Miss Melville," he said gently, "and you will be afforded such an opportunity."

She shook her head decisively. "No. Pardon me if I speak too plainly, but that would be merely to exchange one set of duties for another. It may turn out in the end that this is what I do want, for after all's said, there are those who cannot find fulfilment unless they are necessary to someone else. But I should like to have my freedom for the time being, at least to *try* another way, to discover myself. Does that sound too fanciful? For some time now I have been forming the intention of going away from the manor for that very purpose. Your declaration has served to fortify my purpose, but I am sorry if your disappointment in my answer is too severe."

"That of course, though I have not entirely abandoned hope that you may change your mind. Nevertheless, I understand and sympathise with your feelings. Perhaps you are right in wishing to put them to the test. May I ask where you intend to go? To London, possibly, to sample the delights of that society which you would have entered earlier in life had circumstances permitted?"

"Oh, no!" Her tone was emphatic. "I would cut a sorry figure, I fear, among all those young debutantes! Why, I would most likely be taken for a chaperone, and put to sit with all the gossiping dowagers!"

He started a civil protest, but she cut him short, smiling.

"Now, pray *don't* feel obliged to flatter me, Mr. Aldwyn! Believe me when I say that I am not fishing for compliments. I think we understand each other very well. No, not London. But I think Bath might answer, don't you? It's not so fashionable that I should feel hopelessly outmoded, but I could try my wings a little. Moreover, an opportunity has arisen for me to go there with the full approval of my family. A former friend, who is now a widow and settled in Bath, has invited me to stay with her awhile. You may perhaps have heard Almeria and me speaking of a Mrs. Fordyce on that first day when you called here."

He frowned, considering for a moment. "Yes, I do recollect. But surely a recently widowed young woman will not make the most cheerful of company."

"Mrs. Fordyce shows no signs of melancholy; quite otherwise. I must confess that Louisa says she intends to take me on a round of dissipation if I do go to stay with her. Dissipation!" She laughed. "I must admit, it sounds prodigiously attractive, and quite different from my accustomed life these past years. Exactly what I need at the present time."

"Doubtless you are right. I see now that my declaration was ill timed, to say the least, and that I must abandon all hope of success. Pray forgive me for my importunity, and accept my most sincere wishes for your future happiness, ma'am."

Henrietta looked contrite. "You should rather forgive me for receiving your proposals with such scant ceremony. I have not even spoken of the great honour you do me. Only," she went on, returning to a more natural manner, "I'm quite sure that when you come to consider it, you will feel that you've had a fortunate escape. Perhaps you may yet meet someone else who can make you truly happy, Mr. Aldwyn; for my part, I don't at all subscribe to the view that one cannot love a second time."

He made a gesture of repudiation, almost of distaste.

"Oh, I know you think you don't wish to fall in love," she continued, greatly daring, "but no one can be certain of schooling one of the strongest of human emotions. There, now you think me monstrously impertinent, I don't doubt, and will be glad to be rid of me. Nevertheless, I, too, wish you all possible happiness."

He bowed, rising to take his leave. There was nothing left to say.

He was suddenly conscious of all the confusing emotions within himself, one of which was pique. He had been so very certain of Miss Melville, in spite of his rival the vicar. He had so much more to offer than the clergyman in worldly goods. And he had been persuaded that she liked him well enough to build with him a satisfactory and even mildly affectionate relationship.

The devil fly away with all women. Unpredictable, in-
consistent creatures they were, even those seemingly most
sensible! Surely the confounded female could see that it
was in her own best interests to accept his offer? Freedom
might seem attractive enough in youth, when ties of any
kind were irksome, but surely it had acquired a lonely
look for her by now. With maturing years, the comforts
of hearth and home began to beckon. Had he not reluctantly reached that very conclusion recently himself?
Well, she would come to it, too, in time, most likely too
late. The thought gave him a moment's bitter satisfaction,
after which he at once felt slightly ashamed.

She rose, too, and held out her hand.

"You won't stay for my brother, sir?"

"No." He spoke tersely. "I am not in the mood for social conversation at present. Good day to you, Miss Melville."

He took her hand, hesitated, then carried it briefly to
his lips. It was trembling slightly as she drew it away.

"It may be that we shall chance to meet again in company with others," he said stiffly. "Let me assure you that
suuch meetings need occasion you no embarrassment,
ma'am. I shall make no further reference to this interview."

She nodded. "I think it unlikely that we shall meet
again for some time," she said a little breathlessly, "But if
we do, sir, on my side it will always be in friendship."

He bowed again and left her.

After he had gone, Henrietta stood for some time at
the window, gazing out at the garden, where yellowing
leaves were drifting slowly down from the trees. And all
the while the tears were falling unbidden and unheeded
down her cheeks, blurring the melancholy autumn scene.

✜ Chapter VII

FEW TOWNS COULD equal Bath for its handsome streets, crescents, and squares surrounded by elegant buildings of honey-coloured local stone fashioned in classical style. Centuries ago, the Romans had come there for its curative waters, constructing a series of public baths, which still survived. It was in the previous century, however, that the Spa had become a fashionable resort under its famous Master of Ceremonies Beau Nash. Domestic building began on a large scale, fortunately in the hands of gifted architects, who gave the town its symmetrical beauty. Handsome public rooms were also provided: the Pump Room, where visitors came to gossip or take the waters, and the magnificent Assembly Rooms for balls and other entertainments.

Captain Robert Barclay of the Royal Navy stood before the window of his drawing room looking down into Pulteney Street. He was a tall, lean man in his mid-thirties. His strong, resolute countenance was still bronzed from long exposure to the elements, in spite of almost two years ashore. Although living at present on half pay, his style and manner gave no indication of straitened means, for indeed he had not the slightest occasion for economy, since he had amassed a considerable fortune in prize money during his years of naval service. He occupied a house in one of Bath's most select quarters, at which he kept a stable of blood horses, a smart town coach, and a sporting curricle. Always well turned out, without in any way aspiring to dandyism, he was a very eligible bachelor, a state of affairs the ladies of Bath were determined to remedy.

Lately, however, they had noticed that his attention seemed to be caught by his neighbour, the attractive widow Mrs. Fordyce, not long settled in the town. They could not but feel aggrieved by this; surely when a female

had been once married, she might in fairness leave the
field to less fortunate sisters who had yet to make a first
catch? But far from showing any sporting instinct for the
rules of the game, Mrs. Fordyce seemed bent on playing
it her own way. The captain was only one of several eligible gentlemen who gathered about her.

Captain Barclay's keen eyes quickened suddenly, for
he had detected the flutter of a skirt on the steps of the
house next door. Yes, there she was, looking delectable
in a cherry red velvet gown and black spencerette, with
a high-crowned bonnet of the same colour velvet tied
under her chin with pink ribbons. In a trice he had
snatched up his hat and cane, ready beside him, and
covered the distance to his own front door at a pace more
suited to boarding an enemy ship.

They both reached the pavement outside the captain's
house at the same moment. He removed his hat and
bowed.

"Good morning, Mrs. Fordyce. A fine day. Do you
walk to the Pump Room, ma'am? Perhaps I may accompany you?"

She acknowledged his greeting with a smile that lit up
her fine hazel eyes, and cordially accepting his escort, she
placed her hand in its shapely pink kid glove lightly on
his arm. As they progressed along Pulteney Street in the
direction of the town, she chattered away in her usual
light, airy style. He seldom replied, seeming content to
listen to her while he watched her lively face constantly
change expressions.

"I am prodigiously excited today!" she exclaimed as
they crossed Laura Place. A boy, who had been bowling
a hoop around the central enclosure, almost collided with
them, but drew away quickly when he saw the captain's
warning frown. "I am to have a visitor—a *very special*
visitor—tomorrow!"

The frown remained, and the keen grey eyes momentarily shadowed. "Indeed, ma'am?"

"Well, I would make you guess who it might be," she
said, laughing, "but that you could not, as you have never
met the lady."

He relaxed a little. "A relative of yours, Mrs. Fordyce?"

"Oh, no, I have no relatives—that's to say, no relatives
on visiting terms," she amended quickly. "This lady is a

friend from my childhood days. I haven't set eyes on her these fours years or more. And now she is to come and stay with me for, oh, I don't know how long—as long as I can persuade her to remain!"

"That will be very pleasant for you. Old friends are the most comfortable, after all. They understand us without the need of explanations."

"Now I declare you're prodigiously clever, Captain Barclay! You've such a way of putting matters in a nutshell."

"I'm a plain man, I fear." He shook his head sadly. "But I trust your old friend will not lead you to neglect your more recent ones?"

"Oh, no, certainly not, for I mean to make Miss Melville acquainted with you all. And I know everyone will like her. She's the dearest, sweetest creature imaginable!"

Privately Captain Barclay considered this description best fitted to the lady presently holding his arm, but as he was a shy man where females were concerned, and not given to paying fulsome compliments, he held his peace.

They had by now crossed to the far side of Pulteney Bridge, where they paused to look down on the swans sailing peacefully across the river Avon.

"I always wonder why it is that swans' necks look so yellow," remarked Mrs. Fordyce thoughtfully. "Do you suppose it's because they are too long to wash?"

Captain Barclay laughed. " 'Pon my soul, ma'am, you raise a tricky point there, and one I haven't the knowledge to answer. I suppose we might search it out in some learned library or other."

She wrinkled her nose in distaste. "Oh, no. It's not at all my notion of entertainment to be passing my time in a fusty library! But see, there is Mr. and Miss Dyrham just ahead of us, and doubtless bound for the Pump Room too. Do let us walk a little faster and come up with them, for there is something I particularly wish to ask Miss Dyrham."

The captain obediently lengthened his stride, though he had no real desire to join the Dyrhams. Roderick Dyrham was a personable man approaching forty, and he was obviously quite taken with the attractive Mrs. Fordyce. There were far too many men in Bath, thought Captain Barclay gloomily, who had their eye on this lady and though she showed no sign of favouring any one above the others, it disheartened him, to say the least. As for Miss Dyrham, it was no matter for wonder to the captain that she was still a spinster, in spite of her modishly attired trim figure. He could never abide a gushing female, and moreover, he shared the dislike of most men for being too industriously pursued. As soon as the two couples came together, Miss Dyrham opened up a barrage of arch glances and playful banter in the captain's direction and he was thankful when Mrs. Fordyce drew the lady aside to consult her on a matter concerning female fashion. By the time they reached the promenade in front of the Pump Room, they had been joined by several other of their acquaintances, and the captain reluctantly became separated from Mrs. Fordyce.

The Pump Room was Bath's morning social hub. Here visitors came to drink the waters for reasons of health, while residents and others gathered to meet acquaintances and hear the latest gossip. It was a large, elegant room surrounded by classical columns and extended at each end with a curved recess. In one of these, a fine long-case Tompion clock stood, and above it, in a niche, rested a statue of Beau Nash, who was, in his lifetime, the undisputed ruler of Bath society, and who now looked down upon it in a slightly disapproving fashion.

Once inside the Pump Room, Louisa Fordyce had no difficulty in shaking off Miss Dyrham, who was by no means a favourite with her, and she was soon surrounded by a group of other acquaintances and admirers. Presently Sir Giles Barrington, a pleasant-looking man in his thirties, entered the room with his wife Almeria on his arm. Louisa waved airily to them, and they at once came to join her group.

"My dear Almeria, I must tell you!" began Louisa to her friend. "Henrietta is to come to stay with me tomorrow. Is it not famous?"

"Henrietta?" Almeria's expression was not quite as rapturous as the other had expected. "Oh, is she so? You told me you had the intention of asking her, but I thought perhaps she might—" She broke off suddenly and smiled. "Oh, yes, of course, it will be such fun for you both!"

Louisa regarded her with a speculative frown. "Were you about to say you thought she might refuse?" she asked bluntly.

"Well, yes, I did wonder," admitted Almeria.

"Had you a particular reason?"

Almeria shook her head uncomfortably. "No—that's to say, Henrietta rarely pays visits. I have invited her often enough myself in the past, but I gave it up entirely of late years, since it was always Papa or one of the girls who could not be left. But, of course, there is nothing now to keep her at Westhyde Manor," she said without conviction.

Louisa could not help feeling that her friend was not being entirely frank. But she had her own reticences, and was quite prepared to respect those of others.

"Well, at any rate she is to come, and I leave you to judge how pleased I am! She tells me she wishes to go round the shops while she's here in order to refurbish her wardrobe."

"No, does she indeed?" Almeria drew her friend a little aside, so that no one else might overhear. "Louisa, I do beg you to use your influence to make her purchase some more attractive garments than her present style! I know you are as devoted a friend to her as I am, so I don't scruple to confide in you that Henrietta has allowed herself to become beyond anything dowdy. I collect that it all began because of some pinchpenny attitude of her father's after his wife died, but it's become a fixed habit with her now."

Louisa nodded. "Yes, I recall that even before I left Somerset, she was practising economies in her dress. But there is surely no need. She is possessed of a comfortable fortune, is she not?"

"Indeed she is, but you know how easy it is to go on in the same way, even after the reason for doing so is gone. I declare I could positively *shake* her at times, seeing her wearing hideous caps and odiously depressing gowns just like an old maid. Although she's still an attractive female, one needs to look very hard nowadays to discern it, I vow! You *will* do your utmost possible, won't you?"

"You may rely on me completely," promised Louisa, her eyes twinkling merrily. "By the time I have done with our dear Henrietta, she will be as completely transformed as—as Cinderella after the fairy godmother waved her wand! She will quite shine down all the females of Bath, and have the gentlemen flocking round her like bees around a honey pot!"

Almeria laughed. "If you achieve only half as much

you'll earn my undying gratitude, and Henrietta's, too, I vow."

In her own mind, she added Julian's name to the list of Louisa's debtors in this project. She had been surprised and somewhat disappointed to learn that Henrietta proposed to leave Westhyde Manor just at present. A brief note, which she had lately received from Julian, seemed to suggest that he and Henrietta were going along together very well, and had led her to hope that a declaration from Julian was imminent. It was a pity if Henrietta should remove from his neighbourhood just as he might be on the point of making it. However, Almeria was too sensible not to realise that there was a point beyond which one could not meddle in the affairs of even the closest connections. If Julian had a mind to secure Henrietta for his wife, he would doubtless find his own way about the business. And perhaps a short separation might be no bad thing for both of them, if indeed absence made the heart grow fonder. She sighed; hearts, unfortunately, did not come into this. What a pity it was all so unromantic!

Miss Mynford's Select Seminary for Young Ladies in Queen Square was conducted on liberal lines compared to many other establishments of the kind. Although she required her pupils to retire at eight o'clock every evening, and regularly inspected the dormitories at half past to make sure all bedside candles were extinguished, she was quite aware that the senior dormitory girls did not always compose themselves immediately for sleep. As long as the chatter was conducted in whispers, however, so that the younger girls in adjoining dormitories were not disturbed, she turned a deaf ear to a little clandestine social intercourse, contenting herself with listening at the door of the senior dormitory for a few moments on her way up to bed at ten o'clock. Usually all the young ladies were fast asleep by that time, for they arose at seven o'clock every morning and followed a rigorous regime throughout the day.

On certain special occasions, however, the senior girls considered it worthwhile to miss a few hours of sleep in order to partake of a dormitory feast after their preceptress was safely abed. Birthdays were celebrated in this way, and for some years it had been the custom to hold a feast on the occasion of their reassembling after the long summer vacation. This was a particularly propitious time, as goodies from home could be concealed among their ordinary luggage.

This year there were ten girls in the dormitory, of ages ranging from fifteen to seventeen. When Miss Mynford stealthily opened the door at precisely ten o'clock, her lighted candle revealed ten heads of assorted colours peacefully settled on white pillows, just as they should be. Those nearest to her were sleeping with such angelic looks on their countenances that Miss Mynford, had she not been privileged to know more of their real characters, might have supposed they were not long for this wicked world. She smiled cynically, shut the door quietly, and repaired thankfully after a hard day's work to that haven of rest, her own bedchamber.

Three-quarters of an hour later, ten figures in white nightgowns threw back the covers and, having rekindled the bedside candles, crept cautiously about the room retrieving from various hiding places the ingredients of the feast. This done, one of their number produced a quantity of curl papers, which she passed among the others for use as plates.

"I've brought a cold broiled ham!" hissed a plump girl, in a triumphant whisper.

"Oh, famous!" breathed several others.

"But how shall we slice it?" asked Caroline Bovill.

"We might tear it apart with our fingers, as they did in the Middle Ages," suggested another girl, who was fond of history.

This caused giggles, which were quickly hushed by Charlotte Brisbane, the eldest girl and the ringleader.

"No such thing. We'll use my penknife, stupid. Now where's the lemonade Matty smuggled in for us?"

A small ewer was produced from under one of the beds. There were some exclamations of disgust when it was noticed that a few feathers from the pillows were floating on top of the beverage, but once again Charlotte hushed the group.

"If you don't take care, Minnie will be coming down! Oh, bother. We forgot to ask Matty to bring some cups! Now, what shall we use? I know: the hair-tidies!"

One or two of the girls gasped, and one made so bold as to say she could not fancy drinking from a hair-tidy. The others regarded her scornfully.

"Why not? They've been washed," scoffed Anna Florey. "I tell you what, Sylvia. If you're going to fuss over every little thing, you'd best get back into bed and not join in our feast at all!"

This effectively silenced Sylvia; and after a moment she tried to reestablish her position by announcing that she had brought a plum cake. Someone else produced ginger-bread, another boasted of cheese tartlets (though on inspection, these proved to be a trifle squashed), and others produced more or less intact contributions to what finally looked a well-spread board.

The feasting began. Time and again during its course Charlotte was obliged to utter warnings about the fatal consequences of too much noise; and more than one girl was forced to smother her uncontrollable giggles in the nearest pillow. At last, when appetites were sated and at least one of their number was beginning to feel sick, the girls began to relate their various adventures during the holidays. These all seemed to Anna Florey pathetically tame. Having waited her turn and gained enough time for her creative impulse to do its work, she suddenly announced that she could tell them of the most splendid adventure.

"Well, pray go on, then!" they urged.

Anna, who knew just how to produce suspense in an audience, hedged, saying she was not sure if she ought.

"Why not?" several voices demanded, impatiently.

"We-ell, because," said Anna slowly, "because for one thing it's a secret. It wouldn't do for my mama to know. How can I be sure that some of you may not let it out when she comes here to visit me?"

"As if we would!" came the general chorus. "We're no tell-tales; you know that very well, Anna!"

"But you might let something slip without meaning to do so," she insisted.

"You haven't anything to tell," declared a thin girl, tossing her head scornfully so that her brown plaits whisked about her neck. "You're just trying to gammon us!"

"Yes, yes, that's it," agreed several others. "For shame, Anna Florey! You needn't think you can hoodwink us in that way!"

"I am *not* trying to hoodwink you at all, you stupid things. I really have got the most vastly exciting adventure to relate! Only"—she sank her voice so low that they all had to gather closely round her to hear at all—"you must promise solemnly *never* to breathe a word of it to anyone, not even, not even under *torture!"*

They promised eagerly, looking expectantly into her serious, now mysteriously withdrawn face.

"It happened one day when I'd nothing much to do— nothing of interest, that is. Caro was away from home on a visit, and everything seemed flat and tedious."

They nodded in sympathy, often having experienced such moments themselves.

"So I decided to go for a walk," resumed Anna.

"That isn't very exciting," put in the thin girl.

"If you mean to keep on interrupting, Mary Brent, I shan't say any more," said Anna loftily.

Several of the others informed Mary, in terms that would have deeply shocked their preceptress, that she could hold her tongue or else. She subsided, and Anna continued, enjoying the rapt expression on the faces surrounding her.

"I walked to an old castle ruin about a mile from my home," she said. "You must know of it, Caro: Farleigh Hungerford."

Caroline Bovill nodded. "Yes, I do. But surely your mama wouldn't permit you to go there alone?"

"She wasn't at home, and I managed to dodge the others," said Anna glibly. "When I reached the castle, I decided to poke about a bit, in case there might be something interesting to find—"

"What kind of thing?" demanded a small girl with her head covered in curl papers.

"Have you no imagination?" retorted Anna scornfully. "There's no saying what one might not discover in a place of that kind. Perhaps a murdered body."

There was a sharp intake of breath from the group about her.

"Anyway," continued the narrator, pleased with the impression she had so far created, "I thought I saw a splendid hidey-hole just out of my reach, so I climbed up onto a ruined bit of wall to get to it. But I missed my footing and fell. I must have knocked myself senseless, for I don't recall anything until"—she paused for effect, looking round into nine pairs of wide-open eyes—"until I found myself lying prone on the ground with the most handsome gentleman in the world bending over me!"

"Oooh!"

"He was just like the hero out of"—she paused, doubtful if some of her audience would have read Miss Burney's *Evelina*—"out of the pages of a novel! And besides being as handsome as anyone you can think of, he was prodigiously gallant. He tried to help me to rise, but I had hurt my ankle and couldn't manage it. And so, and so, what do you think?"

"Anna! Never say that he lifted you up in his arms!" exclaimed Charlotte. "That would be vastly improper!"

"But it would be most romantic," another girl remarked wistfully.

"That's just what he did, and it was indeed romantic," declared Anna emphatically. "Moreover, he lifted me on to his horse and rode home with me! It was far and away the most exciting thing that's ever happened to me, I can tell you. I shall never forget it; never!"

A chorus of excited murmurs broke out, followed by a barrage of eager questions, which Anna was only too ready to answer. She must have gone too far on some points, for Charlotte, who had been watching her with narrowed eyes, suddenly declared that she did not believe a word of it.

"I'm positive the whole is a figment of your imagination, Anna Florey!" she accused. "You may well say that this gentleman was like the hero of a novel, for that's precisely where you found him. No such person exists in real life at all!"

"He does, he does!"

"Keep your voice down!" Charlotte hissed at her. "It's of no use to protest, for none of us believes you. Your story is a farrago of nonsense!"

This strong statement from their leader effectively broke the spell that had fallen over the group while Anna told her story. All except Caroline Bovill, whose loyalty to Anna kept her silent, voiced their agreement with Charlotte. They might not be certain what the word *farrago* signified, but they understood the sense well enough.

"But he *does* exist, I tell you, he *does*! He's the Honourable Julian Aldwyn, son of our neighbour Lord Aldwyn, isn't he, Caro? And after that, I went riding with him—and with an older lady, Miss Melville, whom my family have known for ever—and then he came to Mama's evening party, and talked to me for simply ages!

Caro knows it's so, for I told her of it when she returned from her visit, did I not, Caro?"

All eyes turned upon Caroline Boville, who hastened to confirm what her friend had said; though with some uneasy inner reservations about the accuracy of the earlier part of Anna's story.

"Very well, then," said Charlotte finally, "perhaps there *is* such a gentleman, since Caroline knows of him, but I take leave to doubt the greater part of what you've told us concerning your dealings with this Mr. Aldwyn. And it's of no use to ask Caroline to bear witness to the truth of it, for she only knows what you've told her, after all. No"—the girl said firmly, as she saw Anna about to begin arguing again—"we don't wish to hear any more. We must clear up now. Make haste and get back into bed, all of you, and for goodness' sake, do it *quietly!*"

Anna's mouth set into mulish lines as she bustled about with the others in setting things to rights. But after the candles were at last extinguished, and everyone had settled down to sleep, her last waking thought was that somehow or other she would show them.

❧ *Chapter VIII*

FROM THE FIRST MOMENT Henrietta arrived at the house in Pulteney Street, it was as though she and Louisa had never been parted. At once they loosed upon each other a flood of reminiscences about their old times together, laughing heartily over past escapades.

"Oh, we had famous fun in those days!" exclaimed Henrietta, wiping tears of mirth from her eyes.

Then she sobered suddenly. "But, poor dear, you've suffered grief enough since then. I was so distressed to learn from Almeria that you had been widowed, and then that your mother had died early in this year. I need not tell you of my deepest sympathy; I shall always have the kindest remembrances of Mrs. Randall."

"Poor Mama," said Louisa quietly. "The saddest thing was that I did not arrive in Yorkshire in time to see her alive. The journey from Ireland took so long at that season. But her death was not unexpected, for she had been ailing some time. It was a welcome release from her sufferings."

For a few moments, they sat in silence. Henrietta was just about to ask a gentle question about Mr. Fordyce's demise, when Louisa prevented her by taking up the conversation herself in a brisk, cheerful tone.

"Let us speak no more of bereavement and melancholy affairs, my dear. Talking pays no toll, and one must try to leave the painful past behind. We shall make a pact to remember only the happy times. Is it agreed?"

Henrietta perforce assented, though she could not help feeling some measure of disappointment that she was to learn nothing about the late Mr. Fordyce. But if her friend did not wish to speak of a marriage that had ended so tragically, Henrietta could scarcely persist in asking questions. Perhaps later on Louisa might feel better disposed to make confidences.

68

"And why are you not married, Hetty?" demanded Louisa brightly. "Now that your sisters are off your hands and your brother has charge of the manor, you must have leisure at last to consider your own future."

"That is precisely what I intend to do, though I don't think marriage will form part of my plans."

"Why not, pray? Surely it's the natural outcome for a female, especially for one like yourself, who has all the domestic virtues."

Henrietta grimaced. "Have I indeed? It sounds monstrous dull! Well, perhaps marriage seems the natural outcome when one is eighteen or nineteen, but at more mature years, one is harder to please, don't you agree? One becomes more wary, as the years go on."

"Oh, yes, how true that is!" exclaimed Louisa involuntarily. "I myself—but never mind that," she added hastily. "Of course, I know how few eligible gentlemen there were in our part of Somerset when I was living there. But have you met with no one since those days? Surely you don't mean to say that no one has *ever* offered for you? Not that you need tell me anything, my dear," she concluded, in an apologetic tone, "if you do not choose."

'I haven't the least objection to telling you, but I fear there's very little to tell. No halcyon romances, that is. But I have in fact received two offers of marriage, and those quite recently."

"Two?" squeaked Louisa, her hazel eyes bright with mischief. "Upon my word, you *are* hiding your light under a bushel! And never a word about this until I particularly asked you! Now why in the world, dearest Hetty, are you not engaged to either one of these suitors? Were they so very unacceptable?"

"No such thing. Quite the contrary, in fact. Both were agreeable, personable, and eligible from every point of view."

"Hetty, dearest girl! You must be wanting in your wits, if what you say is true! Why, oh why, did you not then accept one or other of them?"

"Perhaps I am wanting in my wits," replied Henrietta. "But the matter, you see, Louisa, is that I knew they wished to marry me for what I consider the wrong reasons. It was my domestic virtues, as you term them, and not myself that attached their interest. One gentleman, our local vicar—though you won't know him as he has come into the neighbourhood since your time—wished to supply his children with a suitable stepmother. The other—oh, he wanted a conformable wife to preside over his household, give him an heir, and make no demands upon his emotions."

"Well, of all the cold-blooded propositions! Do you tell me that he had the effrontery to say as much directly to you? He must be a rare coxcomb, upon my word!"

"No, I don't think he's that," said Henrietta, reflectively. "But an unhappy incident in his youth has set him against entrusting his happiness to a love match. Instead, he wished to marry a woman such as I have described to you. Naturally he thought I would be such a one."

"Did he indeed?" cried Louisa indignantly. "Well, I trust you soon sent him about his business!"

"I did refuse him, of course, but in the circumstances I did not feel insulted. You see, he doubtless thought that I should be glad to accept him, seeing that he is heir to a wealthy estate, while I am neither young, nor the kind of female to inspire a strong attachment in a man."

"Hetty, you shall *not* speak so of yourself! Any man would be so fortunate to have you!"

"As a housekeeper, perhaps." Henrietta smiled wanly. "But it's no use in deceiving myself, my dear. I am not the kind of female to inspire a man with an undying passion. I doubt if any would ever cast me a second glance."

"I'll wager they soon would, if only—" Louisa broke off, looking embarrassed.

"If only what?" urged Henrietta, with an encouraging smile.

"If only—oh, you may not like this, but for the sake of our old friendship, I feel I must say it! My love, you don't even try to win second glances from the gentlemen. True and lasting attachments, I know, are founded on character. But what man will trouble himself to discover a female's nobility of character, unless she first takes his eye by her looks? I refer to your mode of dress, my dear. You are doing yourself an injustice. If only you would take the trouble, you could look so charmingly, and quite turn the heads of every man in Bath! There, I have said my say, and if you feel that you must rush off to pack your trunk again and shake the dust of my threshold off your feet, I'm sure I can't altogether blame you."

Henrietta held silent for a moment, until Louisa began

to fear that she was indeed offended. But suddenly she laughed and affectionately hugged her friend.

"Well, you have only said what Almeria had already hinted to me when she recently visited. I've never before considered such matters, but, somehow, lately—" She paused a moment to consider. "Lately, I've begun to desire a change, not only in my way of life, but in myself. My youth seems to have passed by without giving any of its promised delights: pretty clothes, balls and parties, flattering attentions from gentlemen. Is it too late, do you suppose, to enjoy a few of these frivolities before I am quite settled into confirmed old-maidhood? For so long I've been a sensible woman, I feel a little nonsense wouldn't come amiss by way of a change!"

Louisa gave a gurgle of delight. "Oh, now you are seeing things just as you ought! One cannot be serious all the time, you know. Without frivolity we should be dull creatures indeed. I tell you what, Henrietta, we will go shopping at once and purchase for you everything most modish! There is a capital modiste in Milsom Street; all the ladies of *ton* in Bath patronise her, but I've been a very good customer, and I think I can persuade her to give your order the most urgent attention. Of course, she's expensive."

"Expense," said Henrietta in the grand manner, "is of no consequence. But there is one more consideration, Louisa. Do you suppose we could avoid going into company until I have something more fashionable to wear? I have the most foolish, girlish fancy that a new Henrietta is about to emerge, and I wouldn't wish your friends to meet the old one."

"A new Henrietta indeed! Only wait until I've persuaded you to abandon that hideous cap, and my maid has dressed your hair in a becoming style. I declare you won't even know yourself, my love!"

"In my present mood, I shall be glad to be quit of the old Henrietta Melville." On a sudden impulse, she snatched the cap from her head and tossed it onto the fire. "There! I am burning my boats, as well as my headgear, and I declare I was never so well pleased at anything in my life!"

For the next few days, she and Louisa spent all their time in the shopping streets of Bath, returning home each afternoon exhausted but jubilant. Captain Barclay found to his chagrin that the utmost vigilance was unable to reward him with more than the merest glimpse of his attractive neighbour as she whisked her newly arrived visitor each day into or out of her carriage. They were always accompanied by a maid loaded down with bandboxes and parcels, so he guessed easily enough where they had been. He wondered glumly how long this shopping spree was likely to last, and when he might hope to meet Mrs. Fordyce once again in the Pump Room and the Circulating Library. He contemplated paying her a formal morning call, as he had once done in the early days of their acquaintance; but although as a young lieutenant he had taken part in the bloody battle of Trafalgar, this simple social observance seemed to call for more courage than he could muster. Sooner or later, she would wish to take the other lady about a little to meet people; until then, he must resign himself to waiting patiently.

To Henrietta, it was all delightful. It had been many years since she had gone shopping in Bath, for Pamela and Cecilia had been fitted out for their come-out by their aunt in London. Even in those far-off days when she had come to Bath for shopping, she had never stepped inside such a luxurious emporium as that of Madame Blanche in Milsom Street. At first she thought they must have strayed into some lady of quality's parlour by mistake. The deep pile carpet, the delicate gilded chairs with their green and gold striped satin coverings, the Grecian statues standing in pale green alcoves, all suggested wealthy leisure rather than mundane commerce. Madame Blanche, herself, was quite as elegant as her salon; only her shrewd glance as she eyed Henrietta gave any indication that she was a businesswoman. Henrietta soon discovered that the glance had taken in not only her new customer's measurements to the half inch, but also which colours and styles would be most flattering to her.

A bewildering assortment of garments paraded before her. There were walking dresses, carriage dresses, ball gowns, pelisses and spencers, finest woven Norwich shawls, filmy gauze stoles, fur tippets and muffs. Henrietta admired everything; moreover, she was in the mood to indulge herself, a fact that did not escape Madame Blanche's quick, businesslike eye. Nevertheless, the proprietress was too jealous of her reputation to allow the new client to purchase any gown, however expensive, that she felt did not enhance the lady's appearance; so she shook her head when Henrietta stood pensively before an over-elaborate model with a wealth of floss trimming, sleeves puffed all the way down into ribbon, and finished at the neck with a ruff and three frills.

"I think not, madam. If I may say so, madam should avoid too much frilling and fussiness, and aim to present the quiet elegance that is madam's greatest asset."

"Yes, I'm sure you are quite right," replied Henrietta, when Louisa had supported this view. "It was really the colour that attracted me so much. Isn't it lovely?"

The gown was of cerulean blue silk. Madame Blanche nodded in approval.

"Any soft shades of blue, green, or pink are Madam's natural colours. But, of course, one would not wish to appear too *ingenue,* in the manner of a young lady in her first season. Materials and styling must be well chosen. A successful toilette, madam, is a work of art, and no less. Now this, if I may say so, is exactly in madam's style."

This was a blue silk and wool dress with a plain bodice finished at the neck with a single frill, long straight sleeves, and a full skirt bordered with a few inches of pin tucking.

"If madam would care to try on this model, I do believe it is very much the correct fitting," suggested the modiste.

Henrietta needed no more urging, and very soon she was gazing, entranced, at her reflection in a full-length mirror.

Louisa drew a deep breath. "Oh, it's beyond anything, Hetty! It fits you to perfection, I vow!"

Madame Blanche agreed, though in a more reserved tone. As for Henrietta, she said nothing, but her face expressed all her surprised delight. Surely this slender vision in the mirror could not be herself? The blue of the gown set off her fair skin and deepened the colour of her blue-grey eyes; it even added a glint of gold to the once mouse-coloured hair, which Louisa's maid had earlier arranged in a more fashionable style. This was indeed a new Henrietta Melville, a young lady who looked as though she might well have an interesting future in prospect.

"And now you are ready to launch yourself into Bath society," Louisa informed her when they had returned home. They were sitting in the drawing room, refreshing with a cup of tea. "You have several new gowns already, and more are soon due to arrive. Not to mention three pelisses and any quantity of shawls, gloves, muffs, stoles, and other kickshaws! Upon my word, Henrietta, when I heard you order three dozen pairs of silk stockings, I knew that you had thrown all discretion to the winds!"

"Well, we must do ourselves up in style, as my brother would say. Besides, stockings are odiously fragile."

Louisa's eyes suddenly brightened. "What do you say we call on Almeria this afternoon? It's a wonder we haven't run across her already on our shopping expeditions, for she's often to be found in Milsom Street."

"But surely she cannot always be buying new clothes, Louisa. She would quite run Sir Giles Barrington into the ground, poor man!"

"It would take a great deal to do that. But you must understand that Milsom Street is not only a shopping street, it is also one of the foremost fashionable promenades in Bath. Like Bond Street, in London, you know."

"Now you mention it, I certainly did notice a great many people sauntering aimlessly about, as though they intended to be seen themselves rather than to gaze into shop windows. By all means do let us call on Almeria. Could we walk there? I seem almost to have lost the use of my own two legs since I arrived in Bath, and I miss the exercise of walking and riding."

"Walk all the way to the Circus? I don't engage for *that*, I assure you! Why it's almost as far again from here as the abbey. And the last part, Gay Street, is all uphill, into the bargain! No, you shall walk with me to the Pump Room tomorrow morning, should it be fine enough. That's quite as far as I care to go on foot."

"Oh, shame on you, Louisa! Why, you'll gain weight and lose your slender figure, if you don't have a care."

"Well, at least there's a royal precedent for that. They say the Prince Regent is enormous, in spite of his corset."

Henrietta's few previous excursions to Bath had never afforded her a sight of the Circus, one of the most exclusive areas of the town, and she was considerably impressed by its classical elegance. The magnificent houses were circled by a broad carriage road; the central area was enclosed by railings protecting from general usage a shrubbery and a gravelled walk beside the reservoir that supplied the houses with water.

The butler graciously informed them that his mistress was within, and admitted them to a light, airy drawing room with walls of palest blue plaster surmounted by a scrolled frieze and furnished in modern style. In a moment, Almeria was on her feet to welcome them. But as she was about to embrace Henrietta cordially, she stopped short, staring.

"Oh, my dear!" she exclaimed, involuntarily. "You look so, so"—then, after a pause—"delightful!"

Henrietta was wearing an olive green pelisse with frogged fastenings in black and a black cord tassel. Her bonnet was of the same green with a silk lining in a paler shade, and in the very latest style. She coloured with sudden self-consciousness before Almeria's frankly incredulous gaze.

Noticing this, Almeria tactfully refrained from making any further personal remarks. She invited her guests to be seated, offered refreshment, and settled down with them for a comfortable chat.

"Did you chance to see my brother before you came away?" she asked Henrietta presently in a casual tone. "I had a few lines from him a day or so ago to say that my father continues to make progress, but I wondered if you had any later news?"

She watched closely for any quickening of interest in Henrietta's expression as she spoke, but could detect none.

"Oh, yes, we met at an evening party given by the Floreys, and briefly again some days later. But I believe I cannot have seen him since he wrote to you, so I'm afraid I have no more recent information about Lord Aldwyn's health. I dare say you will be hearing from Lady Aldwyn before long, though, will you not?"

All of which tells me nothing at all of how matters stand between you and Julian, thought Almeria, disappointed; evidently, enlightenment would only come from her brother himself.

If only she had known how it cost Henrietta a struggle to speak nonchalantly of that last meeting with Julian Aldwyn. She was no green girl, Henrietta told herself sternly, to be blushed and confused at the mention of a gentleman who had lately made her a declaration. Had she not dealt easily enough in similar regard with the Reverend Thomas Claydon? There was nothing at all different in having received addresses from the Honourable Julian Aldwyn, which she had been obliged to decline.

Nothing? Well, very little. And in any case, Miss Melville of Westhyde Manor, who wore frumpy clothes and promised by her manner to make a conformable wife for a man with no love to offer, had ceased to exist. In her place was Henrietta, the dashing New Woman, who would marry, if at all, on her own terms.

❧ Chapter IX

AFTER ALL HIS recent disappointments, Captain Barclay was delighted on the following morning to espy the two ladies from the house next door setting out on foot. He guessed they were bound for the Pump Room, which, until recently, had been Mrs. Fordyce's usual morning port of call; so he quickly started off down Pulteney Street in pursuit.

A few long strides soon brought him alongside his quarry. He raised his hat and bade the ladies good day, inquiring in diffident tones if they were walking to the Pump Room, as he was going that way himself.

"We shall be most happy to have your escort," replied Louisa, smiling up at him in a way that made his heart turn a somersault. "May I make my neighbour Captain Barclay known to you, Henrietta? This is my dear friend Miss Melville, Captain—I had almost said old friend, but that sounds much too absurd! Only we have known each other a very long time."

The captain and Henrietta exchanged bows, covertly sizing up each other, and simultaneously reaching a favourable conclusion. No woman could compare with Mrs. Fordyce, in the captain's opinion, but this one was undeniably attractive in a quite different style. She had a warm, friendly smile, which suggested a kind and generous disposition. Henrietta, for her part, judged the captain would be a useful man in a crisis, one to make quick, reasoned decisions upon which he would promptly act. It was plain, too, she thought, that the gentleman was very much smitten with Louisa.

As they strolled along chatting pleasantly together, she could not help looking for any sign that Louisa returned the captain's partiality, but her friend treated the captain in an informal, friendly way, which gave no hint of any warmer feeling.

77

The Pump Room was crowded when they entered. Louisa quickly introduced Henrietta to those acquaintances nearest at hand.

"You'll take a cup of the waters, will you not, Miss Melville?" asked Roderick Dyrham. "Every visitor to Bath must do so, you know; it's one of our unwritten rules."

"Naturally I'm reluctant to infringe a rule, sir," replied Henrietta, smiling. "But can you truly recommend the beverage? My persuasion is that anything with curative properties is bound to taste horrid. What do you think, Captain Barclay?"

The captain considered for a moment. "I've taken worse things in my time, I believe, ma'am, but only in the line of duty."

"Oh, for shame, you naughty man!" trilled Miss Dyrham, fluttering her eyelashes at him. "Now you've quite set Mrs. Fordyce's friend against our famous Bath waters! As a punishment, I shall insist on your taking a glass yourself!"

"Happy to oblige in most things, ma'am, but this time I must ask you to excuse me." He bowed stiffly.

She started a flirtatious protest, but he was rescued by the arrival of the Barringtons. Sir Giles was a tall, fair gentleman with an air of assurance. He and the captain were friends of long standing and were soon discussing sporting matters with Mr. Dyrham, while Almeria chatted to the ladies in the group.

Miss Dyrham drew the reluctant Louisa a little to one side.

"Did you hear what Captain Barclay said to me, Mrs. Fordyce?" she asked in a conspiratorial whisper. "That he was happy to oblige me in most things, I mean? I do declaire, the poor man has conceived quite a *tendresse* for me, and it's so droll, because I never give him the least encouragement."

Louisa scarcely knew how to reply to this. But she need not have troubled herself, for Miss Dyrham was quite accustomed to supplying comments in reply to her own remarks, having found from experience that other people's responses were not nearly so satisfactory.

"He is very shy, poor man," she went on. "I dare say he will never summon up courage enough to make me a declaration. Now, do you think it would be improper in me to give him a little—oh, a very little—encouragement? I ask you, dear Mrs. Fordyce, because I rely utterly on your sense of decorum and good taste. Of all the females in Bath, you are the most discreet, I declare. Why, even to me—and I flatter myself that we are quite bosom bows —even to me, I say, you have never breathed a word concerning the sad loss of your dear lamented husband. What you must have suffered I can well imagine! But you are like myself, you don't care to make a vulgar parade of your sufferings. So it is with sensitive souls. Whenever I hear anyone say of you that you are overly secretive, I always deny it hotly! You shall not find Jane Dyrham lacking in loyalty, I promise you."

"You are very good," replied Louisa shortly, looking around for a way of escape.

"It is nothing. I would do a great deal for you, my dear. This friend of yours, Miss Melville, I suppose must be quite an heiress? That gown she's wearing must have cost a pretty penny, if I'm any judge."

"And indeed you are," Louisa answered coldly, resenting the other's impertinence.

"Yes, I think I may fairly claim a knowledge of such matters," Miss Dyrham said confidently, for she had made a study of every changing whim of fashion. "And has she come to Bath to find a husband? She is a prodigiously attractive woman, and one can scarcely guess at her age, though she can't be younger than three and twenty, I think. Now, tell me, how close am I to the truth?"

But as they were joined at that moment by one of Miss Dyrham's few cronies, an overweight widow of uncertain years who had a liking for gossip, Louisa was enabled to escape at last and promptly excused herself to rejoin her own party.

"I saw you trying to escape from the Dyrham," Almeria greeted her, "but I was too cowardly to attempt a rescue. I had little desire to be gathered into her clutches with you."

"Ah, if only you had her loyalty," Louisa remarked sardonically, setting them all laughing. "Fortunately I was rescued by Lady Hillier, though I fear that, like Sir Peter Teazle in Sheridan's play, I leave my reputation behind me."

"Is she such a dreadful gossip then?" asked Henrietta.

"One of the worst sort," said Almeria. "But I cannot be too severe upon anyone who affords me a little amusement now and then."

"Amusement?" echoed Sir Giles, who had come over to his wife's side with the captain when Dyrham had left them to join some other acquaintances. "Fiddlesticks, my love, the female's a dead bore! For my part, I keep out of her way as much as I can. Feel sorry for her brother, though; a good enough sort of chap."

"Tolerable sportsman," agreed Barclay. "Wish you'd tell me how you contrive to keep out of the lady's way, though, Barrington. Don't seem to have the trick of it, myself."

Sir Giles laughed. "Ah, but I'm an old married man, don't y'know, while you're an eligible bachelor! Only one remedy for you: get yourself leg-shackled. She'll let you alone fast enough then."

Almeria glanced covertly at Louisa, but she appeared to have lost interest in the conversation and was talking animatedly to Henrietta. Soon Henrietta found herself being presented to so many people that she retained only the vaguest impression of their names and faces. Louisa, obviously at home with all of them, seemed quite a favourite with several of the gentlemen. Henrietta reflected that there seemed to be no reason why her friend should remain a widow for a moment longer than she chose. It was equally plain that at present she did so choose; she treated her admirers with the same easy camaraderie that she had shown to Captain Barclay, yet at the same time, she contrived to maintain a certain distance from them. Henrietta remembered that Almeria had hinted to her that Louisa's marriage might not have been altogether happy; that would account for her seeming reluctance to undertake a second alliance.

"How long has Louisa been widowed?" Henrietta asked Almeria quietly.

"I do not know. She will never speak of her marriage, and naturally one doesn't care to pry. I have always assumed that it must have occurred some time since, perhaps years, as she seems completely recovered from grief. But Louisa is a most resilient woman, so it's difficult to judge."

There was no time for more, as they were once more drawn into general conversation, and Henrietta found herself talking to a sprightly, fair-haired young matron, Mrs. Hinton-Wellow, who seemed not to have the slightest objection to her husband's determined attempts at flirtation with every attractive woman under forty in the room. The two ladies soon discovered that they had mutual acquaintances in the Lavertons.

"They're in Bath at present," said Mrs. Hinton-Wellow, "staying in Laura Place, quite close to your friend Mrs. Fordyce. Miss Laverton is a prodigiously attractive young lady, is she not? She's just had a season in London, and I quite expected that she would come back betrothed. However, the Assemblies here are as excellent marriage marts, as are the Almack's in London! Not that a girl should marry *too* young," she added, with a nice display of tact. "One needs to see a little of the world before taking on the duties and responsibilities of matrimony, don't you agree?"

Henrietta appreciated the implied compliment in this; probably Mrs. Hinton-Wellow had set her down as being several years younger than her actual age.

"True, ma'am," she replied. "But perhaps the more one sees of the world, the more reluctant one may be to leave it for the matrimonial fireside."

Mrs. Hinton-Wellow laughed. "Oh, I can see you are quizzical, Miss Melville! And so you regard marriage as imprisonment, a kind of trap? Upon my word, I am half inclined to agree with you!"

"Marriage a trap?" echoed George Hinton-Wellow in a mocking tone, having overheard this remark. "Ay, and if it is so, my dear Olivia, it is we men who are caught in it!"

"For shame, sir!" chided Louisa. "Do you mean to say that we females deliberately set out to entrap you?"

"My dear lady, nothing was further from my thoughts," he protested, gallantly. "But you cannot deny we are helplessly enslaved by your bright eyes and charming ways, so that we have no more hope of escape than has a rabbit from a snare!"

"Intolerable windbag!" Henrietta heard someone mutter at her elbow.

She turned to discover Captain Barclay glowering contemptuously at Hinton-Wellow.

"Oh, Captain Barclay," she said quickly, thinking to provide him with a distraction before he was moved to make further comments. "I think perhaps I will try a glass of the waters, after all. Would you be so very obliging as to procure one for me?"

"With pleasure, ma'am," he responded, a trifle stiffly.

"But I won't put you to the trouble of carrying it to me across the room," went on Henrietta as he started to turn away. "I'll come with you to the fountain."

Excusing herself to the others, she accompanied the captain to the place where tumblers of the healing beverage were dispensed to the public.

"Obnoxious whipstraw!" growled the captain as they moved away.

Henrietta regarded him with mockingly raised brows. "What, I, sir?"

He gave her a startled glance before breaking into a reluctant laugh.

"You know well enough I don't mean you, Miss Melville."

"Yes, I did know," she confessed, smiling at him. "I have a misguided sense of humour, I fear. I collect that Mr. Hinton-Wellow is not a favourite with you?"

"Detest the fellow! What beats me is how his wife can stand smiling by while he ogles every pretty woman in the room."

"It would scarcely raise her consequence to show jealousy."

"Well, it's a pretty sort of husband who puts his wife into that kind of fix. Fellow needs a taste of the rope's end, if you ask me."

"Oh, dear, you *are* fierce, sir. I declare you quite frighten me."

"Take a deal to do that, ma'am," he replied with a shrewd glance, "unless I'm much mistaken. I don't set you down as one of these die-away young ladies who can't say boo to a goose."

"Well, I suppose that must pass for a compliment," said Henrietta judicially.

"You are roasting me again."

"Well, yes, I was. Do you mind?"

"Not a whit. No man should take himself too seriously. Mrs. Fordyce is always joking me, too. I can see why the two of you are good friends: you have a similiar teasing humour."

"Perhaps, but I'll vow Louisa has the livelier disposition, and more puckishness. My amusement comes all too often, I fear, from studying my fellow creatures and remarking their foibles and oddities. I have been doing it forever and can't break myself of the habit, though I'm sure it's a regrettable one."

"Well, it don't seem to have done you any harm, Miss Melville. It's plain enough you have a kind heart into the bargain, and wouldn't make game of anyone's suffering."

"Now you *are* paying me compliments!" she accused him.

"No such thing; merely speaking as I find. But here we are. Will you have a large tumbler or a small one, ma'am?"

"Oh, small, please. I'm not at all sure that I shall care for it, and I've been brought up to abominate waste of any kind."

He smiled and turned toward the attendant at the fountain, where a few people were awaiting service. As he did so, he inadvertently knocked the arm of a young gentleman who was carrying a full glass, causing some of its contents to be spilt.

"I beg pardon. Devilish clumsy of me. Allow me to procure you another glass, sir," apologized the captain. Then, recognising the young man belatedly, he went on, "What, you, Fortescue? I never thought to find you partaking of this brew! All the same, I'll get you another."

"Good God, you don't fancy I'd touch this devilish stuff?" asked the other indignantly. "It was intended for my Aunt Euphemia, who's sitting over yonder."

"Allow me to present Mr. Fortescue to you," said the captain, turning to Henrietta. "This lady is Miss Melville, Fortescue, at present staying with Mrs. Fordyce."

Mr. Fortescue was in his early twenties, a good-looking young man with fair hair and steel blue eyes, but a bored, restless expression that marred what might have been a lively countenance. He was dressed in the height of fashion, with shirt points that put the captain's more modest efforts to shame. He and Henrietta exchanged bows and a few civil words before he strolled back with a refilled glass to join his relative at the other side of the room.

"Evidently a devoted nephew," remarked Henrietta approvingly, as she watched the young man for a moment.

"Hm," returned the captain, noncommittally, handing her the glass he had just procured.

She took it. sipping cautiously at the contents.

"How do you find it, ma'am?"

She made a face.

"Tepid. And so is my enthusiasm for it. Do you think I might tip it away? Or would that be a social solecism?"

"Give it to me and I'll dispose of it for you."

He suited the action to the word, then took her arm to guide her back to their friends, who were still engaged in animated conversation.

"You sounded dubious about Mr. Fortescue's devotion to his aunt," she accused him.

"He dances attendance on her for what he can get out of it," replied the captain bluntly. "He don't mind admitting it, either—to other men, at least. He's one of these young bloods who's always short of blunt; cards and the turf swallow up most of his allowance. Then there's nothing for it but to turn old Lady Bellairs up sweet. The old lady's taking the cure here, and she brought young Fortescue down as escort. Been here two months now. He's not such a bad chap, but would be the better for having some occupation other than gambling."

"You think a few years at sea might help?" said Henrietta, greatly daring. "I am fast becoming persuaded that it's your remedy for every ill!"

"Ay, you may laugh, Miss Melville, but a full-grown man needs man's work, in my view. It's not as if he'll ever have the management of an estate to occupy him, for he's a younger son."

"Ah, well, marriage may settle him," said Henrietta, laughing.

"He's not in the petticoat line. That may change, of course; he's only two and twenty."

"You make yourself sound like a greybeard, sir!"

He regarded her with a severe expression, belied by a twinkle in his gray eyes.

"And you're an incorrigible quiz, Miss Melville!" he retorted. "I can see that I shall need to adopt my quarterdeck manner with you. Well, there's some excuse for me; I can give Fortescue twelve years."

"And you so well preserved!"

He burst into laughter at this, just as they came up with Louisa and her party. Louisa gave them a quick, searching glance before continuing her conversation with the others. It did not escape Henrietta's notice; she wondered whether it was prompted by curiosity alone or by some other emotion. An audacious notion came into her head. If only she could be sure; she must try to win her friend's confidence on the subject. It seemed a pity that such an admirable gentleman as Captain Barclay should wear the willow unnecessarily.

❧ *Chapter X*

THEY WALKED HOME with Captain Barclay, accompanied for part of the way by Mr. and Miss Dyrham, who lived in the same direction.

"We shall all meet at the Assembly ball tomorrow evening, I suppose," said Jane Dyrham, as they prepared to part. "Roderick and I should be happy to take you up in our carriage, Captain Barclay, should you not wish to take out your own. Such a pity to have the horses set to for just one passenger."

"Yes, indeed, Barclay, pray do join us," seconded her brother.

"Very civil of you both, but I've already offered Mrs. Fordyce and Miss Melville a seat in my own carriage. There seemed no point in taking out two vehicles from adjoining houses," answered the captain promptly.

"Oh, well, in that case, of course, five persons would be rather a crush, especially in ball gowns," said Miss Dyrham with a chagrined expression. "Well, we shall see you all there, at all events."

Louisa had quickly checked the look of surprise that started to her countenance on hearing the captain's words, while Henrietta darted the gentleman an amused, appreciative glance. Evidently she had judged his character aright, for he was indeed able to take prompt action when the occasion demanded. It took some time longer to achieve a parting from Miss Dyrham, who always had one more urgent remark to make, while her brother hovered uncertainly in the background, ready to be off at a moment's notice, and uneasily aware that the others must be wishing to be on their way as well. When at last the Dyrhams were out of earshot, Louisa turned a laughing, accusatory face on the captain.

"You must correct me if I'm wrong, sir, but I never heard you ask me to make use of your carriage."

He looked a trifle shamefaced. "Well, no, ma'am. I intended all along to offer, but a suitable opportunity failed to come up. Too many people wishing to talk to you in the Pump Room. Trust you'll pardon the liberty, Mrs. Fordyce, and I beg you will allow me to escort you to the ball in my chaise."

"You know what I think, Captain Barclay? That you're the most complete hand!"

He shook his head. "Wish I were. But may I have the honour? Unless, of course, you prefer to go alone."

"Oh, no, an escort will give us more consequence. Besides, your carriage is a trifle better sprung than mine. Miss Melville and I will be very grateful, sir."

"That must have succeeded in depressing the poor man's pretensions!" remarked Henrietta once they were indoors. "You are very hard on him."

"He deserved punishing a little for easing himself out of an awkward situation by telling an untruth like that," chuckled Louisa. "The effrontery of it!"

"I do believe he was being truthful when he said he'd intended to suggest it. Probably he was trying to summon up his courage, and the prospect of being shut up in a carriage with Miss Dyrham provided the stimulus."

"No wonder. She hangs on the arm of every eligible male in sight, but Captain Barclay's a particular objective. And you're quite right, Hetty: he's uncommonly diffident for a man who's distinguished himself in naval actions. He was at Trafalgar, you know; he was quite young then, of course, for that's eleven years since, and he's only five and thirty now."

"In spite of my having met him for the first time today, I like him extremely," said Henrietta. "And I fancy he's only diffident with females—perhaps more so with you than most."

Louisa laughed. "Why me? Am I so very unapproachable?"

"No such thing, as well you know. But—again, I'm speaking on very short acquaintance—it does seem to me that he is vastly taken with you."

Louisa's mirth vanished. "Oh," she said in a flat tone. "Yet you and he appeared to be dealing extremely well together this morning. He offered to procure you a taste of the waters, which is comparatively dashing for the captain."

"I dragooned him into that. I feared if he remained longer to watch Mr. Hinton-Wellow attempting to flirt with you, he might burst a blood vessel! I tell you, he was downright *jealous*, Louisa!"

"He has no call to be! Evveryone knows George Hinton-Wellow is the most shocking flirt, and no one takes him seriously. It's not even worth troubling to snub him, for he means nothing at all by it. Besides, what right has the captain to be jealous?" Louisa said indignantly. "I have never given him the smallest encouragement."

"That's true, my love, and I may be wrong, of course, in thinking him attracted to you." She hesitated, then went on. "You yourself have no warmer feelings towards him than friendship, I collect?"

Louisa coloured. "I like him better than any gentleman of my acquaintance," she admitted guardedly. "But I must tell you, Hetty, I have positively no intention of marrying again. Nothing can alter my resolution, so it would be monstrous folly in me to allow myself to become attached to anyone." Her tone changed to her usual light-hearted one. "But that's not to say that I may not enjoy the company of gentlemen and flirt a little—quite harmlessly, I vow!—with any who are so disposed. Being a widow, my love, is so much pleasanter than being a Bath miss, for one is not expected to maintain such a high degree of propriety! Of course I do not positively *flout* the conventions, merely bend them a little."

"What an abandoned female you are become!" laughed Henrietta. "Truth to tell, I'm glad myself for the greater freedom of mature years. So many tiresome rules apply to the young."

"Have a care, though, Hetty." Louisa warned her half seriously. "Your mature years, as you call them, are not so evident since you changed your style. Why, even Jane Dyrham said you could not be more than three and twenty—which most likely means that she secretly puts your age at a few years younger than that."

"Oh, dear! No doubt it's vastly flattering, but it may prove tiresome too. You see, I had some notion of setting up my own establishment here in Bath, just as you have done. I thought perhaps a female who's almost six and twenty might be supposed to have the same freedom as a widow. But if everyone thinks me younger, what's to be done? I would need to have a respectable older female living with me. How provoking! Do you think I ought to publish my true age in the Bath *Chronicle?*"

"Can you be serious? Not about your silly last remark, I mean, but about the rest?"

"Never more so, I assure you. There's no place for me now at Westhyde Manor; my sister-in-law has made that plain enough. And I don't choose to make a home with either of my sisters. No, there seems nothing else to do but to settle myself in a home of my own and maintain my independence. I had the intention of looking for a suitable house while staying with you. What do you think? Could I live alone without setting Bath society in a bustle? I must admit I should be at a stand if I had to find an older female to bear my company." Her forehead creased with a thoughtful frown. "I have no unattached relatives, and I wouldn't care for a hired companion. I should always be afraid of putting upon the poor creature."

Louisa stared at her for a moment without replying, then her eyes lit with sudden inspiration.

"Why do you not share this house with me? There is plenty of room; at present, I rattle about in it like a single pea in a pod! I'd willingly relinquish the household management to you, for I don't like it above half and leave most things to my housekeeper. Neither of us would be mistress; we'd share everything equally and could even keep quite separate apartments, should you wish it. You could make any changes you chose, even to tearing down all the hangings and starting afresh! Now pray *do* say you will, dearest Hetty. I should like it of all things!"

By way of reply, Henrietta gave her friend a quick hug. She was laughing, but there were tears in her eyes.

"My dear, you are too generous. Who but you would make such an offer without a moment's reflection? I thank you from the bottom of my heart! But don't you think we should wait awhile and see how we go on together first? For all you know, I may have become old Cattish with advancing years. I must have some tiresome ways, I own, for I never failed to irritate my brother's wife, do what I would."

"By all that Almeria told me, the shoe is on the other foot, and it is Lady Melville at fault," retorted Louisa.

"Let us say that our situation was at fault. You and I would start with the advantage of an old and tried friendship, it is true, whereas Selina and I scarcely knew each other when my brother brought her home to the manor."

"Exactly so!" exclaimed Louisa triumphantly. "Oh, I am certain it would answer splendidly!"

"And I'm just as certain that *you* wouldn't be to blame if it did not, my dear. But all the same, I shall not take advantage of your impulsive good nature. Let us speak of this again after a few weeks."

Louisa agreed, though she would have preferred to settle the matter there and then; to think of an idea, as far as she was concerned, was to put it into execution at once.

Bath's foremost Assembly Rooms had been constructed in 1771 when the city was rapidly developing to the northward and it was felt that the existing public rooms situated near to the river were no longer adequate. The elegant design of the New or Upper Rooms soon gained them the reputation of being among the finest in Europe, and few visitors seeing the interior for the first time could fail to be impressed. Henrietta gazed appreciatively about her as she entered the vast ballroom, which was tastefully decorated in duck-egg blue with handsome plasterwork embellishments and lit by five magnificent crystal chandeliers.

"Oh, dear," she murmured to Louisa, "I'm not at all certain that my dancing is worthy of such splendid surroundings."

Before Louisa could reply, the Master of Ceremonies had come up to welcome them and to offer to make them known to any of those present with whom they were not already acquainted.

"But of course you are no strangers to our gatherings, Mrs. Fordyce, Captain Barclay"—with a bow to each— "and we are prodigiously happy to welcome your friend Miss Melville. I promise you that you'll not lack for partners, ma'am."

This proved to be true, though without the need for much effort from the Master of Ceremonies. Almost all the many gentlemen of Louisa's acquaintance anxiously hastened to partner her attractive friend, who looked very fetching in her gown of pale pink muslin embroidered with gold thread. Henrietta had never before attended a formal ball, and now she felt very much like a young girl on her first night out. Her eyes deepened to blue with exhilaration, and her cheeks were becomingly touched with colour.

One gentleman was introduced to her by Almeria, who, with her husband, was also present. Mr. Thomas Burke, a neighbour of the Barringtons, was a sober man in his late thirties with a kind, sensible face. He was not, he admitted to Henrietta, much in the habit of attending Assemblies, and he apologised for any lack of skill in his dancing.

"Why, sir, I am vastly glad of it, for you won't notice my own faults," she returned with a smile. "I, too, am little enough accustomed to dancing."

"One can scarce credit that, ma'am. You move so gracefully. But 'tis most kind in you to put me at my ease."

"No such thing, I spoke the simple truth. Nevertheless, I am sure we can both contrive to acquit ourselves tolerably well—at least, well enough to escape notice."

As it happened, this was a country dance and both knew the steps. But Henrietta found that not only was Mr. Burke's dancing stiff, but his conversation too.

When the set ended, she was escorted by Mr. Burke to some gilded chairs where Louisa, Almeria, and a group of their friends were sitting. He showed a tendency to linger by her side, but as there was no vacant chair for him there, he soon became swept away by Sir Giles and several other gentlemen going in search of refreshment.

"He seems to have taken quite a fancy to you," whispered Almeria, who was sitting on one side of Henrietta. "Most unusual, I assure you, for he has always until now remained impervious to female charm. But you look so delightfully this evening, it's small wonder. I don't believe you've sat out a single dance so far!"

"No, but I mean to sit this one out, Almeria. Your friend Mr. Burke is no doubt an estimable man, but I must confess to having found dancing with him somewhat of a strain. Is he always so solemn?"

"Invariably. But as you say, he's a worthy man. Come to think of it, the estimable ones nearly always *are* dull, though, don't you think? The rogues are much more fun!" Her green eyes lit with mischief.

At that moment Almeria was claimed by a partner for the set that was forming. She had scarcely left her chair before Henrietta found herself being applied to by the

young gentleman named Fortescue, to whom Captain Barclay had introduced her in the Pump Room on the pre-
ceding day. She excused herself civilly, saying that she
was tired and would like to sit down for a while.

"Sit beside you, ma'am, if you'll permit," he replied
promptly, barely waiting for her permission before taking
the chair left vacant by Almeria. "Suit me very well. No
caper merchant myself, but my aunt thought you might
care to dance."

"That is prodigiously kind in her."

"Introduce you to her if you like," offered Fortescue.
"Don't recommend it at the moment, though. She's got
that devilish female Miss Dyrham with her. Miss Dyrham's been telling my aunt all about you."

Henrietta followed his glance across the room to where
Jane Dyrham, wearing an elegant pale lilac grown, was
sitting engrossed in conversation with a rotund elderly
lady dressed in unbecoming puce satin.

"Indeed?" she asked with a touch of hauteur. "As Miss
Dyrham met me for the first time only yesterday, I cannot
imagine she can tell overmuch."

"Don't you believe it, ma'am. That female knows
everything about everybody in less time than it takes the
cat to lick its ear! Told my aunt you're a baronet's sister,
a friend of the Barringtons and Mrs. Fordyce, that you
had your schooling here in Bath, that you're unmarried,
and you're a considerable heiress into the bargain! Upshot
was, Aunt Euphemia thought I should ask you to dance.
Well, she would, of course," he finished, in such tones of
disgust that Henrietta was hard put not to laugh outright.

"I see—or I think I do," she said in a stifled voice. "So
it was not your own idea?"

"Lord, no. That's to say," he amended hastily, "very
happy to lead you out, of course, ma'am, but dancing
don't just come natural to me. Cards are more in my
line."

He glanced ruefully at Henrietta's face, and seeing that,
far from looking offended as he feared she might, she appeared to derive amusement from his naive revelations, he
felt encouraged to continue.

"Thing is, I wouldn't be at a dashed Assembly at all if I
had my way! But must turn the old girl up sweet, y'know,
and nothing would do but that she must come with myself
on her arm. Wouldn't have minded that so much if I could

have left her here to chat with some of her fusty dowager friends, then slipped off and collected her later. She wouldn't have it, though." He shook his head mournfully. "Says she wants me to get acquainted with eligible females. Not in my line, Miss Melville, and I ventured to say so. Might as well have told it to a brick wall for all the notice she took. I ask you, ma'am, what's a fellow to do?"

Henrietta gave a little shrug and laughed. "Oh, it's of no use to ask me, Mr. Fortescue! All I can say is that in my own experience, it's a mistake to submit too readily to the demands of one's relatives when they run counter to one's own inclinations. Heaven knows I've made that mistake myself often enough."

He shook his head again. "That won't fadge," he said in a melancholy tone. "Mean to say, don't doubt you're right—stands to sense—but not in this particular case. Thing is—"

He broke off, searchingly scrutinising her face for a few moments. Then, evidently satisfied by what he read in her countenance, he continued in a lower tone.

"Think I can talk to you, Miss Melville. You're—what d'ye call it?—sympathetic, that's the word! And dashed if I know anyone else who is, in spite of having more brothers and sisters and other relatives than were begat in the Bible. None of 'em the slightest use to me, come to think of it. But Aunt Euphemia, now, she *is* useful to me. Fond of me in her way, y'see, and ready to come down handsomely when the dibs aren't in tune, which I'm bound to say is a frequent occurrence with me, worse luck. So you can appreciate, ma'am, that it won't do for me to run counter to *her* demands, whatever my own inclinations. Downright folly. Worse than backing a nonstarter."

"I suppose you couldn't learn to hold household?" suggested Henrietta, amused by the confidences of this feckless young man, who appeared to her a good deal younger than the two and twenty years credited him by the captain. "It would solve all your difficulties at one fell swoop."

He shook his head. "No good. Haven't the talent for it. I started outstrippin' my allowance when I was at Eton, and I've never lost the trick of it since."

"Do you mean to say," asked Henrietta incredulously,

"that you have been obliged to manage all these years on a schoolboy's allowance?"

He gave a crack of laughter. "Good God, no, ma'am, not as bad as that! Though it might as well be, for all the difference it makes," he added soberly. "Y'know how it is, though. One's expenses have the most devilish way of rising with one's income—dashed well outpacin' them, in fact. Why, it's a law of nature."

"Law of *your* nature, at all events," she said with an ironic smile. "Someone should take you in hand, Mr. Fortescue. Cannot your aunt or perhaps your parents—"

He interrupted her quickly. "That cock won't fight, ma'am. Oh, they've all had a crack at it, and if endless jawing would do the trick, I'd be a reformed character to-day. M'father's thrown in his hand this age past. Only Aunt Euphemia's willing to frank me nowadays, and even she's startin' to flag, game 'un though she's always been. What d'you think she says now, Miss Melville? The most dastardly thing!"

"I really can't imagine," replied Henrietta, wondering what measures would appear dastardly to this happy-go-lucky character.

"Marriage," he pronounced in sepulchral tones. "Says it will steady me. Must be an heiress, of course, or we'd both be in the suds at the start. That's why she wants me to meet some eligible females; why she suggested I should ask you to dance, as a matter of fact."

He looked so relieved when he had made this admission that Henrietta gave him credit for some small degree of honesty; evidently he was not a natural fortune hunter, however pliable his morals might be in other directions.

"Presumably on the strength of Miss Dyrham's information concerning me?" she asked, with a quiver in her voice.

He glanced at her apprehensively.

"Not up in the boughs, are you, Miss Melville? I beg pardon if I've given you offence. Only you seemed different from these other females—more—I don't know—" he broke off, helplessly. "Got carried away," he concluded lamely. "Do sometimes. Thought you'd understand, somehow. Crackbrained of me."

"But I do understand," she assured him hastily. "And I wasn't at all offended. On the contrary, I was trying not to laugh! You must agreee that this is a—a most unusual conversation between two new acquaintances."

He looked into her eyes, brimful of mirth, and they both dissolved into helpless laughter. No one paid any particular heed to them except Jane Dyrham and Lady Bellairs, the former looking curious and the latter gratified.

"So marriage," said Henrietta when she could command her voice again, "appears to you the most dastardly thing, to use your own words?"

"No doubt of it. Well, I ask you, ma'am, what man wants to get legshackled at two and twenty? Even to a handsome young lady like yourself," he added.

"Oh, now you're trying to turn *me* up sweet. For shame, sir! But since you're so delightfully frank, I don't mind telling you in confidence that nothing is further from my own thoughts than marriage. To anyone," she added, for good measure.

"It ain't? Well, that's capital!" he exclaimed with satisfaction. "Don't you see, Miss Melville, if you'd only agree— But I dare say you'd not like it," he added, downcast again.

Henrietta had quite a fair notion of what he had in mind, but she was looking forward with amusement to hearing him explain himself, so she refrained from helping him.

"Well, we shan't know that unless you tell me what it is you wish me to do," she replied, turning an ingenuous look upon him.

He ran a finger round his cravat. "Dashed awkward thing to ask, matter of fact," he said hesitantly. "I was only thinking that if Aunt Euphemia got the impression I was making up to you, Miss Melville, she'd let me alone for a bit. And since you say there's no danger—that's to say," he amended hastily, "you ain't likely to take my attentions seriously, seeing that you're as set against matrimony as I am myself, I thought perhaps we could make a game of it. Hoodwink the old girl. Might even be some sport in it," he added with a brightening countenance.

"What a reprehensible notion!" exclaimed Henrietta with a grin that belied her words. "Mr. Fortescue, you're a scheming wretch, let me tell you."

"Well, perhaps so, but a fellow's got to protect himself

the best way he can. What do you say, ma'am: will you allow me to do the pretty without openly spurning me?"

"That depends. I wouldn't want you forever hanging on my sleeve."

"God forbid!" he interrupted fervently.

"Or frightening off any other gentlemen who might display a tendency to take an interest in me."

"But I thought you said you didn't want any suitors?" he protested, surprised.

"No, I didn't say that. I said I wouldn't wish to marry any."

"Well, if that don't beat the Dutch! Sounds to me, Miss Melville, remarkably like flirting!"

"And what if it is?" she demanded. "Are you to be the only one allowed to indulge in a little fun?"

"I suppose not," he conceded reluctantly. "But well-bred females aren't supposed to do such things—though I've seen plenty of 'em at it. Thing is, they don't admit to it quite so—so—"

"Brass faced?" supplied Henrietta, laughing. "I might not admit to it with anyone else, but I thought you and I had decided to be frank with each other. I have led a monstrously dull life, Mr. Fortescue, and I intend to permit myself a little fling while I am in Bath."

Mr. Fortescue found himself in complete sympathy with her and readily promised not to monopolize her attention.

"Trust me," he concluded. "Won't overdo it. Too dashed fatiguin', anyway. Just enough to keep my aunt from tryin' to fob me off with other females."

As the dance had now come to an end, Henrietta's companions returned to their seats, displacing Fortescue, who seemed ready enough to go.

He departed well pleased with the bargain he had struck. As for Henrietta, reflecting on the idea with considerable amusement, she intended presently to share the plan with Louisa, knowing that her friend's discretion could be relied upon.

✁ *Chapter XI*

"MIGHT I PREVAIL upon you to come for a walk, Louisa? Or shall I go alone? I simply must have some fresh air and exercise."

"What a restless creature you are. Anyone may see that you're best suited to a country life!" teased Louisa. "Well, I'll take you round the Sydney Gardens. It's only a step away, and you may roam around the walks for hours if you wish. For my part, however, I shall be entirely content to sit quietly on a bench and wait for you."

The Sydney Gardens, situated at the opposite end of Pulteney Street, offered a pleasant promenade to the citizens of Bath. Henrietta was charmed by its tree-lined walks, artificial waterfalls, hidden grottoes, and thatched pavilions. The Kennet and Avon canal, which ran through the grounds, was crossed by two elegant cast-iron bridges in the Chinese style. From one of these, the two friends looked down upon a number of small rowing boats making slow and inexpert progress. Finally Louisa declared that she was fatigued to death and must find a seat at once. Accordingly, they made their way to a bench nearby.

They had been sitting there for some time when they noticed the sound of regimented feet approaching along the broad walk. Looking round, they saw a crocodile of some twenty or so schoolgirls, walking sedately with a first mistress at the head of the line and a second bringing up the rear.

"Oh, Louisa, that carries me back!" exclaimed Henrietta.

"Yes, so it does. What frightful ordeals we endured in our youth! Only look at their faces, Hetty. I'll wager the poor dears would give anything for a chance to run amok!"

Henrietta studied the schoolgirls as they passed, and suddenly discovered one she recognized.

"Why, it's Anna Florey," she said in a voice that carried to the glumly silent throng. "I'd forgotten that she was at school here."

Several heads, including Anna's, at once turned their way, and Anna ventured to raise a timid hand in greeting. Even this small exuberance was firmly checked, however, by one of the mistresses in charge of the party; any communication with members of the public while out walking with the school was firmly discouraged.

"Poor Anna, what a shame!" said Henrietta. "I must call on her and see if I cannot gain permission to take her out for a treat. It should not be too difficult, for she's at our old school, Louisa, and Miss Mynford is still in charge there."

"Never say you actually desire to renew your acquaintance with that old harridan!"

"Oh, she was not so very bad, after all. It would never do to be too indulgent when one has charge of high-spirited girls, and I *have* known her look the other way on occasions."

"I detest constraint of any kind!" said Louisa vehemently. "How one envies men their freedom from interference!"

"I think we only suppose them to be more free. And surely you have less to complain of in that way than most females, my dear? You do as you choose, do you not?"

"I do now. But there was a time—" She broke off and shivered. "I've become chilled, sitting here out of the sun, Henrietta. Let us return home."

They rose and set off in the direction of the park gates. Louisa, now seeming quite in spirits again, chattered away inconsequentially as they walked, but Henrietta answered absentmindedly.

She was reflecting on Louisa's reticence whenever any reference was made to the four years during which they had been separated. Something in that part of the past had hurt Louisa so deeply that she obviously felt unable to speak of it, even with her intimate friend from girlhood, in whom she had always been able to place her trust.

Of course, Henrietta was too scrupulous to attempt to force her friend's confidence. She sighed, impatient with herself. Must she always become involved in other people's troubles? She had come to Bath with the intention of discarding all responsibilities and making a new life for herself. This was surely not a very good beginning.

The afternoon brought several callers, the first of whom were Lady Bellairs and her irrepressible nephew Fortescue. Henrietta had already recounted the extraordinary conversation with Fortescue at the Assembly ball, so Louisa was not surprised to see them, although considerably amused.

Lady Bellairs seemed frankly interested in Henrietta's family and connections.

"You are one of the Somerset Melvilles, I collect," she began. "There is a family of that name in Northamptonshire."

"They are not connected to ours as far as I know, ma'am. I do have some relatives in Wiltshire and Sussex, though my father didn't keep in touch with them."

"I'm glad to learn you're not connected with this Northampton set, at all events. There's bad blood, I hear, and the men are gamesters."

"No, dash it, Aunt, I mean to say!" protested Fortescue, not liking the tone of these remarks.

"Hold your tongue, boy. I wish to become better acquainted with Miss Melville," said Lady Bellairs sternly. "The baronetcy goes back a few hundred years, I'm informed, and your brother holds it at present. And you have two younger sisters, I think? Both married?"

"That is so, Lady Bellairs."

"I think it a mistake to bring out younger sisters while the eldest is unwed. What can your mother have been thinking of?"

Henrietta, who had so far been amused at the dowager's forthright manner, took some exception to this remark.

"That I cannot say," she replied coldly, "for my mother died before any of us came of age. I, for one, would think it monstrously unfair to keep one's younger sisters from enjoying the pleasures of society until their elders were married. Why, the poor dears might be doomed to the schoolroom forever!"

"Naturally you must think as you choose, Miss Melville, though you'll allow that I have a little more experience of the world than you. I am sorry if I seemed to be criticising your mother."

"Oh, Lord!" muttered Fortescue uncomfortably. He had been trying to maintain some desultory conversation with Louisa, rather than be obliged to listen to his aunt's interrogation. "They'll be at dagger drawing next. What's to be done, Mrs. Fordyce?"

But Lady Bellairs, having confirmed most of her information about Miss Melville, now abandoned that topic and launched instead into another that her unfortunate nephew found even more embarrassing. She began to give Henrietta a detailed account of the Bellairs' ancestry, starting a few hundred years back when the family had been ennobled, and working her way laboriously down to the present day.

"Of course, it is not very likely that Roger will ever succeed to the title," she pointed out fairmindedly.

"Not unless I poison off m' father, three brothers, and my uncle," remarked Roger Fortescue with heavy sarcasm. "For God's sake, have done, Aunt, will you?"

"Miss Melville will naturally desire to know these things," said Lady Bellairs calmly.

"Indeed, ma'am, I cannot imagine why you should suppose so!" retorted Henrietta. "It is none of my business."

Lady Bellairs surveyed her for a moment in patent disbelief. "Personally, I always believe in plain speaking. And now that you are informed from a credible source of my nephew's social standing, I trust you will feel secure in allowing him to escort you about the town a little. One must beware of upstarts, Miss Melville, especially when a young woman is, like yourself, possessed of a tempting fortune."

"Your ladyship is very good to take such an interest in my concerns," said Henrietta with a trembling lip. Before she had been divided between amusement and indignation, but now amusement definitely had the upper hand. "I must tell you, however, that for some years I have been used to look after myself, and am not such a green girl as you evidently think me."

Lady Bellairs then rose to take her leave. While she was bidding good-bye to Louisa, with whom she had scarcely exchanged a word during the short visit, Fortescue seized the chance to make a quiet, anguished aside to Henrietta.

"For God's sake don't take a miff, ma'am. I know she's positively Gothic, but don't let her set you against our little arrangement! You've no notion what my life will be like if you fight shy!"

Henrietta nodded. Then, making a graceful bow to both ladies, the young man ushered his daunting relative quickly out of the house.

They had barely left when Almeria arrived, to be regaled with a lively account of the foregoing visit.

"Why, it's incredible!" she exclaimed, when they had all laughed until their sides ached. "I know she's an eccentric, of course, but to act in such a fashion! I trust she did not demand six cows or horses as a dowry."

"Poor young man, he will have thoroughly earned whatever she intends to bequeath to him," said Louisa.

"He may decide to play the man and make a bid for independence before then," remarked Henrietta. "I trust he will. But in the meantime I've no positive objection to playing a part in his little scheme."

"What little scheme?" asked Almeria, opening her green eyes wide.

Henrietta explained, producing more laughter.

"Upon my word, one's neighbours provide endless amusement! I wonder, do they laugh over our antics?"

"You may be certain of it," said Louisa. "Speaking of neighbours, we require your help with one, my dear Almeria. Mr. Burke, it seems, intends to make up a party, which will include the two of us, for the next Gala night at the Sydney Gardens. And we greatly fear that it may turn out an odiously dull affair unless you use your influence with him in the choice of those to be invited. He's almost sure to ask you and Sir Giles, so pray do your best for us."

Almeria readily promised.

🐛 Chapter XII

LOUISA WAS MILDLY SURPRISED to receive a morning call a few days later from Lady Laverton and her daughter, Isabella.

"I scarcely knew the family when I was living at our old home in Somerset," Louisa said to Henrietta when the butler delivered the visiting card. "However, I dare say they are calling on your account. Isabella Laverton was a particular friend of your younger sister, Pamela, was she not?"

"Yes, indeed. Your friend Mrs. Hinton-Wellow told me that the Lavertons had recently arrived in Bath. It's rather surprising that we haven't encountered them before."

"The town is so crowded during the social season that it's easy to miss people," replied Louisa. "You may show the ladies in, William."

It could never have been said of Lady Laverton that she would so far forget herself as to stare, but her hand travelled momentarily to her lorgnette as she first set eyes on Miss Melville. Henrietta wore a gown of blue percale and had dressed her hair becomingly so that small ringlets framed her face. As for Isabella, being less experienced in the social niceties than her mother, she did stare quite frankly before recollecting herself.

"It was quite a surprise to learn that you had come on a visit to Bath," remarked Isabella to Henrietta. "You said nothing of it when we met at the Floreys' evening party."

"I hadn't made up my mind to it, then. Did my sister-in-law inform you?"

"No, it was Mr. Aldwyn. He dined with us a day or two after you left."

At the name, Henrietta's pulse seemed to miss a beat, and she sternly reprimanded herself not to be foolish. If she had only to hear his name to go into a flutter, what likelihood would there be of her carrying off the situation

102

with credit should they chance to come face to face? Not that a meeting between them was at all probable for some time, she consoled herself.

Even while these thoughts were chasing through her mind, she schooled herself to ask after Lord Aldwyn's health with a proper degree of neighbourly interest.

"Oh, Mr. Aldwyn said that his father continues to make good progress and that Lady Aldwyn is beginning to go out a little once more. Mama tells me Lady Aldwyn has never left his side in all these months. She is a most devoted wife and mother. Have you seen much of Lady Barrington? We called there yesterday, and she gave us your direction."

"We've met almost daily," replied Henrietta. "Mrs. Fordyce takes me around to all the meeting places of Bath: the Pump Room, the Assemblies, the theatre, shopping in Milsom Street."

"Yes," said Isabella, "I can see you have been shopping. You won't think it impertinent in me, I trust, Miss Melville, but I do think you look beyond anything in that gown. Why, it's in the first stare of fashion!"

"I'm so glad you like it," she said casually.

For the next half hour, they talked about fashions and style, until finally Lady Laverton and Isabella made their farewells and rose to leave.

"Mama, did ever you see anything like it?" demanded Isabella, as the front door closed behind them. "Miss Melville, I mean! I could almost bring myself to call her by her first name. She used to look so frumpy and old-maidish; I can't believe it's the same person!"

Her mother frowned thoughtfully. "Yes, it is rather a drastic change, isn't it?"

In the days that followed, Henrietta thought with amazement how changed her life had become. She had never lacked occupation at Westhyde Manor, but her activities there had been vastly different from those that now engaged her. The quiet country pursuits that she had always so much enjoyed had now given place to the activities of a fashionable town. Shopping in the elegant thoroughfares, attending lively social gatherings in the various public rooms, going to private dinner parties, and making morning calls occupied most of her time. Sometimes she missed her solitary walks or rides among the familiar hills of her own countryside, and she told herself that a town life was not really for her an ideal existence. But it was all new and exciting, and after being so long on her own, the companionship of Louisa was especially welcome.

Like Louisa, she was popular with the gentlemen, and at first was a little embarrassed by the fulsome compliments of flirts such as Hinton-Wellow. On one occasion, when she had delivered a blighting snub to that gentleman, Louisa took her to task.

"Don't be so heavy-handed with him, my love," she advised. "You made everyone stare."

"Much I care!" said Henrietta hotly. "He is an odious wretch to behave in such a way with his wife standing by, doing her best to look unconcerned, and, if I know anything, almost dying of shame!"

"But if you show that you take him seriously, surely it must make it worse for Olivia Hinton-Wellow? Turn his gallantries off with a laugh, and she can at least keep up the pretence to others that it is simply his joking way."

"I dare say you are right. The trouble is, I have no experience of flirting."

"Then it's high time you acquired some. Only study me!" replied Louisa shamelessly.

Although Henrietta laughed, she had already noticed Louisa's skillful handling of admirers. She knew it for a useful talent, so she set herself to learn the trick of it.

They were shopping one morning in Milsom Street, where Louisa purchased a new bonnet.

"What a pity that I shan't have an opportunity of wearing it until tomorrow. I never can *bear* to wait before trying out something new, can you? But nowadays you are forever wearing something new, you lucky creature. I declare you're quite giving me a disgust of my own wardrobe, and I shall be obliged to discard most of it and start again!"

"Oh, dear, I should be sorry to think that I have been the cause of leading you into extravagance," replied Henrietta primly. "Do you think I should perhaps wear one of my old gowns to the concert this evening?"

"That you can't do, for I told my maid to bundle them up and give them to charity," said Louisa with a chuckle.

At that moment a passing curricle drew into the sidewalk alongside them, and they saw that the driver was Captain Barclay.

"I trust you have your carriage close by," he said, after greeting them cordially, "for I see you've some cargo there."

"No, we walked into Milsom Street," answered Louisa. "We had no intention of doing any shopping when we left home, but I saw the most delightful bonnet, and so—"

"And so you had to purchase it," he said, his eyes twinkling. "But could the shop not deliver it for you?"

"Well, you see, I had just carried it off from under the nose of another customer, and I couldn't bear to entrust it to the milliner. Mistakes can happen so easily, you know."

The twinkle became a broad grin. "Wanted to make sure of your prize? Don't blame you, ma'am. Well now, I'd be happy to take you home, but this vehicle's no good for more than one passenger, so what do you say if I relieve you of that bandbox?"

Louisa looked doubtful. "Oh, but it will roll about and mayhap become damaged. I think I had best carry it myself, but thank you all the same, Captain."

"Not a whit. I promise to hold onto it all the way," he insisted.

"Then you'll be obliged to drive with one hand," she pointed out.

"Nothing easier, assure you. Will you hand it up to me, ma'am?"

Louisa was about to comply when Henrietta noticed Lady Laverton and Isabella approaching along the sidewalk. It seemed a pity to deprive the captain of the chance of a few moments alone with his lady love.

"See, here are the Lavertons," she said quickly. "Why do not you go home with Captain Barclay, Louisa, and then you can take care of your precious headgear yourself? I will return with Lady Laverton and Isabella, and if they haven't quite finished shopping, I shall be quite content to go round with them."

Louisa protested that she could not abandon her friend in that way, but Henrietta clinched the matter by at once going over to the Lavertons. After a moment, she turned to nod reassurance, and Louisa, realising that the captain could not keep his horses standing any longer, allowed him to assist her into the curricle. She settled herself beside him, the bandbox held securely on her knee, and the curricle moved off smoothly.

"And what have you been doing with yourself all day?"

she asked, smiling up at him. "I often wonder how gentlemen do contrive to pass the time that we females fill with shopping and such like."

"I've been over to Bristol, ma'am," he said, checking his horses as they came to a temporary traffic jam. "Deuce take it," he exclaimed involuntarily, "what does that fellow in the whiskey think he's about? The merest whipster could have done better."

"He certainly doesn't seem very expert," allowed Louisa.

"Expert!" The captain snorted contemptuously. "Fellow ought to be driving a dogcart."

"Well, we are in no particular hurry," said Louisa soothingly.

"Ah, we're getting through at last," said the captain with satisfaction, as the road ahead cleared and they were able to proceed. "I beg your pardon, Mrs. Fordyce. You'll be thinking you'd have done better on foot, after all."

"Not at all," replied she politely, then added, with irresistible mischief, "This is infinitely more diverting! Tell me, Captain, are Clifton Downs as pleasant as ever? They are the only diversion in Bristol I can remember."

He was now able to give his attention to her, and once more experienced the heady sensation produced by meeting her dancing hazel eyes.

He cleared his throat uneasily. "The Downs are certainly pleasant, but I go to Bristol to walk around the docks and look over the vessels lying at anchor. West Indiamen, mostly, unloading their cargo or refitting for the next voyage; tidy craft, by and large, though not to be compared with a naval ship, of course."

"You're not really happy ashore, are you, sir? You would prefer to have a command again, I believe."

"That's not likely in these times, now the wars are over. There's many a sailor—ay, and a soldier, too—who must content himself with a less adventurous life. And I dare say, provided a man has a home and family, there are compensations. It's lonely at sea, ma'am. Voyages sometimes last for years. It's a capital life for a young, unattached man, but I've known married officers who found the separation from their families a tremendous strain. And the time comes to most men when they want to settle down and raise a family."

Louisa stirred uneasily in her seat. She had never before heard Captain Barclay talk in quite this vein, and moreover, she felt a little nervous of where the conversation might be leading. She did not answer him for several minutes, pretending to be engrossed in watching the pedestrians in the street, and he, taking one look at her averted face, sighed and gave exaggerated attention to his driving.

"I dare say you will not attend the concert in the Rooms this evening," she said at last, when she felt the silence had lasted too long.

"A concert, is there?" He came back from what appeared to be some distance. "I didn't know of it."

"No, but then you don't like music," she said accusingly.

"I don't? What makes you think so, ma'am?"

"Why, I heard you tell Miss Dyrham so on one occasion, when she was teasing you to attend a concert," she reminded him, her eyes dancing with mischief.

"That—!" He checked himself, quickly substituting a more suitable phrase for the one he had intended to use. "That *lady* spurs too hard for a body to bear and no man likes to be ridden! I'll admit, Mrs. Fordyce, that one or two ladies singing round the pianoforte after dinner is more to my taste than a full-scale concert lasting for several hours, but I am not averse to music altogether. No such thing, I assure you. I suppose you and Miss Melville are to go?" he added.

She assented, and he looked thoughtful.

"Well, I may look in," he said presently.

"You may find it difficult to secure a ticket, sir, for I suppose you are not a subscriber?"

"To the balls, yes, also to the Card and Reading rooms, but not to the concerts. But never fear, I shall find a way of procuring a ticket, all right and tight."

Glancing at his confident expression, she did not doubt that he would find a way to achieve his objective. He was a gentleman who inspired one with a comfortable feeling of security. She sighed; security was something that she had good reason to value highly.

He set her down at her door. Then, deep in thought, he drove the curricle round to the mews. Why, he asked himself bitterly, could he never bring matters to a head with this enchanting lady, the only female he had ever met whom he would wish to make his wife? Had he not always been a man to go straight for his objectives, determinedly surmounting any obstacles in his path? Why then, in this instance, was he behaving like any young middy under fire for the first time? Love was a devilish business, quite different from any other. If only this lady would give him some sign, some small encouragement, he might be emboldened to put the question. But her manner towards him, though lively and natural, was no different from that she showed to many other men in Bath. And surely it was not fancy on his part that, whenever he seemed to be approaching closer to her in spirit, she drew off, holding herself aloof? He dared not offer her his hand, he concluded disgustedly, because he was afraid of rejection, of losing the little that he had and might still keep, as long as he remained silent.

By the time he entered his own house, he was decidedly out of charity with himself.

✦ Chapter XIII

THE ASSEMBLY card rooms, though well patronised, were decidedly too tame for such a determined gambler as young Roger Fortescue. He had not long been lodged in the town when he chanced to learn of a discreet gaming establishment called Lorimer's, where a taste for higher play might be indulged. He made up his mind to pay the place a visit as soon as he could evade the watchful eye of his aunt.

His first time at Lorimer's, he came away several hundred pounds lighter in pocket, but he had at least made some fortunate acquaintances. Many gentlemen of *ton* patronised Lorimer's, for only the affluent could afford to game there, and it was the one place in the town where a newcomer might find a quick introduction into Bath society with nothing more to recommend him than the ability to play and pay.

Fortescue's ability to pay being unfortunately restricted, his visits were not as frequent as he would have wished. Then, too, there were always his aunt's demands upon his time.

These same irritating demands caused him some disappointment and embarrassment on the evening of the musical concert at the Assembly Rooms. He had managed to slip away to Lorimer's on some pretext earlier in the afternoon, but as nothing would do for Aunt Euphemia but that he should escort her to the concert, at six o'clock he was obliged to make his excuses to the three gentlemen with whom he had been playing.

"Beg you'll forgive me," he said, consulting his watch and pushing back his chair from the table. "Got to escort my aunt somewhere this evening; the most devilish thing, but can't be avoided!"

George Hinton-Wellow, one of the four at the table, looked at Mark Kennett, a crony of his, and winked. The fourth man in the game, a newcomer to Bath called Paul Colby, saw the gesture and misinterpreted it. He laughed.

"Sure and I trust your aunt will be looking as pretty as a picture and will reward you suitably, Fortescue," he said in a voice that held just a hint of an Irish brogue.

"You're faint and far off, m'dear fellow," retorted Fortescue, with an embarrassed smile. "This really *is* my aunt, worse luck! Can't afford to upset the lady, so must make my apologies, gentlemen. Shall we settle?"

They did so, Fortescue leaving the gaming house with only a few coins to jingle together in his pockets.

"A lively youth," remarked Colby after Fortescue had departed. "Dependent on his relative for funds, I collect?"

Hinton-Wellow nodded. "Just so, and the old dragon has him dancing attendance on her for most of his time. Still, who pays the piper calls the tune, what?"

"He should look out for an heiress instead," suggested Colby. "I dare say there are some to be found in Bath."

"Indeed. We've some rare little charmers! Mrs. Fordyce, for instance—now there's a bewitching female! Though I fancy young Fortescue would be a trifle brash for that lady's taste, as she's a widow. She needs a man of more experience."

"Someone more like yourself, for instance?" quizzed Mark Kennett with a ribald chuckle.

"Precisely, my dear chap. But, alas, I'm a married man and out of the running."

"Not noticeably," retorted Kennett.

"Fordyce," Paul Colby repeated thoughtfully. "I knew a lady of that name once."

Henrietta and Louisa arrived at the concert early. They selected seats with plenty of space alongside so that any of their friends who might chance to appear could sit beside them. This turned out to be not altogether an advantageous move when presently Mr. Burke entered, looked about him for a few moments, then came over to the chair beside Henrietta.

"Are you saving this place for anyone, Miss Melville?" he asked, having greeted them both gravely.

"Oh, no," answered Henrietta quickly, then added, "That's to say, not positively, though I did think perhaps if Lady Barrington should be coming—"

"Then possibly you would prefer me to sit somewhere else," he said, looking a little crestfallen.

Henrietta's kind heart could not persist in repulsing him. "Not at all; she may not come, after all. Pray sit here if you've a mind to do so, sir."

"Thank you," he replied, seating himself with the deliberation that characterised all his actions. "Are you fond of music, Miss Melville?"

"Yes, indeed, though I'm not very knowledgeable on the subject, I fear. I enjoy simple chamber pieces rather than the grand orchestral style. But then I have not had the advantage of attending concerts frequently."

"That is a pity, but I am sure your natural taste must be good. My dear mother was very fond of music, and I accompanied her to almost every concert that was held in Bath."

Just then Henrietta was pleased to see Almeria and Sir Giles seating themselves next to Louisa; with more mixed feelings, she noticed Fortescue about to settle Lady Bellairs in the adjacent chair to Mr. Burke. Having performed this office, Fortescue moved behind Henrietta to whisper in her ear.

"Dished, b'God, and by a man who'll certainly cut me out! But see if I don't make a recover when there's an interval!"

She smiled up at him, then leaned forward to greet Lady Bellairs, who responded with an affable nod. Fortescue, reluctantly sitting down on the other side of his aunt, fidgeted in his chair a great deal and looked extremely bored.

The concert began with a pianoforte concerto by Haydn, after which Mr. Burke told Henrietta about a child of only four and a half years who had played this same work at a concert held at Ranelagh some twenty years previously. He continued talking until the next item on the programme began, when Henrietta silently breathed a sigh of relief.

During the interval that followed, Lady Bellairs, who had shown increasing signs of impatience with Mr. Burke's chatter, finally took a hand in matters by forthrightly demanding that the gentleman should change places with her.

"I do not see at all well in this seat. That female in

front of me with the ridiculously towering headdress quite obscures my view!" she complained in a loud voice.

The lady in question directed a hostile stare at her critic before defiantly arching her neck so that her head-gear gained several inches in height.

"No, really, Aunt!" protested Fortescue feebly.

Mr. Burke, however, with the impeccable manners that had never been known to desert him, at once changed places with Lady Bellairs, and since he felt that it would be uncivil to separate the lady from her nephew, he politely urged Fortescue to take the chair now vacated by his aunt.

"That is much better," declared Lady Bellairs as she settled herself next to Henrietta. "My dear Miss Melville, you must be quite tired of that man's insipid conversation! In a little while I shall change places with Roger so you may enjoy a comfortable cose together. He can be a most entertaining companion, Miss Melville, if I say so myself."

Henrietta had the greatest difficulty in repressing a laugh.

"But I thought, ma'am," she said in a low voice, "that you wished to change places because you could not see over the lady in front?"

"Oh, pooh, that was an excuse, my dear, to come next to you. Besides, if I must confess the truth, I don't see too well in any case. I simply wanted to give you and my nephew the opportunity to become better acquainted. He really is an admirable young man, though at times I find him a trifle irritating. But what elderly female does not find a young man irritating, I'd like to know? Youth goes to youth, as the saying is."

Henrietta scarcely knew what to reply, but there was no need, for Lady Bellairs began again with scarcely a pause for breath, this time condescending to lower her voice.

"I dare say you may think Burke quite a good catch, Miss Melville, and so he is, in a way. That's to say, he has an income of twenty thousand a year and is well connected. I think he'll prove a hard man to bring along; he's not the marrying kind, take my word for it. He's never had any time for females. You'll not mind my dropping a friendly warning in your ear, I feel sure, my dear. Take it from me, you have positively no hope of Burke."

"Indeed, Lady Bellairs, there is no occasion for you to

speak at all on this subject," replied Henrietta stiffly. "Mr. Burke is the merest acquaintance."

"Ah, now you've taken umbrage. I only meant well, you know. No matter. Fortescue will change places with me. You'll be more in charity with him, I'm sure."

The exchange of seats was made, but Henrietta, still ruffled, had turned to Louisa and the Barringtons, so for some time Roger Fortescue had only a view of her back. She did not turn until the next item began, and immediately after it was over, there was a long interval for refreshments, and she and her friends rose and left their seats.

"Oh, that dreadful woman!" she exclaimed to Almeria and Louisa. "You'll never credit what she said to me!"

Sir Giles had moved away to join some of the gentlemen present, so Henrietta was able to repeat the conversation with Lady Bellairs for the edification of her friends. They were most amused, and in the end, she was forced to laugh herself.

"I have never met anyone quite like her," she said. "And how to answer her outrageous comments civilly has me in a puzzle!"

"Actually, there's a good deal of truth in what she says of Mr. Burke," Almeria judicially remarked. "I've noticed he's taken a fancy to you, Hetty, but I don't truly believe he'll ever marry. He's a born bachelor—far too long under his mother's thumb."

"If only everyone was not quite so busy matchmaking on my behalf!" declared Henrietta. "Is it of the slightest use my telling you all that I have no intention whatsoever of marrying?"

She noticed Almeria's eyes resting thoughtfully upon her and wondered for an embarrassed moment if Mr. Aldwyn had confided in his sister about his unsuccessful declaration. If so, it seemed odd that Almeria had never mentioned it. But perhaps Almeria was tactfully waiting for her friend to broach the matter herself.

"Oh, yes, Henrietta and I have quite decided to abjure menfolk and set up a *ménage à deux!*" said Louisa airily.

"No. Truly?" Almeria seemed astounded.

"Well, it is not quite settled yet," amended Henrietta. "But we are certainly considering it."

"Considering what?" demanded Sir Giles, who joined them at that moment, accompanied by Captain Barclay.

Almeria turned a face of mock protest toward him. "Truly, my love, you have the most odious habit of intruding into other people's conversations."

"I'm much too well intentioned to be odious, my dear. See, I've brought Barclay to join our party. Found him skulking by himself at the back of the room, looking like a fish out of water."

"I may be wrong, Barrington, but I don't think a landed fish skulks," protested the captain. He bowed to the ladies. "I trust you're enjoying the concert?"

The party moved into the refreshment room, where they found themselves caught up with other acquaintances. After the interval, seats were resumed for the second half of the performance. There proved to be no difficulty in accommodating Captain Barclay, as a couple who had been previously sitting beside Sir Giles had now moved to other seats. The captain was placed between Almeria and Louisa, and seemed quite content to be there.

No sooner had Henrietta sat down than Fortescue, who was still her neighbour, claimed her attention, his aunt being absent for the moment.

"No need to give me the cold shoulder," he said in a low tone. "Oh, I know she put you in your high ropes—enough to send anyone off the top, I'll agree! But don't forget our bargain, ma'am, or I'm in for the most devilish time of it, give you my word."

"It seems to me that I'm in for a devilish time, myself, Mr. Fortescue, if I stick to our bargain, as you call it."

He turned a comic look of dismay on her. "You'd never cry craven, would you, ma'am? Well, I ask you, what can I do with her, short of gagging her, I mean to say? I may as well admit that I feel just as devilish as you do, when she starts spouting her mouth. Makes me look such a confounded fool, dammit!"

Henrietta could withstand him no longer. She gave a merry gurgle of laughter, and for the rest of the evening exchanged light banter with him whenever an opportunity occurred. Lady Bellairs, who resumed her seat just as the next item was about to start, looked on complacently, while Mr. Burke, on her other side, appeared sunk in gloom.

The last item on the programme was Beethoven's Sonata Number 14. Henrietta began to make images around the slow, langorous notes of the first part of the piece. She was beside a lake, watching the moonlight caught in its quiet ripples; but underlying the peace, she felt a poignancy that moved her almost to tears. And then the mood of the music changed; the waters of the lake became turbulent, and a deeper, stronger emotion took possession of her, leaving her shaken at the final chords.

She glanced at Louisa, whose eyes were turned upon Captain Barclay. The expression on her friend's face for that brief moment surprised Henrietta, as it would have done the captain, had he been fortunate enough to catch it.

Louisa was in love with Captain Barclay; there could be no other explanation of such a look, so intense, yet so sad. But why, then, did she conceal her true feelings, when the captain was awaiting only the slightest sign of encouragement to declare himself?

Henrietta could find no satisfactory answer.

🐌 Chapter XIV

A FEW DAYS OF CLOUDY SKIES and sudden showers set in, making the two ladies' daily outings hazardous if ventured out on foot. They had no intention of remaining cooped up indoors on this account, however, so they made use of the carriage to visit their usual haunts.

One morning, Louisa wished to call at her bankers in Northgate Street before going on to the Pump Room. Henrietta accompanied her in the carriage to the premises, but declined to enter, insisting that instead she would take a stroll into nearby Bond Street to look through the shops.

"Well, don't get caught in a shower," Louisa warned her. "There's no thoroughfare for carriages in Bond Street, as it's far too narrow, so I cannot take you up there. You had much better wait here for me."

"Oh, it will not rain just at present," declared Henrietta rashly, looking up at the unpromising skies, "and I have been doing too much sitting. I would dearly love a short stroll."

"You'll have strolling enough in the Pump Room. But if you must go, pray take the umbrella."

Henrietta decided otherwise, confident that the skies would hold during the ten minutes or so she intended to be out of doors. Dismounting from the chaise, she made her way into Bond Street and was soon engrossed by the elegant window displays to be found there.

As it happened, weather prophecy was not one of her talents. While she was gazing into a jeweller's window, entranced by a delicately chased gold pendant necklace set with sapphires, the sky rapidly became overcast, and a torrent of rain descended.

She drew back quickly into the shelter of the doorway, reproaching herself for leaving behind the umbrella, for, although she withdrew as far as possible, the slanting rain followed her. The situation was saved by the jeweller's assistant at once opening the door and politely inviting her to sit inside the shop until the storm abated. She was very glad to accept his offer and to watch the shop door close upon the deluge outside.

As she took the chair placed for her by the thoughtful assistant, she noticed two gentlemen standing before the counter examining a tray containing snuff boxes. They half turned at her entrance, and she recognised one as Fortescue.

"Miss Melville!" he exclaimed, coming over to her. "Gad, you've picked a devilish morning for shopping! Are you very wet, ma'am?"

"Oh, nothing to signify. It's my own folly entirely, for I wouldn't trouble to bring an umbrella. I left Mrs. Fordyce making a call at the bank in Northgate Street. The carriage is waiting there for me."

"Glad you're not soaked through. Allow me to present Mr. Colby to you, ma'am. He's not long arrived in Bath from London. Colby: Miss Melville, who's also a recent arrival."

Henrietta looked up into a pair of blue eyes alive with mischief.

" 'Servant, ma'am," said Colby with a graceful bow. "It's a soft day, as they say in Ireland, but I trust you'll take no harm from it."

"A *soft* day?" echoed Henrietta, smiling incredulously. "And it's raining as hard as can be. Only the Irish could be so paradoxical, I fancy!"

His answering smile was full of charm. "Sure, an' you're in the right of it, ma'am. But in fairness to my fellow countrymen, I must own that the phrase is more often used to describe conditions of mist and drizzle."

"So you are Irish, Mr. Colby."

"I admit the impeachment, Miss Melville, though like many another from that fair isle, I have spent most of my time in other countries."

"Have you indeed? How interesting, Mr. Colby."

"Doesn't seem to be easin' off, ma'am," said Fortescue as he cast a glance outside. "Looks as if you'll be here for some time."

"I hope not. Mrs. Fordyce will be anxious about me. She will have concluded her business by now, I expect."

"Tell you what, I'll dash round to Northgate Street and

let her know you're shelterin' here," offered Fortescue, unfurling an umbrella that he had propped up beside the counter. "Won't take a minute."

"Oh, no. It's very good fo you to offer, but you'll be soaked! I couldn't put you to so much trouble," protested Henrietta.

"Pooh, no such thing, with this, ma'am," brandishing the umbrella. "Besides, don't regard a drop of rain. Happy to oblige."

Before she could protest any further, he had darted through the shop door and was seen hurrying past the window.

Left alone with Mr. Colby, Henrietta began to study him covertly. He was of middle height, broad shouldered and well built, with crisply curling, light brown hair brushed onto a face that could fairly be described as handsome. His tailoring was elegant, but his air was more that of a Corinthian than a dandy, and the humorous twist to his mouth suggested a man who rarely took matters seriously. She was immediately attracted to him, and not at all loath to be left in his company.

"I collect you're a newcomer to Bath like myself, ma'am. Do you like the town—in its more sunny moods, that is?"

"Oh, yes, indeed I do, and so far I've been more fortunate than this in the weather."

"It's a pleasant enough place, though a trifle slow after London, as I'm sure you'll allow."

She shook her head. "I'm very little acquainted with London, sir."

His eyes held a look of mocking incredulity. "What, were you never there for a season, Miss Melville? I thought all young ladies made their come-out in the metropolis."

She smiled. "My sisters certainly did so, but I am a country mouse, I fear."

"A country mouse! No, no, ma'am, I'll not believe that! Such elegance, such town polish could not belong to a rural maiden! You are roasting me, Miss Melville."

At that she laughed. "You are very gallant, Mr. Colby, but nevertheless what I say is true. I have lived in a Somerset village called Westhyde for the whole of my life."

"And that, of course, is an unconscionable time," he replied with a quizzical smile. "No, I am not seeking to find out, for I know well that ladies never tell their age. Besides, I already know it."

She raised her eyebrows. "You know it, sir?"

"Indeed I do. You are sweet seventeen, and not a day older," he pronounced solemnly.

"Oh!" she exclaimed with a little chuckle. "I do believe, Mr. Colby, that you are the most shameless flatterer!"

"I speak only what appears to me to be true. I can't think now why I should have asked you if you had spent a season in London. Obviously you are by far too young to have already made your come-out."

"Now you're doing it too brown," she warned him, her eyes twinkling. "Were I as young as you pretend, I would not venture abroad without my chaperone."

"But you've brought one, I collect? A Mrs.—what was it now—a Mrs. Ford, I think?"

"Fordyce," corrected Henrietta.

"Ah, yes, Fordyce. A lady of estimable years and high moral tone, no doubt."

"You are quite out, sir," she laughed. "Mrs. Fordyce is of my own age,—somewhat older than seventeen, I must own—and we are lifelong friends. I am staying with her at present."

He nodded. "The lady lives in Bath with her husband, one supposes. So, after all, you are well chaperoned, Miss Melville."

"Not unless we chaperone each other, for there's no husband in the case. Mrs. Fordyce is a widow."

"The Widow of Bath," he repeated mockingly. "It was Chaucer, was it not, who wove a story around one such? But perhaps you're not of a literary turn of mind, Miss Melville."

"Within reason, though I had only the usual hamble-scramble kind of education that is thought suitable for females."

"And rightly so. What a pity it would be to wrinkle the fair charmers' brows with overmuch study of prose when they might browse lightheartedly in the Book of Life," he replied, with a comical sententiousness that made Henrietta chuckle once more.

"Mr. Colby, I fear that you are sadly lacking in the ability to take matters seriously," she said amiably.

"Indeed I am, ma'am. It's a heinous fault, but I trust you'll overlook it."

He made an attempt to look contrite but spoilt it by breaking into a laugh. He gestured toward the window, where Fortescue, giving his umbrella a vigorous shaking, had just come into view.

"It's just stopped," he announced, entering. "Mrs. Fordyce was in the carriage when I got there, and bids you not to go through the rain on any account, as she don't mind waiting."

"Since it's stopped, I'll go at once," said Henrietta, rising from her chair.

"I'll escort you," said Fortescue. "You'll be glad of an umbrella, in any case, because of all the confounded drips from the awnings and so forth. You coming, Colby, or are you making a purchase here?"

"No, I shall look in at another time. Perhaps Miss Melville would prefer my umbrella, as yours is deuced wet, old fellow."

Henrietta expressed her thanks to the jeweller for giving her shelter, and the trio were bowed out courteously. Once in the street, Colby raised his umbrella and offered Henrietta his arm, leaving Fortescue to walk on the outside. As she placed her gloved hand on Colby's sleeve, ste felt a little tingle of excitement. He was the kind of man, she thought, who could scarcely fail to raise a spark of interest in any woman.

A few minutes' walking brought them to the waiting carriage. As they drew level with it, Louisa opened the door and leaned out.

"Did I not tell you, Henrietta, that it would surely rain if you ventured out?" she began. "Foolish creature, you should have—'"

She broke off abruptly, staring at Henrietta's escort, who had lowered the umbrella and was about to assist his charge into the coach.

"May I make Mr. Colby known to you, Mrs. Fordyce?" said Fortescue punctiliously.

Colby helped Henrietta into the coach, executed a graceful bow, and fixed his eyes in an intent look upon Louisa.

"Mrs. Fordyce and I have already met," he said in an ambiguous tone. "I trust I see you well, ma'am?"

"Oh—yes—thank you," stammered Louisa, with none

of her usual assurance. "I think—perhaps we should not keep the horses standing longer."

"I look forward to renewing our acquaintance," said Colby smoothly. "Miss Melville, it has been a pleasure."

Fortescue, too, took his leave of the ladies, and the carriage moved away.

"Well, I'm damned!" exclaimed Fortescue. "Met the charming widow before, have you? Not in Bath, I presume; you've scarce had time."

"No, it was on one of my travels," replied the other evasively, and quickly went on to speak of other matters.

Meanwhile, Henrietta was asking the same question of her friend, with no more result.

"I met Mr.—Colby—in Ireland," replied Louisa, somewhat unsteadily. "He was—acquainted with my husband, but—"

She seemed unable to continue.

"But?" prompted Henrietta with a tentative smile.

"Oh, I don't wish to speak of him," returned Louisa petulantly.

"Then we won't do so, love, though I must say I find him a most charming man. There, I have done, never fear! Are we bound for the Pump Room?"

"Would you mind very much if we went straight home, Hetty? I have a little headache. Nothing much, but there's always such a clatter in the Pump Room."

Henrietta agreed at once, expressing concern. When they were seated at home in the parlour, she was able to study her friend's face and found it paler than usual. She suggested that Louisa lie down for a while.

"No, no, it is nothing, I assure you. I shall be perfectly recovered if only I may sit quietly for half an hour. I am so sorry to have spoilt your morning."

"Goose! As if a lost visit to the Pump Room could ruin my morning. Now, do you sit quietly, and I will read my book without saying another word."

Accordingly, she picked up a novel she had begun read- and was soon engrossed in it. Louisa, however, far from sitting quietly, sprang up out of her chair within minutes and began to pace restlessly.

After a little while, Henrietta looked up from her book.

"My love, why do you not keep still? It can't possibly improve your headache to go on in this way! I tell you what, do you happen to have a Dr. James' powder in the house? I always found them most efficacious whenever my sisters had the headache."

To Henrietta's consternation, Louisa began to laugh in a hysterical way.

"Powders!" she gasped, in between the outbursts. "P-p-powders! Oh, what g-g-good can a p-powder do? If only it sh-should be as s-simple as that!"

Henrietta seized her firmly by the shoulders and shook her vigorously.

"Louisa! Stop it at once! *At once,* do you hear me?"

Louisa's hysteria subsided after a moment, and releasing herself from her friend's grasp, she dropped into a chair and burst into tears.

Henrietta knelt beside her, taking the shaking form into a comforting embrace.

"My love, whatever is amiss to upset you so? Only tell me, dearest Louisa, and there's nothing I wouldn't do to help you!"

For a few moments Louisa clung to her friend, sobbing violently. Presently, she ceased and gently disengaged herself from Henrietta's arms, wiping away the traces of tears from her face.

"No one can help me," she said in a more composed voice, "but I dare say I shall manage."

"If only you would tell me what the trouble is! You must know you can trust me. Recollect our girlhood, and all the secrets we shared! I haven't changed so much, I assure you."

"Oh, I know you haven't, my dear. No one could wish for a truer, kinder friend. But there are some things——" She broke off, leapt to her feet and took a turn or two about the room, then went on, in a lighter tone. "Forgive me for enacting such a Cheltenham tragedy, my love! You know there are times when a female is prone to attacks of the vapours. Pray think no more of it, for it's merely a health matter. We will eat our luncheon, and afterward you shall choose some diversion for the rest of the day."

Henrietta had also stood up and was regarding her friend in some perplexity. Obviously something other than female indisposition was responsible for Louisa's outburst, but she saw that there was nothing further to be done at present to win her friend's confidence.

Later, when they were just sitting down to their customary midday meal of cold meats and fruit, a footman entered and handed Louisa a note. Henrietta saw that the superscription was in a bold, flowing hand, which Louisa, judging from her expression, recognised at once. She jumped up from the table with a muttered apology and quitted the room.

It was some time before she returned, muttering an apology for interrupting the meal.

"That's no matter," said Henrietta. "I trust, though, you've not received bad news?"

"Bad news? Oh, you mean the letter. No, that was merely a little matter of business. Pray do have some of this pressed tongue, Hetty. It's one of Mrs. Rudge's specialties."

Throughout the meal, she chattered away at a great rate, and though Henrietta suspected the animation was a trifle forced, she found her friend more composed than before. Perhaps, after all, the previous outburst had been due to a temporary bout of the humours.

They decided to pass the afternoon in a visit to Almeria, and set out as soon as luncheon was over. Almeria was fortunately at home and delighted, as always, to see them. They found her browsing over some recent copies of *La Belle Assemblée,* consulting the fashion plates with a view to having some of the designs copied for her own wardrobe. They were all quite willing to assist her, and so spent a lively afternoon debating the merits of various designs. But at five o'clock, Louisa suddenly said that they ought to be going.

There could be no reason for this that Henrietta could see, unless her friend felt that a quiet evening at home might be beneficial. It was not for her to argue, however, so she and Louisa departed with assurances of meeting Almeria again soon.

"I am sorry if you would have preferred to stay, Hetty, but we have been racketing about so much of late, that I thought perhaps you would not object if we were to remain quietly at home for once."

"Not at all. Indeed, there are some letters I must write if I am not to alienate all my relatives," replied Henrietta agreeably.

"And I think I shall rest in my room until it's time for dinner," said Louisa with a sigh.

"You don't still feel unwell, my dear?"

"Oh, no, merely a little fatigued. A short rest will soon set me up again. I'll come down just before dinner, and in the meantime you'll be able to write your letters in peace."

Henrietta looked anxiously after her as she mounted the stairs. It was quite unlike Louisa to complain of feeling tired; her energy always seemed boundless.

She tried to dismiss her worry, however, and made her way into the parlour where a small oak writing table was set against a window looking out on to Pulteney Street. There she settled down to write a letter to her sister Cecilia. For some time she wrote fluently, then inspiration failed, and she took to gazing abstractedly out of the window. When she at last recalled her errant attention to the task in hand, daylight was fast fading.

She rose to light the candles, but hearing outside the squeak of an unoiled iron gate, she again glanced at the window, in time to see a cloaked and hooded figure emerging from the gate that led down to the servants' basement. The figure gave one quick, backward glance before stepping hurriedly into the street and turning in the direction of Sydney Place.

Henrietta stood stock still in amazement. It was Louisa. Where on earth could she be going at this time of day on foot, and why had she made no mention of her errand? Obviously she was leaving the house by the servants' exit and keeping closely wrapped to escape recognition.

As these thoughts raced through Henrietta's mind, she was seized by a strong feeling of uneasiness. Louisa's behaviour had been altogether so odd over the past few hours that perhaps she ought not to be allowed to venture out of doors alone. With some thought of stopping her, Henrietta hurried from the parlour. No servants were about in the hall, so she quietly let herself out of the front door and started in pursuit.

The lamplighter had not yet reached that part of the street, and consequently a friendly gloom shielded her from inquisitive onlookers who might otherwise have wondered at seeing a lady without either cloak or bonnet rushing in such an unseemly way down Pulteney Street.

Henrietta walked briskly. Turning into Sydney Place, she hesitated and looked anxiously about for any sign of

Louisa. At last she espied the cloaked figure close by the Sydney Gardens.

She was on the point of moving forward to cross the road in pursuit, when her progress was arrested by the sight of a second figure moving out of the shadows to join her friend. She gave a gasp of dismay. In spite of the fast-gathering darkness, Henrietta could tell at once that the second person was a man.

Uncertain what do do, she shrank back against the railings of the nearest house and watched the pair move into the shadow of the trees overhanging the gardens. They seemed to be talking earnestly together, oblivious of their surroundings.

Recovering herself, Henrietta decided that this was no place for her to remain. Although such had not been her intention, she was now in the invidious situation of spying on her friend. She retraced her steps with the same haste as before and was soon knocking at the door of the house. The footman who admitted her may have been surprised at her appearance, but he was too well trained to show it, and Henrietta's perplexed state of mind did not allow her to feel self-conscious.

She returned to the parlour, where the candles were now lit and the blinds drawn, but she was in no mood for finishing her letter. Instead, she sat staring into space, trying to make sense of what had occurred. Louisa's reason for leaving the house so mysteriously was now plain. She had been keeping a clandestine meeting with a man. But why should she do so when she was at liberty to meet anyone she chose quite openly? And who was this mysterious man?

❦ Chapter XV.

ON THE FOLLOWING MORNING the weather was sufficiently improved for the two ladies to walk to the Pump Room. Captain Barclay, whose ever vigilant eye had been watching for their departure from the house, escorted them. Louisa seemed her usual carefree self, delighting the captain with her lively conversation on the way. Once at their destination, they soon found themselves surrounded by friends and acquaintances. Henrietta fell into conversation with Olivia Hinton-Wellow, whom she was beginning to like very much. She was not best pleased when presently the lady's husband bore down upon them, greeting her with one of his extravagant compliments, but she brightened a little on seeing that he was accompanied by Mr. Colby. Hinton-Wellow drew Colby forward to introduce him to the ladies, and seemed surprised that he was already known to Henrietta.

"Been stealin' a march on us, eh, my dear fellow? And who can blame you for losin' no time in making the acquaintance of one of Bath's fairest flowers?"

He kissed his fingers to Henrietta. She achieved a strained smile in reply, and wondered why it was that she found Hinton-Wellow's compliments so objectionable, when only yesterday she had been listening with complacency to very much the same kind of nonsense from Mr. Colby. She had no time to develop these thoughts, however, for with considerable address, Colby succeeded in separating her from the others.

"I trust you've suffered no ill effects from yesterday's exposure to the elements, ma'am," he said with a twinkle in his blue eyes. "But there, need I ask? Flowers are always the fairer for a drop of rain."

She pursed up her lips in disgust. "Oh, pray don't repeat such tedious nonsense, sir! Why will so many gentlemen suppose that females enjoy being subjected to fulsome flattery?"

"Because most of them do," he returned promptly. "But am I to understand that you completely despise the gentle arts by which men seek to recommend themselves to members of your sex?"

"Yes—no," she answered, then started to laugh. "Oh, I lost my sense of humour for a moment. Pray forgive me! I suppose I appreciate a compliment as well as the next female, if it is sincere. But that kind of—of *patronising* flattery in some way makes me feel insulted. I don't wish to be looked upon as a pretty plaything!"

"Oh, dear," he said with a rueful smile. "Then I fear that I must have offended you deeply yesterday."

"No such thing, for I knew you were only funning."

"Not even sincere," he answered with mock humility. "Lud, ma'am, can I ever retrieve my position? Only tell me if there is a way!"

"By not talking nonsense," she said severely.

"I promise it from this moment forward, ma'am. And as a token of your forgiveness, will you not permit me to drive you out tomorrow? I am told that there is a particularly fine view of the city from Beechen Cliff, a verdant hill that you must have noticed in the distance when walking about the town. As newcomers, it is our bounden duty to inspect all such places of beauty, so that we may give pleasure to the residents by praising their surroundings."

He said this with such a comical air of seriousness that Henrietta was obliged to laugh again.

"You consider it should be an object with us to give pleasure to the residents?"

"Oh, undoubtedly. Their pride in the town would be deeply mortified, else." He struck an attitude. "We drove to Beechen Cliff yesterday, upon my soul, I never saw a more beautiful spot, never looked at a more extensive view, never passed a more delightful hour, etc. etc. etc. All this is balm to a patriotic spirit, and cannot help but result in cordial invitations to dine out or take tea, according to the generosity of the hearer."

"What a complete hand you are, Mr. Colby!" she chuckled. "And you call this *sense!*"

"Well, my invitation—no, supplication—to you was

sense, at all events. Now, pray say you'll honour me, Miss Melville, by accepting."

She sobered a little. "I don't quite know. Louisa—Mrs. Fordyce—"

"Sure, you'll not be wanting to live in each other's pockets," he said soothingly. "I don't doubt that Mrs. Fordyce will be quite content to spare you for an hour or so."

"I dare say, but it would be vastly uncivil in me not to mention it to her first, as I am her guest."

"Just so, ma'am. And may I wait on you later in the day to learn my fate?"

The conversation ended at this point, for they were joined by others.

To Henrietta's surprise, Louisa seemed doubtful when she was told of the scheme.

"Do you think it would be improper for me to drive out with a gentleman I've only just met?" teased Henrietta. "I'm not a Bath miss, you know!"

"Not that, no, of course not. But Mr. Colby—" She broke off, frowning.

"Do you know something to his discredit?" demanded Henrietta, her curiosity aroused by her friend's reticence. "I realise that your previous acquaintance with him must make you a better judge of his character than myself, but for my own part, I must say I do so enjoy his company. He is so absurd!"

"Yes, he is that, and knows well how to charm a woman. But, Hetty, don't fall in love with him, will you? It would bring you nothing but misery!"

"A womaniser, is he? Have no fear, my love, I am in no danger of losing my heart to the first agreeable rogue I meet. But did you not yourself bid me take a leaf from your book and learn to flirt a little?"

Louisa relaxed and laughed. "I didn't realise what an apt pupil you would prove, Hetty. Oh, very well, go with him if you wish."

Accordingly Henrietta went, and so much enjoyed the outing that she agreed to another a few days later. At the next Assembly ball, she danced no less than three times with Mr. Colby, a fact that did not go unremarked by the gossips of Bath. Fortescue, anxiously soliciting her hand for one of the remaining dances, was moved to protest.

"Dash it, Miss Melville, you're forgetting our bargain! That devilish Dyrham female has been cacklin' to my aunt that you're smitten with Colby, and now I'm in the suds! She's been plaguin' my life out either to cut the fellow out, or else to switch my attentions to someone else. Got her eye on someone, too: Miss Laverton. It's the most devilish business, give you m' word!"

"Well, you might do worse," Henrietta consoled him. "Miss Laverton is an extremely pretty girl, and just the right age for you."

He groaned. "Don't I tell you that I've no wish to fall into parson's mousetrap? I did think I could rely on you to keep me clear of it, but I suppose I was a fool to trust a female!"

"I'm truly sorry," she said, laughing.

He looked at her resentfully. "Must say, you sound it!"

"Well, I'll do my best to make amends by fiirting with you outrageously for the rest of the dance," she offered magnanimously, "if you'll play up to me."

He brightened.

"That's the ticket. Always knew you were a right one."

He proceeded to give such a spirited imitation of a young man in the throes of desperate passion that Henrietta had the greatest difficulty in schooling herself to respond without laughing. She could not help noticing that several bystanders were watching this performance, among them Colby himself. She wondered what he made of it. It would do him no harm to see that she did not favour him above other gentlemen; at the same time, she studiously avoided considering whether or not his was true.

The following morning brought Henrietta the first letter she had received from her brother since coming to Bath, a hastily scrawled page containing little news beyond the continued good health of himself and his family and an enthusiastic description of a new mare, which had recently been purchased by Mr. Florey.

"There's far more about the wretched animal than there is about Selina and the children," she remarked, laughing to Louisa. "As though I could care a whit about prime steppers and rare bits of blood! But I tell you what, Louisa; it does put me in mind of Anna Florey. I still intend to call at Miss Mynford's to solicit a half-holiday for the child. May I bring her here one afternoon? Perhaps your Mrs. Rudge would make some of her delicious little cakes; school fare is so depressingly stodgy and dull."

Louisa agreed readily to this suggestion, but was firm in refusing to accompany her friend on the visit to Miss Mynford.

"Pray excuse me, Hetty, but you know I have the utmost dislike of raking over the past, and I know just how it will be: every feeling is revolted! But should you care to go this morning, I have an appointment for a fitting of my new spangled ball gown at Madame Blanche's, and that is sure to occupy the best part of an hour, I dare say. We could go together to Milsom Street, and it's but a step from there to Queen Square. Anna Florey may come this afternoon, if Miss Mynford agrees."

It was settled accordingly, and shortly afterwards Henrietaa parted from her friend outside Madame Blanche's premises. She had just turned the corner into Quiet Street when she heard someone speak her name and, turning, she saw Mr. Colby.

"Where are you bound for, all alone?" he asked, surveying her with his mischievous look.

She explained her errand.

"Then may I walk there with you? I understand that the streets of Bath are extemely hazardous for unprotected young ladies."

"What, in full daylight? I never heard such nonsense! One may see females shopping here without escorts every day, as well you know, sir."

"Ah, but that was until today," he replied solemnly.

She threw him a suspicious glance. "And pray what has occurred today to alter the usual state of things? But need I ask! You've this moment invented it. You should be ashamed, Mr. Colby!"

"Ashamed to invent reasons for the pleasure of walking beside you? Never, Miss Melville."

"You talk more nonsense, I believe, than any gentleman of my acquaintance," she said severely.

"More than young Fortescue?" he asked quickly.

She laughed. "Mr. Fortescue is certainly a most entertaining gentleman."

"You seemed to find him extremely so at yesterday's ball. I was in two minds whether or no I should call him out."

"Dueling has gone out of fashion, has it not?"

"Not in Ireland," he assured her.

She was silent, wondering for a moment how well he

had known Louisa in Ireland, and if she could possibly put the question to him. He seemed to sense her thoughts.

"I dare say your friend Mrs. Fordyce will have told you a deal about life in that country."

She shook her head. "No, she never mentions it. But then, Louisa dislikes most of all things to dwell on the past. That was why she didn't wish to accompany me today on my visit to our old schoolmistress."

"She is very wise," he said with emphasis. "The present is all that matters."

Then he adroitly steered the conversation to more lighthearted topics, keeping Henrietta amused until they reached their destination.

"What a remarkably handsome frontage that is," he said, gazing at the buildings on the north side of the Square. "Indeed, the town is resplendent in fine building, altogether. Can you spare a moment, Miss Melville, to walk over to that obelisk in the centre of the square? I would like to see the inscription."

"By all means, if you wish, though I can almost recite it to you by heart. The obelisk was erected by Richard Nash in 1738 in honour of the Prince and Princess of Wales."

They walked together along one of the gravel paths bordered by symmetrical flowerbeds until they stood before the obelisk.

" 'In memory of honours conferr'd and in gratitude for benefits bestow'd in this city,' " he read aloud. "H'm. I wonder now, did His Royal Highness come down handsomely to Nash himself in order to earn such an eulogy?"

"I see you are somewhat of a cynic, Mr. Colby."

"Sure, you'll succeed in making out my character before long," he said, twinkling at her again. "The prospect puts me all in a dither, I assure you, but if it's a way of keeping you in my company, I'll do my best to humour the inclination."

She smiled back, reflecting on the charming twinkle that so often lit his blue eyes.

They retraced their steps to the school, where Colby, ringing the iron bell hanging outside the door, declared that it put him in mind of a nunnery.

"No doubt you frequently visit nunneries?" asked Henrietta demurely.

He was laughing as the door opened to reveal a little

housemaid in mob cap and apron, whose face lit up as she saw Henrietta.

"Why, Matty!" exclaimed Henrietta. "I did not expect to see you on the doorstep! And how are you?"

"I'm nicely, thankee, Miss Melville. Didn't ought to answer the door by rights, but the footman didn't come, an' bein' as I was in the 'all—"

She broke off, shrinking, as an imposing figure in livery bore down upon her. He gestured her imperiously away. She scuttled off with a smile and a backward glance for the visitors.

"I shall hope to be allowed the pleasure of escorting you back to Milsom Street, ma'am, after your call is made," said Colby, bowing to Henrietta as she was admitted to the house. "I shall be strolling about in the vicinity meanwhile."

Miss Mynford was delighted to see her ex-pupil. Unlike her friend, Henrietta found it no penance to recall her schooldays; indeed, on reflection she decided that it was perhaps the most carefree period of her life until very recently, when she had left Westhyde Manor for Bath. And even here, in spite of her new-found freedom, there were disturbing moments.

Anna was presently summoned. She was very much on her best behaviour, as befitted a girl in the presence of her headmistress, but still managed to convey something of the eagerness with which she received Miss Melville's invitation to spend an afternoon at Mrs. Fordyce's house. Any respite from the monotony of the schoolroom was welcome of course, but this particular outing held a special appeal for her.

"Miss Melville has kindly arranged for a coach to call for you at two o'clock," Miss Mynford informed her pupil in her magisterial way. "The maid Matilda will accompany you, and you must return to school punctually at five o'clock. You will wear your best white muslin, and I trust I need not remind you to conduct yourself in the manner I expect from all my young ladies. That is all. Make your thanks to Miss Melville and then you may leave us."

Thus adjured, Anna expressed her gratitude in a few formally polite phrases and made her very best curtsey before quitting the sanctum. Once outside the door, she gave vent to her feelings in a deep sigh of relief, only wishing that it might have been possible to let out a loud whoop and jump for joy. She was to be free of restraint for a whole afternoon, and moreoever, for once she would be able to talk about her hero to her heart's content. She fell into a pleasant reverie, wondering what he was doing now and if she would ever be fortunate enough to see him again.

✥ *Chapter XVI*

JULIAN ALDWYN, with a gun over his arm and a weary but contented dog at his heels, strode through the ancient stone archway that led into the gardens of Aldwyn Court. The imminent arrival of his sister Jane with her husband and entire family had thrown him into such a fit of gloom that he had felt obliged, as he put it to his father, to go out and shoot something.

"Don't blame you, m'boy," Lord Aldwyn agreed. "Damme, if I felt equal to it, I'd join you, but I'm not quite in prime twig yet, more's the pity. Much improved, of course, though there's no saying but what your sister's visit won't cause me to suffer a relapse. Why the devil your mother should agree to it passes my understanding! But there we are, she don't realise what a trial I find Jane and her brood. Hyde's not a bad chap; dull, of course, but don't jaw your head off, like my daughter. God knows who she takes after; not myself, I trust, and your mother's a peaceful woman enough."

In truth, the threatened visit of the Hydes was only adding to a subdued mood that Aldwyn had been experiencing ever since Henrietta Melville had rejected his proposal of marriage. It was intolerable, he thought angrily, that after screwing himself up to the point of offering for the wretched female when he had no real wish to marry her—or anyone else, for that matter—she should have turned him down without a second's hesitation. And just as he had begun to think that they would deal admirably together, in view of their many shared interests and the possession of a similar sense of humour. A sense of humour was a rare virtue among females, in his experience, and it could add greatly to the comfort of domestic life. Indeed, he had even begun to envisage a time when he might become quite fond of Henrietta Melville, for she had many endearing characteristics.

But what must the silly creature do but throw all these rational, comfortable prospects aside for the sake of a foolish, romantic whim? In her situation, one would have supposed that she would grasp eagerly at a man so obviously a brilliant match for her. It was not as though she disliked him personally; there had been many little evidences of friendship that had encouraged him to hope for an acceptance. But there it was, friendship was not enough for her, and as he had no stronger feelings to offer, that must be the end of the matter.

In his first fit of pique, he had looked about the neighbourhood for other likely candidates, and taken to calling on the Lavertons. Isabella Laverton was pretty enough to please any man, she would certainly make a suitable future mistress of Aldwyn Court, and she seemed to have an agreeable disposition. She was, however, too much like all those other young ladies whom he had met in London for him to view the prospect of marriage to her with any enthusiasm. He was relieved, therefore, when she and her parents left for Bath before there had been time for his visits to raise any serious expectations. He needed more time to consider. It was the devil's own business, he thought, to know that he must marry, yet to have no smallest inclination for it.

The Hydes arrived later in the day, and at once the house was in an upheaval. Jane kissed her parents and Julian rapturously, then began fussing over the children.

As soon as he could, Aldwyn escaped from the house and rode over to Westhyde Manor. He had not been there so frequently since Miss Melville had departed for Bath, but now he felt the inclination to hear some news of her.

He was not to be disappointed, for Sir Nicholas had lately received a letter from his sister, and was soon volunteering information.

"Kicking up no end of larks, by the sound of it," he said, laughing. "Balls, concerts, evening parties, driving out with admirers—not that she calls 'em so, but why else should a fellow drive a female around? Dare say she may find a husband before long. Trust she will, for Hetty was never cut out to be an old maid."

"I'm delighted to hear she's been kept entertained," replied Aldwyn sourly.

The truth was that he felt far from delighted, though on his way home he failed to discover any reason for this.

Miss Melville had confided to him her desire to lead a new life free from duties and responsibilities; at the time, he had acknowledged that she certainly had earned some such change. Yet now, when it seemed her aspirations were realised at last, his attitude was grudging.

Admirers! he thought resentfully, jerking his horse's head so sharply that the animal suddenly shied. But why not? There was something—yes, damn it all!—something about her that drew forth affection, if not that more heady feeling against which he was determined to guard himself. She might well meet some man who would wish to marry her for love rather than as a matter of convenience. It was much more probable in Bath than here, in this restricted rural community.

His jaw set with determination. He would not relinquish her to some other man without putting up some show of resistance, damned if he would! He would go to Bath himself. In any event, he had no pleasure in staying at Aldwyn Court while the Hydes were visiting. Almeria would welcome him, or if his visit should prove inconvenient to her, he could always put up at one of the town's excellent hotels.

When he reached home, he informed his father of this intention.

"Bath, eh?" said Lord Aldwyn, with a knowing look. "Didn't you say the Lavertons were there, m'boy? Yes, go by all means."

When Aldwyn presented himself on the following morning at his sister's house in Bath, he was welcomed even more cordially than he had hoped.

"Devilish awkward of me, I know, turning up like this without a word of warning," he said apologetically as he embraced her. "But if it puts you out to have me here, I can easily quarter at one of the inns. York House and the White Hart both provide excellent dinners—"

"You'll do no such thing!" declared Almeria emphatically. "There's plenty of room for you and your servants —I suppose you've brought your man and a groom with you? Yes, well, I'll instruct the housekeeper to make the front guest bedchamber ready at once. Giles, do you look after Julian while I see to it."

She sailed out of the room, full of housewifely importance, while Sir Giles ordered some liquid refreshment.

"And what brings you here in such a pelter?" asked Sir Giles, grinning. "Escaping from your creditors or some too importunate female?"

"Escaping from m' sister Jane's damnable brats," corrected Aldwyn, taking a long pull at the foaming tankard that had been placed for him. "Another day of 'em would have turned me into a fit subject for Bedlam! I only hope they may not cause my father to suffer a relapse."

"They're certainly resty little devils, by what I've seen of 'em," conceded Sir Giles, stretching his long legs comfortably before him.

"It ain't so much that, it's Jane's absurd attitude toward 'em. Only to be expected that lads will be high spirited, of course, but they must learn to keep in line, and no one in that household seems prepared to instruct 'em. I think Hyde would like to take a hand, but Jane's got him in her pocket. Same with their nursemaid: wretched woman's got no authority."

Almeria had come back into the room in the middle of this speech and endorsed her brother's views. "How would you like to occupy the rest of the morning? Giles and I were about to stroll down to the Pump Room. You may meet some old acquaintances there," she concluded meaningfully.

"H'm, I've not much acquaintance in the town to my knowledge," he replied, not wishing to understand her.

"Oh, come, now, this will not do! Sir Richard and Lady Laverton are here with their daughter Isabella, and you can't pretend that you won't know them, since you've been acquainted with them for most of your life!"

"True, I was aware that they had come to Bath. But one swallow, my dear, doesn't make a summer."

"There's another swallow, too, if that's not an oddly inadequate way of describing her. I mean Henrietta Melville," persisted Almeria, determined to force some reaction from him. "And when you do see her, I dare say you—"

She broke off suddenly. She had been about to say that he might indeed find it difficult to recognise Henrietta, so changed was she now from the dowdy female whom he had met at Westhyde Manor. But her sense of mischief prompted her to let him make this discovery for himself. It would serve him right, she thought impishly. He'd been far too secretive about his dealings with Henrietta. Yet, Almeria did not care to put a direct question to him on that matter, hoping instead that he would readily confide in her after a few days under the same roof.

He sensed that she was holding something back.

"Dare say I'll what?"

She shrugged. "Oh, nothing of consequence."

He was content to avoid the subject of Miss Melville. Knowing his sister's disposition, he was well aware that she was bursting with curiosity as to whether or not he had made her friend an offer. At present, he was in no mood to enlighten her. Was it not enough that a man should have made a fool of himself over one woman in his lifetime? The only saving grace in this second affair was that his heart had not been broken. Perhaps that was something that could happen only once. Remembering the grief and suffering of that boyhood affair, he fervently hoped so. At all events, he had no intention of making himself vulnerable ever again.

Almeria could not guess what was passing through his mind, but she did notice his grim expression, and her hopes faded. Evidently there had been some hitch in her splendid plan to make a match between him and Henrietta. No doubt when it came to the point, he had been unable to carry through his cold-blooded scheme to marry for convenience only. She of all people realised that underneath his cynical facade, her brother was a warm-hearted, affectionate man, who needed to love and be loved in return. Surely somewhere there must exist a woman who could truly care for him, whose love might succeed in breaking down the barriers he had raised to protect himself? She had thought that Henrietta, herself a loving individual with no present object for her affections, would be the very one to lead him to happiness. She sighed; there was little she could do to help him, it seemed.

She soon recovered her spirits as they all strolled down to the Pump Room, entertaining him with Bath gossip in the intervals of meeting and greeting passing acquaintances. There was much more of this once they reached the crowded Pump Room, so that Aldwyn began to feel almost as confused as Henrietta had at first.

"For God's sake, Almeria don't introduce me to anyone else," he said at last. "I've done nothing but bow and smirk for the past half hour!"

"I promise you I will not," she said, laughing. "Now at last you shall meet someone whom you already know quite well: Henrietta Melville."

An enigmatic expression appeared on his face. "Indeed. Where is the lady?"

"Over there by that pillar, in conversation with three gentlemen and a lady. But I fear you don't at all know two of the men and you'll have forgotten the lady, as it's so many years since you last met her. She's Louisa Fordyce, the Randalls' daughter. Louisa was at school with Henrietta and myself, and Hetty is her guest at present."

"Yes, I remember the Randalls, though I've no recollection at all of their daughter. But I don't see the group you mean. At least, I see a group of five persons by the pillar, but Miss Melville is not among them."

"Are you quite sure?" asked Almeria in a teasing voice. "Pray look again, more closely!"

His gaze switched from one to the other of the two ladies in the group, then came to rest incredulously on the one attired in a stylish royal blue merino pelisse trimmed with fur and a tall, crowned bonnet decorated with ostrich feathers. At that moment her face turned toward him, and there could be no mistake.

"Good God!" he exclaimed weakly. "Can that be *Miss Melville?*"

Almeria studied his expression with some satisfaction. "Yes, quite a change in her, is there not? But come, we'll go and speak to her."

Sir Giles had become caught up in conversation with two other gentlemen, so brother and sister made their way across the room toward the group. As they drew nearer, Henrietta looked up and saw them.

Her expression, which had been animated, changed all at once. She and Aldwyn looked into each other's eyes; hers were shy, his incredulously admiring. Colby, standing close beside her, was instantly on the alert, watching them.

"Henrietta, here is my brother come to renew his acquaintance with you. He's staying with me for a few days."

Aldwyn bowed and Henrietta inclined her head in response, but for the moment, neither found anything to say beyond a formal greeting. He was studying her face, attractively framed by the becoming bonnet and the soft curls that clustered under it onto her forehead. It struck him that he had never before realised how lovely she was.

For her part, Henrietta was making an effort to disregard a strong feeling of embarrassment and to appear unconcerned. Almeria assisted her in this by presenting Julian to the other members of the group: Louisa, Colby, and Fortescue. Captain Barclay was already known to Aldwyn from previous visits to Bath. During the general conversation that followed, Henrietta recovered her poise sufficiently to talk and laugh with Colby and Fortescue. Aldwyn observed this performance without any outward show of interest, meanwhile taking his part in the conversation of the group.

"You will certainly bring your brother to the Assembly ball tomorrow evening, will you not, Almeria?" asked Louisa in full hearing of the others. "Are you fond of dancing, Mr. Aldwyn?"

"I wouldn't rate my feelings on the matter quite so high, ma'am," he replied with a laugh. "Dancing is well enough, but I suspect it was really invented for the pleasure of the ladies."

"I must disagree with you, my dear sir," Colby challenged him. "There are few more delightful experiences than stepping down a ballroom with a charming partner."

"Rather sit down to a hand of cards, myself," said Fortescue. "That is"—turning to Henrietta with belated gallantry—"most times I would, but I hope to be privileged to lead you out tomorrow evening, Miss Melville."

Aldwyn darted a swift glance at him, a slight frown wrinkling his brow.

"And may I add my name, ma'am," said Colby, bowing sedately but with a mischievous twinkle in his blue eyes, "to the doubtless long list of applicants for the favour? Now pray, don't say you have no dances left!"

Aldwyn's frown turned to something suspiciously like a scowl, but recollecting himself, he speedily banished it, smoothly informing Louisa that he certainly intended to be present at the ball, and he hoped to be allowed to dance with her. She gave the assurance readily enough, and the conversation turned to other topics.

Presently Sir Giles and the Hinton-Wellows joined the group, and soon George Hinton-Wellow was carrying on his usual flirtations with every female present except, of course, his wife. As neither Captain Barclay nor Aldwyn had any taste for watching this kind of exhibition, by common consent they drew a little apart and fell into conversation.

They discovered several mutual sporting interests, and made an appointment to meet and go together to watch a boxing contest on Claverton Down.

"Barrington's unluckily engaged elsewhere on that day," said the captain, "otherwise he was to accompany me. I'll take you up in my curricle, if you like, Aldwyn. Don't know what kind of vehicle you've brought with you, but no place for a chaise, as I needn't tell you. Too devilish crowded."

"I've brought my own curricle, as a matter of fact. But thank you, I'll be glad to accept your offer." He paused, looking back at the group just behind them. "Who *is* that fellow—forget his name—the one standing beside Miss Melville? Does he reside in the town?"

The captain cast an unloving look at Colby. "Name of Colby. Putting up at the York House Hotel. Came into the town a few weeks back, don't know from where. Don't know much about him, in fact, but he's one of Hinton-Wellow's cronies. He met the chap at that gambling hell close to the theatre, shouldn't wonder; goes there a bit. So does young Fortescue, silly halfling!"

"I seem to think I've seen him somewhere before— Colby, I mean," said Aldwyn musingly. "Can't just place him at the moment, though. The name ain't familiar. Doubtless it will come back to me."

The captain agreed. "Don't mind admitting to you I don't care for the fellow above half," he went on. "Maybe I'm imagining things, but I get the impression that Mrs. Fordyce is made uneasy by him."

Aldwyn glanced at the group again and saw that Colby was standing very close to Miss Melville and laughing with her.

"Do you? Well, it may be because she don't care to see him paying such very particular attentions to her friend Miss Melville. Not," he added dryly, "that the fellow seems to be alone in that."

"If you refer to Hinton-Wellow, he's always making up to the females. Sort of chap who can't help himself; nauseating! Some husband will give him a leveller one day, and I only hope I'm there to see it. Like to do it myself, matter of fact, but it ain't any of my business."

Sir Giles and Almeria came over to them to say that they were ready to leave. Aldwyn readily agreed, and a distant bow to Henrietta was all he attempted by way of leave-taking.

❧ Chapter XVII

"ALMERIA'S BROTHER is a most personable man, is he not?" asked Louisa when they were once more at home. "I suppose you met him occasionally while Almeria and he were staying at Aldwyn Court. Is he as agreeable as his looks suggest?"

"My acquaintance with him is really very slight, but, yes, he is certainly agreeable."

"I did not think you could have known him very well. You had so little to say to each other. In truth, there seemed a certain coldness in your reception of him. Is there perhaps something about him which you don't quite like?"

"No such thing. As far as my knowledge of him goes, he has everything to recommend him that a gentleman should have: good looks and address, an estimable character. And moreover, a sister of whom I'm especially fond. There, will that satisfy you?"

Louisa smiled. "Not quite. There is an underlying reticence in your praise that gives me the impression you're keeping some matters hidden."

"Then we may cry quits, my dear, for I have the very same impression when you are speaking of Mr. Colby," retorted Henrietta with a laugh.

Louisa's expression altered. "Yes, well—"

She broke off, staring into space for a while. Henrietta watched her curiously, but wisely refrained from prompting her to continue, knowing that if she did so, Louisa would most likely turn the subject off with a laugh and a shrug. Her forbearance was rewarded, for presently Louisa once more took up the conversation.

"Hetty," she continued, with a serious look, "are you quite sure that you're in no danger of falling in love with —Colby? He is a man who knows to a nicety how to charm women, and you have little enough experience of

143

such men, I dare say. I would not have you hurt for anything! Not even if I were obliged—"

She broke off again, evidently in agitation.

"If you were obliged to do what?"

Henrietta could not resist the question, but it brought no intelligible response.

"Oh, nothing," replied Louisa with a despondent shrug.

"Well, my love, I wouldn't wish to oblige you to do nothing." Then, seeing that her friend could not even force a smile at this modest quip, she continued, "Come, there's no need to look so serious! Haven't I told you already that I'm merely indulging myself in a harmless little flirtation? I am just getting into the way of it, you know, what with Mr. Colby and young Fortescue! I might even spread my wings wider still and attempt to draw Mr. Burke into the game. But, no! I fear he's not the man for light dalliance."

She had the satisfaction of seeing Louisa's expression lighten.

"What an abandoned female you are become! Is this all my doing, am I to suppose?"

"Not quite all, for I came to Bath with the fixed intention of enjoying all those frivolous pleasures that I missed in my first youth. But you've proved an apt mentor, I must say!"

At that Louisa laughed outright.

"I fear Mr. Fortescue stole a march on the captain by offering to take us up in his carriage tomorrow evening for the ball," went on Henrietta. "I don't know if you noticed Captain Barclay's face, but if looks could have killed, Fortescue would have dropped dead on the spot!"

"Yes, I did see he was not best pleased. Moreover, it's not nearly such a convenient arrangement for us from any point of view. And who could wish to share a carraige with Lady Bellairs?"

"Not I, certainly. But I didn't like to refuse, in view of my promise to help Fortescue with his aunt. I wonder, though, how he thinks it will all end? She is bound to be pestering him presently to make me an offer, and then what is he to do?"

"Oh, I believe he's a young man who considers that trouble postponed is trouble averted. As long as he's gained a breathing space, he'll let the future take care of itself. I think, you know," said Louisa thoughtfully, "that I'm of a similar disposition myself. It has much to recommend it."

In her present mood, Henrietta was inclined to agree.

Punctually at a quarter to eight on the following evening, a smart town coach with a crest on its panels drew up before Louisa's house. Fortescue, looking extremely handsome in knee breeches and an impeccably cut dark blue coat, which set his fair hair off to advantage, leapt out of the carriage to follow the footman to the door. The ladies soon appeared on the threshold and were courteously escorted to their seats.

Lady Bellairs greeted them affably, remarking on their charming appearance. "And what do you think of Roger, Miss Melville?" she asked. "Does he not appear to prodigious advantage in evening dress? I know you've never seen him in that particular coat, which was ordered especially to please a certain lady not so very far from here. And pray what is the point of going to all that trouble and expense," she demanded, seeing her nephew make a repressive gesture, "if I am not to draw anyone's attention to it?"

Fortescue muttered an imprecation and fidgeted with his gloves. Feeling sorry for him, Henrietta was about to make some frivolous remark, but she was swept aside.

"So I hear Lady Barrington's brother has arrived in Bath," continued Lady Bellairs. "Miss Dyrham tells me he is heir to a title and a large estate situated not many miles away. It seems he's a bachelor into the bargain— though such an eligible party will prove hard to get, mark my words. A gal can't be too careful, either, about setting her cap at others whose birth and circumstances are not so well known. I refer to another new arrival to the town, Mr. Colby."

Henrietta and Louisa exchanged a quick glance, and Fortescue looked even more uncomfortable than before, if such a thing were possible.

"May recall, Aunt," he interrrupted with an apologetic air, "I did mention to you that Colby was known to Mrs. Fordyce before he came to Bath."

"So you did, Roger. Well, in that case, ma'am, you can enlighten us as to the young man's antecedents?"

Louisa's chin went up. "I suggest you apply to the gentleman himself, my lady," she replied coldly. "I have no information to offer on the subject."

"Hoity toity! There's no occasion to get in a miff, Mrs. Fordyce! It is only right and proper that young ladies should know something of the men whom they are meeting, so that they may not be taken in by encroaching *mushrooms*. That is why I was so careful to give you, Miss Melville, an account of my nephew's birth and expectations. You are not perhaps in your *first* youth, but you are still young enough to require the guidance of an older woman in these matters. Mrs. Fordyce is a *married* woman, of course, and as such must be considered capable of looking after her own affairs, but she is scarcely old enough to take you in her charge."

"For pity's sake, Aunt!" interjected Fortescue, looking thoroughly abject.

Henrietta had been about to make a sharp retort, but seeing his misery, she bit it back and laughed instead.

"I appreciate your concern, madam, but believe me, I need no one to take me in charge. Now tell me, how is your health, Lady Bellairs?" she went on, quickly turning the subject to one that Fortescue told her was of overwhelming interest to his aunt. "Do you find the hot bath is of much benefit to you? Are your rheumatics at all improved since you began to take the cure?"

The ruse succeeded, and though the ensuing monologue—skilfully fed with brief comments by Henrietta from time to time—was of no greater interest to the coach party, at least she was free of further embarrassment.

"I positively *refuse* to return with that woman!" exclaimed Louisa emphatically as they stood together in the cloakroom, having evaded Lady Bellairs once they entered the Rooms. "How you bear with her, Hetty, passes my comprehension!"

"I do so only for her nephew's sake. Poor young man, it must be a sore trial to possess such an uninhibited, not to say rude, relative! Never fear. We'll find some excuse to return in Captain Barclay's carriage; I'm sure *he'll* be only too ready to contrive something, if I explain how matters are. And he is a gentleman on whom one can confidently rely, don't you think?"

"Oh, yes, indeed he is. There is something so very—he gives one rather a sense of security," replied Louisa, sounding a little confused.

After they entered the ballroom they became separated for a time, and presently Henrietta seated herself beside Olivia Hinton-Wellow in a row of gilt chairs where there were so far few occupants. They were soon chatting animatedly together, until they were joined by Mark Kennett's wife, Julia, a sophisticated woman in her early thirties whom Henrietta did not like. Seating herself beside Henrietta, she began to cast a blight on the conversation by complaining about the crush in the Rooms and the general insipidity of Bath entertainments.

"So different from London," she said in her usual bored drawl. "Have you been lately in town, Miss Melville?"

Henrietta had no intention of aiding Mrs. Kennett's obvious attempt to patronise her, so she answered that she had been in London last year.

"But as I was then in mourning, I naturally did not go about to places of entertainment," she added.

"A pity. There is nothing to equal Almack's, but it's not at all easy to obtain vouchers, you know. The patronesses are most strict, which is just as it should be, of course. They say that in Beau Nash's day things were regulated in much the same way here in Bath, and only persons of *ton* were to be met with in the Assemblies. But nowadays of course . . ." She finished with a shrug of contempt.

"You are too nice in your judgments, Julia," said Olivia Hinton-Wellow warmly. "I'm sure we have very good company here, and there are always scores of amiable and interesting visitors arriving to prevent our becoming bored with each other."

"If you say so, my dear Olivia," said Mrs. Kennett with a yawn behind her fan. "Ah, here is your husband," she continued in a slightly more animated tone. "My dear George, pray take pity on us and join our party."

Without awaiting a second invitation—which in any case would not have been forthcoming from either his wife or Henrietta—Hinton-Wellow advanced, beaming, upon the group.

"What man could possibly resist such a heaven-sent opportunity of resting awhile in this oasis of beauty and charm. But pray, fairest Julia"—the Hinton-Wellows and the Kennetts were on first-name terms—"do be so good as to move into this chair so that I may have the felicity of being seated in the midst of your entrancing group."

Julia Kennett was not pleased at being asked to move so that Hinton-Wellow might sit between herself and Miss Melville, but she complied without protest. He began to settle himself into the chair she had vacated, deliberately making an awkward business of it so that he was obliged to rest his arm against Henrietta's bare shoulder. Instinctively, she shrank away, but his hold tightened for a moment while he apologised for his clumsiness with a smile.

At that very moment, Henrietta heard Almeria's voice greeting her. Looking up, to her acute embarrassment she saw that not only Almeria but Sir Giles and Mr. Aldwyn were passing before her. She was just able to ctach a cynical sneer on Aldwyn's face before she hastily lowered her eyes, too confused to do more than murmur a greeting. When she did venture to look up again, the three had already moved away.

Nothing could be more humiliating than that Mr. Aldwyn should have seen her practically in the embrace of such a notorious flirt! What must he think of her conduct? But the expression of disdain on his face had made his feelings obvious. She would have given almost anything to undo this mischief, which was not of her making; yet why, she asked herself impatiently, should she be so overset? It could scarcely signify now what Mr. Aldwyn might think of her. Had she not voluntarily put an end to any connection between them? All the same, she was forced to admit that she would have preferred to retain his good opinion. Perhaps Almeria would explain to him that a man like Hinton-Wellow needed no encouragement, and that Henrietta herself was not to blame. But she doubted that such a cynic as Mr. Aldwyn would be comvinced.

Tormented by these incoherent thoughts, she was quite unable either to fend off Hinton-Wellow's gallantries or invent a plausible excuse for escaping from his company. Then the orchestra began to play.

"I believe this is my dance, Miss Melville," said a welcome voice.

Henrietta looked up with a start to see Colby standing there. She gave him her most radiant smile and stood up instantly. He took her hand and led her onto the floor.

"Sure, and you look as though you were a Christian escaping from the lions, ma'am," he said with the familiar twinkle in his eyes.

"Do I? Well, perhaps you are not so far out in that."

"Hinton-Wellow?" he asked, cocking an eyebrow.

She nodded.

"Oh, there's no harm in the man. It's a lion with the teeth drawn."

"It is vastly unpleasant, sir, to be pestered with undesired gallantries."

"Sure, an' I'll remember that," he promised, smiling. "But would you like me to give him just a hint now?"

"Oh, no!" She looked taken aback. "You have no occasion—that is to say—"

"I haven't the right? That is so, of course, unless the right of a friend who has your interests very much at heart."

He watched her closely but could read only the lingering traces of embarrassment in her expression. Too experienced to make a false step, he said no more.

"The only thing, then, ma'am, is to avoid the gentleman."

"So I do, as much as possible. But, tell me, why do you suppose he does it?"

He shrugged. "Why do *you* suppose, Miss Melville? Because he enjoys it."

"And is that to be the sole criterion of anyone's conduct?" she asked indignantly. "Is there to be no consideration for the feelings of others?"

His eyes twinkled again. "Perhaps our friend is more to be pitied than blamed. When a man has been married for a number of years, he sometimes requires the reassurance of flirtations with a pretty female or two. And since most females find such attentions flattering, what harm can there be? It gives pleasure all round, does it not?"

"Not to me," she said emphatically. "And not to his wife."

They were separated then by the movements of the dance and Henrietta shook away her feelings of irritation to rejoin her partner in a lighter mood. He sensed this at once and began to entertain her with his usual amusing chatter, until they were both smiling and laughing together as they went down the dance.

This did not escape Aldwyn, who was dancing with Almeria, and a cynical light came into his eyes.

"Miss Melville seems very pleased with her partner," he said.

Almeria glanced round to see where her friend was in the set. "Oh, Mr. Colby. Yes, he's a favourite with us all. The most attractive man, with just the hint of a rogue about him."

"Indeed? Well, I've seen the fellow somewhere before, unless I'm much mistaken. What do you know of him?"

"What does one know of most visitors to Bath? I believe he came here from London. But you should ask Henrietta, for she's been seeing more of him than most of us," she added with a hint of mischief.

He made no answer to this, but she saw that he was watching the other couple again. On whose account, she wondered, Henrietta's or Colby's?

"Dance with her, and perhaps you will discover something further."

He shrugged. "It's of no importance. Besides, I am engaged to Mrs. Fordyce for the next dance."

In fact, Aldwyn employed most of his dance with Louisa covertly watching how Miss Melville fared with her present partner, the young man Fortescue, whom he had met yesterday in the Pump Room. He was not at all pleased by what he saw, and he remarked later to his sister that Miss Melville seemed in a fair way to becoming an accomplished flirt.

"And why not?" retorted Almeria, who considered that he needed a lesson for never mentioning how he had fared with Hetty in his matrimonial purpose. "Poor Henrietta has led such a restricted life; it's high time she indulged herself in a little flirtation and fun!"

"Doubtless, if it gives her satisfaction," he replied dryly.

"It must give any woman satisfaction to be so much admired. I may tell you that she's a prodigious favourite with all the gentlemen," went on Almeria, determined to bring home to him what he had lost by not offering for her friend. "And so she deserves to be, for don't you think she looks charmingly tonight?"

Aldwyn's eyes rested for a moment on Henrietta, who was now standing a short distance away with Louisa and two other ladies, attended by several gentlemen. She was wearing a gown of blue muslin spangled with silver, cut in a low V at the neckline. Her hair—had he once thought it mouse coloured?—was drawn high on her head and confined by a chaplet of artificial flowers from which curls depended at the back, while a few curling tendrils framed her face.

His glance kindled for a moment, but his expression was guarded as he turned to his sister.

"Oh, prodigiously charming! Indeed, I scarcely know her for the same female I met at Westhyde Manor. She is altogether changed—whether for better or worse, I leave you to determine."

Almeria pouted. "You're foolish beyond permission, Julian! She is *not* changed, except in having realized how to appear to her best advantage. She is the same dear girl that ever she was! And if you doubt that, you've only to make some push to renew your acquaintance with her, and you'll soon discover the truth of it for yourself!"

He looked amused. "You're as cross as crabs now, ain't you, dear sister? But if it will please you, I'll ask her to dance."

"If it will please—!" echoed Almeria in disgust. "Oh, pray don't put yourself out, sir!"

"Indeed I shall," he said provokingly and made his way over to Henrietta's group.

But when he made his request she looked apologetic.

"I am so sorry, but I'm promised to Mr. Burke for the next dance, sir. Perhaps the one after—"

"No, no, Miss Melville, that is mine," put in Colby, who was standing next to her.

Aldwyn bowed stifly. "In that case—"

She rapped Colby over the knuckles with her fan, laughing. "No such thing! You know very well that you have not bespoken it."

"Dear lady, I've bespoken every one of your dances," he said, smiling down at her in a way that made Aldwyn long to give him a facer.

"Can't be done, Colby," said Fortescue. "That's my privilege."

She coloured a little. "Oh, you are too absurd, both of you. Pray have done! Mr. Aldwyn, I shall be happy to dance the next but one with you, if you please."

She looked up shyly into his sombre eyes. He bowed brusquely and moved away.

"Then *you* must take pity on me, Mrs. Fordyce," said

Colby to Louisa, "and accept me as a partner for that particular dance."

There was a hint of command in his tone that brought him a frowning look from Captain Barclay, who was one of the party.

"Don't care for that fellow's manners," said the captain peremptorily as he led Louisa onto the floor. "Queer way to ask a lady to dance, by my notions."

"Oh, it's just that he has known me a long time," replied Louisa airily. "He was a friend of my husband's—in Ireland, you know."

"Is that so, ma'am? I never realised that you and Colby were acquainted before he came here."

She shrugged. "I never chanced to mention it before."

"I suppose then, as an old friend—"

He broke off and looked at her shrewdly, seeing a slight shadow dimming the liveliness of her hazel eyes.

"I have sometimes thought," he went on in his direct manner, "that you were not completely easy in that gentleman's company, ma'am, old friend or not."

She made no answer to this, but seemed very intent on the steps of the dance.

"I would like you to know, Mrs. Fordyce," persisted the captain, "that if there is ever any way in which I may serve you—any way at all—you have only to mention it."

She turned a laughing face upon him. "Yes, there *is* a way, Captain Barclay. You may oblige me by keeping in step!"

There was nothing for him to do but apologise, although he knew he was being fobbed off. Thereafter the subject was dropped.

When Henrietta danced with Mr. Burke, owing to her own abstraction, their conversation was even more stilted than usual. There could be little doubt, she thought uneasily, that given the evening's events Mr. Aldwyn must have formed a most unfavourable notion of her conduct. To be sure, it was delightful to talk nonsense with Colby and Fortescue when she felt in the mood, but Mr. Aldwyn's presence in some way destroyed her girlish pleasure in these vanities. Well, let him despise her if he would, she thought defiantly. *He* was not to be the arbiter of her conduct.

She was in this mood when she took the floor with

him. For a time, neither spoke. Aldwyn was studying his partner, thinking how well the soft blue of her gown set off her fair skin and deepened the colour of her eyes; whenever she turned her head, the cluster of brown curls swung gracefully from side to side in a way that must have enchanted a man less determined to resist feminine charms, Even he felt his determination waver a fraction, and soon he was smiling at her in the old way.

"I need scarcely ask, Miss Melville, if you are enjoying your visit to Bath?"

"Oh, prodigiously!"

He had not intended to make any reference to that final conversation between them at Westhyde Manor, but the temptation was too great.

"And is your new-found freedom of as much benefit as you had hoped, ma'am?" he went on. His brown eyes were mocking but not altogether unkind.

She gave him a reproachful smile that was calculated to cover her embarrassment.

"Shame on you, sir, for putting serious questions to me at a ball, of all places! Besides, you must realise that I've not had time to get a satisfactory answer."

"Possibly I can supply some of them for you," he said lightly.

She looked up quickly, and a flicker of apprehension crossed her face.

"You have discovered, for instance," he continued smoothly, "that, like most females, you infinitely prefer shopping in Milsom Street to such simple rural pleasures as, say, the visiting of historic sites."

She shook her head vigorously, setting her curls swaying in a seductive motion.

"What a poor creature you must think me!" she challenged him. "Because I have discovered a new delight—and I'll freely admit that I take prodigious pleasure in buying pretty things—it's not to say that I've totally renounced the old ones! Indeed"—with a small sigh—"sometimes I miss my simple rural pleasures, as you term them."

He nodded. "Well, then, you've learned a little about yourself. At least you now know that town life cannot be completely satisfying to you."

"And yet I've almost made up my mind to settle here in Bath," she countered.

He looked at her keenly. "You have? May I ask—but no, that is none of my business."

"I'd have no objection to telling you if my plans were certain, but they depend upon another person."

They were separated by the movements of the dance at this juncture, so she missed the mortified expression that came over his face. When they came together again, his manner was more constrained and the ease had gone from his voice.

She found it almost a relief to exchange her present partner for Colby when the next dance began. She noticed that Aldwyn was leading out Isabella Laverton, who looked ravishing in a gown of yellow silk under gauze. He too, judging by his expression, appeared well pleased with the change.

It came to her suddenly that he could have misunderstood her last remark to him, that he might have taken it to mean she was at last contemplating marriage, to someone whom she had met here in Bath. *But how nonsensical I am*, thought Henrietta scornfully, *to trouble my head over Mr. Aldwyn, when there is a gentleman at my side only too ready to please and be pleased in turn!*

She gave herself up without reserve to the entertainment of Mr. Colby's company.

❦ Chapter XVIII

THE BOXING MATCH at Claverton Down had provided some splendid sport, as Aldwyn and Captain Barclay agreed on their way home. Indeed, they were looking forward to giving Sir Giles a full account of the proceedings later on, as the captain had been invited to dine that evening with the Barringtons.

"Mustn't bore your sister with it, though," the captain remarked, as they drove past the Theatre Royal. "Females don't care for sporting talk."

"Oh, Almeria will have Mrs. Fordyce and Miss Melville to keep her company. No doubt they'll chatter away nineteen to the dozen on their own concerns," replied Aldwyn carelessly. "I say, isn't that young Fortescue and that fellow Colby coming out of the house yonder? Looks a bit down in the mouth, don't he? Fortescue, I mean."

Barclay glanced across the road and nodded. "Don't intend to stop, though, Aldwyn, if you've no objection. Can't keep my cattle standing."

The two men on the street looked up as the curricle passed them; recognising the occupants, they touched their hats in salute.

"Yes, I dare say the youngster's got cause enough to look blue-devilled," said Barclay. "They've just come out of the gaming house I told you of; stakes pretty high, and no doubt Fortescue's lost. Colby will have won a bit, though; he's the more experienced gamester. A downy bird, that one, in my opinion."

Aldwyn suddenly clapped a hand to his head. "That's it!" he exclaimed. "Knew I'd seen the fellow somewhere before, but never could think where! It was in London, at one of the less reputable gaming halls. I was out on the town one night with a few friends—you know how it is—and they looked in at this place. Didn't stay long; too devilish queer by half, full of flats and sharpers. But I

155

had this chap pointed out to me as a wrong 'un. He was fleecing a mutton-headed young sprig at the time. They did mention his name, but it escapes me now. Not Colby, though, I'll take my oath."

"Sure there can be no mistake?"

Aldwyn shook his head. "I was only in the place for an hour or so, but I'm positive it was the same man. He had a slight Irish brogue, too, like this fellow."

Barclay looked glum. "Damned awkward," he said thoughtfully. "Don't know if you're aware of the fact, but Mrs. Fordyce had some acquaintance with Colby when she was living in Ireland."

Aldwyn started. "Good God, is that so? I'd no notion of it. It follows then that she must know something about him, perhaps even his other name."

"Not necessarily," replied Barclay, firm in defence of Louisa. "What the lady actually told me was that Colby was an acquaintance of her late husband. She herself might know very little about the fellow; plenty of wives are little acquainted with their husbands' friends."

"True enough," agreed Aldwyn in a propitiatory tone.

"Another thing," went on Barclay. "If she knew anything of that kind about this chap, I'm confident she would discourage her friend Miss Melville from seeing so much of him. She's very attached to Miss Melville, y'know."

"Has Miss Melville been seeing so much of him?"

"Driving out a few times, dancing at balls, and so on. Considering the short time he's been in Bath, yes, I'd say she has seen him a great deal."

"Then perhaps someone should drop the lady a hint," said Aldwyn grimly.

"Your sister, perhaps?"

"I'll have a word with her."

He did broach the subject with Almeria later, just before their guests arrived for dinner. She heard what he had to say without exhibiting either surprise or alarm.

"Well, I guessed he was a bit of a rogue, of course, because he's so prodigiously attractive," she said airily. "If you'd told me he was a womaniser, I wouldn't have been at all surprised. A gamester, yes, I can believe that, too. But my dear Julian, are you positive that he actually *cheats* at cards? I can't conceive that he'd take in experienced gamesters like Hinton-Wellow and Kennett. Indeed, it was Hinton-Wellow who first introduced him into Bath society, and whatever George Hinton-Wellow's faults may be, I can't imagine his sponsoring a shady character. I think perhaps there may be some mistake."

"And I tell you my informant was reliable," replied Aldwyn, testily. "Dare say the fellow has too much sense to try his tricks on experienced players, though no doubt he'd consider a youngster like Fortescue fair game. Not much one can do about that; the boy will have to learn the hard way. I'm more concerned on Miss Melville's account. By all I hear, she's been seeing a good deal of Colby."

"Oh, so you *do* take some interest in Henrietta's affairs?" asked Almeria with deceptive innocence.

"I would not care to see a close friend of yours duped by some rascal, naturally." His tone was defensive.

"Is that all? And what happened to that scheme we two had for Henrietta's, and your, benefit? You've been odiously secretive on that subject!"

"It came to nothing," he answered tersely.

"Why, Julian? Did you change your mind about a marriage of convenience, or did she——"

"I prefer not to discuss it."

She saw from his expression that she would get no other answer from him at present, so she wisely refrained from further questioning.

"Nevertheless," he continued, "I trust you will have a word with your friend?"

"I'll consider it," she temporised, "but I believe Henrietta is well able to manage her own concerns, and she may not thank me for any interference."

He strode away, displeased with her attitude.

By the time their guests arrived, however, he was ready to play his part in entertaining them. The three gentlemen discussed the day's sporting event over a glass of sherry, while the ladies enjoyed a quiet cose together, then everyone sat down to dinner in a relaxed, congenial atmosphere, which promised well for the rest of the evening. Giles and Almeria were seated at each end of the table, with Julian and Henrietta on one side and Louisa and Barclay on the other. The three ladies looked charming. Almeria was in rose satin, Louisa in golden brown velvet, and Henrietta in aquamarine silk; their hair—

black, chestnut, and brown—appeared burnished by the light from the chandeliers.

"Upon my soul, we're lucky fellows to be sitting down in such prodigiously attractive company!" exclaimed Sir Giles gallantly. "I give you a toast gentlemen. To our ladies, the fairest of their sex!"

The other two men responded with alacrity.

"I do declare, Giles, you sound for all the world like Hinton-Wellow!" protested Almeria, laughing.

"How like a wife to turn a compliment into an insult," remarked Aldwyn. "At least, Almeria, you can credit your husband with sincerity."

"Yes, indeed, for unlike the other fellow, who seems to have a store of 'em on the end of his tongue, I don't pay compliments every day."

"I sometimes like to indulge myself with the fancy that Hinton-Wellow sits up burning the midnight oil in order to con over suitable phrases for future use," said Louisa with a mischievous smile.

"Do you think so?" asked Henrietta. "Perhaps one day he will publish his efforts under some such title as 'Pretty Phrases, or How to Commend Oneself to the Fair Sex'. Only he doesn't commend himself well," she added more seriously.

"Poor Hetty," said Almeria with mock compassion. "I noticed your sufferings at the Assembly ball."

"Why, what was this?" demanded Louisa. "I saw nothing."

"Oh, it's only my nonsense," replied Almeria, airily.

Soon afterward, the ladies retired to the drawing room.

"And now tell me," said Louisa, "what was it that you had to suffer from Hinton-Wellow at the ball, Hetty? Was he being more than ordinarily obnoxious?"

Henrietta explained.

"Well, but my dear, it wasn't so very bad, surely? I know how you dislike him; and, of course, no female wishes to be positively *mauled*, but—"

"I found it humiliating in front of my friends. They might have supposed that I'd been encouraging him," replied Henrietta defensively.

"But your friends know both of you too well ever to suppose any such thing, Hetty! Besides"—with a mischievous smile—"would it not have been worse had he offered such familiarities *in private?* I should have thought you'd prefer to have your friends present!"

"Absurd creature!" said Henrietta with a reluctant laugh. "Have it your own way. But I was upset at the time."

Almeria had listened to this exchange with a knowing little smile, and her curiosity was more aroused than ever. What exactly had occurred between those two after she had left Aldwyn Court? If only Julian would not be so odiously secretive!

Throughout the rest of the evening, she covertly watched them for any clue to the mystery. They neither avoided each other nor sought to sit together, and whenever they conversed, it was in an sociable, light-hearted style. Only once did she detect any sign of discomfort between them, and that was when they were all enjoying a musical interlude which had been suggested by Sir Giles, who on occasion liked to hear a few songs played on the pianoforte.

"Pray don't expect me to sing," pronounced his wife, "for you know very well I have a voice like a corn crake! But I'll accompany Louisa and Henrietta, if they'll oblige us."

Both ladies protested the inadequacy of their performance, but were soon overruled, and Louisa proceeded to give a spirited performance of 'Cherry Ripe,' which was loudly applauded.

Henrietta was then applied to, but she hung back, saying she did not know a suitable piece.

"Well, you certainly know this," said Almeria, producing some music with a flourish from atop the instrument. "I've heard you sing it often in the past. Come now!"

Henrietta glanced at the music. "Oh, dear, it's a trifle sentimental, don't you think? Perhaps there's something more suitable—"

"No, no, you shan't escape in that way!" laughed Almeria. "I insist you sing *this!*"

She struck the opening chords of 'Robin Adair,' and Henrietta obediently began.

She had a pleasing, light voice, not strong enough to fill a large drawing room, but adequate for this small parlour. The melancholy words soon exercised their effect on the audience; they listened intently, their eyes fixed on the singer's face.

Henrietta herself focused her gaze a little above them, for she would have found it disconcerting to look directly at them. She was not used to performing anywhere but in her own family circle, and that she had not done for a good many years. But when she reached the final verse, some compulsion forced her eyes downward until she met Aldwyn's steady look.

> "But now thou'rt cold to me,
> Robin Adair.
> Yet he I lov'd so well
> Still in my heart shall dwell.
> Oh, I can ne'er forget
> Robin Adair."

Almeria knew the music by heart. She watched her brother and caught the sudden spark of emotion that flashed for a brief moment in his dark eyes. And when Henrietta turned at the conclusion of the song to thank her accompanist, Almeria saw that her friend's eyes were suspiciously luminous also.

"Oh, dear, I knew I should cast a gloom over you if I sang that," Henrietta said to her audience, "but Almeria would have it! If only you could see your melancholy faces! Perhaps we should sing something lively now, all together, as an antidote."

The suggestion was taken up with enthusiasm, and the somber mood of the party soon changed to conviviality. What a consummate actress her friend must be, Almeria reflected. Was it only in her imagination, she wondered, or did there exist some emotional involvement between these two, even if as yet unsuspected by themselves? It was an intriguing notion.

☙ Chapter XIX

ON SUNDAY MORNINGS the pupils of Miss Mynford's Seminary, demurely dressed in their best white
muslins, trooped into the Abbey. They carried prayer
books in their hands and maintained angelic expressions
on their faces. Their deportment, as might be expected
under the alert eyes of their accompanying tutors, was
always exemplary. But on this particular Sunday morning,
the conduct of the senior girls departed from that usual
high standard.

It all started with Miss Anna Florey. She had been
gazing innocently about her, expecting to see nothing out
of the ordinary, when her gaze became riveted upon a
group of people seated in the opposite aisle. She recognized Miss Melville, Mrs. Fordyce, and the Barringtons, but it was not the sight of those two ladies that had
caused her to gasp in a way that brought a warning
nudge from her neighbour, Caroline Bovill. Rather, it was
the presence beside them of Mr. Julian Aldwyn!

With surreptitious movements of her head and darting
messages from her expressive eyes, she contrived to direct Caroline's attention.

"Mr. Aldwyn!" she whispered, greatly daring. "Now
they'll see! Pass it on!"

Pretending to aid her neighbour in finding the place in
her prayer book, Caroline whispered the message, and
before long, it had reached every one of the girls who
had heard Anna's story at that memorable dormitory
feast. This was not accomplished without incurring warning frowns and dark looks from the schoolmistress at the
end of the pew. Although the girls knew very well that
some retribution must eventually follow, they were young
and sanguine enough to disregard this hazard.

As for Anna, she paid no heed whatever to the sermon

161

from that moment, being far too occupied with watching Mr. Aldwyn's every movement as far as she was able.

At the conclusion of the service, the school party filed out of the Abbey to pause and chat with the groups of parishioners and visitors loitering in the open space before the doors of the great church.

Anna lost no time in gaining permission to go over and speak with Miss Melville and her companions. Everyone greeted her kindly as she made her curtsey, but her shy glances at Mr. Aldwyn prompted him, as once before, to be especially charming to her, even though his mood was far from convivial. For several minutes, she was granted the rapture of a tête-à-tête with him. Conscious that the curious eyes of her schoolfellows were riveted upon the two of them, Anna felt jubilant. Her credit, which had suffered sadly after Charlotte Brisbane's denunciation of her story, would now be triumphantly restored.

Another gentleman came to join the group while she was standing there, and Miss Melville, with her usual thoughtfulness for the feelings of young girls, introduced Anna to Mr. Colby. He, too, spoke to her in a jovial way that normally would have pleased and flattered her, for one of her greatest desires was to be treated as an adult and not just a schoolgirl of no consequence whatever. But she noticed that Mr. Aldwyn drew off a trifle from the others on the advent of Mr. Colby, as though he did not wish to converse with the newcomer. She therefore edged up to him, and for a further few delightful moments was able to claim the whole of his attention.

The mistress in charge then gave a signal that Anna dared not ignore, and she reluctantly took her leave of Miss Melville's party. She gave one last backward glance at her hero as she took her place in the school crocodile, and she was rewarded with a parting smile and wave from him. As she marched home with the others, her heart sang. It had all gone splendidly, even better than she had imagined in her wildest dreams! Now she had really and truly *shown* them, just as she had promised, though the promise had been made with more optimism than expectation of fulfilment.

The group she had quitted soon broke up to go their separate ways, Colby offering to escort Miss Melville and Mrs. Fordyce home. Aldwyn, who had exerted himself to be pleasant for little Miss Anna's sake, now reverted to the sombre mood that had possessed him all morning and had increased with Colby's arrival.

"Blue-devilled, Julian?" quizzed Sir Giles as they entered the carriage. "Dashed dry sermon was enough to cast anyone into the sullens! Only thing to do was take forty winks, but we'll try a stronger remedy when we get back, I promise you."

Almeria, however, thought she knew better what was the cause of her brother's mood. His aloof air, during the short time they had been chatting to the others, had been marked; he had scarcely uttered a word to anyone except the little Florey girl. Moreover, he had not appeared to be enjoying himself vastly on the previous evening at the gala. Was it possible that he was jealous of Henrietta's admirers? Was he falling in love? She would have liked to think so, but it was far more probable, she reflected with an exasperated sigh, that he was merely suffering from pique. Though he did not want Henrietta for himself, he disliked seeing others paying court to her. Yet Julian had never been a dog in the manger; his spirit was too generous for the indulgence of such petty feelings. If only he would talk openly to her on the subject, she might understand. It was a melancholy reflection that however close one might be to a member of one's family, there must always be some confidences denied, some reticences that could not be overcome.

Meanwhile, Henrietta had not walked far with Colby before Captain Barclay caught them up. Louisa was especially glad to have his company, and soon they were walking a little way ahead of the others.

"It's not difficult to see," remarked Colby to Henrietta, "that our gallant captain is *épris* in that direction." He nodded toward Louisa.

"Why, yes, I think he may be," replied Henrietta cautiously. "But Mrs. Fordyce is a general favourite with the gentlemen of Bath—indeed, with everyone, male and female alike. And deservedly so, for she's so good-natured, and such lively company. But I scarce need to tell you that, for you were acquainted with her in Ireland, were you not?"

"I had some slight acquaintance with the lady's husband. Do you suppose your friend to share the captain's partiality? Or perhaps"—with a glance at her reserved expression—"I ought not to ask, since you ladies never betray each other's secrets."

"Of course not," returned Henrietta, smiling up at him. "So even if I knew, I could not possibly tell you. But I must admit that I do not know."

"How little any of us do know about each other, after all!" he said with conscious sententiousness, then adroitly changed the subject. "Your little friend Miss Anna—was her name Florey, did you say?—seems to be fathoms deep in hero worship for Lady Barrington's brother. All the time he was speaking with her, her eyes were shining like twin stars, and I'll swear I caught a distinct whiff of incense!"

Henrietta laughed. "Oh, yes, poor Anna has certainly set Mr. Aldwyn on a pedestal! I dare say you're aware that girls of that age are very prone to such transports, but they quickly recover. Indeed, I'm surprised that Anna has not already done so, for it began when she was at home for the summer vacation and had nothing much to occupy her attention. I thought that surely once she returned to school and became caught up in her normal interests, she would forget all about it."

"I collect you are all near neighbours, your family, Aldwyn's, and young Anna's?"

She nodded. "The Floreys are nearest, only two miles away from my brother's house. Aldwyn Court is four miles off, and I've seldom visited there since Almeria wed Sir Giles and went to live in Bath. But I've known young Anna ever since her birth."

"And I dare say," he said with a twinkle in his eye, "that even in those days she was cradled in luxury."

"Why, yes, I suppose so, for Mr. Florey is a warm man, as the saying goes. Anna is his second daughter; the elder is now Lady Abdale, and lives in London. There's also a boy in the family, a scamp named Ben, only ten years old. But, gracious, here I am talking about our neighbours in the country, and it must be the most boring subject imaginable for you, sir! Pray, why did you not stop me?"

"Sure, and I could listen to you reciting the days of the week over and over, without feeling the slightest twinge of boredom," he assured her with a smile. "Why, the changing expressions that flit across your face are to me a never-ending source of delight."

She pursed her mouth, but her eyes were laughing. "Oh, pooh! You're being flowery, sir."

"Then I'll inflict no more of it on you, even though I was saying nothing but the sober truth. Never frown at me, ma'am! I have done."

True to his word, he paid her no more compliments, sincere or otherwise, and entertained her for the remainder of the walk home with his usual amusing chatter. She was grateful to him for making her laugh, as her mood had been subdued ever since the events of yesterday evening. When they reached Louisa's house, she parted from him with a pang of regret, and realized she was looking forward with pleasure to their engagement for the following day.

Louisa made no further attempt to dissuade her from keeping his company, but on the contrary seemed almost to approve. Perhaps, thought Henrietta, she would be glad of a few hours left to herself.

This notion was given substance the next day, for on Henrietta's return from what had been a most enjoyable outing in Mr. Colby's curricle, Louisa was not at home. She had left a message with the housekeeper to say that she would be back by three o'clock. As it was then almost two, and Henrietta was made hungry by her ride in the fresh air, she decided not to wait for Louisa but to eat her luncheon alone and at once. Accordingly, the housekeeper sent a tray into the parlour, set out with fresh, crusty bread, cold meats, and fruit.

Henrietta had just finished when the footman came into the room bearing a visiting card on a salver. Henrietta glanced at the name, casually at first, then a second time with more attention.

Her heart missed a beat. She hesitated for a moment, uncertain what to do.

"You may show the gentleman in," she said at last, with a composure she was far from feeling.

The footman departed and presently returned with the visitor.

It was Aldwyn. One look at his face showed Henrietta that he was not in a pleasant mood.

"Is Mrs. Fordyce at home?" he asked abruptly, with only a cursory bow in greeting.

"No, she is gone out, but I expect her back within the half hour," replied Henrietta, glancing at the clock. "Did you wish to see her, sir? Perhaps you would care to wait?"

"No, it is you I came to see. I suppose if I were to observe the proprieties, I should not remain here while you're alone. But since you pay scant heed yourself to matters of the kind, I intend to stay. What I have to say to you will not take long."

"I trust not," returned Henrietta coldly, for his manner set up her hackles, "if you are to address me in such an uncivil style."

"I'm well aware that you have become more accustomed to fulsome flattery, ma'am, since you came to Bath and I regret that it's quite beyond my powers to emulate your many admirers. However, I did not come to quarrel."

"You astound me, Mr. Aldwyn! I should certainly have supposed from your harsh, not to say ungentlemanlike, manner, that quarrelling was exactly what you had in mind!"

"All right, cut up at me if you will, but believe it or not, the office I'm here to perform is that of a friend. I tried to persuade my sister to undertake it, but since she won't, the duty devolves on me."

"And if it's an unpleasant duty, as I suspect, I'm sure you'll enjoy it vastly," she retorted with her chin in the air.

He raised his brows in the familiar cynical gesture. "Spitfire, eh? But you're wrong in that. I don't relish my errand. I'll spare you, therefore, all unnecessary preliminaries. What I've come to say concerns that fellow Colby, whose attentions you're been encouraging."

"I have been *encouraging!* How dare you say so!"

"Do you attempt to deny it? How else, then, would you explain the marked preference you show him in all the public places in Bath, not to mention that you are in the habit of driving out with him alone?"

Twin spots of colour showed on her cheeks. "I do not require to explain anything concerning my conduct to you, Mr. Aldwyn! Besides, I have *not* driven out alone with Mr. Colby; there has always been a groom present. I think you yourself were once kind enough to explain to me"—it was now her turn for sarcasm—"that the presence of a groom made any such outing perfectly proper."

"So it does in the normal way, but not with a fellow like that. I must warn you that he is not at all the thing."

"Indeed? I may tell you that I have always found him charming, attentive, and prodigiously entertaining company—unlike some I could mention!"

"Oh, I don't doubt the fellow's an accomplished lady-killer," he replied scathingly. "I dare say you fancy he's head over heels in love with you, but allow me to inform you that he's much more likely to be after your fortune! I'm sorry, but it's the very truth of the matter."

"You're not at all sorry. You're enjoying every moment and every insult you make upon me. And pray what substance is there, if any, in these accusations against Mr. Colby?"

She had not invited him to sit, and now they both stood angrily scowling at each other.

"I ran across him in London at a gaming house and was warned that he was a wrong 'un. What's more, he was going there by some other name, though I can't recollect what it was. Is that sufficient evidence for you, ma'am?"

She made no answer for a moment. She was trying to think, but her heated emotions were scarcely conducive to the exercise.

"You could be mistaken," she said in a calmer tone. "It is only hearsay, after all. We all know how little credence can be placed in gossip."

"My informant was certainly not the man for idle gossip," Aldwyn replied coldly. "However, I see how it is, Miss Melville. You're too infatuated with this rogue to see him for what he is."

"Infatuated!" she exclaimed indignantly. "It's no such thing! I find him excellent company, charming and—"

"Well, if you're not infatuated, you give a devilish good imitation of it, let me tell you! But of course I am forgetting what an accomplished flirt you are become, madam."

"How—how dare you!"

"It's not only Colby, is it?" he continued ruthlessly. "There's that young chap Fortescue. Cradle snatching is the only way to describe that conquest! And then there's the worthy Mr. Burke, though perhaps you have deeper designs on him than a mere flirtation, who knows? Evidently you are much changed from the female whom I once thought suitable to be my wife, fool that I was," he said bitterly.

"Well, I was not foolish enough to accept you, at all events, for which I'm prodigiously thankful!" she retorted, her eyes flashing. "I am seeing a side of your character that I never before suspected. And so you think that I may be entertaining hopes of a match with Mr. Burke, do you? Well, allow me to tell you, sir, that had I been *that* kind of female, I would have accepted *your* offer, since it would have held out the promise of far greater status!"

"I'll allow that *once* you were not that kind of female. But that was before you gained the freedom to try out a new way of life—I believe that was *your* phrase—and so to discover what you really wanted for yourself." His tone was heavy with irony. "It appears that your aims have been achieved. You've now settled for a romantic infatuation with one man, flirtations with many others, and marriage with a wealthy suitor whom you can lead by the nose. I congratulate you, Miss Melville; the change in you is nothing short of miraculous."

She gave a furious gasp.

"Oh, I detest you!" she cried. "Go! Go at once, and never speak to me again!"

Almost beside herself, she stepped forward and raised her arm threateningly, as if to strike him in the face.

But he seized the arm with one hand and held her tightly.

For a long moment, he looked deeply and searchingly into her eyes, while conflicting emotions raged within him. Meeting his blazing look, she became confused and frightened, yet even more determined to stand her ground. He pulled her closer and she steeled herself to withstand his strength. So they stood, tense, poised, motionless. . .

Then he released her so abruptly that she staggered, and he strode out of the room, closing the door with a resounding slam.

✑ Chapter XX

FOR SOME TIME after he had gone Henrietta stood without moving, as if paralysed. Gradually thought and emotion crept back, and she threw herself down into a chair and gave way to a passionate outburst of weeping.

She rarely allowed herself the indulgence of tears, but there was no one else present to be disconcerted by this relief for her overtaxed feelings.

The storm soon subsided, spent by its very violence. She was attempting to mop her face with a hopelessly wet handkerchief when the door opened to admit Louisa.

Her friend stood staring for a moment, then uttered an exclamation of concern.

"Hetty! You've been crying! What is it, my dear? Not bad news, I trust?"

Henrietta shook her head. "No, no, nothing of that kind. I'll tell you in a minute. But pray lend me a dry handkerchief."

Louisa supplied one and watched anxiously while her friend wiped away her tears.

"It's not anything to do with—with Colby, is it?" she asked with a worried frown. "You were out with him this morning, and if he's distressed you in some way—"

"No, it's nothing to do with Mr. Colby. At least, only indirectly," replied Henrietta, now rapidly gaining control of herself. "We had a most pleasant drive together. But when I returned I had an unexpected visitor."

"Do you wish to tell me who it was? You need not if you'd rather keep it to yourself, you know."

"It was Mr. Aldwyn," replied Henrietta in an unnaturally calm voice.

Louisa started. *"Mr. Aldwyn!"* she repeated in astonished accents. Then, as an afterthought occurred to her,

169

"Hetty, is there something wrong at Almeria's? Is that why—?"

"There is nothing wrong with anyone except myself, and it appears there's too much wrong with me," said Henrietta bitterly. "Mr. Aldwyn called to set me right on one or two points in my conduct."

"Mr. Aldwyn!" repeated Louisa. "But you scarcely know him!"

Henrietta coloured. "I fear I've not been entirely open with you, Louisa.

"Well, as to that," put in her friend hastily, "there's no reason why you should be. But if you're certain you wish to tell me—"

"It would be a relief," replied Henrietta with a deep sigh. "Louisa, you may perhaps recall my telling you of two proposals of marriage I received before coming to Bath?"

Louisa nodded.

"Well, one of those was from Mr. Aldwyn."

Her friend sat down abruptly, staring in amazement.

"Mr. Aldwyn! Well, this is certainly a surprise!" She was silent for a moment, then continued. "Since he is *not* a widower with children, I take it that he must be the other suitor you mentioned, the one seeking a conformable wife?"

Henrietta nodded, a faint blush mounting to her cheeks.

"But was he not to all intents and purposes a *stranger* to you when he arrived at Aldwyn Court? He must have gone to work prodigiously fast to make you an offer in such a short time!"

"Yes, that's true, and I did puzzle over his apparent determination to pursue the acquaintance since I knew well it could not have been"—she choked a little, then quickly turned it into a strangled laugh—"because he had fallen a slave to my charms! There was a degree of calculation in his manner that quite gave the lie to anything of that nature, even had I been naive enough to expect it," she concluded wistfully.

"Stuff!" said Louisa forcefully if inelegantly. "But pray continue, Hetty. I am fascinated!"

Henrietta gave a wan smile. "When I look back and consider matters, Louisa, I think perhaps Almeria may have given her brother the notion by telling him something of my circumstances at home. She had confided to me that Mr. Aldwyn had begun to think it his duty to marry, in view of his father's poor health. She also said that it would be only a marriage of convenience, as he was determined to avoid any further emotional disasters. There was something in his youth—I don't know if you ever heard anything about it—"

"Oh, yes, I recall Mama hinting at some scandal connected with him, but naturally I wasn't allowed to know the full story at the tender age of sixteen," said Louisa with a chuckle. "No more were you, I dare say. But no matter for that; I'm the last person to desire to delve into what's past and done."

"I must say that the details of that story as related to me by Almeria filled me with compassion. He was only twenty, you know, and shamefully used! However, I only mention this to explain his attitude toward marriage, which might otherwise appear somewhat cold-blooded."

"What a magnanimous creature you are, Hetty! Here's a man who made you a proposal of marriage for reasons that any other girl would find insulting, and who has to-day upset you dreadfully in some way, and yet you're actually defending him!"

"I'm certainly not defending his conduct today—that was monstrous!" Henrietta's eyes kindled at the remembrance of it. "But one must be fair, and I don't consider he can be blamed in the other matter. He could scarcely think it an insult to offer to make me mistress of Aldwyn Court one day, whatever you and I may feel about a loveless marriage. And I dare say, you know, Almeria may have given him a hint that I would be relieved to have an establishment of my own. After all, she didn't know that I had already refused one offer of a marriage of convenience."

Louisa considered for a moment. "I must say that does seem likely. Almeria would welcome you as a sister-in-law more than any other female of her acquaintance, for you've been devoted friends since childhood. So all this is doubtless the reason why you and Mr. Aldwyn appear so very reserved with each other? But tell me, Hetty, what did occur today to upset you so? Never say that he came to renew his proposals and that you quarrelled in consequence?"

Henrietta shook her head. "Far from it! The impression he left was that he wouldn't marry me if I were the last woman on earth! No, he came to warn me about my friendship with Mr. Colby."

Louisa started so violently that she knocked her hand against a side table close to her chair. She nursed the hand for a moment, looking down at it to avoid Henrietta's eyes.

"Warn you?" Her voice sounded strained.

"Yes. It seems that while Mr. Aldwyn was in London, he saw Mr. Colby in some gaming house and was told by a friend that Mr. Colby was—I use his words—'a wrong 'un'. I don't know precisely what that signifies, but the implication is plain enough. And he said that Mr. Colby was, at the time, going under another name."

She paused and tried to make Louisa meet her eyes, but without success.

"Louisa," she continued in a pleading tone, "you must know if any of this is true. After all, you did have some acquaintance with Mr. Colby when you were both in Ireland."

"A woman learns little about the *bachelor* friends of her husband," replied Louisa evasively. "It's different with married friends, of course, for wives will chatter to each other."

"But you must know something of his background and character," persisted Henrietta, "else how could you have warned me that he was a—a womaniser, and that I mustn't take him too seriously?"

Louisa looked uncomfortable. "That much I could observe," she answered reluctantly. "But I have the impression that since meeting you, he has turned over a new leaf and will not look at any other woman."

"Oh, we amuse each other vastly, and that is all! But was he a gamester in those days in Ireland, Louisa? Did you have any reason to suppose—"

"Most gentlemen are gamesters," interrupted Louisa quickly. "The world doesn't seem to think any the worse of them for that, I believe. But tell me, was this the reason you quarrelled with Almeria's brother, because of what he said about Colby?"

"I suppose it started with that." She passed a hand across her eyes, trying to recall exactly what had been said during that heated interview. "He told me not to flatter myself that Colby was—in love with me, because it was far more likely that he was after my fortune! That made me angry to begin with, but then he went on to make things worse. He said I had become an accomplished flirt. He mentioned Fortescue, as well as Colby, and even suggested that I might be angling for a marriage with Mr. Burke, with the intention of—oh, I can't tell you! It was too monstrous!"

"I believe I can hazard a guess. He thought you were willing to accept a wealthy husband who would be complaisant while you pursued affairs with other men, did he not? You know what I think, Hetty? He is jealous, my dear! He sees you have blossomed into a woman whom other men admire, and he's regretting that he lost you."

"If so, it is only pique," said Henrietta scornfully. "He really seems to believe that I've changed my character, so he cannot now feel even the *respect* that once he avowed. But don't let us speak of him any more. I wish I might never set eyes on him again, I can tell you!"

Louisa considered her thoughtfully for a moment, then abandoned the subject. But inwardly she was troubled by thoughts she could not share.

After Aldwyn had quitted the house, he set off at a rapid pace along Pulteney Street, but he had not covered more than a hundred yards when he changed his mind and retraced his steps to the house next door to that of Mrs. Fordyce.

"Is Captain Barclay at home?" he asked the footman who appeared in answer to his knock.

"I will inquire, sir," replied the man, taking the proffered visiting card.

Aldwyn stepped inside and watched while the servant knocked upon a door leading off the hall at the rear of the house. In another moment the Captain emerged.

"This is an unexpected pleasure, Aldwyn," he said cordially. "Come into my snug."

Aldwyn followed him into the room he had just left. The captain's snug, as he termed it, was a thoroughly masculine apartment, furnished for comfort rather than elegance. Two of the walls were lined with books, and against one of the others stood a mahogany bureau bookcase with a revolving globe close beside it. What space remained on the walls was covered with maps and pictures of seascapes. Several deep armchairs, a table, and a small sideboard with decanters set out upon it, completed the furnishings.

Aldwyn looked about him with perfunctory approval before seating himself. He was still in a black mood.

"What can I offer you, my dear chap?" asked Barclay. "Ale, a glass of wine, or something else?"

Aldwyn accepted a glass of wine, and, having civilly toasted his friend, drained it in uncivil haste. The captain raised his eyebrows but made no comment, merely rising to refill the glass.

"Sorry. I needed that," said Aldwyn, treating the second glass with more ceremony. "Just made a damned fool of myself, Barclay. At least—no, hell and the devil, I don't altogether regret what I said! But you won't have the least notion what I'm talking about. I've just been paying a visit next door."

The captain looked startled. "To Mrs. Fordyce?"

"No, to her friend. Mrs. Fordyce was not at home."

"Quite right. Saw her go out earlier."

"I needn't tell you that I'm not in the habit of calling on females of quality when they're unchaperoned," went on Aldwyn with a cynical twist to his mouth, "but on this occasion I considered my action justified. You know that business about Colby we spoke of the other day?"

Barclay nodded; he was all attention now.

"Well, I tried to get my sister to give Miss Melville a hint, but she wouldn't, so I decided to tackle the matter myself. Damned idiot that I was!" he finished explosively.

"She didn't take to your kindness?"

Aldwyn shifted uncomfortably. "My fault, in a way. I put the thing badly—said she was encouraging him."

"H'm, no, dare say she wouldn't care for that."

Aldwyn gave a short, mirthless laugh. "She left me in no doubt of it. And then the business went from bad to worse. Don't know what came over me, but I said wild things—made devilish accusations—"

He drained the second glass; once more, Barclay refilled it and poured another for himself.

"I may have a wrong impression," he said carefully, as he reseated himself, "but I had the notion that you and Miss Melville were only slightly acquainted, in spite of your families being neighbours."

"Yes—and no. We formed an acquaintance while my

sister and I were staying at Aldwyn Court on account of my father's illness. I—oh, you may as well know the whole, and a damnable business it is! I made her an offer of marriage at the time."

Barclay choked a little over his wine. "The devil you did! I collect she did not accept?"

Aldwyn explained briefly how matters had stood.

"So there it was, you see," he concluded. "I had decided to settle down and take a wife, and Miss Melville needed an establishment of her own. Seemed an ideal arrangement, but it didn't suit the lady."

"A—er—convenient arrangement, at all events," amended Barclay. "No question of, um, affection in the matter?"

"On the contrary, I was becoming quite fond of the girl, for we had a deal in common and were quite well suited, you know. But if you mean one of these headlong passions, which is what she evidently wished for—no fear of that!"

"Odd word to use; fear," commented the captain, shooting his guest a curious glance.

"Manner of speaking. But, to tell you the truth, fear's not so far off the mark. I was in love once, but never again! It's like the measles, thank God: you don't catch it twice."

"I knew a chap who had measles twice. I was at school with him," retorted the captain, chuckling. "So don't be too cocksure."

"Anyway, I'll take good care it don't happen to me."

The captain reflected that possibly the stable door was being slammed too late. To his shrewd eye, it appeared his friend was already showing a rash.

✺ *Chapter XXI*

HENRIETTA SLEPT BADLY that night. As she tossed and turned, every detail of the distressing scene between herself and Mr. Aldwyn, every word that had passed, came clearly before her again and again. It was odd that when she had tried to recount the story to Louisa, she had been unable to remember exactly what had been said, yet now, in the dark solitude of her bedchamber, she appeared to have gained total recall. It was the last thing she desired; far better to banish it from her mind forever.

In particular would she have wished to bury in oblivion the memory of the final incident of that interview, when he had crushed her to him in an embrace that held nothing of tenderness, but only a fierce intent to hurt and humiliate her. It had been an insult. And yet, to her secret shame, she had felt a moment of exhilaration in his rough, contemptuous grasp.

She could not blame herself for the quarrel. His attitude had been uncompromising from the start. Although he had claimed to be performing the office of a friend, he had gone about the business in a way that no woman of spirit could possibly tolerate. It had seemed as if his real intention had been to criticise her unmercifully and to heap insults upon her. Could it be, as Louisa had suggested, that he was jealous of the attentions paid her by other men? Jealousy was an emotion of insecurity, suffered by those who loved but doubted a return of their affections. Obviously that did not apply here. Pique, then? From what she had learnt of his character while they were together in the country, she could not bring herself to believe that he was capable of allowing such a petty feeling to govern his actions. She knew that he was not a small-minded man; in spite of all her indignation against him, she still could accord him a grudging respect.

It seemed far more likely that he was disappointed in her. During their meetings at home, a friendship had been ripening between them based on mutual liking and respect; what he had seen of her conduct since coming to Bath had made him feel that she was no longer the kind of woman to whom he wished to offer friendship.

This was such an upsetting thought that she found her pillow wet with tears before she pulled herself together sufficiently to remember that *she* was the injured party. What right had he to criticise what was only harmless fun? And if *he* had not found her attractive enough to fall madly in love with her, why should he complain because there were others who took a different view? It would do him good to see that Henrietta Melville was a woman whom men could desire.

One thing was certain. He was not going to browbeat her into giving up her friendship with Mr. Colby.

On the following morning she and Louisa were about to set out for the Pump Room, when Fortescue was announced.

"Something to show you," he said importantly. "Outside, if you care to take a look."

Curiosity impelled them to comply with this request. They were rewarded by the sight of a brand-new curricle with bright yellow wheels, drawn up before the house. Two handsome bay horses were harnessed to the vehicle, their mettlesome qualities admirably controlled by a liveried groom who touched his hat to the ladies.

"Ain't they prime bits of blood?" said Fortescue proudly, walking round the horses to show off their points.

Louisa had little knowledge of horseflesh and less interest. But Henrietta, reared in the country sporting community, was able to join in his raptures.

"Altogether a spankin' equipage, wouldn't you say?" he went on enthusiastically. "A present from my aunt—my birthday, you see."

They both congratulated him on this event, and agreed that the gift was certainly handsome.

"Wondered if you'd care to take a turn about the town with me?" asked the young man diffidently. "Just to try their paces, y'know."

He looked at Henrietta as he spoke, making it clear that the invitation was meant only for her.

She glanced doubtfully at Louisa.

"Why, yes, I'd be delighted, but the truth is that Mrs. Fordyce and I were about to set out for the Pump Room at present. Perhaps some other time—"

His downcast countenance bore completely the appearance of a child disappointed because he could not show off a new toy. Fortunately, at that very moment, with his usual careful timing, Captain Barclay emerged from the house next door and came up to the group. He, too, was ready to appraise and admire Fortescue's equipage, an operation that took some time and caused the horses to fidget.

"Mustn't keep 'em standing any longer, my dear chap," warned the captain. "They're craving exercise."

Fortescue agreed. "I was trying to persuade Miss Melville to accompany me on a short drive," he added, "but it seems the ladies are bound for the Pump Room. Pity."

"Oh, but there is no reason why Miss Melville shouldn't go with you, if she wishes," put in Louisa quickly. "I can perfectly well walk to the Pump Room alone, as I was always used to do before she came to stay."

"If you'd do me the honour to accept my escort, ma'am," said Barclay promptly, "I was bound that way myself."

Henrietta was assisted into the curricle, Fortescue seated himself beside her and took up the reins, while the groom climbed nimbly up behind into the dickey seat.

They started along Pulteney Street at a spanking pace. At first Henrietta was a trifle nervous about her driver's expertise. To her, Fortescue had always appeared a mere boy, in spite of his three and twenty years. She soon saw, however, that it was not the first time he had driven a spirited pair, for he was quite capable of controlling them.

"It is certainly a splendid gift," she remarked presently. "Lady Bellairs is very good to you."

"Yes, the old girl generally turns up trumps," he answered. "Talking of trumps, wish I could do the same! The devil's in the cards for me, lately. I've dropped a packet. Scarce know which way to turn, to own the truth."

"You play cards with Mr. Hinton-Wellow's set, do you not?"

"That's so. Play quite a bit with Colby, though, just the two of us. Dashed good player, Colby; lucky, too," he added enviously.

"Do you think he has more luck than most players?" she asked, forcing a casual tone.

"Oh, I don't know. Never thought about it. All I know is that he's luckier than I seem to be."

She would have liked to press the point further, but decided against it. In spite of her repudiation of Mr. Aldwyn's warning against Colby, an uneasy doubt had invaded her mind at Fortescue's words.

"Well, you will just have to give up cards for a time," she said lightly, "until you've come about."

"A fellow's got to have some diversion," he complained. "Squirin' my aunt to all these dashed balls and concerts ain't my notion of fun, I can tell you! Another thing"—he glanced at her uncertainly—"don't like to mention it, but I'm at point non plus as far as you're concerned."

"I? What can you mean?"

"This maggot my aunt's got into her head about you," he replied gloomily. "Thought it would answer if I made up to you, but no such thing! Dashed poor notion that turned out to be!"

"Oh, dear," said Henrietta in an apprehensive tone. "Do you mean—?"

He nodded. "She wants me to pop the question at once. Says if I don't, Colby will get in first, or even that prosy fellow Burke. What's to be done? Devil of a coil ma'am!"

Henrietta sighed. "Indeed it is, but I must say, I anticipated such an eventuality. I suppose I was foolish to agree to your scheme."

"Oh, I don't know. It was a bit of a lark, after all, and it did hold her off from thrusting other females at me. I suppose," he went on, his expression brightening, "you wouldn't consider marryin' me? Come to think of it, if I must marry, I'd as lief have you as anyone. You're a rare sport and a dashed pretty girl beside! I'll wager that if I put my mind to it, I could fall in love with you in less time than it takes the cat to lick its ear!"

Henrietta could not help laughing. After a moment, he looked ruefully at her and joined in himself.

"What a very odd declaration, to be sure!" she said, sobering. "But I beg you won't—fall in love with me, that is. I think you ought to postpone that process for several years yet, and then choose a girl younger than yourself."

"I'm three and twenty now," he protested. "And you're no more than that, I'll stake my last penny!

"Alas, you'd lose it. You have no more talent for wagers than you have for cards, I fear. I can give you more than two years, you know."

"You can?" He seemed genuinely amazed.

She nodded, laughing again. "Yes, but there's no need for you to blazon the fact abroad! No female likes to be thought older than she is, and to be thought younger is extremely pleasant."

"No fear of that. Doubt if anyone'd credit it, anyway. But even so, that's no bar to our gettin' wed, is it?"

"Not that alone, no," replied Henrietta slowly. "But there are other reasons."

"Colby?" he asked with a shrewd glance.

To her annoyance, she found herself blushing, but she merely shook her head in reply.

"Not sure, y'know, that he'd be any safer bet than I am," he said. "Devil of a gamester, by all I've seen. No, for a nice, steady husband, Burke's your man, though I'll wager a filly of your spirit would die of boredom in a twelvemonth if you were hitched to him! Still, as Aunt Euphemia's always saying, females must do the best they can for themselves, and God knows I ain't a good catch! Most likely gamble your fortune away in no time. Come to think of it, wouldn't be sportin' to let you take the chance. I may be a rum 'un, but I ain't as rum as that, damned if I am."

She laid a hand gently on his arm. "No, you are not," she said softly. "Under all that nonsense of yours, you've a good heart."

He gave a shaky laugh. "What, me? You're thinkin' of some other chap, Miss Melville! A care-for-nobody, that's Roger Fortescue!"

"You'd like to make everyone think so, at all events.

But can't you possibly bring yourself to face up to Lady Bellairs and tell her that you don't wish to marry at present?"

He whistled. "Tall order, that. She'd most likely cut off the dibs straight away."

"But surely you could manage to live within your income if you really set your mind to it?" insisted Henrietta.

It was evident from Fortescue's strained expression that he was bringing his by no means disciplined intellect to the consideration of this problem.

"Might go on a repairin' lease to my brother's place in Leicestershire for a bit," he said at last. "Come to think of it, the huntin' season's not far off, and I'd get some famous sport there. Not sure, though, about facin' up to Aunt Euphemia; she's got the devil of a temper."

"But she's very fond of you, so it's unlikely her anger will last. Besides, she can only respect you, however unwillingly, for insisting on your right to decide matters for yourself. I dare say she still thinks of you as a boy. It's for you to disabuse her of the notion."

"Ay, and lose the best part of my funds in playin' the man!" he retorted with a wry grin. "But never fear, I'll have a touch at it, if only to please you. Y' know, ma'am," giving her a glance compounded of affection, exasperation, and amusement, "you're a powerful advocate! Reckon you ought to set up as a missionary, or— or go into Parliament!"

Henrietta shook with laughter.

"A female in Parliament! That would be the day!"

"I don't know," he said judicially. "Lot of old women there already, to my way of thinkin'."

Aldwyn, insisting that he really must take his chestnut mare out for some exercise, declined his sister's invitation to accompany Sir Giles and herself to the Pump Room that morning. Sir Giles showed an inclination to ride with him, but was put off by the impression that his brother-in-law did not wish for company.

The events of yesterday were still occupying Aldwyn's mind, even though he had found some relief in unburdening himself to Barclay. Polite conversation must be something of a strain until his equilibrium should be restored, and he judged that exercise was the one method certain to achieve this desired end.

A brisk canter through Weston and the neighbouring villages northwest of Bath however, brought him back in much the same mood as before. He was riding down the Lansdown Road toward home when he casually noticed a very new equipage in the press of traffic coming toward him. Something vaguely familiar about the lady passenger made him look more carefully; he recognised Miss Melville.

She looked extremely attractive in a claret-coloured pelisse and straw bonnet trimmed with pink flowers and ribbons, and she was leaning toward the driver of the curricle in a very intimate way, smiling up at him. They were evidently much too engrossed in each other to notice anyone who was passing, so Aldwyn went unacknowledged, for which he was thankful.

After luncheon, a meal at which he was unusually silent, he seized the first opportunity that offered of a private conversation with his sister.

"I shall be returning home tomorrow, Almeria," he announced without preamble.

She looked surprised. "But why, Julian? There was a letter from Mama this morning saying that all is well with Papa, as I told you. Moreover, Jane is still there with her family. There was some trouble about the apple loft and Mama's workbox, which I didn't trouble to read out to you for you didn't seem in a mood to enjoy it. But it did sound as though those three boys are in splendid form."

"I dare say I shall manage to survive," he replied brusquely. "Anyway, I've made up my mind to go."

"Is it anything I've done, Julian?" she asked in a small, pathetic voice. "You are vexed, I know, but I cannot think why. I wish you will tell me."

He gave her a quick hug. "Absurd creature! No, it's certainly nothing to do with you, or Giles, for that matter you've both been ideal hosts. But I feel restless. I must be on the move."

"There was a time," she said, still in that unhappy voice, "when you would have confided in me. And it's of no use for you to pretend that there's nothing to confide, for I know you too well, my dear."

He studied her dubiously for a moment. She was over-playing her part, of course—artful female. But underneath he sensed some genuine feelings of hurt and disappointment. Perhaps he owed her an explanation.

"Very well, I'll tell you the whole." His tone was resigned. "But it may take some time."

Almeria indicated that she had all the time in the world to spare for him, and settled down to listen. During the early part of the recital, she restrained herself as much as possible from any kind of interruption, tempted though she frequently was to comment.

She soon learned of all that had passed before Henrietta's arrival in Bath, and felt that she had formed a tolerably accurate understanding of events.

"It wasn't only Jane's brats who drove me to come here," he confessed. "They were simply the means of hardening a resolution I'd been forming not to let matters between Miss Melville and myself come to an end so easily. She and I dealt so famously together, seemed so well suited—in short, I determined to make one more throw for success, woo her, if necessary." He gave a snort of contempt. "Woo her! I had no notion that I should find plenty of other men about the same business," he went on bitterly. "Of course, I found her vastly changed from the dowdy female I first knew. She'd become instead an attractive, desirable woman, whom any man—well, no matter for that! But her character seemed changed, and she was flirting outrageously with every Tom, Dick, and Harry who came in her way. Of course, she had told me before that she intended to try a new way of life, become a different person, so I suppose I was fairly warned."

Almeria shook her head vigorously. She could not let this pass without comment.

"Of course her *character's* not changed, just because she wishes to enjoy herself some! Why, I myself flirted outrageously during my London season, and so I suppose does every young girl, given the opportunity. But Hetty never had the opportunity to behave as a young girl; she was obliged always to act sensibly and with a maturity beyond her years. Can you truly find it in your heart to blame her if just for a short space she attempts to recapture the lost delights of those earlier years? She would never be satisfied with that way of life forever, as you surely must realise if you've arrived at any understanding of her true nature."

He was silent for a time, digesting what she had said.

"Well, you may be right," he acknowledged presently, "but all the same, it sickens me to witness it! Why, only just now, as I rode home, I passed her with that young chap Fortescue in a curricle, making eyes at him for all she was worth. And he still wet behind the ears! Faugh!"

"Oh, Fortescue!" exclaimed Almeria and burst out laughing.

"Why, what's so amusing?" he demanded irritably. "Making a cake of herself, I call it!"

"I see I shall have to explain it to you," said his sister, and proceeded to do so.

"And perhaps you'll see from that," she concluded, "how little Hetty's character has changed, for since first I knew her, she was always ready to lend a helping hand. How we've laughed over this, the three of us! Louisa's in the secret, too, of course."

"Well, of all the corkbrained notions! That young fellow must have windmills in his head, and Miss Melville too! But, good God!" he exclaimed, belatedly realising the implications of what she had just confided to him. "I flung an accusation at her yesterday—oh, but I'd better tell you about that too. Might as well make a clean breast of the whole!"

He proceeded to give her a full account of yesterday's quarrel for, like Henrietta, he could recall every word. When he had finished, she was shaking her head and looking grave.

"Oh, dear. You said some monstrous things."

"Realise that now, of course," he said awkwardly. "Although I believed them at the time. Felt as angry as fire, I can tell you." He hesitated a moment, then went on. "Do you think she does mean to marry Burke? Seems to me she's receiving his attentions seriously—making no effort to repulse him, at any rate, and certainly not treating it as one of these light flirtations that you seem to think"—he gave her a provocative grin—"will do her so much good."

Almeria considered for a moment.

"It is difficult to say," she replied at last. "I don't think Henrietta will ever marry without affection. But whether she has any such feeling for our neighbour Burke—"

"No," interrupted her brother explosively. "Any feelings she has are for that damned worthless fellow Colby! She's positively infatuated with him!"

"Did she tell you so?"

"I don't need telling. I can trust the evidence of my own eyes."

"Well, I would have said that *is* only a flirtation," pronounced Almeria. "I don't believe either party is serious."

"He's certainly not. Fellow's after her fortune, as I informed her."

"That must have placed you high in her favour," remarked Almeria ironically.

"As I told you, she said she never wished to speak to me again."

She looked up at him with a pleading expression in her eyes.

"Julian, couldn't you possibly bring yourself to apologise to her?"

He hesitated. "For some things, though not for all," he said presently, with a sudden flash of his eyes. "It's true that I went about the business badly. Vented my spleen instead of sticking to the matter of warning her against Colby, as I'd intended at the start. I was uncivil and ungentlemanlike, and I'd apologise for that, if I thought it would do any good. But I told you what she finally said: she won't hear me."

"Perhaps I could—"

"Oh, no, you don't, sister!" he interrupted her firmly. "Damned if I'll hide behind any woman's skirts! I got myself into this devilish mess, and I'll get myself out of it. Seems, the best thing is for me to clear off. People will certainly notice when we blatantly ignore each other. Less embarrassing all 'round if I leave Bath."

This was the last thing Almeria wanted; Julian had revealed a great deal more to her discerning inner eye than he could realise.

"Well, of course it won't be possible for you to ignore each other completely, as Henrietta herself must realise when she has time to consider the matter. The forms of civility must be observed. But since you've never given the impression in company of sharing anything more than a very slight acquaintance, I'm sure that no change will be noticed by anyone in our circle."

"That may be so, but what is the point of my remaining here? I've told you what I had in mind when I arrived. There's no prospect now of furthering that scheme!"

"One never knows," said Almeria cryptically. "In any event, if you're still seeking a wife, you're more likely to find one in Bath than at Aldwyn Court. There are scores of eligible young ladies here."

"Truth to tell, I'm more disinclined for marriage than ever, sister. However, there may be something in what you say. I suppose"—with a twinkle in his eye—"you have Miss Dyrham in mind?"

"Why, certainly!" laughed Almeria. "She would make the most delightful sister-in-law!"

Nevertheless, she saw that for the present he intended to remain, and this gave her hope that all might yet be well.

✥ Chapter XXII

ON THAT SAME AFTERNOON Henrietta was entertaining Anna Florey.

"Now what would you most like to do?" she asked, once the door of the seminary had closed behind them. "I'm quite at your disposal. Always provided," she added cautiously, "that you don't suggest anything *too* outrageous."

"As if I would!" Anna giggled. "But what I'd really like is to stroll about the town a little. We always go out in a crocodile, you know, and are never allowed to stop and gaze into shop windows or, indeed, to do anything in the least bit interesting! It would be such a treat to be able to look for as long as one pleases."

"Yes, by all means let us spend an hour or so in Milsom Street," replied Henrietta agreeably.

Anna hesitated, evidently having had second thoughts. "Are you quite sure you wouldn't perhaps prefer to call on one of your friends—Lady Barrington, for instance?" she suggested slyly. "She is always so kind, I don't suppose she'd object the least little bit to my accompanying you."

Henrietta smiled at this transparent attempt to engineer a meeting with Mr. Aldwyn.

"I didn't rescue you from the rigours of the schoolroom in order to plunge you into a round of social calls! Besides, Lady Barrington and I will meet this evening, at the Assembly ball."

"Oh, how lucky you are!"

"What, lucky to go to the ball, or to see Lady Barrington?"

Anna laughed. "You are a quiz, Miss Melville! Well, yes, you are lucky to be going to a ball, but you must know that when I speak of seeing Lady Barrington, I really mean—"

"Yes, well, we won't go into that at present," replied

187

Henrietta briskly. "I tell you what, Anna. How would you like to help me purchase a new bonnet?"

"Oh, of all things!" Anna looked admiringly at her companion's present headgear. "But I must say, Miss Melville, that you don't seem in need of one! Mama says one should never make personal remarks, but it does seem a shame when one only wishes to pay a compliment, and I do think yours is one of the prettiest bonnets I've ever seen! Such a heavenly shade of blue, and the feathers drooping so gracefully from the crown! I only wish"— with a heartfelt sigh—"that I might wear such a lovely bonnet!"

"Why, so you will one day soon."

"But not for ages and ages. And our school clothes are monstrous; we all detest them!"

Henrietta nodded sympathetically. "So did I and my schoolfellows. I think all schoolgirls feel the same. But cheer up, Anna. Only consider what prodigiously attractive clothes you have at home for wearing during the holidays. I recall that on the day we rode to Farleigh Hungerford castle you were sporting a dashing new riding habit, which quite put my ancient one to shame."

"Oh, did you truly like it? I do hope so. Not because I'm vain, you know, ma'am," she added hastily, "but because—well, for quite another reason."

"I'm relieved to learn that it wasn't vanity, otherwise I should feel obliged to return you at once to the seminary and recommend Miss Mynford to set you to reading improving extracts from some such volume as Fordyce's sermons."

This mock severity sent Anna off into a fit of the giggles, which drew the attention of a gentleman strolling on the other side of the road.

Recognising the pair, he crossed over and approached them.

"How d' you do, Miss Melville? And Miss—Florey, is it not? May I enquire into the source of your amusement, or is it a secret not to be entrusted to a mere male?"

It was Colby. He smiled at Anna as he put the question but although she curtseyed and returned his greeting civilly, she answered with unsmiling reserve. She had noticed on Sunday that Mr. Aldwyn seemed not to approve of this gentleman.

"Oh, it was only some nonsense, sir."

Colby quickly sensed her attitude and guessed easily enough at the reason for it, for he had kept his eyes open during their meeting on Sunday. This chit was of no consequence as far as he was concerned, but Miss Melville seemed attached to her, so he decided it might be wise to try and foster a better feeling toward himself in Miss Anna's youthful bosom.

He used his charm to thaw her out as they all three walked together in the direction of Milsom Street. Anna's reserve, never very long-lived, was not equal to his experienced assault and soon she was chattering away in her usual free, uninhibited way. Henrietta noticed his ploy with some amusement, and could not help comparing it with Mr. Aldwyn's past efforts at setting Anna at ease in his company. There was a difference, she decided. There seemed less of kindness and more of calculation in Mr. Colby's approach, but perhaps she was imagining this. In any case, she had no wish to dwell on thoughts of Mr. Aldwyn.

She allowed Anna to talk on uninterrupted, and soon Colby had learnt almost all there was to know about the regimen of Miss Mynford's Seminary and the various pranks practised by its older pupils. Several times the girl attempted to drag Aldwyn's name into the conversation, speaking of him in almost reverent tones; at such moments, when Colby would look to catch Miss Melville's eye, he noticed that she was quick to steer Anna away from this topic.

He accompanied them as far as the milliner's shop.

"And here we must part, sir," she said, smiling, "for Anna and I are about to embark on some very serious and feminine business: choosing a new bonnet."

"Ah, yes," he said, with the familiar twinkle in his eyes, "I shall certainly be *de trop* there! But I shall hope to view the article of your choice on some future occasion, even though you are unlikely to wear it to this evening's Assembly ball. I do trust you will be there, and that you will grant me the honour of the first dance?"

She gave a laughing assent, and he took his leave.

"I think, you know, Miss Melville, that Mr. Colby admires you," remarked Anna as they entered the shop. "But who could help it? For you look so delightfully nowadays. Oh, dear!" She clapped her hand over her mouth with a crestfallen expression. "Pray excuse me—I shouldn't have said that—Mama would say it was impertinent, I fear!"

"It must be a great comfort to your mama to know that you pay so much attention to her rules of conduct," said Henrietta in a teasing tone. "Now let us see what the milliner can show us."

The succeeding hour they passed most agreeably. Several delightful bonnets were brought out, exclaimed over, and examined from every angle; Anna was even permitted to try on one or two herself, posturing before the mirror and declaring that she positively adored this one or looked a frightful quiz in another. Finally, a choice was made and instructions given for its delivery.

Afterward, they discovered that there was no time to attempt anything further before returning Anna to the seminary. Accordingly, she was safely delivered to its portals, and parted from her companion with heartfelt thanks for a most enjoyable afternoon.

On her way home, Henrietta decided to look in at the Circulating Library in Milsom Street, for although she had little enough time for reading, she always liked to have a book at hand.

The library appeared deserted at present, so she was able to browse along the shelves uninterrupted. She was ensconced in a corner behind a fixture, which had been constructed at right angles to the wall, when her concentration was disturbed by voices coming from the other side of a row of books on the shelving.

She would have moved away at once, had she not immediately recognised the voices of Louisa and Colby.

"You must see that this can't go on!" Louisa exclaimed in a low, agitated tone. "You cannot possibly require more so soon!"

"Sure, Bath's a devilish expensive place," replied Colby. "But if you were to use your influence in a certain quarter, m'dear lady, I think you might find your own situation a trifle easier, now."

"I—I can't," gasped Louisa. "You ask too much. It would be a, a gross betrayal!"

"Better that, perhaps, than another kind of betrayal," he muttered grimly. "Consider that, ma'am."

There was a silence, during which Henrietta thought she could detect muted sobs. For a moment, an impulse came over her to rush round the partition and confront the pair. She fought it down, realising that Louisa might not welcome her interference.

Very quietly, she left her corner and hastened out of the library.

Once in the street, she walked along without paying the slightest heed to the press of people about her, her mind full of what she had just overheard. What could it mean? Colby had seemed to threaten Louisa. And now that she came to consider it, Henrietta realized this was not for the first time. There had been something said to Louisa on a former occasion, about memory—now what exactly had it been? Something to the effect that he was possessed of an accommodating memory, able to recall or forget at will, and that this was fortunate for some. She had thought then that he meant an underlying threat, but she had later concluded that she was reading too much into his words.

There could be no doubt, however, that the gentleman did exercise a somewhat sobering effect upon Louisa's spirits. Henrietta knew that she had not been the only person to notice this: Captain Barclay obviously did as well. But it was no use, she reflected despondently. She had done her utmost to persuade her friend to confide in her, but Louisa had resisted all these efforts. That being so, it was quite impossible for Henrietta to interfere.

When Louisa reached home some time later, she went to her room with only a brief greeting to Henrietta. Although Henrietta studied her friend's expression closely during the few moments they were together, she could see no signs of distress; and when Louisa, dressed in an amber gown of shot silk with a double flounce at the hem, eventually came downstairs, she seemed in her usual high spirits. Henrietta began to wonder if once again she had been allowing her imagination to run away with her, and her mind gradually turned to speculations about her own dilemma: in all probability, Mr. Aldwyn would be present at the ball this evening.

It would, she knew, be impossible altogether to avoid speaking to Mr. Aldwyn when they chanced to meet in company but it would obviously be an object with both of them to ensure that such meetings were infrequent. She, too, had thought of leaving Bath as a way out of the difficulty, even though to do so would involve her in manufacturing a plausible excuse for the benefit of Louisa and her other acquaintances. It was not this that persuaded her against such a course, however, but a stubborn pride. Why should she allow him to drive her away when she was enjoying herself so much? She had a suspicion that the time might come when her present diversions would pall, but for the moment she was caught up in the excitement of it all.

Nevertheless, she entered the ballroom in some apprehension and was relieved to find it so crowded that she saw nothing of Almeria's party. She and Louisa were soon surrounded by a group of friends, among them Captain Barclay and Mr. Burke. The latter greeted the ladies in his usual solemn way and proceeded to request of Henrietta the pleasure of the first dance. He looked downcast when she replied that she had already promised it.

"I am sorry, Mr. Burke. I chanced to meet Mr. Colby this afternoon in Milsom Street, and he made his request to me then."

"Then perhaps I may hope to lead you out for the second dance, Miss Melville?"

She readily assented, and he seemed mollified.

"Oh, dear," whispered Louisa in her ear, "we seem to be in some trouble with your admirers, don't we? They'll be calling each other out next!"

Henrietta pulled a face at her, which set them both laughing.

The band then struck up, and Colby came to claim his partner.

He was as amusing as ever, but this evening she found it difficult to respond. Her glance kept flickering away from him over the other dancers, a fact that did not escape his quick eye.

"And who is the lucky man for whom you are looking, Miss Melville?"

She started. "Looking? I? What do you mean, sir?"

He smiled knowingly. "Ever since we took the floor you've been searching the room for someone. Now I wonder who he can be?"

"What nonsense! I am merely looking about me a little. And even if I were looking for someone in particular, there's no reason why you should suppose it to be a gentleman."

"Is another female at all likely to arouse so much interest in any lady? But I see what it is: you are tired of

my trivial conversation and are wishing to hear some of
the worthy Burke's profound discourse instead."

She laughed, and thereafter forced herself to abandon
the search for Aldwyn that had caused her to neglect her
partner. At the conclusion of the dance, she found that
Almeria and Sir Giles had joined Louisa's group, but
there was still no sign of Aldwyn. Perhaps he had decided not to come. She was longing to put the question to
his sister, and suffered all the frustration of one who is
obliged to chat upon indifferent subjects while avoiding
the one topic uppermost in her mind.

During her dance with Mr. Burke, Henrietta at last
saw Aldwyn. He was dancing with Isabella Laverton and
paying no heed to anyone else. This was scarcely to be
wondered at, thought Henrietta, as Isabella's gown of
pale pink muslin set off her dark beauty to perfection.

She returned to Louisa's party in a sober, slightly apprehensive mood, which was not lightened by finding
Almeria and Sir Giles had rejoined the group. In a moment or two her fears were realised by the advent of
Aldwyn himself. She at once began an animated conversation with Almeria and Louisa. But the dreaded confrontation could not long be postponed. A bow, a stiff
smile, a formal greeting from each, and the thing was
done. When no one present appeared to notice any lack
of cordiality, Henrietta breathed a sigh of relief.

Determined to keep as much distance as possible between Aldwyn and herself for the remainder of the evening, she responded to a signal from Jane Dyrham to
join her apart from Louisa's group.

"You may have noticed, Miss Melville, that my dear
friend Lady Bellairs is not here this evening?" Miss
Dyrham said with calculated restraint.

Henrietta admitted that she had not.

Jane Dyrham gave a sceptical smile. "Well, I must say
I'm surprised, for her nephew has been paying you a certain amount of attention, and a female generally notices
the absence of an admirer. Or perhaps I should say," she
corrected herself, "a seeming admirer, for as matters have
turned out, it looks as if you may have been sadly de-
ceived in the young man's attentions."

Henrietta laughed. "No such thing, I assure you! Mr.
Fortescue and I have talked a deal of nonsense together,
but at no time have I ever thought him serious."

"Well, naturally you would say so, my dear, and I do not blame you for that. One has one's pride, after all. But it may surprise you to learn that the young man has quitted the town for good, this very afternoon!"

This did surprise Henrietta, as her expression showed.

"I called in upon Lady Bellairs about four o'clock to ask if she would be at the Assembly Rooms this evening," continued Miss Dyrham with scarcely a pause, "And I found her in the most dreadful passion! Indeed, had we not been such close friends, I must have taken offence. However, I hope I made allowance for the heat of the moment, and in no time I learned the cause of her vexation. She told me that she and her nephew had just had the most violent quarrel!"

"Oh, dear!" exclaimed Henrietta, with foreboding. "Why? But perhaps," she added, hastily, "you ought not to tell me anything more."

"I can't see why not, when it will be all over the town by tomorrow," replied Jane, with the confidence of one who intends to see a thing accomplished. "He told his aunt flatly that he would no longer allow her to order his life for him, that he had no intention of marrying, so there was no use in her attempting to throw females at his head"—here she gave Henrietta a malicious glance—"and in short, he flouted her authority in the most vehement way! I must say, after all she has done for him, it's the most flagrant ingratitude ever I heard of!"

"No young man of spirit would for long submit to the kind of autocratic treatment that I have seen Lady Bellairs mete out to her nephew," replied Henrietta.

"Well, there's no denying she's a woman of strong character and likes to get her own way," allowed Miss Dyrham. "But only picture to yourself the kind of scene that ensued! She storming and raging, saying that he need never expect another penny from her and that he could leave her roof instantly, and he flinging the curricle and pair in her face—not literally, of course,—telling her he wouldn't accept it, and that she might dispose of it as she wished! I had it all repeated to me, every word, for he'd only departed just before I called there. She was in a monstrous rage, I can tell you, and she intends to quit Bath tomorrow! Now, what do you think of that, Miss Melville?"

"Why, to a certain extent I am sorry for it," said Henrietta slowly, "as I believe that they are both fond of each other, in a curious kind of way. But such a breach was bound to come, and perhaps when they've both had time to cool down a little, they'll be reconciled—and with a better understanding of each other's dispositions than before. A man of three and twenty doesn't relish being treated as a boy, you know."

"Perhaps not when he's financially independent, but beggars can't be choosers, Miss Melville. However, I thought it only kind to let you know that one of your beaux"—she gave an audible sniff—"is, to use vulgar parlance, no longer in the running."

"Thank you, Miss Dyrham, but I never considered that he was. Now pray excuse me, for I see my partner is waiting for the next dance."

She stood up and went toward Sir Giles, who had been hovering in the background, evidently reluctant to break in on their conversation.

"Been regaling you with a prime piece of gossip, I dare say," he said with a laugh as he led her onto the floor.

"Oh, of course," replied Henrietta lightly. "But I won't tell you the details, for I'm sure that would spoil the lady's fun."

As they moved about the ballroom, she caught sight of Aldwyn dancing with Louisa; once she intercepted a glance from him in her direction, but it was quickly withdrawn. Now, however, her mind dwelt a little on what she had just learnt, preventing her from that uneasy concentration on Aldwyn that had previously obsessed her. Her words to Fortescue that morning must have been responsible for the quarrel between him and Lady Bellairs, but she could not repine. Some such confrontation, with or without her influence, had been inevitable before long, and she believed, as she had told Miss Dyrham, that it was all for the best.

By the time the ball ended, she had danced twice with Mr. Colby, but refused to grant him a third, and she had noticed that Aldwyn had taken out Isabella for a second time. Perhaps he was now transferring his attentions to that quarter, but it was a matter of indifference to her.

Captain Barclay handed Louisa into the carriage first,

then turned to perform the same office for Henrietta. As he did so, he surreptitiously pressed a small folded piece of paper into her hand.

"Aldwyn asked me to give you this, ma'am," he said, so quietly that Louisa could not posssibly hear. "He begs you will read it."

Chapter XXIII

HENRIETTA COULD SCARCELY WAIT to be alone so that she might read the note, which she had hastily slipped into her reticule. When she did at last reach the privacy of her bedchamber, she quickly dismissed her maid and with eager fingers unfolded the crumpled piece of paper. There were only a few lines, penned in a firm, decisive hand.

"Madam," it began in an austere way.

Since you have forbidden me to speak to you, this is my only recourse. I rely upon the generosity of your nature in trusting that you will read it. I wish to apologise sincerely for my lack of civility toward you yesterday. My intention was but to safeguard your interests, but in the heat of the moment, I fear I expressed myself in a way I cannot hope you will forgive. It is my hope that this expression of my deep regret will make it possible for us to meet in the future, if not as friends, at least with a socially acceptable degree of tolerance.

JULIAN ALDWYN

She read it again and again, through eyes dimmed with tears. At every reading, her feelings underwent a change. Her first sensation was one of relief mingled with gratitude; he did not, then, despise her, nor believe her capable of all the monstrous things of which he had accused her. He had spoken hastily and now was truly sorry and anxious to restore good relations between them. And he was properly diffident: "I cannot hope that you will forgive" he had written.

Subsequent readings brought less satisfactory reflections, however. The tone of his note was cold and stiff. Could it have been dictated merely by pride? Realising

that his behaviour had fallen short of gentlemanly propriety, was he offering an apology merely as a concession
to social form? And those final lines gave yet another in-
terpretation: they suggested that he was concerned principally with keeping up appearances within their social
circle.

After an hour's anxious perusal and cogitation over the
note, she had no idea what to make of it. At last she went
to bed in an unhappy frame of mind, deciding to seek
Louisa's opinion in the morning. Her friend would take a
more objective view.

Accordingly she handed the note to Louisa at the
breakfast table and watched closely while it was being
read.

"Why, this is capital, is it not?" said Louisa brightly,
handing back the paper. "He has made an honourable
amend and now you can both be comfortable again! Not
that I should be too quick to show forgiveness, were I
you, Hetty. He deserves some punishing."

"You talk as if he really cares whether or not I forgive
him."

"You believe he does not? But why else should he
trouble to write such a handsome apology?"

Henrietta proceeded to outline the other possible motives that had occurred to her the previous night.

Louisa looked doubtful.

"Well, there may be something in what you say," she
allowed. "After all, you know him much better than I do,
so you must be a more reliable judge of his conduct. But
to me it seems that he truly regrets having behaved so
outrageously and has done his best to express his contri-
tion. It's always difficult to do justice to one's feelings in
a letter, I find, and I dare say men may be even more in-
hibited than we would be. At all events, his apology,
whatever may be his true motives for making it, will
mean that you can meet publicly without undue awk-
wardness. And as we two are such intimate friends of his
sister, that's something to be thankful for."

Henrietta agreed, though she could not help feeling
that Louisa's final remarks gave credence to the notion
that Mr. Aldwyn was chiefly concerned with keeping up
appearances.

"Do you think I should make any reply to this?" she
asked doubtfully, taking back the note.

Louisa hesitated, then spoke decisively.

"Oh, no, you won't wish to be involved in a correspondence with the gentleman; that would be too tedious! You might perhaps mention having received his letter—just casually, you know—when next you meet."

Henrietta nodded and changed the subject. It had been a relief to confide in Louisa, for now she hoped to put the whole affair out of her mind. She only wished that her friend would be as ready to confide in her, especially after yesterday's incident with Colby in the library.

As the morning weather was mild, they decided to take a stroll to the Pump Room. For once, Captain Barclay did not join them, nor did they see him there when they arrived. Most of their other acquaintances were present, however, and it was not long before Henrietta found that Miss Dyrham had been at work, for everyone was talking of the quarrel between Fortescue and his aunt.

"This must be a sad blow to you, Henrictta," remarked Almeria with her tongue in her cheek, as she joined the group where Louisa and Henrietta were standing in conversation. "I trust you won't dwindle into a decline on his account."

"I believe I may safely promise that I shall not."

"What a pity for Jane Dyrham! She would like to have some such evidence to support the story she is spreading of your having had strong expectations in that quarter."

"Well, of all things!" protested Henrietta indignantly, drawing away from the others so that she and Almeria could be private.

"I shouldn't trouble your head over that, my dear. Everyone knows what a monstrous gossip she is. But I wouldn't be at all surprised to learn that you know rather more of the inside story of this quarrel than even Jane Dyrham does."

"Would you not?"

"I see you're determined to tease me. But I happen to know that you and Fortescue were out driving together early yesterday, and knowing my Henrietta of old—"

"Oh, did you see us?"

"No, but Julian did and told me of it. And by the way, Hetty, I trust you won't mind, but I let him into the secret of your seeming flirtation with Fortescue."

"I don't mind," replied Henrietta slowly, "but I expect he thought it a nonsensical business, as indeed it was."

"Well, yes, he did."

Almeria hesitated for a second, wondering if she should say more. Julian had made it plain that he would not thank her for interfering in his concerns; on the other hand, the temptation was very great.

"He confided to me what had passed between you before you came to Bath," she continued. "I'll not reproach you for refusing him, much as I could have wished . . . However, I understand and respect your reasons, dearest Hetty, so I'll say no more on that head. He said something, too, of a recent disagreement between you."

Anxious not to venture too far on such delicate ground, she paused and searched her friend's face. Beyond a faint flush, however, it betrayed nothing.

"I dare say you'd prefer not to speak of it," she said at last. "But I must just assure you—indeed, Hetty, I cannot be entirely silent, loving you both as I do—that he is truly sorry for having given you offence."

Henrietta was unable to answer, but she pressed Almeria's hand affectionately before they both, by common consent, moved into the group again.

Some time later, as they wandered about the room chatting to various acquaintances, Henrietta saw Aldwyn laughing with Isabella Laverton over by the fountain. She experienced a sharp pang and quickly turned away her head. Colby came up to her shortly afterward, and she greeted him rather more effusively than otherwise she might have done.

"And so our young friend Fortescue has bolted from the hand that feeds him—having bitten it, so I hear," he said lightly. "He'll be a great loss to the gaming establishment of Bath, but otherwise I believe we may manage to go on tolerably well without him. What do you say, Miss Melville?"

"Oh, for my part I shall miss him. He was always such fun," she answered lightly.

"Then we must contrive to keep you from pining, ma'am, by providing you entertainment. What do you say to a drive out into the country tomorrow? I have it on good authority that the day will be lovely."

"Is there such thing as a good authority on that subject?" she demanded, smiling.

"Well, there's *Old Moore's Almanac,* which promises no end of blessings for this particular week. And then there's the aged ostler at my hotel, who always tells the weather by his rheumatism, and swears he doesn't feel a twinge at present. Of course"—his eyes lit up with mischief—"his prognostications might possibly have been influenced by the quantity of ale he consumed at my expense last night. I must confess, however, that I have yet to consult the stars, but I'm positive that they'll prove propitious if only you'll consent to come, ma'am."

She scolded him for being nonsensical, but she did agree to go, for in spite of some misgivings about him, she always found him a most entertaining companion. She remained at his side, talking and laughing, until she suddenly noticed Julia Kennett eyeing them with a cynical expression. This made Henrietta realise that perhaps they had been too long together, so she parted from him, having arranged that she would be ready when he called for her at half past eleven on the following morning.

Henrietta found the Lavertons with Louisa's group, but to her relief, Mr. Aldwyn was not there. The relief proved short-lived, however, for soon Almeria came over, accompanied by Sir Giles and her brother, to bid good-bye. For a time, it looked as though nothing more was to pass between Henrietta and Aldwyn than the brief bow with which each had acknowledged the other as a matter of course.

An adroit movement on his part, however, brought him close enough to her side to speak without danger of being overheard.

"I learned that you received my note, Miss Melville," he said in a low tone, fixing an earnest look upon her. "Dare I hope that you were charitable enough to read it?"

She was quite unable to speak for a lump in her throat, so she merely nodded. His expression showed that he misunderstood her silence, believing her determined not to answer.

"You forbade me to speak to you again, I know, but good God, ma'am! How else can I convince you that I'm sincerely sorry? Impossible to explain oneself in a letter. If only you would grant me a few minutes alone with you . . ."

She swallowed and managed to speak, keeping her voice steady by a strong effort.

"That will not be necessary, sir. I accept your apology."

"But you can't bring yourself to forgive what I said? I understand," he replied in tones of deep mortification.

There was no time for more even had she been sufficiently in possession of her wits to think of anything to say.

She watched his retreating figure across the room and felt a wild impulse to run after him, to tell him that she forgave everything.

But such conduct was forbidden by propriety and pride alike.

Captain Barclay had decided that morning to make one of his frequent trips to Bristol. He would have liked to feel that he would be missed by Mrs. Fordyce, but knew he could not indulge himself with any such hope. That fellow Dyrham or any one of the lady's other admirers would do equally well to keep her company, he thought bitterly. The only consolation in his frustrating situation—if consolation it might be accounted—was that so far she did not appear to favour any other above himself.

The captain did not allow himself to brood over his unfortunate love affair for long. The morning sky was clear and the early October air exhilarating; his horses took him at a spanking pace along the good turnpike road, which was lined with trees slowly shedding their gold, brown, and russet leaves to make a crisp carpet for travellers afoot.

Arrived in Bristol, he left his curricle at The Bush, a hostelry in Corn Street that supplied excellent dinners, and then set out upon his accustomed leisurely tour of the docks and waterways. His heart lifted when, reaching the drawbridge, he was greeted with the nostalgic sight of tall masts all along Broad Quay. He loitered there for some time, turning a keen eye on the ships and their rigging before watching the men cranking hand cranes to lift the cargoes ashore. There were kegs of wine from France, Spain, and Portugal, sugar from the West Indies, and bales of cloth brought by coastal vessels from other parts of Britain. The kegs and bales were loaded on to horse-drawn sledges or pack horses to be conveyed to the many Bristol warehouses and to places farther afield.

When he had looked his fill at this bustling scene, he moved onward to that part of the wharf called The Grove, where there was a dock for larger ships, and here, for a while, he watched the Great Crane at work, an ingenious mechanism erected on fourteen cast-iron pillars and powered by treadmills. He fell into conversation with an officer from one of the merchantmen and eventually invited him to take a glass at the Llandoger Trow in nearby King Street, his favourite port of call in the area.

Dusk was descending as they went into the tavern, which was already crowded. They managed to find two seats in a nook not far from the door and were soon pleasantly occupied in an exchange of seafaring talk, tankards in hand.

The Llandoger was a timbered, low-ceilinged building with several small rooms opening out of each other, all dimly lit; a haze of tobacco smoke clouded the atmosphere, for several of the customers were puffing away at clay pipes. From time to time, Captain Barclay gazed incuriously about him, but on one such occasion his glance suddenly sharpened and remained fixed for a moment.

Two men were sitting in earnest conversation close together on one of the window seats at the other side of the room. The intervening space between them and himself was thronged with other customers, but intermittent movements in the crowd brought them now and again into view. In spite of the dim light and haze in the room, Barclay recognised one of the men instantly as Colby.

It was no more remarkable that Colby should have decided to pay a visit to Bristol and look in at the Llandoger Trow than it was for Captain Barclay to have done so, but anything concerning that gentleman was always a matter of interest to the captain. Whenever a gap in the crowd permitted, his eyes returned to the pair, and he soon decided that Colby was keeping some unexpected company. The man beside him was certainly not a gentleman, nor did he have the look of a seafaring man. His sharp-featured face had an unpleasantly shifty expression, and his dress was rather like that of an impecunious clerk from one of the warehouses. What could the elegant, well-turned-out Colby possibly have in common with such a man? Business, perhaps, thought the captain, but what kind of business was likely to be conducted in the taproom of the Llandoger Trow?

The captain's sharp eyes observed Colby quickly withdraw a small package from his pocket, and the second man as stealthily transfer it to his own. It was the work of a few seconds only, and no one less keenly interested than Barclay would have noticed the manoeuvre. A few moments later, he saw that Colby had risen and was shouldering his way through the crowd toward the door. The captain quickly turned his back in that direction, confident that he would escape the other man's notice.

The man to whom Colby had been talking remained in his seat for a short time after his companion had left, then, before leaving the tavern, rose to exchange a few words with the landlord. The captain cast a swift, appraising glance over him as the man passed on his way to the door. Certainly an odd business, all this.

Chapter XXIV

ON THE FOLLOWING MORNING Barclay and Aldwyn chanced to meet in Milsom Street.

"By the way, Aldwyn," said Barclay, after they had been chatting for a few minutes, "I've something to tell you I think you may find of interest. Saw a friend of yours—ours, you might say—while I was in Bristol yesterday."

"In Bristol, were you? Thought I missed you in the Pump Room. By your tone, I collect the friend you mention may have been a horse of a very different colour. Miss Dyrham, perhaps? Or Colby?"

"Your second guess scores the bull's eye. Colby it was, in the Llandoger Trow in King Street. Often go there myself for a chat with other seafaring men, but wouldn't have thought it was his touch. Especially not in such devilish odd company."

Aldway raised his brows.

"Well, always up to the mark, Colby, ain't he?" said the captain. "Not the chap to hobnob with the lower orders. But there he was with a seedy individual, tall, thin man who'd got a cast in his right eye, talking in a mighty intimate way, as if their business had some importance. Saw Colby pass the other man a packet of some kind, too; furtive about that, to my way of thinking. Seems the seedy character was known to the landlord, though, as they exchanged a few amicable words after Colby had left the tavern."

Aldwyn looked thoughtful. "Yes, that is certainly interesting, in view of what I already know about Colby."

"May be nothing in it," admitted Barclay. "I don't mind owning to an obsessive curiosity over Colby's concerns, of late. You know my reasons well enough. Thing is, I'd like to have more information about the fellow. He's too much of a dark horse for my liking."

205

"Mine, too," agreed Aldwyn emphatically. "Do you know, Barclay, I've half a mind to—well, I'll be damned!"

The exclamation escaped him at sight of a curricle proceeding along the street toward them in a press of traffic. Barclay's attention alerted, they both watched the driver of the equipage feather-edge neatly around two other vehicles so that he could let his horses out a little. This achieved, he passed by at a fair rate without noticing the two men on the pavement. His female passenger was similarly oblivious, laughing up at the driver in approval of his expertise.

"Talk of the devil!" said Barclay. "Colby and Miss Melville! Neatish pair of bays he's got there," he added approvingly.

"To hell with his bays!" exploded Aldwyn.

"Just so," agreed the captain. "Well, must be on my way. Got an appointment with my tailor. Devilish bore. I'll see you again, my dear chap. Tell you what, are you doing anything this evening?"

"Nothing of importance. My sister and Giles are spending the day with some of his relatives and will be dining there. Wanted me to accompany them, but the prospect didn't appeal."

"Don't blame you for that. Join me for dinner, then, at my place? Pot luck, you know, but I dare say you won't mind that. Shall we make it six o'clock? Earlier, if you like."

"Six will do nicely."

"Good then. Till dinner, old chap."

After the captain had gone, Aldwyn strolled aimlessly up and down the street, lost in thought. He was intrigued by what Barclay had told him. What kind of business would anyone of Colby's cut be likely to have with a down-at-heel man in a waterside tavern? Likely some kind of barter, since a package had passed between them. Like the captain, Aldwyn felt an overpowering interest in anything concerning Colby; there was something havey-cavey about that man, and the sooner his subterfuges were brought into the light of day, the better for all concerned. It was not only, he persuaded himself, that Henrietta Melville was implicated.

Suddenly his mind was made up: he would try his hand at investigating the business. He strode purposefully back to the house and ordered his curricle brought around to the door. As his sister and brother-in-law were not in, he suffered no delay beyond what was needed to change into driving clothes.

He took the road for Bristol, driving at a spanking pace, which caused his groom to cling on to the dickey seat grimly at times. Arrived in the town, he made for King Street, where he alighted and handed the ribbons to his groom with instructions to await him at the Bush hotel.

There were few customers in the Llandoger when he entered, and a quick, searching glance assured him that the man described by Barclay was not among them. This did not disappoint him, however, for he had scarcely expected such good fortune. In truth, he had entered impulsively on this venture with no clear plan of campaign, trusting to his wits to serve him should anything helpful transpire.

The landlord appeared promptly, and Aldwyn ordered a tankard of ale. He leaned against the counter as he drank, engaging the landlord in casual conversation meanwhile. After a few minutes, he decided to broach the real business of his visit.

"A friend of mine was in here yesterday evening with a man who seemed to be known to you—tall, thin individual with a cast in his right eye. Can you direct me to that person? I've a message to pass on."

The landlord's face, which was of a healthy, ruddy colour, paled slightly, and his eyes shifted uneasily to a point immediately behind Aldwyn. The latter turned his head sharply and saw that a man had approached soft-footed to his elbow. He was a head shorter than Aldwyn, but more thick set, and it crossed Aldwyn's mind that he would make a powerful adversary in a fight. He was wearing a dark coat of undistinguished cut, serviceable brown breeches, and boots. In spite of the man's ordinary appearance, however, to Aldwyn's military eye he conveyed an impression of assurance and authority.

"And what might be the nature of that message, your honour?" the stranger asked softly, so that no one but themselves could hear.

"That I will reveal to the man I am seeking," replied Aldwyn curtly.

The other nodded. "Just so. I think, sir, you and me could do with a bit of a talk. If you'll be good enough to step this way. Landlord, see to it we're not interrupted."

Aldwyn hesitated a moment before following him through into a small, empty room. Having gestured toward a bench against the far wall, the man seated himself beside Aldwyn.

"Keep an eye on the door from here," said the other. "Always put your back against the wall, take my tip. Now, sir, who might you be?"

"I might be anyone," replied Aldwyn stiffly.

The other chuckled. "Ay, well said, but you ain't, sir. You're quality—that much is easy to tell—and been a military or naval officer not so long since, I'll be bound. Also you're a bit o' a sportin' cove: good muscles, in spite o' that natty tailoring, and a handy bunch o' fives, I'd opine. But none o' that gives me your name."

"You're an observant fellow," said Aldwyn, "but can you give me any good reason why I should tell you?"

"Plenty, and never doubt that I'll know the answer, choose how. I'll also want to know why you comes in here askin' after felons," replied the man grimly.

Aldwyn's eyes glinted. "Felons, you say? You mean the individual I'm looking for is a criminal?"

The man considered him carefully for a moment. "Ay, well, mebbe you needs to ask that, and then again mebbe you doesn't. First, we'd better know who *you* are—and then who's this friend of yours who came here last night."

"You'll learn my name when I discover your authority for demanding it!" snapped Aldwyn, but already he was beginning to have an inkling of the man's identity.

The other nodded. "As you say, sir."

He eased a short, thick truncheon from his pocket, displaying the Crown stamped on its head before returning it smartly.

"Jack Trimble, sir, Bow Street Runner, and here's my warrant, too, should you be disposed to doubt my *bona fides,* as they say."

He produced a warrant card signed by the magistrate at Bow Street. Aldwyn nodded and drew out his own visiting card.

"Suspected something of the kind," he said, handing over the card.

The Runner studied it, then consulted a notebook which he took from his pocket.

"Aldwyn Court, north of Frome in Somerset," he said.

"Proprietor Lord Aldwyn—your parent, sir?—and a Justice of the Peace. Ay." He returned the notebook to his pocket, closing Aldwyn's card inside it. "And how," he continued sternly, "does it come about that the Honourable Julian Aldwyn has a friend who hobnobs with felons, eh, sir?"

"The fact is," replied Aldwyn, "he's no friend of mine, though it seemed expedient to tell the landlord so, in order to gain the information I required."

"Which is, sir?"

"The man I falsely described as a friend of mine is a gentleman who goes by the name of Colby," began Aldwyn.

Trimble cocked an eyebrow. "You have reason to suspect that's not his real identity?"

"Indeed I have, for when I encountered him previously in London, he was going under another name."

"Ah, London," said the Runner in a satisfied tone. "Tell me what you know of this cove, sir."

"Precious little. I came here today in the hope of discovering more. However, I'll put you in possession of such facts as I have. About ten days ago I came to Bath on a visit to my sister, Lady Barrington, who lives in the Circus. I found this fellow Colby had recently arrived in the town and had quickly moved into the first social circles, although no one knew anything about him. I recognised him as a man I'd been warned about when I paid a visit with some friends to a London gaming house. There was no doubt in my mind that this was the same man, though for the life of me I was unable to recall the name under which he was going at that time."

"I might just be able to assist you there, sir. But go on, please."

"Naturally, I'd no desire to see my sister and her frriends imposed upon by a wrong 'un. I issued a timely warning, but it had little effect. The fellow's plausible enough, and a great favourite with the ladies," he added with a hint of bitterness.

The Runner eyed him shrewdly and decided there was most likely a female in the case. "Yes, go on."

"A genuine friend of mine chanced to be in this tavern yesterday evening, one Captain Barclay, a naval man who resides in Bath. He noticed Colby sitting with the man I was inquiring about just now. He, too, has little trust in this Colby, so he took some interest in the pair. They seemed an ill-matched couple, yet were talking very intimately together, and at one point, a packet of some kind passed between them. They were pretty furtive about that, so the captain said when he told me of the incident."

"Just so. A smallish packet, that would be?"

"None of this seems to come as a surprise to you, Mr. Trimble," remarked Aldwyn, studying the other intently.

"No, sir, can't say as it does. So do I take it that you came here in hopes of meeting your man Colby's companion of last night and interrogating him?"

Aldwyn nodded. "Seemed a slim chance, but worth a try," he acknowledged. "Well, I've revealed to you what little I know, but so far you've given no information in return, and I strongly suspect that you've a deal to tell. You referred to Colby's companion as a felon?"

He looked inquiringly at the Runner, who gave a knowing wink.

"Name of Ned Bly. A known receiver of stolen goods; fence is what we calls 'em. He was apprehended this very morning on account of information we received from a pawnbroker."

Aldwyn whistled. "Stolen goods, b'God! Then do you mean that Colby—?"

"Suppose you describe this Colby, Mr. Aldwyn, sir. Just so's there's no slip-up, as you might say."

Aldwyn proceeded to do so, and the Runner appeared satisfied.

"Ask the public to describe anyone and ten to one it's no help at all," he commented. "But you, sir, you know how to use your eyes. You've got this cove off pat, as you might say. Slight Irish brogue, too; that tallies. Does the name Clavering mean anything to you?"

"Clavering. Yes, that's it!" exclaimed Aldwyn. "That's the name mentioned to me in London! Damned if I could ever call it to mind before, try as I would."

"There's quite a tale to our Mr. Clavering alias Colby," said Trimble thoughtfully, "and seeing as I'm satisfied about your *bona fides,* sir, and what's more you may be of some assistance to me in the pursuance of my inquiries, as they say, I'm minded to make you cognisant of it."

"I'd be devilish obliged if you would. As for any assistance, you may count on me, right enough."

"He first came to our notice when a complaint was laid

against him at Bow Street by a wealthy London merchant," began Trimble. "Seems he'd been courtin' the merchant's widowed sister; after her money, as the family was quick to see. They put a stop to it, or the silly widgeon would've wed him, so what does he do but clear out takin' her jewels with him, worth I dunno how many thousands. I was hired to track him down and recover the loot, a guinea a day and expenses. I've been on the job for a month now, so you can tell my client's well breeched, eh?"

Aldwyn nodded, too interested now to interrupt.

"Found out he'd left London by mail coach and arrived in Bristol. We've quite a number of sources for information, you know, sir: tollkeepers, inkeepers, coaching offices, and the like, not to mention petty felons and bawdyhouse women. All anxious to keep their own noses clean," he added cynically. "All the same, we lost track of him in Bristol, so I pops over to Ireland, see if he'd gone back there. He told the widow woman he came from Dublin, reckon it was the only true tale he did tell, for we caught up with his past there, all right and tight."

He went on to relate in detail Colby's nefarious adventures in his native town, concluding with an event that had made it imperative for his immediate removal to a healthier locality.

"So he left for London," went on the Runner, "and being a card-sharper by profession, he tried to get a living at it again. That's when you'll have come across him, sir. But although there's plenty o' flats in London gaming hells, there's plenty as knows their onions, too, so in the end he was rumbled and kicked out. That's when he tries his luck in the city instead of Mayfair, and uses his charm to catch himself a wealthy widow."

"Good God, I knew about the card-sharping but I'd no notion he was such an unmitigated scoundrel," exclaimed Aldwyn. "You came back to Bristol when you discovered he'd not returned to Ireland?"

"Correct. And I had news then of one of the stolen pieces being handed into pawn shortly after our man had reached Bristol from London. Bow Street sends out lists of stolen goods to the dealers, you know, but it don't always click with them—or they don't want it to. After that of course we went round warnin' them all, me and my assistant, Tom Kemp, that we must know on the in-

stant when any other item from that same little lot came
in. We also told 'em to keep tabs on whoever offered it.
Sure enough, they turns up trumps this time, and we nab
Bly with another of the pieces. Says he bought it off a
bloke in the Llandoger, and swears he don't know the
bloke from Adam. So here I am, waitin' for someone who
wants to meet Ned Bly, and in comes you."

"Naturally you took me for Colby—I mean Clavering."

"Yes and no, sir. I'd a pretty good description of our
man from the interested parties in London, and you didn't
fit: taller by a head, slimmer build, and dark hair instead
of light brown. Course, a man can dye his hair, but I
never heard tell of one who could add a cubit to his stat-
ure, as the Good Book says. What's more, you'd nay a
trace of Irish brogue. But I was interested in you, on account of you asks for Bly. Thought perhaps you might
have been sent here by the man Clavering."

"Believe me, he and I are certainly not on those terms,"
said Aldwyn grimly. "But should you wish to satisfy yourself as to my identity, I am known at The Bush in Corn
Street, where my curricle is awaiting me."

"No need for that, sir," the Runner reassured him. "But
I'll thank you to tell me where I may find the man Clavering, for he and I must have a chat."

"He's putting up at the York Hotel in Bath."

"I'll need to get a warrant sworn. You can help, sir,
since you've a speedy vehicle in the town. Convey me to
the nearest Justice and then to Bath, if you'll be so good."

"Of course." Aldwyn stood up. "Shall we take a hack
to The Bush?"

"May as well walk, it'll be as quick. I'll just tell my assistant to hang on here and keep his peepers open, just in
case. Be with you in a moment."

It was getting dusk as they drew up outside the York
Hotel. Aldwyn alighted with the Runner and waited in
the coffee room while the latter made his inquiries. It was
not long before Trimble returned, a frown on his face.

"Greatly fear our bird's flown," he said, shaking his
head. "They tell me he came in about an hour and a half
ago, then left shortly afterwards, carrying a portmanteau.
I've been up to his room though, and he's left a few
things—to disarm suspicion that he'd done a bunk, I
opine."

"What will you do now?"

"Watch here for a bit, see if he turns up. If by any chance you sets eyes on him, get word to me at once, will you, sir? I expect I'll be about somewheres; otherwise leave a message for me with the landlord. I'll tell him to look out for it."

"Wonder where he's gone?" asked Aldwyn, frowning. "I don't quite see how he could have got wind already that you were on his trail."

"No more do I, but there's no accountin' for the way information leaks through to the criminal classes. And times we're mighty glad of it ourselves, I can tell you, sir. Well, thanks for your assistance. Don't forget, tip me the wink the moment you sees our friend."

"You may be very sure that I shall," replied Aldwyn emphatically.

⚜ *Chapter XXV*

HENRIETTA HAD almost regretted her promise to drive out with Colby that morning. Shortly before he was due to call for her, she confessed her misgivings to Louisa.

"I don't feel in the least inclined to go with Mr. Colby," she said. "Do you think I could make some excuse? Or would that be too shabby?"

"It would be a trifle uncivil. But why don't you wish to drive out with him? It's a splendid morning, and you always say that you enjoy his company. Don't you feel well? I must say you *look* in the pink of health!"

"Oh yes, so I am, and I scarce think I could convince him that I'm suffering from so much as a headache. But perhaps I could make you my excuse, Louisa, for *you* do look a trifle peaky, now I came to study you closely. Would you not prefer me to stay and keep you company?"

There was a pleading note in her voice, which her friend chose to ignore.

"No such thing!" she replied lightly. "I've no intention of allowing you to sacrifice your pleasures on my account. Besides, I have planned several things for today, knowing I should be on my own. I intend to do some shopping, then call on the Lavertons."

"Oh, very well," said Henrietta in a flat tone. "If there are things you wish to do, that's splendid."

"You didn't answer my question, though," persisted Louisa. "Why do you not wish to drive out with Mr. Colby?"

Henrietta shrugged. "I'm not perfectly certain of the reason myself. A general disinclination is all I can find. Although," she added slowly, "lately my feelings toward him are become somewhat contradictory. When we are together, I do enjoy his company; he's quite the most entertaining person of my acquaintance. But when we're apart, I must admit to some doubts."

"Doubts? What kind of doubts?" Louisa asked sharply. "If it's what Mr. Aldwyn said to you, I shouldn't refine too much upon that. There could be some mistake, you know."

"I suppose there might, but something that Fortescue also said to me did make me wonder."

"Did he make accusations against Mr. Colby? You never told me this before."

"Oh, no, not accusations. Indeed, I don't believe that any such thought had crossed his mind. But he made some remarks about Mr. Colby's extraordinary luck at cards that suggested to me, perhaps quite wrongly, that there might be more than luck in the matter."

"I'll tell you what I think, Hetty. Have you never noticed how it is that whenever one is told of some particular fault—or virtue, for that matter—in another person, one is forever looking out for it afterward? It's no more than prejudice. Take my advice and forget it, my dear! You admit that you find pleasure in Mr. Colby's company, so enjoy it and put away your suspicions."

All this seemed reasonable enough, and since Henrietta could not bring herself to mention what she had overheard between Colby and Louisa in the library, she said no more.

Indeed, after sitting beside him in the curricle for ten minutes or so, she forgot her misgivings. He was in a particularly entertaining mood, relating amusing anecdotes about their mutual acquaintances, spiced with touches of mimicry, for which he had quite a gift.

"What a loss to the stage you are, Mr. Colby!" she exclaimed, laughing. "You must have kissed the Blarney stone while you were in Ireland, I vow!"

He turned an incredulous look on her, his eyes sparkling with mischief.

"Sure, ma'am, and no Irishman worthy of the name would ever kiss anything as cold as a stone! How can you suppose it? Warm red lips, now—ah, that's another matter!"

His impudent, laughing gaze rested for a moment on her own mouth, and she turned away, colouring slightly.

But the next moment he was giving a spirited rendering of a conversation between Miss Dyrham and Captain Barclay that he had overheard in the Pump Room.

"The poor man was doing his best to escape from the lady," he chuckled. "He looked this way and that, like a cornered animal, and kept answering in short gasps: 'Just so, ma'am,' and 'Indeed, ma'am?' I felt in charity bound to draw off her fire myself, for which I earned the only kindly look I can ever recall receiving from that quarter."

Henrietta laughed. "Oh, that is exactly right! I've heard similar exchanges between those two, time and again!"

"She must be of a prodigiously optimistic disposition, for anyone can see that the only lady who interests Barclay is Mrs. Fordyce," remarked Colby in a more serious tone. "Well, perhaps he will win her in the end."

Henrietta shook her head. "Louisa says she will never marry again."

"Indeed?" His tone was noncommital.

"Do you know why, Mr. Colby?" she asked impulsively. "Was her first marriage unhappy?"

He made no reply, and at that juncture on the narrow lane they were following, they caught up with a farm wagon, which he passed with only inches to spare.

"Oh, that was splendidly done!" exclaimed Henrietta, forgetting her question in sudden admiration of his expertise. "How I wish I could drive like that!"

"Do you drive, then, Miss Melville?"

"Why, yes, I drive a gig sometimes at home, but I've never taken out anything more dashing! I did once ask my brother if I might try with his curricle, but my sister-in-law said she thought it would be unbecoming in a lady. Of course, she may simply have feared that I would put the vehicle in a ditch!" she added, chuckling.

"Sure, and you shall try now," he said promptly.

"Oh, may I?" Her eyes sparkled. "But are you quite sure? I may perhaps do some damage to your vehicle, as I've never handled a pair before. And these are blood horses."

"Pooh, this is only a hired vehicle," he said disparagingly. "One more scratch on it would never be noticed, I assure you. I've carriages of my own at home, but when I'm travelling about, I must perforce hire. Come, let us change places, and I'll show you how to go on. I'm sure you'll prove an apt pupil."

He summoned the groom with a gesture of his head, and the man leapt down to come to the horses' heads while the exchange of seats was made.

Full of inner qualms, Henrietta took up the reins. Colby at once leaned toward her, placing his hands over hers to guide her movements. His close proximity made her feel a little breathless and confused, so that at first she did not manage at all well, and the vehicle wandered from side to side in a way that made the groom lift expressive eyes heavenward. Colby seemed not at all perturbed, smiling at her encouragingly and issuing instructions in a lazy, relaxed tone.

It was not long before her performance improved sufficiently for him to remove his hands from hers. He still sat close to her, however, ready to intervene should it prove necessary. She was now able to maintain a straight course, keeping the horses at a gentle trot. She turned a triumphant, smiling face to him.

"There! I'm beginning to master it, am I not? Though I fear it will be a very long time before I attain quite to your standard!"

"You must drive out with me every day, and then you'll soon be handling the ribbons in style," he promised her. "Just around this bend we shall come out onto the turnpike road. Do you feel competent to meet the traffic, or shall I take over?"

Although pleased with her progress, she did not care to meet the challenge of a busy road just yet, so she readily yielded the reins to him. While changing places, he put an arm around her to assist her into the seat, and he patted her hand encouragingly before taking up the reins himself. She did not relish this as much as she might have done earlier in their acquaintance; he was still personable and charming, but her feelings had subtly changed.

They had driven only a short distance along the turnpike road when they came to an inn. There he turned into the courtyard and reined in his horses.

"After your recent exertions, perhaps some refreshment would be welcome, ma'am," he said, smiling. "I understand the coffee is tolerable here."

Henrietta was not at all sure that she wished to be seen

alone with a gentleman in a public inn, but she told herself that such qualms were ridiculous in a mature female. Moreover, a cup of coffee would be most welcome. She allowed him to lead her inside, and was relieved to see that, although it was by no means crowded, they were not to have it to themselves. An elderly lady and gentleman were already seated at a small table by the window. They looked up briefly as the newcomers entered, but showed no curiosity and were fortunately quite unknown to Henrietta.

Colby settled her at a table on the other side of the room and made his wants known to a stout, dour-looking waiter. The coffee was brought to them, together with some small cakes, which both found very appetising. Altogether, it was a pleasant interlude with Colby at his most amusing, and when they finally left the inn, Henrietta was in a happy, relaxed frame of mind.

This lasted until they had once more mounted into the curricle, which had been brought round from the stables by an ostler instead of Colby's groom. Colby gathered up the reins and prepared to start the horses.

"But where is your groom?" asked Henrietta. "Shall we not wait for him?"

"I've given him the afternoon off," Colby replied casually. "The fellow has some relatives living in this village, and I said he might visit them."

Henrietta felt disconcerted. "Oh," she answered in a flat tone of voice.

He gave her a mischievous glance. "You don't mind, surely? Are you anxious for your reputation if you drive the five miles back to Bath with only myself for escort? I can't believe that the Miss Melville I know would be so missish, at all, at all!"

She smiled reluctantly, remembering how she had once considered herself past the age for troubling about those excessive constraints that were proper in a young girl. Why should she think differently now? She told herself she was being absurd.

Her confidence returned as Colby tooled his horses at a smart rate along the busy turnpike road, keeping up a flow of light banter that frequently set her laughing. Presently, he turned off into a quiet byroad and eased his horses to a gentler pace.

"Have I told you how very charmingly you look to-day?" he asked, looking earnestly into her eyes. "Today and all days. To me you always appear more lovely, more desirable than any other woman."

Under his gaze she blushed and turned her head away.

"No mere compliment, my dear Miss Melville," he went on, "but a sincere expression of my feelings."

"I wish you will not," she protested, embarrassed.

"Ah, but I must," he insisted in a voice of tightly controlled emotion. "How can I be with you almost every day and never yield to the overwhelming impulse to tell you how much—how very much!—I admire and love you! It was so from the first, Henrietta: from the moment we met, I knew that you were the only woman in the world for me!"

He took the reins into one hand while with the other he caught and held one of hers. She tried to draw away, but his hold tightened.

"You *shall* hear me! I've been silent too long; flesh and blood can stand only so much! And I can't believe that you're entirely indifferent to me either, my dearest."

"Pray don't make so free with my name and these endearments, sir!" she said in a frigid voice. "You are not behaving as a gentleman should."

"I'm behaving as any man of spirit will who wishes to tell a lady of his love!" he retorted passionately. "Do you misunderstand me, I wonder? Can that be it? I offer you no insult, Henrietta, but an honourable proposal of marriage. Say that you'll accept me, my dear, dearest girl!"

She succeeded in drawing her hand from his at last, and moved hastily away from him into her own corner of the seat. Her heart was beating furiously with apprehension. Why had she allowed herself to become placed in such an awkward situation? She should have refused to drive home with him unless the groom accompanied them. No doubt he had planned it all from the start. Could she believe in his protestations of love, or had Mr. Aldwyn been right when he had said that the man was only after her fortune? Whatever his feelings might be, she thought feverishly, at least she was certain of her own.

"Come, Henrietta, won't you answer me?" His tone was coaxing now. "You can't be so cruel as to keep me in suspense! One word now, only one! And I'll be the happiest man alive!"

Swallowing resolutely, she took a grip on her confused thoughts and emotions. Something must be said, and that quickly.

"I fear you won't, sir, because the word is not what you wish to hear. I am very conscious of the honour you do me in making your proposals—"

"Bah! Such sad stuff is not for us, my beloved! Speak from your heart!"

He leaned toward her and slid his free arm about her waist, pulling her closer.

"Very well, I will!" she exclaimed angrily, doing her best to thrust him away. "I do not return your affection and have no intention of marrying you!"

"But that's nonsense! It must be!" he insisted. "Can you pretend that you haven't been attracted to me from the first, just as I have to you? Haven't we laughed together, danced together, driven out together until all the gossips of Bath have been coupling our names?"

She felt her cheeks flush. "It's true that we've had some pleasant times together," she conceded. "But that kind of entertaining companionship is very different from—from being in love."

"How so? If only I hadn't to keep an eye on these confounded animals, I'd soon show you there isn't any difference at all! Sure, if I could but take you in my arms, I'll wager you'd realise that you're as madly in love with me as I am with you!"

In his eagerness, he took his attention from the horses for a moment and tried to grasp her with his driving arm. Resenting the sudden jerk on their mouths, the animals reared, and he was forced to bring both hands to the task of controlling them again. Meanwhile Henrietta, hoping fervently that they would not be overturned, clung tenaciously to the side of the curricle.

He was an experienced whip, however, and soon had matters in control again.

"If you don't love me, then I can only conclude that you're the most shameless flirt it's ever been my misfortune to meet!" he snapped, scowling at her. "But I see what it is: you think Burke will be a better catch."

"How fortunate that you understand me so well!" Her

tone was mocking, but inwardly she was now very angry.

"You mean you're not after him? Well, I can't see why you should be, as it can be no object with you to marry money; you've plenty of your own. And he has nothing else to tempt you, such as a title."

"What a prodigiously flattering notion you have of my character, Mr. Colby. And pray how do you know that I have a fortune? I don't recall ever having mentioned that to you."

"Anyone who consorts with the Dyrham female may know the circumstances and history of anyone in Bath," he retorted. "I'd not been in her company five minutes before I knew everything about you."

"And yet," she said in a sarcastic tone, "you seem to have succeeded in guarding your own past from her searching scrutiny, if not quite from that of others."

His glance sharpened. "What the devil do you mean by that? Has Louisa Fordyce been blabbing some trumped-up story to you? If so, b'God, she'll live to regret it!"

"All that Louisa has ever told me about you is that you have a reputation as a womaniser."

He laughed unpleasantly. "That doesn't seem to have put you off. You've been oncoming enough."

Her eyes flashed. "The rest of my information came from another source. And I only wish I'd heeded it!"

"What information? What source?" he snapped.

"If you must know, from Mr. Aldwyn. He saw you some months ago in a London gaming house and was warned that you're an undesirable character. At that time you were known by a name other than Colby."

This seemed to upset him to an alarming degree. His face paled under its tan and took on a murderous expression. Suddenly he whipped up the horses into a gallop, setting the curricle rocking from side to side. Henrietta involuntarily let out a scream of fright and clung grimly to the side of the vehicle with both hands, convinced that he intended to throw her out into the ditch.

His wild progress continued until they came to the village of Weston, where he was forced to pull up because a wagon loaded with farm produce was blocking most of the narrow street. He swore roundly.

Henrietta came to a quick decision.

"Put me down here!" she commanded breathlessly. "I'm going no farther in your company."

He glared at her. "As you like, damn you!"

He pulled up and watched maliciously as she dismounted without any assistance. A few moments after she had reached the ground, the wagon turned off the road into a farm, and she saw Colby drive off in headlong style with never a backward glance.

Thankful to be rid of him, she took the road home. To one of her country habits, the walk of a mile and a half was no hardship; indeed, had she been in a mood to appreciate it, she would have enjoyed the jaunt. But the anger and disillusionment that seethed within her made her oblivious of her surroundings. Mr. Aldwyn had been right about her friendship with Colby, and she had been wrong. She ought to have been warned by her own increasing doubts, instead of persisting in seeing the man and so bringing on herself a most unpleasant experience. She shivered as she recalled that last mad gallop, that had almost thrown her overboard, and the hatred in his eyes when she had left him. Yet how could she have realised that so charming and entertaining a man would behave in such a fashion? Not only was he a rogue, he was a dangerous rogue, and she felt lucky to have escaped so lightly.

When she reached home, she was still in a state of agitation. Louisa was at the parlour window, anxiously looking out for her. As soon as she was admitted by the footman, her friend ran out into the hall and embraced her fervently.

"Oh, Hetty! I've been so anxious! You're so much later than I expected! I didn't know what to think—an accident, or something frightful! Thank God you're safe!"

"I'm sorry, Louisa, but I was delayed," replied Henrietta as calmly as she could manage. "Let us go into the parlour, and I'll tell you all about it."

They walked in and shut the door. Henrietta removed her gloves and bonnet, then sank gratefully into a chair.

"What is it, Hetty? Something has occurred, I can tell," said Louisa, with troubled eyes searching her friend's face.

"I've received a proposal of marriage from Mr. Colby, Louisa. And in such fashion!"

Louisa turned deathly pale. "Marriage?" she repeated in a shocked whisper. "Oh, no! No, Hetty"—her voice rose, and a distracted look came into her eyes—"you shan't marry that—that villain! I don't care if I have to ruin my life to save you. Save you I shall! He knows my my secret, and he's been blackmailing me ever since he came here, but I don't care anymore, so long as I can save you from him!"

❧ Chapter XXVI

HENRIETTA STARED in amazement. *"Blackmailing* you? What on earth can you mean? What secret?"

"Oh, I might have known it was no use," said Louisa despondently. "Once he had arrived in Bath, it could only be a matter of time before the mischief was out! I purchased his silence with money and—oh, I can't possibly tell you what else. I'm too ashamed to think I could ever have even considered such a thing!"

Henrietta looked grave. "Louisa, my dear, can you possibly mean that you consented to, to become his mistress?"

"No. *No!"* replied Louisa in tones of revulsion. "It was not I he desired, but *you,* Hetty. And your fortune. Nothing matters so much as money to Clavering. That's the name I knew him by in Ireland, though whether it's his real name—"

She broke off and shrugged.

"Part of his price was that I should use my influence to try and persuade you into marriage with him. He wanted it all settled speedily for fear that your brother might interfere. He was always set on schemes that he hoped would enrich him quickly, and when they turned out badly, he'd be forced to flee—as no doubt he fled from London. But as much as he tried to force me, Hetty, I could not so far forget our friendship as to positively *urge* you into marrying him. I—I tried to make light of your doubts concerning him and to recommend him to you as far as I could force myself to do so. But all the while I was reproaching myself bitterly for the betrayal of such a dear, dear friend!" Her voice broke. "But what was I to do, faced with such a dire alternative? I have nearly gone mad over the past few weeks! At least now I can comfort myself now with the thought that, though all is over for me, I've had the courage to save you from a fate similar to my own! You will not wish to marry him after hearing just what manner of man he is!"

"Let me reassure you on that point, my love. I never had the faintest intention of marrying Colby, or whatever his name is, and I told him so in no uncertain terms this afternoon."

Relief flooded Louisa's face. "Oh, I was so afraid that you were falling in love with him!"

"I'll admit to being captivated by him at first," confessed Henrietta. "He certainly knows how to use his charm to good effect, and just when I needed the reassurance that a man's admiration gives to a female. But, although I didn't realise it at that time, there were reasons why my heart was never in danger. But no more of that," she added purposefully. "You've said too much now, Louisa, not to confide to me the whole. What is the secret that placed you in this horrible man's power? I've known for so long that there was something troubling you, and often wished I could win your confidence so that I might try to help."

"No one can help," replied Louisa in despair. "But I'll tell you; indeed, it won't be long before everyone in Bath knows. Clavering will wreak his spite by betraying me; I know him too well to expect otherwise."

"Your true friends will stand by you, dearest, you may count on that."

"They can do nothing in such a case. I've been living a lie, Hetty, while I've been in Bath. I'm not a widow. My husband is alive in Ireland. I ran away from him, hoping he would never find me again. Then Clavering came, and now—and now—"

She broke down completely. Henrietta, after a moment of astonished immobility, gathered her into a comforting embrace.

For some time there was no sound in the room but that of Louisa's racking sobs. Henrietta, recovering from the first shock of her friend's confession, was beginning to understand much that had previously puzzled her, but there was still a great deal to be explained. Finally Louisa became calmer.

"Tell me all about it, dear, right from the beginning," Henrietta said gently. "No doubt you've been keeping everything cooped up inside you for months, perhaps years."

Louisa heaved a deep sigh. "I would like you to know just how it was, so that you won't judge me too harshly, Hetty. You see, I was so much in love with Lucius, my husband, once. It seems a long while ago and almost in another world. We had not been settled in Harrogate, Mama and I, above a year when he came there on a visit from Ireland. I know now that he came to catch a rich wife," she added bitterly, "but no such thoughts troubled me then, and I had neither father nor brother to protect my interests. He was just such another as Clavering, handsome and charming enough to turn any girl's head—especially one such as I, for you know, Hetty, I was always lighthearted in those days, and not very prudent."

Henrietta smiled affectionately. "So you were, my love, and even now you're not so completely changed, thank goodness."

"I was not when you first came to Bath. But let me tell you about the early days of my marriage. As soon as the wedding was over we left for Ireland, and Lucius took me to his house in Dublin. It was situated in one of the best parts of the town, and as luxuriously appointed as any bride could wish. I did not realise until long afterward that none of it was paid for, that it had been made ready by Clavering, acting on my husband's behalf, to receive me after the wedding."

"You mean that it was not your husband's own home, but one he had recently acquired in the town?"

"Exactly so. I doubt if he ever had a home in the sense that you and I understand it, although he must have lived somewhere or other as a child, I suppose. He never spoke of any family, and I never questioned him. Whatever his origins, he had managed to acquire at least the outward marks of a gentleman—sufficient to impose upon a silly girl such as I was then. For the first few months of our marriage, I was radiantly happy! He plunged me into a whirl of pleasure such as I had never experienced before —balls, dinner parties, picnic outings, visits to the races. And of course he wagered heavily, though I never troubled my head over that. I was too enchanted with it all! He was most attentive and never left me alone for a moment, for I truly think he was just a little in love with me at that period of our marriage"—her voice wavered for a moment, then strengthened as she continued—"as well as being after my fortune. But that I never suspected until later."

"Did you have any company beside that of your husband? Female friends of your own, I mean?"

Louisa shook her head. "Most of Lucius's acquaintances were bachelors, although they were usually accompanied by rather dashing, smart females, who were congenial enough but not the kind with whom I would wish to make friends. Even in the early days, I often thought longingly of you and Almeria. I did wonder a little, too, that Lucius appeared not to be at all acquainted with our nearby neighbours, but drew his companions from other, less reputable quarters of the town. But when one is in love, one shrugs off suspicion. For those first few months of our marriage, we went on famously, and I was as happy as I'd ever been in my life. Then things changed."

She paused, lost in her unhappy thoughts.

"Circumstances, do you mean?" prompted Henrietta. "Or did your husband change toward you?"

"Both. I didn't realise it at that time, but he was rapidly running through my fortune. This fact made him decide to turn once more to his former way of making a living." Her voice was full of scorn. "I discovered later that he and Clavering, both accomplished card-sharpers, had always lived by their wits. They decided to set up a gaming house of their own, in a less select part of the town, naturally, using what remained of my dowry. From then onward my husband had less time to spare for me. But I think what finally detached his interest was the news —only imagine, I thought it exciting!—that I was breeding."

"Oh, my poor love!" exclaimed Henrietta. "So far from your mama and friends, and with an unsympathetic husband."

"One couldn't expect a man of his stamp to welcome a family," put in Louisa in a hard, brittle voice. "He suggested various remedies for my situation, all of which I opposed vehemently. That was when my disenchantment began—and I'd been married only four months! I don't know how long I could have continued to withstand his wishes, enforced by ill-temper and even an occasional blow"— Henrietta winced. "—but nature came to my

aid, quite unsupported by any act of mine. I suffered a
miscarriage."

She glanced at her friend, then quickly away again, for
Henrietta's eyes were brimming with tears.

"I was ill for quite a time after that, and poor company
for a husband, so he sought out other females for consolation. When I recovered, he had the brilliant notion of
forcing me to act the role of hostess at his gaming house.
I had no choice. I had married him, and I was his to treat
as he would until death did us part. Clavering was most
always present in our household. He treated me with indifference, as a person of no consequence. I preferred
that to being made the object of his attentions, as were
many of the females who visited our establishment from
time to time. Both he and my husband had always a mistress in tow; I cannot recall how many, nor what were
their names. I soon ceased to make any protest, for my
feelings had dried up, my former love for Lucius had
been replaced by something akin to hatred. I even found
it hard to pity the foolish young men who nightly gamed
away their fortunes at my husband's tables. So many went
to ruin and misery."

Henrietta wiped her eyes. "Did you write and tell your
mama of all this?" she asked.

"No. Would you have done so in my place? She was
separated from me by many miles and had grown increasingly frail since my father's death. I wrote to her, of
course, but I forced myself to keep my letters in a cheerful
vein. I have sometimes since wondered if I ought not to
set up as a lady novelist, for those letters were the purest
fiction! The only realistic note was when Lucius sometimes
compelled me to ask Mama to assist us with money. I always told her that it was a loan, and managed to make it
sound as though our embarrassments were temporary. I've
reason to think now that she saw through all this subter-
fuge. I didn't see Mama again while she was alive, as you
already know; but my Aunt told me Mama suspected misfortune in my life. I suppose it's not easy to deceive someone who knows you so thoroughly, but what could she
have done? He was my husband; no one could interfere
between us."

"When did you decide to run away, and how did you
manage it?"

"I thought of it often—often! But where else could I go

but back to Mama? And apart from upsetting her in her
poor state of health, he would know where to find me and
would have fetched me back. I was too useful as a source
of funds for him to let me go. Then news came that Mama
was seriously ill and asking for me. I pleaded with him to
allow me to visit her. He was not opposed to this, for of
course we both realised that in all probability it was a ter-
minal illness"—here Louisa's voice faltered for a moment
—"and he knew I was her sole heir. What made him hesi-
tate was the fact that he couldn't accompany me at that
juncture, since Clavering was absent on one of his nefarious money-making schemes, and there was no one else
whom he could leave in charge of the gaming house. With
an inheritance at stake, Lucius would have preferred not
to trust matters to me," concluded Louisa bitterly.

"He must indeed be a monster!" exclaimed Henrietta.
"Oh, my poor love! But I collect you did manage to persuade him to allow you to go in the end."

"Do you know how I went to work on him, Henrietta?
You'll never credit how guileful I was, nor how much I
despised myself for the deception I was forced to practise.
He didn't know Mama's disposition—how gentle, how loving she was, how she would have given me her all at any
time—"

Her voice choked with emotion and she was obliged to
break off for a while. Presently she resumed in the same
hard, bitter tone as before.

"He judged everyone to be as hateful as he was. So
when I said that Mama, if I did not answer her summons
and go at once to Harrogate, might change her will and
leave everything to my aunt, he was quite convinced that
there was a real danger of losing the inheritance. He allowed me to go alone, without so much as a servant to attend me. Fortunately, my experiences since marriage have
made me more self-reliant than most gently bred females."

Henrietta nodded. "I can well understand that. And afterward, after the funeral, how did you contrive? Since
you didn't return to Ireland, I suppose your huband must
eventually have followed you to Harrogate."

"I've often puzzled over that point since. Lucius did
not follow me, although I received a letter from him during the time I remained at my aunt's house, in which he
announced his intention of joining me as soon as Claver-

ing had returned to Dublin. That letter finally made up my mind, Hetty! I was now possessed of a considerable fortune, and I was determined that my worthless husband should never get his hands on it. I ran away in earnest. I went to a remote village in the Dales, and there hid away for four months. No one knew where I was, not even my aunt, though she would never have willingly betrayed me to Lucius. I could not afford to take the risk of his persuading her by force."

"She must have been most anxious for you."

"We did finally communicate," replied Louisa. "That is how I knew my husband had never come seeking me in Harrogate, nor written to me again."

"It is certainly odd that he did not," mused Henrietta.

Louisa shrugged. "I've learnt simply to accept it thankfully and not to seek reasons. After five months had elapsed since my leaving Dublin, and there was still no word of him, I began to feel safe. Can you imagine what it was like, Hetty, after months of anxiety, at last to be able to feel tolerably secure? By that time, I was heartily sick of my solitary confinement in the country; you know I am not a lover of rural pursuits, and I was longing for a dash of town life! And so I took a house in Bath, not so far from the place that had been my childhood home. I'd already been passing myself off as a widow in the Dales, and Bath is just the place for widows!"

Her voice was more lively now, and for the first time, she laughed.

"So I came here in June, and was soon settled in and as nearly content as I might be. I had almost forgotten all the misery of the past, for you know I am not one to dwell on gloomy thoughts, and I'd resolutely put by all my fears of discovery. There was only one circumstance that marred my new-found peace of mind. And that"—she gave a deep sigh—"can never be removed, alas."

"I know," said Henrietta softly. "Captain Barclay."

Louisa nodded, her cheeks colouring.

"Is it so obvious?" she asked with a catch in her voice.

"Not to anyone but myself, I assure you. And I was watching you very closely on the only occasion when you gave any sign. It was at one of the concerts, when they played that sonata of Beethoven's with the sweet, rippling notes—you know the one."

"Yes, I do know." She paused a moment, then went on.

"It's not a young girl's infatuation, such as I felt for Lucius, but a deep, sincere, mature love founded on respect and trust. He's so much everything that a man should be: kind and considerate, yet firm in principle, modest, perhaps too modest to feel that he has any chance with me! Hetty, if only you knew what it might mean to me to find security at last in such a man's affection! But talking pays no toll," she finished. "There can never be anything between us. I am married, and nothing can remove that obstacle."

Henrietta was silent, unable to offer any consolation beyond an affectionate pressure of her hand on Louisa's shoulder.

"Many things are clear to me now, my love," she said after an interval. "I always wondered why you were so insistent that you would never marry again, especially after I'd guessed that you cared so for the captain. And there were several incidents I never understood, which now I can comprehend. You seemed upset after meeting Colby that morning in the rain, when he and Fortescue escorted me to your carriage. Tell me, Louisa, was it he who sent you the note that you received later that day?" she asked.

"Yes, it was. Of course, I was expecting to hear from him after that encounter, and I knew he would find some way to turn my situation to the best advantage for himself. Therein lay my only hope, after the dreadful shock of finding him in Bath! If I could but buy his silence . . . It was the one glimmer of light! His note suggested a meeting for that same evening, and I kept the rendezvous."

"I already know of that," said Henrietta quietly. "I saw you leave the house, and I followed you. It was perhaps not an honourable thing to have done, but I was so concerned for you, Louisa. You seemed quite unlike yourself, and I thought you shouldn't be out alone in that state of mind."

Louisa stared. "You followed me? Did you see me meet Clavering, then?"

"I saw you with someone but couldn't recognise that person, although I knew it was a man. It came over me suddenly that I ought not to be spying on you, and that if you chose to meet a gentleman clandestinely it was none of my business, so I slipped away before you could discover me."

"I see. Well, at that meeting we came to an agreement. I was to keep silence about his concerns and in return— and for a fee, besides!—he would not betray me to my husband. He started by asking me if I'd heard anything from Lucius since I'd left Dublin, and seemed gratified in some odd way when I told him there'd been no news since that first letter. I asked him if he knew the reason, but he didn't answer, and I have never since been able to extract any explanation from him. I was past caring, however, so long as he would promise to keep my secret. I knew, of course, that I could depend on his silence only as long as it suited his fancy. That was why I had to agree to help him, once he had formed the intention of marrying you. You do see that, don't you, dearest Hetty? I hope you can find it in your heart to excuse me a little, for in the end I couldn't bring myself to the ultimate betrayal."

"Of course I forgive you. What else could you do, my poor love? And what can you do now, I wonder?"

They embraced each other, both shedding tears. Presently Louisa disengaged herself, a resolute look on her face.

"I must run away again, perhaps somewhere much farther off. The Continent, somewhere overseas," she said determinedly. "It will be a while before Lucius can arrive here, for first Clavering will need to inform him of my whereabouts. That should give me time enough to make my arrangements and disappear completely."

"Oh, no!" exclaimed Henrietta in dismay. "There must be some other way than exile, alone and friendless! Are you quite certain that Colby will inform your husband? I should have thought that a man of his cupidity would prefer to keep your secret so that he could continue to extort payment for doing so."

"You don't know his vile temper. He'll do anything to pay me out for your refusal, which he'll attribute principally to me. Besides, he knows well that when Lucius gains control of my inheritance, he himself will benefit. Those two have always worked together and shared the spoils, though why they should do so is a mystery to me. They are both ready enough to cheat everyone else! Of course, if he could have succeeded in marrying you, he might have agreed to keep my secret. But now he must realise that I'll have told you of his villainy, and this will make it difficult for him to remain in Bath. Moreover, he's finding the town too expensive for his purse, even with the contributions to it I have been forced to make. No, I fear I cannot at all rely on his silence any longer. And you must see, Hetty, that even if he did agree to stay here and say nothing, my own situation would now be intolerable. I always knew that there must come a time when I couldn't continue with matters as they stood, but I was at my wits' end to know what else to do!"

She pressed her hands to her face in a distracted gesture.

"That's not to be wondered at," replied Henrietta in a gloomy tone. "It's a dreadful dilemma."

She brooded for a few moments, then suddenly brightened.

"I tell you what, my love, it needs a man's experience of the world to grapple with this affair and try conclusions with Colby! We are no match for such as he! I wonder, now; Captain Barclay would do anything to serve you. Could you not—"

"Oh, no!" exclaimed Louisa. "Of all men, I could not approach him! Besides, what if he were to call out Clavering? It would involve him in the most monstrous scandal! No, far better that he should never see or hear from me again, than that I should bring disgrace upon him!"

Henrietta nodded.

"I understand your feelings. Then what about Sir Giles? If you were to confide in Almeria, she could ask his advice. And I'm sure you won't object to taking Almeria into your confidence, for haven't we all three shared our secrets since we were girls together? Let us go to her now, Louisa, for I'm sure there's no time to be lost."

"Well, if you think it will be of any use, I shall seek advice from Sir Giles, though I've little hope that anyone can see a way out of my particular difficulty. Lucius is my legally wedded spouse, and nothing can alter that."

"Still, one never knows," said Henrietta in a rallying tone. "As I said before, gentlemen have more experience in dealing with rogues." She glanced at the clock. "Shall we go to Almeria's now? It's close on five, and we should find her at home at this hour."

Louisa agreed, and had the carriage brought from the stables in readiness. She was about to go and put on her outdoor attire, but she paused irresolutely with one hand on the doorknob.

"You'll think me craven, I know, Hetty, and so I am, but I positively dread facing Almeria. Our girlhood scrapes were one thing, but this—the shock will be severe! Do you think I could explain it first in a letter, so that she has time to recover a little before she and her husband come to discuss matters with me? I wouldn't then find it so difficult to talk to them."

"Of course I understand, dear. The strongest spirit would quail before such a task," said Henrietta gently. "But a letter would also present difficulties, I think. I have a much better notion," she went on, energetically. "Why do not I go alone to explain it all to Almeria? Then, after she has informed her husband, they can both accompany me back here to consult with you. I'm sure once they know how desperate is your plight, they'll be ready to come immediately."

Louisa thanked her with tears of gratitude, and Henrietta at once set out on her errand.

✒ Chapter XXVII

HAVING PARTED from the Runner Trimble at the York Hotel, Aldwyn drove home and went straight up to his room to change from his buckskins and Hessians into something more suitable for his evening engagement with Barclay. It was just after five o'clock. His invitation had been for six, but Barclay had said that he might go earlier if he chose. No point in delaying for another half hour, he thought, especially since there was a good deal to impart to the captain.

He had just taken up his hat and cane and was on the way to the street door when the knocker sounded. The butler, always alert, moved smoothly past Aldwyn to answer its summons; opening the door, he revealed a lady, quite unaccompanied, standing on the step. She was immediately invited to enter. But when she began to enquire urgently for Lady Barrington, he shook his head.

"I regret, madam, that Sir Giles and milady are from home," he replied.

"Oh, dear, how unfortunate! When do you expect them back?" she asked anxiously.

It passed through the butler's mind that it was not his place to know the exact time when he might expect his employer's return, but he suppressed this, answering instead that he could not be certain, but he thought they might be rather late.

"Oh, dear!" exclaimed the lady again, evidently perturbed.

The butler was about to mention that Mr. Aldwyn was at home, when that gentleman himself came forward.

"Miss Melville." He bowed. "You wished to see my sister on a matter of some urgency? Perhaps I could deliver a message for you. Be pleased to step in here, ma'am."

He opened a door leading off the hall. After a moment's hesitation, Henrietta entered the room and Aldwyn followed, closing the door behind him.

"Pray be seated, ma'am."

Henrietta took the nearest chair, perching uneasily on its edge. She did not quite know what to do. She had been confident of seeing Almeria.

Something of her trouble showed in her face and was not missed by Aldwyn's keen eyes.

"You are in some kind of difficulty, Miss Melville, I believe," he said quietly. "My sister's absence has evidently put you out. Is there any way at all in which I may serve you in her place? Assure you, I am only too willing."

His kind tone, so very different from the one in which he had addressed her at their last meeting alone together, brought tears to her eyes. He saw this, too, and with difficulty restrained himself from taking her hand in a comforting clasp.

"You are very good," she said, faltering a little, "but I think I must not trouble you. Perhaps the delay may not matter as greatly as I fear."

"Delay in communicating some news to Almeria, do you mean, ma'am?" he asked swiftly. "May I inquire if it's of importance to her or to yourself?"

"To neither of us directly, but only as friends of Mrs. Fordyce. It concerns her. Louisa urgently wished to consult Almeria—I should more correctly say Sir Giles, for it is a matter in which she requires a gentleman to advise, rather than another female. But since neither your sister nor her husband are here—"

"If Barrington would have served your purpose, why not myself?" he demanded with a reassuring smile. "I'm here on the spot and more than willing to assist in any way possible. I've no wish to brag, of course, but I think I may safely promise to accomplish whatever it was you were about to ask of my brother-in-law."

She considered for a moment. It was quite true that Sir Giles would be no better able to advise than Mr. Aldwyn in such a seemingly hopeless situation, and at least the latter was already aware of Colby's dubious character. She could not think that Louisa would raise any objection to admitting the brother as well as the sister into her confidence. But how on earth should she begin the story? The recent quarrel between Julian Aldwyn and herself did not make matters any easier; she naturally still felt some constraint with him.

He attributed her hesitation to this latter cause and hastened to do his best to reassure her.

"I understand how you must be feeling, ma'am," he said in a diffident tone. "Your recent experiences with me cannot have encouraged you to place me in the role of confidant. But if for the moment you will forget—though you cannot forgive—my transgressions, and allow me the privilege of rendering you some assistance by way of expiation, I will do my utmost on your behalf, assure you. Or on Mrs. Fordyce's," he added.

"It's not that," she replied hurriedly. "Our—disagreement is quite swallowed up in my present distress on my friend's account. Yes, I do think you might be able to help quite as well as Sir Giles, though indeed I fear that the business is past anyone's help."

"Tell me exactly what is the trouble," he urged, leaning forward in his chair and fixing a gaze of keen concentration on her anxious face.

"I hardly know where to begin," she confessed with a helpless little shrug. "Mrs. Fordyce has just made the most astounding revelations to me! And she is in such distress that I cannot think she would object to my repeating the story to you in your sister's stead. After all, it may soon become common knowledge if the worst ensues."

"You may rely absolutely on my discretion, but I trust you'll realise that."

"Indeed I do, though discretion may be impossible," she replied despondently. "First I must tell you that Mr. Colby plays some part in this affair."

His face hardened. "Colby? You don't surprise me! I've learnt a good deal more about that villain today than I knew formerly, and all of it bad! His real name's Clavering, and the Runners are after him. I talked to one of them about him at some length only a few hours since."

"The Runners?" she gasped. "Do you mean the Bow Street Runners? Oh, you must tell me everything you know at once. This may mean a reprieve for my poor Louisa!"

His eyebrows shot up at this remark, but he decided to let it pass for the moment.

"Willingly, ma'am."

He proceeded to explain the circumstances that had led

to his meeting with Trimble in the Llandoger Trow, and
to give her an account of their conversation. She listened
without any interruption beyond an occasional involuntary
exclamation, but at the conclusion she looked downcast.

"You think he has gone for good?" she asked anxiously.

"That was the conviction the Runner had, and he must
be experienced in such matters. He said Colby had left a
few personal items of no value lying about the hotel room,
doubtless in order to give the impression that he'd be returning. He hadn't paid his shot, so the landlord re-
ported."

"Oh, dear, then I fear my friend's case is desperate indeed." Her lip trembled, and she was obliged to bite it
hard. "He'll most likely be bound for Ireland again and
will betray Louisa's whereabouts. He has been blackmailing her ever since he arrived in Bath."

"The damned scoundrel! I beg your pardon, ma'am, but
only oaths can do justice to that fellow! I think perhaps
you'd better now tell me the nature of Mrs. Fordyce's secret. Has she"—he paused, wishing to put this as delicately as possible—"has she perhaps become unwittingly
involved in some of the nefarious schemes that her husband and Colby put into execution? They were two of a
kind, by what I heard! Poor lady, I pity her sincerely,
whatever she may have done."

"No, she has never taken part in any of their frauds,
except to the extent of acting as hostess at their gaming
house in Dublin, and that was forced upon her by her
brute of a husband. No, Louisa's only fault—if fault it
can be called, when her married life was such a misery!—
was to run away from her husband and pass herself off as
a widow. She came here in January to attend her mother's deathbed alone, for her husband couldn't leave Dublin at that time, owing to Colby's absence. Colby and Mr.
Fordyce were partners in a gaming house." She repeated
the details of Louisa's story, ending with Clavering's part
in the matter. "He knew the truth about her and extorted
money to keep her secret."

Aldwyn leapt to his feet with fists clenched.

"If I could only lay hands on that"—he substituted a
more seemly word for the one that first sprang to his lips
—"that unmitigated scoundrel, I'd choke the life out of
him! He was practising the most damnable deception on

Mrs. Fordyce in order to blackmail her, for there was no secret to keep—at least, no one to whom he could betray that unfortunate lady. Her husband was dead by then; she was in very truth a widow."

"Louisa's husband *dead?*" Henrietta repeated his words dazedly. "Are you quite positive, Mr. Aldwyn? There can't be some mistake?"

"None. I had that information together with the rest from the Runner. He gave me chapter and verse, for when they were searching for Colby after his flight from London, they made a full investigation in Dublin, thinking he might have returned there. They discovered that Colby had been at the gaming house early in February when a brawl took place in which his partner Fordyce was shot dead by some infuriated youngster who had been fleeced by the pair. Naturally the law was brought in, and Colby fled to London to escape reprisals. It appears," he added grimly, "he spends most of his time on the run. It seems odd that no one should have informed Mrs. Fordyce of her husband's death."

Henrietta shook her head. "No, because no one but Colby would know where she had gone. There were no relatives on her husband's side, moreover, and she had made no friends. Who would be likely to take the trouble to trace her? It's not as though there would be an inheritance in the case; I expect her husband left nothing but debts."

He nodded. "So I was informed."

Henrietta had so far been too astounded by his news to realise the full importance of it, but now she leapt excitedly to her feet, her face alight.

"Oh, I must go at once to Louisa and tell her the good news! I suppose," she added more soberly, "it's a dreadful thing that one should view a man's death so joyously, but if indeed you knew how she has suffered!"

"I can well imagine, tied to such a man. Yes, you will wish to return to her at once. Did you come here in a carriage, Miss Melville?"

She nodded. "It's waiting outside. I told the coachman to walk the horses up and down a little."

He rang the bell, and directed that a servant should be sent out to summon the coach to the door.

"I'm bound for Pulteney Street myself, to dine with Barclay," he said. "I had intended to walk, but I'm a trifle late for that, now. Would you have any objection, ma'am—"

She broke in before he could frame his request, a happy smile on her face.

"Why, of course you must share my carriage! I haven't yet thanked you, Mr. Aldwyn, for your kindness in listening to me, but I certainly do so now. Oh, if only I could have known what a weight would be lifted from my shoulders, and all through your agency! Of all things, it is the most wonderful!"

"I'm happy to have been the means of bringing you relief, though such a small service scarcely warrants thanks," he replied as he escorted her to the street door.

He handed her into the waiting carriage and stepped in after her.

"Should Mrs. Fordyce require further details of this affair," he said as the vehicle moved away, "you will know where to find me."

"You are very good," she replied warmly.

He said no more for a while, but studied her covertly by the soft light of the street lamps. He thought how lovely she was, how loyal in friendship, this, the only woman he would ever desire for his wife. He had guarded his heart so rigorously against this emotion that flooded his being. And now only an iron control could prevent him from expressing his feelings to her in fervent words. He never doubted that this control was essential after all that had previously passed between them, how could his addresses be other than unwelcome to her now?

He did not speak again until they were crossing over Pulteney Bridge; Henrietta had likewise been silent.

"I shall of course tell Barclay what I've discovered today concerning Colby," Aldwyn said at last. "He put me on the trail, so he's entitled to know. Do you consider that Mrs. Fordyce would prefer me to withhold that part of the story that most nearly concerns her? I promised you my discretion, and I'll not go back on my word. I imagine, though, that you'd have no objection to my sister knowing, since you intended originally to confide in her."

"Oh, yes, certainly you may tell Almeria. Louisa would eventually do so herself, I know, especially since the outcome is so much brighter than we had feared! As to Captain Barclay—do you know," she said impetuously, "I believe Louisa would like him to be told, though I'm cer-

tain she would shrink from saying anything herself. She
has a special regard for him. Oh dear, that was indiscreet
of me, but at present I feel so lighthearted, my tongue
runs away with me, I fear!"

"Has she so?" Aldwyn smiled. "How difficult it is for a
mere male to fathom the workings of the female mind!
But she had good reason, of course, to dissemble any interest she may have felt. That barrier is now removed.
Shall I join you in being indiscreet, and tell you that
Barclay . . . But perhaps you've already divined the poor
fellow's secret. Ladies are so very expert in such matters."

"I think half Bath must know of it!" said Henrietta with
an attractive little chuckle. "Don't you agree, sir, that it
would be a pity for two such delightful people to remain
apart, when their friends might contrive a little to bring
them together? Now, if you were to relate Louisa's history
to Captain Barclay—"

She broke off, turning a face alight with mischief toward him. He caught his breath, resisting with difficulty a
strong impulse to seize her in his arms.

"What incurable matchmakers you females are!" he
exclaimed in as light a tone as he could manage. "But I'm
exactly of your opinion, so I'll tell Barclay the whole. It
won't be easy to encourage him, for he's a devilish modest
chap, but I'll do my possible!"

She burst out laughing, and after a moment he joined
in. Just then the carriage pulled up outside Louisa's house.

"I fear we're a pair of wicked conspirators, sir! But
how impossible it seemed when I set out from here less
than an hour since, that I would come back laughing!"

"If I were a philosopher," remarked Aldwyn as he assisted her to alight, "I might find some suitably profound
comment. As it is, I can think only of trite sayings, so I'll
spare you. Good night, ma'am, and I trust your friend's
heart will soon be as light as yours."

As he plied the knocker on the captain's door, he reflected that amidst all this rejoicing he seemed to be the
only one with no reason to be happy.

❦ *Chapter XXVIII*

FOR A TIME after Henrietta had left him, Colby's temper continued at white heat. Having passed through the village, he tooled his curricle along at a rate that it was ill constructed to endure, even if constant hirings had not undermined its original condition. His thoughts were bitter. He had been so sure of the Melville female, damn her! She had seemed to prefer him far above the other men who paid her attentions. It was a thousand pities that he had been obliged to hurry the business on and pop the question so soon; perhaps another few weeks would have taken the trick. Impossible to delay longer, however. Bath was a damnably expensive place, and he had been disappointed in the sums received for the jewels he had so far managed to trade. Louisa Fordyce's extorted contributions had helped a little, but he needed much larger funds to continue to keep up his part in style. He had lost another source of income, too, when that young whelp Fortescue had left town. No use playing off his tricks on men of the stamp of Hinton-Wellow and Kennett; they were downy birds who would soon rumble him.

It began to look as though he would be well advised to quit Bath without more delay, and not only for financial reasons. If his dubious dealings in the London gaming houses were known to Aldwyn, that gentleman might soon make it his business to convey the information to others beside Henrietta Melville. It was damnably bad luck that Aldwyn should have come lately from London. Yes, on the whole there seemed nothing for him now but to clear out and make a fresh start elsewhere, but the question was where? Spas were useful places for meeting rich widows of mature years who would be particularly susceptible to his brand of whimsical Irish charm. Tunbridge Wells, perhaps?

belonged to a less privileged social class and possessed the caution of her kind.

"I only wondered, Miss," she said haltingly, "that letter not bein' in Miss Melville's writing, which I knows from the letter of reference she give me for Miss Mynford when I first comes 'ere."

"Isn't it Miss Melville's handwriting? I hadn't noticed. Anyway, what does that signify?" asked Anna, sweeping the objection aside. "I dare say she was too busy to pen it herself, so asked someone else to do it for her. Now pray, don't waste any more time, Matty, or I shall never get changed in time for dinner!"

Matty obediently repeated the instructions she had earlier received from Mr. Colby. A carriage was to be waiting in the square at eight o'clock, the hour at which all the pupils retired to their dormitories. Matty was to smuggle Anna out by way of the servants' staircase and the side gate. Anna would be brought back to the seminary promptly at a quarter to ten, when Matty must be ready and waiting to conduct her by the same route to the dormitory, so that she might be safely in bed when Miss Mynford made her final room check.

"She won't notice my absence at half past eight when she comes to see that our bedside candles are out," said Anna thoughtfully. "The dorm will be in darkness, and she only peeps round the door. But I'll have to confide in the others, as they'll know I've slipped off somewhere. Yes, and then, you know, they can do something to help. Put a bolster in my bed and cover it up so that it looks as if I'm there," she added with a giggle. "Minnie never looks properly, but still, it's just as well to be prepared."

There was no time for any further discussion, as already most of the young ladies were dressed and starting to brush their hair. Matty left the dormitory, while Anna, with more haste than care, flung off her daytime attire and scrambled into her muslin.

"And just what have you been whispering about to Matty?" demanded one of her schoolfellows. "Some mischief, I'll be bound!"

"Why, yes, it is," admitted Anna cheerfully. "Come here, all of you, and I'll tell you a famous secret! But I mustn't speak too loud, so come close."

ing nothing that might at some time be turned to his advantage.

His ill temper disappeared in a flash, and a wide grin spread over his face as he began to elaborate a plan. It would require the assistance of Mick Byrne and his doxy, and also of the housemaid at the seminary. Now what the devil had the brat's name been? Molly, Mary—Matty, that was it, Matty! And she came from the Melvilles' village, as Henrietta had explained on their way home. Do anything for Miss Melville, most like, and Anna Florey had said that Matty was a sound ally in any of the pupils' escapades.

Yes, the plan seemed plausible, and it would kill two birds with one stone, he thought maliciously. No doubt that Henrietta Melville was very fond of the Florey chit, so he would pay her out nicely for turning him down and thereby forcing him to quit Bath.

Matty had for some time been awaiting a suitable opportunity for a quiet word with Miss Anna, but it did not arise until five o'clock when the young ladies went up to the dormitory to change into their evening white muslins.

Quickly drawing Anna apart from the others, Matty handed her a letter.

"From Miss Melville, Miss," she whispered urgently. "That gent Mr. Colby brought it, who came 'ere with her once. You'd best read it quick, Miss, as you and me's got things to talk over."

Thrilled immediately by this scent of mystery, Anna unfolded the note and skimmed hurriedly through its contents, then turned a radiant face toward the maid.

"Oh, Matty, what famous news! A fête at Kelston Park with fireworks! And Mr. Aldwyn to be present, as well as Miss Melville! No time to apply for permission to Minnie, she says; just as well, for I'd never obtain it, not for an *evening* outing! Miss Melville says you know all about the arrangements. Tell me quickly, please. Oh, I'm so excited, I can scarce draw breath!"

"Yes, I will, but—but you're sure it's all right, Miss Anna?"

"All right? Of course it is! It may take some contriving to slip out without being detected, but that only makes it more fun!" declared Anna rapturously.

Matty was much the same age as Anna Florey, but she

One thing was certain, he dared not return to either London or Dublin. It was useful that he possessed a handy bolt hole in Bristol where he could find lodging for short spells. Mick Byrne and that shrew who might or might not be his wife had been useful allies in the past and would help him again as long as their rewards were commensurate with their trouble. It was they who had put him onto Ned Bly; though he now considered that he might have made a better bargain elsewhere. Had Byrne taken an extra cut from Bly in addition to what had already been agreed, or had Bly himself done all the milking? No end to the frauds that could be perpetuated when one was forced to employ agents.

Fordyce and he had agreed long ago that the best way to ensure an effortless life of luxury was to marry a wealthy woman. Fordyce had done quite well at it. Even if his bride had come to him with only a moderate dowry, as she was the only offspring of a wealthy mother in failing health, expectations of her were considerable. No male relatives to put a rub in the way, either. Bad luck that Fordyce had got himself killed just as he was about to reap the full harvest. Colby wondered idly how long it would be before Louisa Fordyce learnt the truth; perhaps never, as no one in Dublin would be interested enough to inform her, and she would certainly keep away from Ireland. It seemed a pity that he had to abandon this lucrative sideline, but he had an instinct for trouble, and that meant moving on. His main object must still be to make a wealthy marriage. The difficulty was that he would need considerable funds to set himself up in another town in the proper style to rub shoulders with the right company. If he could find a really profitable market for the rest of the jewels, now . . .

At this moment he was passing by Queen Square and chanced to observe the tail end of a crocodile of young ladies returning to Miss Mynford's Seminary. At once his fertile mind was struck by a new idea. He remembered the day when he had met Henrietta Melville and the Florey girl in Milsom Street. The chit had run on endlessly about all the details of her daily routine at the Seminary. He had automatically stored the information away in his mind, not because he then expected that it would ever be useful, but because of a lifetime habit of overlook-

They all gathered round while Anna explained what was afoot.

"Oooh, Anna, you are lucky!" exclaimed Sylvia. "No one ever offers to take me on exciting outings!"

"Are you sure you ought to go?" asked Caroline Bovill anxiously, for Anna was her particular friend and Caroline well knew the other girl's impetuous nature. "There'd be a frightful fuss if you were found out!"

"I must say," remarked Charlotte Brisbane disdainfully, "that it seems a little odd for an older lady to suggest a clandestine expedition of the kind. My married sister would never for one moment entertain such a shocking notion!"

"She must be as stuffy as you are then!" retorted Anna hotly. "I know what it is: you're jealous, all of you! And I *am* going, so you may say what you like. I dare say I'll manage very well without your assistance—that's to say, so long as you're not mean enough to give me away."

There was a general outcry at this; whatever their feelings might be about the wisdom of the escapade, no one would dream of informing on her. Caroline and another of the girls at once promised to put a bolster in Anna's bed, and other offers to help were eagerly made. Charlotte contented herself with reminding the others sharply that if they did not make haste with this foolishness, and present themselves in the dining room, they would all be in serious trouble. Recognising the wisdom of this warning, they hastened to complete their toilet and were ready to go downstairs as soon as the first note of the dinner bell sounded.

Anna's appetite was usually as hearty as that of anyone present at the senior girls' table; but tonight she ate little, feeling replete with excitement, and thus earned an unwonted reprimand from the mistress in charge.

She suffered agonies of suspense when the girls repaired to the drawing room for their nightly recreation of board games, music, and conversation. When at last they were dismissed to the dormitory, she headed the procession up the stairs instead of being, as usual, one of the dawdlers at the tail.

Once in the dormitory, she quickly slipped out of her muslin and into the more serviceable daytime gown, changed her light slippers for half boots, and took out a dark, hooded cloak. By which time Matty had breathlessly arrived, bringing the good news that all was clear on the backstairs and in the kitchen through which they would need to pass. After a brief exchange in excited whispers with her schoolfellows, Anna quickly followed the maid from the room.

Her heart was beating fast with excitement and apprehension as they tiptoed down the servants' staircase, through the dim, deserted kitchen, and out into the kitchen gardens. On this unknown terrain in the darkness of the moonless night, Anna clung closely to her guide. There was only one bad moment, when they disturbed a marauding cat that scuttled across their path, causing Anna to let out a startled, hastily stifled cry. At last they reached the side gate; Matty opened it stealthily, and they emerged into the square.

A hackney carriage was drawn up and waiting. The door of the vehicle was opened at once, and a gentleman alighted; they saw that it was Mr. Colby, who beckoned to them imperatively. They went toward him, and he held out his hand to assist Anna into the coach.

Almost bursting with pent-up excitement, she started to enter; then paused with one foot on the step, disconcerted at seeing that there was no one inside.

"Miss Melville; where is she?" she asked in a whisper.

"She was obliged to leave earlier with Mr. Aldwyn and a party of other friends, but she sends her apologies and hopes you'll allow me to escort you to Kelston in her stead. It's only a few miles, but there's no time to lose, so jump in, there's a good girl."

Anna allowed few social scruples to deter her when in the middle of a splendid adventure, but her mama's oft-repeated precepts had not entirely fallen on barren ground, and it did now just cross her mind that perhaps she ought not to travel even a few miles unchaperoned in the company of a gentleman.

"But, but I thought she would be here," she protested feebly. "Do you think . . . Perhaps we ought to take Matty with us?"

"Then how will you get in again, do you suppose?" he demanded, concealing under a charming smile his impatience to be gone. "No, you need a helper from inside the building; they'll lock up soon, I dare say. But pray hurry, or else the fireworks will have started, and you wouldn't want to miss that part of the fun."

"Indeed not!" Anna agreed. "Let's go at once!"

She jumped into the carriage without further objection. After all, Mr. Colby was a particular friend of Miss Melville's, and if she had sent him, it must be all right. As her caution disappeared, her excitement returned in full force. In a little while, she would be in the company of another gentleman—one she found infinitely preferable to Mr. Colby. And only to think that all the while she was enjoying this most famous adventure, her schoolfellows would be lying tamely in bed!

But Matty, as she watched the carriage move off, was beset by qualms. It had not struck her as odd when the gentleman had been explaining what he wished her to do, for she was not a quick-witted girl and he was very persuasive; but now on reflection it did seem an unusual way for Miss Melville to behave. Had Miss Melville herself been waiting in the hackney, Matty would have passed by the unconventional manner of this outing, even though it did strike her as odd. But Miss Melville's absence was not as readily accepted. Gentlefolk were always so careful of their young ladies, making sure that they were properly chaperoned and the like. Would Miss Melville have thought it right that Miss Anna should travel alone in a carriage with a gentleman she scarcely knew? And after dark, at that. Would she have arranged such a thing? And if she would not, then what was going on, and what ought she, Matty, to do about it?

Only one thing occurred to her: to go to the house where Miss Melville was staying and assure herself that everything was what it seemed to be. For a moment she shrank at the thought; the servants would be too high and mighty to talk to such as her, and most likely they would not permit her to see their mistress either. Her pinched little face set in an obstinate line. She would force her way in, if need be. Miss Melville had been a benefactress not only to her but to all her family, and she should not find Matty behind-hand in doing her duty.

✥ *Chapter XXIX*

LOUISA AT FIRST greeted Henrietta's news with bemused incredulity. She found no difficulty at all in believing that Colby had a Bow Street Runner on his trail, and she declared that the scheme that had brought this about was typical of the man's wicked plots. But that Lucius Fordyce was dead and she herself made a widow in fact seemed to be more than she dared to credit. She made Henrietta repeat again and again the exact words Mr. Aldwyn used to retell this part of his account; and even at the third recital, still fearing there might be some error she could only shake her head.

"I assure you there is not," insisted Henrietta in firm tones. "Mr. Aldwyn is not at all the kind of gentleman to mistake what is said to him, nor yet is a Bow Street officer likely to be in error over the facts of an official investigation. Let me explain matters once more to you, Louisa. The Runners traced Colby to Bristol when he left London with the jewels, but searched in vain for him there. They then thought he might have returned to Dublin—he'd let drop that he came from Dublin to that poor female he was trying to trap into marriage—so they pursued inquiries of him there. It was then that his association with Lucius Fordyce came to light. The local legal authorities knew Fordyce had been killed in a gaming house brawl during February, and Colby had disappeared from Dublin soon after in order to avoid the stir it caused. All this was authenticated by and vouched for by the Bow Street officer, so there can be no mistake, I assure you. But if you'd prefer to have Mr. Aldwyn's account at first hand, he kindly undertook to place himself at your disposal. I mentioned that he's next door, dining with the captain. Shall we request him to step round?"

"Oh, goodness, no, I wouldn't wish to disturb them!" exclaimed Louisa quickly. "It's not that I don't think you've told me precisely what you heard, my dear, it's simply that I just can't believe, after all I've suffered, that at last I am free! Perhaps it is shameful, but indeed I cannot mourn for my husband. The man I loved died in my eyes long ago. Since that time, my marriage has been a mockery."

"Now you have nothing left to do but forget the past," said Henrietta encouragingly, "and start a new life without the shadow of a guilty secret hanging over you. I expect Colby will soon be found and taken into custody, so that will be an end of his machinations, thank goodness. What an evil man he must be. Mr. Aldwyn was enraged when I told him what Colby had done to you. I think he would have dearly liked to get his hands on the rogue!"

"How did you go on with Mr. Aldwyn?" asked Louisa curiously, for she was at last beginning to recover from her shock. "I haven't had wits enough until now to think about it, but you must have found it most embarrassing to be obliged to confide my troubles to him."

Henrietta coloured. "I was so full of your need for help, I didn't have time to feel embarrassment on my own account. Moreover, he was so kind, so understanding, that in the end we were almost restored to the old footing, and were even able to share a mild jest together!"

"I'm glad that you've made up your quarrel. Well, as you say, Hetty, I must put aside the past and look to the future. Have you further considered coming to live with me permanently? I believe it would answer splendidly for both of us."

Henrietta shook her head. "I'm not so certain of that. You may soon have other plans."

"Why, what can you mean?"

"If you *will* play the innocent! I mean that there is now no reason why you and the captain should not make a match of it. You have already confided to me what your own wishes are, if you recall."

Louisa turned a glowing face toward her.

"Yes, but that's not to say that his will be the same. He's so much everything that a female could possibly desire, that I'm sure he could have anyone for the asking!"

"You're doing it too brown, my love," answered Henrietta with a chuckle. "Possibly he could have anyone, but *you* are the only woman he desires. Mr. Aldwyn agrees, and half Bath is aware of it!"

"Oh, so you've been discussing the relationship between the captain and myself with Mr. Aldwyn, have you? A nice thing, I must say!"

"It merely came up in passing," said Henrietta mendaciously. "But gracious, look at the time! Dinner will be on the table in twenty minutes, and I've scarce had a chance to tidy myself all day, so rackety has it been!"

During dinner, Louisa's spirits gradually rose until she was once more the carefree companion she had been prior to Colby's arrival in Bath. Henrietta felt lighthearted herself in consequence. They laughed and talked of all the things they would do during the coming week, including a plan to hold a rout party, which Louisa had suggested when Henrietta first came to Bath.

"I hadn't the heart for junketings at all," Louisa confessed, "and was hard put to it to keep appearances at the Assembly balls and other social functions we've attended recently. But now it shall all go as I planned originally when you came to stay. We'll have such fun, you shall see! And maybe we can find a more dashing suitor for you than poor Mr. Burke, who seems, by the way, to have withdrawn a trifle of late. Have you been snubbing him, Hetty?"

"I fancy he's had second thoughts, if, indeed, he ever did think seriously of me."

"No doubt of that. Almeria declared she'd never seen him so much *épris!*"

"At all events, I don't return his regard, so it's as well he's got the better of his inclination. I think, you know, that he's the kind of gentleman who would be happiest in the bachelor state."

"That may be, but you aren't the sort of female who ought to remain a spinster," declared Louisa emphatically. "So I warn you, my love, that I am about to embark upon a most determined campaign of matchmaking on your behalf!"

"A waste of time, I assure you."

"Fustian! You are not so impervious to the appeal of the opposite sex, I know! Very well, I'll not tease you over your flirtations of the past; one of those at least you'll be glad to forget. But there are better fish in the sea. What do you say to Roderick Dyrham, for instance?"

Henrietta laughed. "That he's likely to be wearing the willow for you for a very long time, poor man!"

"Well, Mr. Aldwyn, then? He proposed to you once and might do so again with a little encouragement. Yes, and now I come to think of it, those demonstrations of pique that led to your quarrel might well have been the result of jealousy. I did suggest it at the time, though you pooh-poohed the notion."

"I beg you won't talk such nonsense," said Henrietta with a little constraint. "Or, since I see you must because you are feeling in high spirits, pray choose another subject."

"I vow I'm beginning to wonder," said Louisa with a mischievous twinkle in her eye, "if you have not a particular reason of your own—"

She broke off as a knock came on the door, and her footman entered, looking a trifle flustered.

"Beg pardon, madam," he said deferentially, "but there's a young person in the hall who insists on seeing Miss Melville. I told her it wasn't for the likes of her to interrupt ladies at their dinner, but I couldn't get rid of the wench no how. Pushed her way in, she did— Well, I'll be danged!"

The last exclamation was forced out of him as a small, dishevelled figure erupted into the room.

"Now look here, you!" he growled, starting to lay hands on the intruder.

"No, leave her be," Henrietta commanded quickly. "Matty! Have you taken leave of your senses? What does this mean?"

"Beg pardon, Miss Melville, but I've got to talk to you!" gabbled Matty in a scarcely intelligible voice.

She had run all the way from Queen Square, and her altercation with the footman had almost exhausted what little breath was left to her.

"Very well, so you shall," said Henrietta in soothing tones. "But first you had best sit down for a moment to recover your breath."

Louisa rose from the table and dismissed the footman, who showed a tendency to linger and satisfy his curiosity. Matty obediently collapsed into a chair and waited until she could speak more clearly.

"Once I knowed you was here instead of where he said you'd be, I had to tell you at once, ma'am! I don't know what's goin' on, but something's not right, and you'll know what's to be done!"

It was scarcely surprising that neither of the ladies could make head nor tail of this speech. They looked at each other with puzzled frowns.

"Of whom are you speaking Matty, when you say 'he'?" asked Henrietta, pouncing unerringly on the most significant word.

Her tone was patient and encouraging; for she could sense that the girl was extremely worried, and any impatience in dealing with her would render her even more incoherent.

"Mr. Colby, Miss Melville! He said you were at, at— I can't remember the name of the place, but it's in the letter, and I've got that, 'cos Miss Anna put it down, an' I picked it up for fear one o' the teachers might find it."

Henrietta's face turned pale. *"Mr. Colby!* And Anna! Matty, tell me the whole, from the beginning, at once! And you'd best give me this letter if you have it with you."

In a few moments, Matty had explained the situation. Henrietta seized the letter and read it in mounting horror. Louisa read it over her shoulder.

"Good God!" exclaimed Louisa faintly. "He's abducted Anna Florey! Is there no end to his villainy? Hetty, what's to be done?"

Henrietta valiantly forced down her fears and tried to bring her wits to bear on the crisis.

"They must be pursued at once. The Bow Street Runner, Louisa! He's in the town! Mr. Aldwyn—we must send for Mr. Aldwyn immediately!"

Louisa nodded and moved to the bell; when the footman appeared, she charged him with an urgent message to the house next door. Henrietta turned to Matty, who, at the mention of abduction, burst into tears.

"I wouldn't never 'ave helped her, Miss Melville, if I 'adn't thought as you wished it! And I'd 'ave gone with 'er in the coach; she suggested it, but that Mr. Colby said no, as she couldn't get back into the school without me there, which was all nonsense, as he never intended she should come back. And what's more, I've got the back door key and the key to the gate in my pocket, so we could've got back in any time we liked, no trouble at all!

Oh, ma'am, what's to become o' me an' poor Miss Anna
if you can't rescue 'er from 'is clutches?"

"Calm yourself, Matty. We *shall* rescue her. You've
both been very foolish, but never mind that now. You'd
best stay here for the moment. Go down to the kitchen,
the footman will show you the way, and I dare say Cook
will give you a hot drink to help calm you. Stay there until I send for you."

Matty obediently departed, snivelling.

"You don't think he means to force that poor child into
marriage?" asked Henrietta shakily.

"No, not for a moment," said Louisa reassuringly.
"Clavering would never wed anyone who wasn't in possession of a fortune. No, older females are his quarry.
Depend upon it, he means to hold Anna for ransom. He
mentioned to me lately that he had reliable accomplices
in Bristol with whom he stayed before coming to Bath. I
expect he'll take her there—or try to, at all events.
Hetty, I dare say this plan struck him as a means of paying you out, as well as putting him in funds. I told you
he's a malicious monster."

Aldwyn arrived quickly. When he heard what had
happened he characteristically wasted no time on unes-
sentials.

"He's had almost twenty minutes start," he said, glancing at the clock. "What kind of vehicle has he; how many
horses?"

"Matty said it was only a hackney," replied Henrietta,
already feeling better now that he was in charge.

"That can't set much of a pace. You say he's making
for Kelston, on the upper road to Bristol. Can we depend
on that?"

Louisa quickly explained her reasons for thinking that
Colby's real objective was Bristol.

He nodded. "Seems probable. We'll try the upper road
first, since he named Kelston. I'll need you to come along,
ma'am"—this to Henrietta—"so that you can take
care of the girl when we catch them. And we shall, never
fear. I'll pick up the Runner on our way. That means
taking a coach to accommodate the three of us."

"Shall I send round to the stables for mine?" asked
Louisa, moving toward the bell.

"No, I'll borrow Barclay's light travelling carriage and

four of his prime steppers, no trouble about that. I'll be off and see to it, if you'll make yourself ready, Miss Melville. Bring anything you think the girl may need."

Less than ten minutes later, Captain Barclay's coach went racing through the town, pausing for only a few minutes at the York Hotel to take up the Runner, complete with pistol and handcuffs ready to lay his man by the heels. Then the coach swept onward to the Bristol road, the hoofbeats of its powerful horses shattering the silence of the night.

Inside, Henrietta sat tense and anxious, wondering how Anna was faring, and praying that they would succeed in overtaking Colby's vehicle.

🎨 *Chapter XXX*

IT WAS SOME time before Anna realised that anything was wrong. They reached the village of Kelston by half past eight and passed through without her knowing it, for she was not at all familiar with the road, and it was too dark to read signposts. Shortly before they came to the town, Colby had lowered the window and shouted up at the jarvey.

"For God's sake, spring 'em, can't you?"

"What d'ye expect, guv'nor?" yelled back the jarvey tartly. "These bain't sixteen-mile-an-hour tits, y'know; more like six is their mark!"

"Dammit, use the whip then!"

He drew in his head and put up the window again, cursing under his breath. Evidently the jarvey paid some heed to his protest, as the pace mended for the next half mile before relapsing into its former lethargy.

"Is it far, now?" asked Anna anxiously.

She was thinking of the fireworks and hoping that she would not miss the start.

"Far enough at the rate we're going," he replied ungraciously.

"But you said it was only a few miles," Anna insisted, "and we seem to have come that distance already."

"Manner of speaking." His tone was curt. "Don't worry your head. Sit quietly, now."

Anna saw that he was not in the best of tempers, and she wisely decided to hold her peace. But when they halted farther on at a turnpike gate to pay the toll, she felt bound to ask again.

"Surely we must be nearly there, sir?"

He made no reply. Peering at him in the dim light afforded by the carriage lamps, Anna decided that he had dropped off to sleep. At once she became worried. Would the jarvey know when they reached their destination, or

was he relying upon Mr. Colby for precise directions?
Kelston Park would be a big house, perhaps up a side
turning off the main road; if they missed the turning because Mr. Colby was asleep, much precious time would
be wasted. She might even miss the fireworks altogether!
Dare she wake him?

She pondered this for several minutes before a pothole
in the road accomplished her purpose by causing the vehicle to jolt Mr. Colby out of his doze.

"Oh, I'm so glad you're awake, sir!" she exclaimed,
seeing him open his eyes. "I was beginning to wonder if
the jarvey had perhaps mistaken the direction, as we've
been travelling for such a long time. Surely we must be
nearly there, or has he gone wrong?"

"Don't fuss," he growled. "We'll get there all right and
tight."

"But surely it must be very late now?" persisted Anna.
"Please, Mr. Colby, what is the time?"

"What's it matter?"

"When we started out, you said we must hurry or
we'd miss the fireworks," Anna said plaintively. "And
now we've come quite a long way, and there's still no
sign of Kelston Park! Please, sir, how much longer will it
be before we reach there?"

"Hold your tongue, can't you? Never knew such a chit
for gabbing!" he declared in disgust.

This made Anna indignant.

"I think you're vastly uncivil, sir. And what's more, I
shall tell Miss Melville so when I see her!"

He chuckled. "Will you, now? Sure, it makes no odds
to me, for I shan't be there to hear it."

Anna stared at him, nonplussed. "What do you mean?
Aren't you staying for the fête?"

He grunted something, she could not be certain what,
then lapsed into silence once more. Anna, too, managed
to sit quietly for another ten minutes or so, but she was
growing increasingly uneasy as they journeyed onward
with never a sign of turning off the main road. At last
she could bear it no longer.

"We must be nearly there now. We've come miles and
miles, I'm sure! Oh, please, please tell me how much
farther it is!"

"Another six miles, I should think," he replied carelessly.

"*Six miles!* But we've been travelling for *ages*—almost an hour, I should think! And you said it was only a few miles to Kelston Park when we started out! I—I don't understand."

"You may as well know that we're not going to Kelston Park. We're bound for Bristol."

"*Bristol!*" Anna was astounded. "But why? The fête, has it been changed to another place? Miss Melville said in her letter it was Kelston Park. Yes, and you said so too, when we started out! What does it mean?"

"It means you've been hoaxed, my girl, that's what," he said roughly. "You may as well know the score now, since the sham's served its purpose. That letter was a fake. I wrote it myself. Had to take the chance that you'd be too excited to notice the handwriting, but I'm a gambler by nature. There's no fête, at Kelston or elsewhere. I'm taking you to Bristol, just the two of us, see?"

Anna stared in stupefaction for a few moments. Then gradually the implications of what she had just heard began to seep into her confused mind. She turned pale and started to shake with fright.

"W-why?" she croaked, her voice constricted by panic. "Wh-what d-do you want w-with m-me?"

He laughed, unmoved by her pitiable state.

"Been reading too many trashy novels, eh?" he mocked. "Think I'm going to ravish you, no doubt?"

Anna shrank into her corner, terror-stricken; that frightful thought had indeed entered her mind.

"Make yourself easy," he said contemptuously. "My taste don't run to school girls. No, the only use I have for you is as a fund raiser. I'm holding you to ransom. Papa will pay up instanter, I don't doubt, and by what the Melville female told me, he's well breeched. A note delivered to him from his darling daughter in captivity should bring quick results, eh?"

Terrified though she was, Anna's spirit was not entirely quenched. She gathered all her forces together to hurl a desperate defiance at her captor.

"I won't write it. I *won't!* Papa will set the law on you, you'll see!"

"Oh, yes, you will write it, miss, make no mistake about that." The menace in his tone made her shudder again. "There are ways, quite unpleasant ways, of making you do as I say. Don't think I'm too squeamish to employ them, either. As for the law, I shall make it quite clear to your father that he'll never set eyes on you alive if he tries anything of that kind. He'll not risk it, believe me."

Anna did believe him; she knew also that this man would stop at nothing to coerce her into writing the note. Terror burst its bounds and she emitted a loud, piercing scream.

Immediately he was upon her, one hand clamped roughly over her mouth, while his arm pressed her back into the corner of the seat.

"Yell like that again, and I'll knock you cold!" he growled, his face menacingly close to hers.

The scream had reached the ears of the jarvey, who reined in his horses and drummed with his whip on the roof of the coach. He yelled something that could not be heard clearly by the occupants of the coach but indicated alarm. Keeping his hold over Anna's mouth, Colby wound down the window and curtly shouted to him to continue on his way.

At the same moment, the sound of fast-galloping horses was heard from behind them. Colby looked back and saw the lantern on a coach and four rapidly approaching.

He cursed; it was a devilish inconvenient moment to be overtaken by another vehicle. But at the rate it was going, it would soon be past and away, with no time for noticing anything untoward.

As he expected, the coach and four swept past. Then it swerved suddenly right across the road, blocking their path.

Two men jumped out. One of them levelled a pistol at the alarmed jarvey.

"Halt, name o' the law!"

The jarvey felt not the slightest inclination to disobey this command. He obediently reined in his horses and sat, mouth agape, watching what followed as best he could by the intermittent light of a fitful moon.

No sooner had he heard the Runner's call than Colby, abruptly releasing Anna, leapt out of the offside door of the hackney and raced off through the trees that bordered the road at that side.

Aldwyn had run toward the coach on the driving side and jerked open the door before he realised what had happened. With a quick word to Anna that Miss Melville

would look after her, he darted in pursuit. Seeing that the
jarvey would present no problem if left unguarded, Trimble followed.

It was easy enough for the two men to follow in Colby's tracks as he went crashing through the undergrowth,
but sighting him among the trees was another matter, for
at the moment the moon was totally obscured by cloud.
Moreover, they did not seem to be gaining on him at all,
a fact upon which the Runner commented in a few brief,
colourful words. Aldwyn, saying nothing, put on an extra
spurt.

Suddenly the sounds of pounding feet ahead of them
stopped.

"Damn the fellow, he's gone to ground!" muttered
Trimble, panting slightly. "Best split up, sir, one each side
o' his trail. You take the left, I'll keep to the right. Shout
if you spot him!"

Aldwyn swung a few paces to the left, advancing now
more stealthily and peering through the gloom ahead
for the slightest sign of movement. It carried him back to
his campaigning days and the tactics of the Spanish guer-
rillas in the struggle against the French. There was plenty
of cover here, and for all he knew, their man might be
armed, so it would not do to take chances.

He had advanced only a few yards when the moon,
which had so far seemed to side with the fugitive, suddenly emitted a faint gleam from behind its cover of
cloud. He could now make out the dark outline of some
species of bush a little in front of him. As he was steering his way round it, his keen eyes suddenly detected a
streak of white in its midst.

He halted, peering more closely, struck by the notion
that the glimmer of white was just about at the right
height for a man's cravat, should he be standing upright
concealed in the bush. He leapt forward.

Simultaneously, Colby sprang out upon him.

The two men struggled together. They were well
matched in strength and fitness, although Aldwyn had
some advantage in height. For a few moments the contest raged with equal honours. Then Aldwyn unluckily
stumbled over a tree root and his antagonist broke away.

Incensed, he made a quick recovery and sprang after
Colby. Seizing him by the shoulder, he swung him round,

and with all the weight of his body behind it, drove his right fist at the other man's chin.

Colby went down like a log just as the Runner came on the scene. He chuckled with satisfaction.

"Said you'd a handy bunch o' fives, now didn't I?"

He bent over the recumbent form, swiftly going through the pockets with expert fingers.

"Ah, here we are, then!" he exclaimed as he discovered a leather bag.

He pulled back the strings and exposed the contents to view. The moon, in full glory now that it was not needed, glinted on the diamonds and rubies of a beautifully wrought bracelet.

"The evidence," he said, fastening the bag again and transferring it to his own pocket. From another, he drew out a pair of handcuffs and snapped them in place on his captive's wrists.

Colby stirred, shook his head, and sat up. His eyes fell on his captors. A stream of curses left his lips.

"Tch, tch!" reproved Trimble. "Come along now and no nonsense, or you'll stop a bullet."

They hauled Colby to his feet and frog-marched him back to the waiting vehicles.

"You," Trimble addressed the jarvey peremptorily, "I'm commandeering your vehicle, my man, in the name of the law, understand? You can drive me to Bristol gaol. And you'd best let them broken-winded nags o' yourn have their heads, seein' as I don't intend to be all night about the business."

The jarvey, being a sensible man, waited patiently while Colby was bundled into the hackney, the Runner keeping his pistol levelled in that direction while he exchanged a few words in an undertone with Aldwyn.

"Obliged for your assistance, sir. Couldn't hardly have brought it off on my own."

"One thing," said Aldwyn. "I hope it won't be necessary to charge him with the abduction of Miss Florey, in addition to his other crimes. If we can keep the girl's name out of it, we're hoping to hush up her escapade."

The Runner winked. "Girls will be girls, eh? Never fear, sir, we've got enough on this beauty as it is, and my job was to restore them jewels to their rightful owner and apprehend the bloke as lifted 'em. Mum's the word."

Aldwyn expressed his thanks in a practical way by slipping a banknote into the other man's hand, with instructions to drink his health; then they parted.

Henrietta had been engaged in restoring the much shaken Anna to a more equable state of mind. She quickly transferred the girl from her seat in the draughty hackney carriage to one in the well-upholstered comfort of Captain Barcley's snug chaise, placing a rug about the shivering shoulders. Then she gathered Anna into a comforting embrace.

At once tears of relief came to the girl's eyes. Henrietta said nothing beyond the incomprehensible little endearments with which a mother soothes her weeping child. Presently Anna's sobs terminated on a hiccup, and she burst into an indignant recital of the evening's events. Inserting a question here and there, Henrietta was relieved to discover that only just before the rescue had Anna really become terrified.

"He said he would make me write the letter!" she cried, with another shudder. "He said there were unpleasant ways of making me, and, and he wouldn't scruple to use them! Oh, Miss Melville, I can't tell you how scared I felt!"

"There, there," soothed Henrietta. "It's all over now! He'll be caught and locked away where he can't do you any harm ever again. You must try and forget it, my dear. Think of it as merely a bad dream that can never recur."

She was still speaking when Aldwyn appeared at the door of their coach.

"I'll ride outside," he said to Henrietta, "and leave Miss Anna to your ministrations. All's well. That scoundrel's on his way to Bristol gaol, and we'll be back in Pulteney Street in no time."

He closed the door and mounted onto the box beside the coachman. The coach was turned neatly in the road and at once began heading back the way it had come, with horses at the gallop.

Anna was silent for a while. When at last she did speak, it was evident that she had recovered sufficiently from her experience to begin speculating about what lay ahead.

"What time is it, Miss Melville?" she asked.

"I think it must be about a quarter after nine, Anna.

When we came up with you, it was close on nine o'clock."

"I've been wondering," said Anna in a small voice, "whether I'll be able to get back into the seminary in time. Oh, Miss Melville, I think I shall positively *die* if Miss Mynford has to hear about all this! She'll expel me, I know she will! And then Mama and Papa—"

She began to cry again.

"Hush," soothed Henrietta. "Don't worry, I'm sure it won't come to that. The horses are galloping along like fury, can't you hear them?"

Anna listened for a moment, then said that she could.

"Judging by the speed at which we came, we can be back at Mrs. Fordyce's house in a little over twenty minutes. We've only to collect Matty from there, you know, and take you both back to Queen Square. She has the keys, and I'm sure you'll be able to creep in with no one the wiser."

"Minnie comes upstairs soon after ten and listens outside the door of our dorm, but she doesn't usually open it," said Anna thoughtfully. If only Matty and I can reach the house with ten minutes to spare, I think I can manage to get into bed, even if I haven't time to undress until later. Oh, if only I can come safely off from this, Miss Melville, I shall never, *ever* wish to have another adventure!"

Henrietta could not forbear a smile. "Well, not an adventure such as this, at all events, though I shouldn't care to think that your spirit was quenched for all time. I dare say you'll eventually make a recovery. But Anna, you will promise to be more cautious in your conduct for the future, won't you? Tell me, did you have no doubts when you read that note? You must have thought it an odd scheme for me to suggest; or do you credit me with being a rackety kind of female? And surely you realised that the note was not in my handwriting?"

"Well, now you mention it, of course, it does seem not at all the kind of thing you'd suggest," agreed Anna. "And Matty said the note wasn't in your hand. She even fussed a bit about whether I ought to go. But the fact is, I wasn't in the mood to pay heed to her warnings. I was so excited at the thought of an outing, and with Mr. Aldwyn there too."

The note of worship in her voice made Henrietta resolve that it was high time to quash this schoolgirl fantasy.

"Oh, yes, Mr. Aldwyn," she said quickly. "He has been put to a vast deal of trouble in this business, Anna. I only hope"—drawing on a sudden inspiration—"that he may not suffer in health because of it."

"Why, what can you mean?" asked Anna, astounded.

"Only that he is not perhaps as hardy as he appears," continued Henrietta unashamedly. "He has the rheumatics, you see, and the night air isn't good for him."

"*Rheumatics!*" Anna's mouth almost fell open.

"Yes," continued Henrietta, relentlessly pursuing her fiction. "He always wears a flannel waistcoat because of his affliction."

"A *flannel*—! But my *grandfather* does that! Surely that's only for elderly gentlemen."

"Mr. Aldwyn is past his first youth, after all. He is nearly thirty," pronounced Henrietta, unscrupulously adding two years to Julian Aldwyn's age. "You may remember, my dear, that you once said you considered thirty to be the end of the road."

"Oh, yes, but still, I must say he doesn't look in the least bit old," said Anna in an uncertain tone.

"He bears up tolerably well, considering, but I believe from what Lady Barrington tells me that the strain is severe."

Anna was silent for several minutes, during which Henrietta had time to reflect with some amusement on what Mr. Aldwyn's reactions would be, were he but privileged to overhear this conversation.

"A *flannel waistcoat!*" exclaimed Anna in tones of disgust, breaking the silence at last. "Oh, Miss Melville! And I thought him like Lord Orville! I was never so taken in before!"

"You may perhaps recall that I myself never could see the slightest resemblance in Mr. Aldwyn to Miss Burney's hero. I fear it's all in your fancy, my love."

Anna brooded in silence.

"Of course, he is a most worthy gentleman," went on Henrietta, delivering what she trusted would be the final blow to Anna's castle in the air. "And doubtless some elderly spinster, finding in him some of the qualities with which your fancy endowed him, may be content to spend her life fashioning flannel waistcoats for his use."

Anna shuddered.

"But that's not in *your* style, Anna! It's not so very long now before you'll be making your come-out, and if I'm not much mistaken, you'll find among the younger gentlemen you'll meet in London one very like Lord Orville. And apart from that, you'll have all the fun and excitement of a London season to look forward to, only consider!"

This happy remark succeeded in giving a new turn to Anna's daydreams, so that by the time they reached Pulteney Street, she was almost her usual ebullient self. Nothing further was said of poor old Mr. Aldwyn, and Henrietta judged that the gentleman had at last been tumbled off his pedestal, through the unexpected agency of a flannel waistcoat.

❧ *Chapter XXXI*

HENRIETTA AND LOUISA both came downstairs late on the following morning, as they had sat up until the small hours talking over the extraordinary events of that day.

Louisa's anxiety had been severe until Henrietta's return with Anna, safe and apparently little the worse for her unpleasant experience. Mr. Aldwyn had insisted that Henrietta should remain at home while he escorted Anna and the maid back to Queen Square.

"Your part in the business is done now, ma'am," he said firmly, "and you must be worn to the bone! When I return, I'll send in a message to say that all's well, but I don't intend you should be disturbed again tonight. If I may, I'll do myself the honour of calling on you ladies tomorrow afternoon."

Matty had been summoned from the kitchen, hastily bundled into the coach, and whisked away with Anna almost before she had time to realise what was happening. The promised message was brought round later by Captain Barcley's footman; it stated cryptically that the packages had been safely delivered.

"But of course," said Henrietta as she and her friend sat at breakfast, "I still don't know if Anna managed to slip into the dormitory undetected. I promised her that I'd call on Miss Mynford this morning so that if matters had turned out badly, I might be at hand to intercede for her. I can only hope that I'll not be required to do so, however, for what extenuation in the world can be pleaded for her offence?"

Louisa declared airily that Henrietta would surely think of something. She was in her brightest spirits this morning, and announced her intention of walking with Henrietta as far as the Pump Room.

"I'll just look in for a while, and you may join me there

266

if you choose, Hetty, when you come away from the seminary. How very pleasant to turn with real enjoyment to our familiar pursuits."

Once they were out in the street, Henrietta half expected that Captain Barclay would join them, but there was no sign of him. She noticed Louisa glancing surreptitiously behind her once or twice as they walked along. A shade of disappointment crossed her face for a moment, but was soon gone. She could not be gloomy today.

They parted outside the Pump Room, and Henrietta continued on her way to Queen Square. Miss Mynford, gratified by this attention from a former favourite pupil, received her amiably. For a time they chatted inconsequentially, and Henrietta became more and more convinced that Anna's secret must be safe. If not, surely something would have been said by now. She decided, however, to put the matter more definitely to the test by asking after Anna.

Miss Mynford shook her head gravely. "I regret to tell you, Miss Melville, that I am at present seriously displeased with Anna Florey."

Henrietta's heart sank. "Oh, dear, I am sorry. What has she done, ma'am, to incur your displeasure?"

She hardly dared to put the question and waited in some trepidation for the answer.

"One of the teachers came to me this morning with a complaint about the girl's conduct that I cannot overlook," replied the principal in a severe tone. "So I fear that if you were intending to ask permission for Anna to accompany you on an outing, I shall be obliged to tender you a refusal."

It required all Henrietta's presence of mind to prevent her from showing her alarm. Anna's escapade must have been discovered; nothing else could account for the degree of Miss Mynford's severity. Poor Anna! Was there anything that could be urged in her defence that might prevent the ignominy of expulsion? It would be such a dreadful blow to her parents, even if Anna herself might pretend not to care.

She decided, however, to wait before launching into a defence of the girl. There was just the faintest possibility that Miss Mynford might be speaking of some other misdemeanour.

"No, I had no such intention today," she said as calmly

as possible. "But may I know, ma'am, precisely what
Anna has done?"

"She has neglected her pianoforte practice," pronounced the principal, as though naming one of the seven
deadly sins.

"I—I beg your pardon?"

The words came out weakly, for Henrietta's relief was
so overpowering that she could scarcely speak.

Miss Mynford looked at her in a kindly way.

"I can see, my dear, that this defection distresses you
as it should. You may recall that all my senior girls are
required to spend one half hour in turn every day at the
pianoforte. The music mistress informs me that she has
just discovered Anna has not been taking her turn over
the past week, but has persuaded one of the other girls to
perform in her stead. Such duplicity cannot be counte-
nanced."

"Oh, dear, no," agreed Henrietta, trying very hard not
to laugh.

"Of course, Anna Florey has no real talent for music,
while the girl who took her place is very fond of it," conceded Miss Mynford. "But that's quite beside the point.
Playing and singing are necessary drawing-room accom-
plishments, and as such, are essential to a young lady's
education. I am sure you will agree."

Henrietta would scarcely have dared to do otherwise.
She did venture to remark, however, that unfortunately
such subterfuges were not uncommon among schoolgirls.

"Of course I realise that only too well, with my many
years of experience," replied Miss Mynford, mellowing
slightly. "The girl is no worse behaved than many of her
companions, but they must all learn the lesson of obe-
dience. So I have decreed that Miss Florey will for the
next week spend *one hour* at her practice under super-
vision. The girls are not usually supervised as you know;
nothing is so trying to a teacher's nerves as listening to a
pupil's practising," she said, with an austere smile.

Henrietta remarked that she was quite sure Anna
would benefit in more than one way from her punishment, and would not err again. She reflected with amusement that she wished she could be more certain of this.
Such a high-spirited girl was decidedly a handful; thank
goodness she was at least cured of her adolescent attachment to Mr. Aldwyn.

Soon afterwards, Henrietta took her leave and strolled back in the direction of the Pump Room.

Inside, she could see no sign of Louisa. She did catch sight of Almeria and Sir Giles, however, and was about to go over to them when she was detained by Miss Dyrham. The lady had an expression on her face that betokened she was bursting with the latest gossip.

"Have you heard the news, Miss Melville?" she demanded in a malicious tone. "It seems that the charming Mr. Colby has run out of the town, leaving debts behind him at the York Hotel, and dear knows where else! I always had my doubts about the creature, as you may recall, but of course there was no turning you against him, such a favourite as he was. I quite compassionate you, my dear! You are not very fortunate in your choice of beaux!"

"I'm beginning to be persuaded that I'm not very fortunate in some of my acquaintances, at any rate," retorted Henrietta dryly, giving her a meaningful look. "Pray, don't waste your compassion on me, ma'am; no one could be less in need of it. As I once told you, I came to Bath in search of entertainment only, and that I have found in full measure. Indeed, I am grateful to you for helping to contribute toward it."

This speech, unusually biting for Henrietta but not, she felt, unwarranted, seemed to have routed her opponent for the moment. Before she could make a recover, Henrietta went over to Almeria, who had that moment seen her and was already approaching.

"My love, I must talk to you!" began Almeria. "Let us go and sit down on one of those chairs in the far corner, where no one will disturb us."

She took Henrietta's arm, steering her through the crowd until they reached their objective.

"There, that's better!" she exclaimed. "I've heard such a tale from Julian, and I simply can't wait to learn what you think about it all! Who would have thought that our engaging rogue Colby would turn out to be such a monster of depravity?"

She gave Henrietta an anxious, searching glance.

"Dearest Hetty," she went on in a hesitant voice, "I do trust . . . That's to say, I've often wondered if perhaps you might not have come to care for him more than you realised. If so, any ill-judged levity—"

To her great relief, Henrietta laughed.

"Jane Dyrham has just been sympathising with me—in her own peculiar style, of course—over that very matter, so for Heaven's sake, don't you begin! This should teach me the folly of attempting my hand at a flirtation. It's plain that I'm not near so expert at it as Louisa, for no one ever credited her with being serious!"

Almeria understood her too well to suppose that she was acting a part.

"I'm so glad, for now I can ask you everything I'm dying to know," she confessed. "Julian told me something of this extraordinary affair of Louisa's, but men have not the slightest talent for relating such matters. Poor, dear Louisa! She must have suffered dreadfully, and yet one could never have guessed. Do tell me the whole, Hetty."

"But haven't you seen Louisa herself this morning? She intended to come here, for I left her at the entrance less than an hour since, while I went on to Queen Square. I quite expected to find her waiting here for me."

"No, we've not set eyes on her. But then we didn't arrive until about a half hour since. Possibly she looked in and then went on to somewhere else."

"She never mentioned any such intention," said Henrietta in a puzzled tone. "But then, she's always impulsive, and today she was in such a lively mood that there's no saying what may not have taken her fancy! I'm sure she'll return presently, however. Would you not rather wait until she comes and then ask her about it?"

Almeria shook her head. "Don't you feel, Hetty, that it would be an unnecessary reopening of old wounds? She was obliged to explain matters to you, of course, but I dare say now her most fervent wish might be never to speak of the past again. But it will be more comfortable for her if her most intimate friends know her history, so I'm sure she would not object to your confiding the whole to me."

This so exactly echoed what Louisa herself had said on the subject yesterday evening that Henrietta was bound to agree. She therefore set about filling in those details that she had thought it better to omit from the story when she had related it to Almeria's brother.

Almeria listened almost without interruption and was evidently much moved.

"If only she can find happiness now!" she whispered

at the conclusion. "Poor love, she has suffered enough for one lifetime."

Henrietta agreed and, glancing across the room, saw that Louisa had just entered. After a moment, she caught sight of her two friends and made her way toward them, weaving in and out of the gossiping groups standing about the room.

Henrietta at once realised that Louisa was in an even more exuberant mood than when they had parted. Her hazel eyes shone and her whole face was radiant.

"And where have you been?" Henrietta asked, laughing. "I quite thought to find you awaiting me here."

"Oh, not far away," replied Louisa with a roguish smile.

"You look to me as if you've been enjoying yourself prodigiously, wherever you may have been," said Almeria.

"I took a stroll round the abbey."

"The abbey!" they both exclaimed in chorus.

"Yes, why not? It's very quiet there on weekdays."

"I dare say," said Almeria, giving her a quizzical glance. "But you don't look like someone who has been passing her time in peaceful meditation! Come now, you may as well tell us what you've really been up to!"

Louisa sat down beside them and leaned across, speaking in an excited whisper.

"Very well then, but you mustn't exclaim or make any fuss, for I don't wish to broadcast it today. Promise?"

Her mysterious manner carried the others back to their far-off schooldays, and they could not suppress their answering chuckles. Henrietta, however, had a shrewd notion of what was to be revealed.

"I am betrothed," announced Louisa, still whispering, "to Captain Barclay!"

They wished her joy in muted accents, but with full hearts.

"Hush!" she warned, looking warily about her. "He's gone to insert a notice in the Bath *Chronicle,* and until it appears, we've agreed to tell no one but our closest friends. Oh, I'm so happy! Too happy, too confused to remain here taking part in idle chatter with all these people! Hetty, would you dislike it very much if we went home now? And then, you know," she added naively, "I can tell you all about it."

She was still engaged with the same topic when Mr. Aldwyn called after luncheon. Henrietta thought he looked very handsome in his buff pantaloons and cinnamon brown coat that set so well over his shoulders; but she wondered why his expression should be so grave.

After greeting them both, he went on to wish Louisa joy.

"I heard the news from Barclay himself when I called in next door before coming here," he said. "I never saw a happier fellow, assure you! But I rather think he'll be telling you of that himself presently, ma'am, as he declared his intention of following me here before long to try and persuade you to join him in a stroll about the Sydney Gardens. Of course," he added with a twinkle, which for a moment relieved the seriousness of his countenance, "I dare say he has small hope of success."

Louisa laughed and blushed.

"I've so much to thank you for, Mr. Aldwyn," she said warmly. "Had it not been for you and dear Henrietta, my situation must have continued wretched indeed! How can I ever adequately express my gratitude, or make a return for your kindness?"

"My part was little enough, but by all means thank Miss Melville. She's a lady with a deal of initiative and perseverance," he replied, smiling at Henrietta. "I dare say she'll tell you that your present happiness is all the thanks she needs. But I must let her speak for herself."

They were interrupted by the arrival of the captain to make his request. Henrietta gave him her warmest congratulations, but soon sent Louisa upstairs to don her pelisse and bonnet. It was evident from the looks exchanged between the newly betrothed pair that very little sense would be obtained from them at present. They civilly invited Henrietta and Aldwyn to join them in their walk, and succeeded tolerably well in concealing their gratification when the offer was declined.

"I can think of nothing less appealing than playing gooseberry," said Aldwyn with a chuckle after the couple had departed. "But I must not take up any more of your time, ma'am."

He rose to go. Was it the rules of propriety that urged him to depart, or did he wish to be rid of her company? Henrietta could not decide; she only knew that she did not want him to go, and sought desperately for a way to detain him, if only for a little longer.

"I haven't told you about my visit to the seminary this morning," she began, resolutely remaining seated. "I went to see the principal, thinking that if, after all, Anna had been discovered last night, I might be able to urge something in her defence. Well, I had such a shock!"

The ruse worked, for he seated himself again, a look of dismay crossing his face.

"Turned out badly, did it? I am sorry."

She disclaimed hastily, then proceeded to relate her interview with Miss Mynford. He laughed genially when she had finished.

"I can imagine what an unpleasant shock you must have had when the principal spoke in such terms of Anna's conduct. What a resty little chit she is. I dare say her parents find her a bit of a handful. By the way," he added, "she made one remark to me last night in parting that puzzled me somewhat. She thanked me prettily enough, then went on to say she hoped the night air hadn't affected me adversely—for all the world as if I were a septuagenarian!"

He noticed Henrietta's guilty look and glanced at her quizzically.

"I'm afraid that was my doing," she admitted.

"I can see that from your expression," he accused, smiling at her. "Out with it, ma'am; let me know the worst!"

"Well, I trust you won't be vexed, sir, but I was obliged to humbug Anna a trifle. You may not perhaps have noticed it, but she had developed a—a schoolgirl attachment for you. One of these adolescent romantic fancies, you know."

"Good God!" he exclaimed in failing accents.

"I don't know how it is with boys, but girls are very prone to such transports," went on Henrietta. "In general, they quickly recover, once they realise their idol sports clay feet, so to speak. I considered it was time to put a period to Anna's infatuation, seeing that it had indirectly caused her to fall into a dangerous situation. Colby had observed it, you see, and used it as a bait for his trap. When he mentioned in his letter that *you* would be present at this supposed fête, all caution was driven from

Anna's mind, and she agreed to the scheme without a second thought."

"What it is to inspire such devotion!" he remarked cynically. Then, in a kinder tone, "But after all, I understand well enough, since once I myself fell into a similar trap. Poor Anna; adolescence is a painful business."

For a moment, neither spoke. Then he regarded Henrietta with an air of amused challenge.

"Do I collect that you, Miss Melville, set about displaying my clay feet? Not too difficult a task, but I'm consumed with curiosity about your method. Pray, enlighten me!"

"Oh, dear!" She gave an embarrassed little laugh. "You see, she thought of you as a romantic hero such as Lord Orville—"

"Lord who?" he interrupted.

"The hero of Miss Burney's novel *Evelina*. You may not know the book, sir, but Anna is a devoted novel reader."

"Oh, I see. Yes, I have read it, some time ago. Devilish stick of a fellow, if my recollection serves me. I must say, I don't feel at all flattered by the comparison. But pray continue, ma'am."

"My object was to make her think of you as rather old and—and decrepit, so to speak," went on Henrietta, glancing nervously at him from under her long lashes. "I told her that you were almost thirty—Anna thinks thirty is the end of everything, you know—and that you were afflicted with rheumatism, so that you were obliged always to wear a flannel waistcoat."

"Good God!"

He glanced down at the waistcoat he was wearing, a stylish garment of striped silk, and shuddered.

"I think it was the flannel waistcoat that carried the day," she said, trying hard not to laugh at his outraged expression. "She confessed herself quite taken in! Then I went on to say that you were a most worthy gentleman—"

He groaned, covering his eyes with one hand in a theatrical gesture.

"—and that, although some elderly spinster might value you sufficiently, it was scarcely to be supposed that Anna would relish the task of fashioning your warm waistcoats. Well, that completed your downfall. I'd only to refer to the pleasures of her come-out, not so very far ahead, and all the eligible *young* gentlemen she would then meet, to give her thoughts quite another direction!"

His eyes met hers, and they both burst out laughing.

"You wretch!" he exclaimed as soon as he could speak. "You scheming female! I dare say you positively enjoyed making me out such a figure! I suppose now the only thing for me to do is to look for this elderly female who is addicted to needlework. Had you anyone in mind?"

"There's always Miss Dyrham. She is very fond of needlework of all kinds. And I dare say," she added, greatly daring, "that she would make you a conformable wife."

Suddenly the laughter had vanished. She saw the intense look in his eyes, and quickly lowered her own gaze.

"I don't want a conformable wife," he said in a voice charged with feeling. "I thought I did once, so that I might order her life as I was trying to order my own emotions. But in the end, I was forced to succumb to the headlong passion I had despised. I fell deeply in love with a woman possessed of her own individuality, one who could be a partner and not a chattel."

Her heart seemed to have leapt into her throat. She dared not again lift her eyes to meet his, for fear they should betray her. Suppose he should be speaking of someone else—of Isabella Laverton, for instance?

He leapt to his feet and stood over her.

"Miss Melville—Henrietta! I offended you deeply recently in a fit of jealousy, but your attitude toward me over the past twenty-four hours encourages me to hope that I am, in part at least, forgiven. You're too honest to make sport of me as another woman once did. Tell me at once if I have any hope of gaining your affections. I love you with all my heart! You refused me once when I offered you only a marriage of convenience." His voice shook a little. "That may make no difference to you; I don't know, and dare not hope. Oh, for God's sake, my dearest girl, say something and put me out of this torment of uncertainty!"

Speech was impossible. She raised her face to his and let him read the tender message of her eyes.

He gathered her to him, pressing his lips upon her hair, her cheek, and, last of all, her lips. She surrendered herself gladly to his kiss, and his arms tightened about her as though he would never let her go. For some time they stayed thus, caught in the heady ecstasy of love's first embrace. Time did not exist. There was neither past nor future, but only this moment of unimagined bliss.

Presently he released her and, putting his arm about her waist, led her to the sofa, where they sat down side by side. She nestled close, letting her head rest on his shoulder, and found her voice at last.

"I love you, too," she said shyly. "I did from the first, I think, but I tried to put my feelings aside since it was plain that you didn't share them. When did you begin to care for me? Was it"—she peeped up at him with a roguish expression—"was it when you saw me tricked out in a modish gown? I realise now what a dowd I must have looked before I came to Bath."

"Do you really think I've fallen in love with a fashion plate? No, my darling, I had begun to care for you before you left Westhyde. Why else did you suppose I followed you to Bath? The thing was, I fought against my feelings. I didn't wish to become involved again in the bittersweet of love. I'll admit that when I saw you with your natural attractions and charm enhanced by pretty gowns, I had my work cut out to resist you! You were my Waterloo, beloved: a glorious defeat!"

"You speak very well," she teased him, putting up caressing fingers to his cheek.

"And can suit the action to the words!"

He held her close, his lips pressed firmly on hers. Then he lifted his head for a moment. "You once wanted me to say that your beauty maddened me, Hetty. It does, b'God! How soon will you marry me?"

"As soon as you wish. As soon as the banns are called," she promised, smiling into his ardent dark eyes.

"I'll go to Aldwyn Court tomorrow and arrange it. You wish to be married at home, I suppose, and not in Bath abbey?"

"Oh, yes, at home." She sighed contentedly. "To think it should come to this, when once I believed that I wanted only my freedom."

"You're not regretting that?" he asked with slight anxiety.

"Not that, nor anything. I did discover myself, you see, dearest, after all. I know now that I'm the kind of woman who can never exist for herself alone. I need a family about me."

"My sweet life, it shall always be my most earnest endeavour to supply your needs," he said with a small, quizzical smile.

She tried to hide her blushing face against his shoulder, but he tilted it up to kiss her again and yet again.

The bestselling romantic suspense of

Rona Randall

"Rona Randall draws her readers on enticingly ... serving up just what they long for in the way of thrills and chills." —*Publishers Weekly*

14   NE-8

Denise Robins
LOVE

Seven enchanting volumes containing more than one novel of irresistible romance—and there are more to come!

"Nobody has delved so deeply into a woman's heart." —Taylor Caldwell